THE
EVER
STORMS

ALSO BY AMANDA FOODY

The Accidental Apprentice
The Weeping Tide

3

WILDERLORE

THE EVER STORMS

AMANDA FOODY

Margaret K. McElderry Books

New York London Toronto Sydney New Delhi

MARGARET K. McELDERRY BOOKS

An imprint of Simon & Schuster Children's Publishing Division

1230 Avenue of the Americas, New York, New York 10020

For information about special discounts for bulk purchases, please contact Simon & Schuster Special Sales at 1-866-506-1949 or business@simonandschuster.com.

The Simon & Schuster Speakers Bureau can bring authors to your live event. For more information or to book an event, contact the Simon & Schuster Speakers Bureau at 1-866-248-3049 or visit our website at www.simonspeakers.com.

Interior design by Karyn Lee

The text for this book was set in Georgia.

Manufactured in the United States of America

1222 FFG

First Edition

10 9 8 7 6 5 4 3 2 1

Library of Congress Cataloging-in-Publication Data

Names: Foody, Amanda, author.

Title: The ever storms / Amanda Foody.

Description: First edition. | New York : Margaret K. McElderry Books, [2023] | Series: Wilderlore ; 3 | Audience: Ages 8–12. | Audience: Grades 4–6. | Summary: Thirteen-year-old Barclay and his fellow Lore Keeper apprentices are excited to travel to the Desert to study at the respected University of Al Faradh, but when dangerous, unnatural sandstorms and a magical library appear, more than their exams are at stake.

Identifiers: LCCN 2022017720 (print) | LCCN 2022017721 (ebook) | ISBN 9781665910750 (hardcover) | ISBN 9781665910774 (ebook)

Subjects: CYAC: Apprentices—Fiction. | Imaginary creatures—Fiction. | Adventure and adventurers—Fiction. | Fantasy. | LCGFT: Fantasy fiction. | Novels.

Classification: LCC PZ7.1.F657 Ev 2023 (print) | LCC PZ7.1.F657 (ebook) | DDC [Fic]—dc23

LC record available at https://lccn.loc.gov/2022017720

LC ebook record available at https://lccn.loc.gov/2022017721

TO DAISY,
WHO LOVED SUNFLOWER SEEDS AND
NAPS—BOTH MOST PARTICULARLY WHILE
IN HER HAMSTER WHEEL

ONE

Barclay Thorne groaned and covered his ears, trying to muffle the ferocious rumbles of the dragon's stomach—the dragon he was now riding.

This was Barclay's first time traveling by carrier dragon, and for the most part, he liked it. The passenger caravan strapped to the Beast's back was comfy and spacious, with wide windows perfect for admiring the breathtaking views. And the speedy flight had shortened an otherwise thirty-week journey on foot to a mere four days.

What he didn't like was all the *noise*. The wind whizzed shrilly in his ears. The pilot hollered directions from his saddle, no matter the time of day or night. And the carrier dragon, named Justine, was clearly suffering from a bad case of indigestion.

"Are we there yet?" Barclay grumbled.

"For the fifth time, no," answered his closest friend, Viola

Dumont, who sat cross-legged on the window bench beside him. "We'll land at sundown."

As she spoke, Mitzi—Viola's own dragon—reached a silver wing over Viola's shoulder and clawed at one of the hundreds of gold pins on her tunic. Viola yelped and shot Mitzi a dirty look.

Mitzi used to be sneakier—and a *lot* smaller. Only a baby whelp when Barclay had first met her, Mitzi had since grown to the size of a sheepdog. Two nubby horns had sprouted between her ears, and the feathers on her tail now climbed up her back and wings. But despite how much she'd changed, Mitzi still loved nothing more than all things shiny.

"Mitzi, we talked about this," Viola scolded her. "You need to be better behaved."

Mitzi paid her no mind. She jabbed a talon at a glimmering button on Viola's sleeve.

Both Justine and Mitzi were Beasts, which were animals with magical powers called Lore. Beasts came in many shapes and sizes, from tiny, harmless creatures to gigantic, terrifying monsters, and they dwelled in six regions of the world known as the Wilderlands. The people who lived there with them, like Barclay and Viola, were called Lore Keepers, and they bonded with Beasts in order to share their magic.

"You should try to relax," Viola told Barclay, ignoring Mitzi's pokes and prods. "Haven't you read that book twice already?"

Barclay peeled his attention away from *Beastly Biographies of Brilliant Keepers*, which Viola had gifted him for his thirteenth birthday earlier that Summer. "But what if I missed something? There are going to be apprentices from all across the Wilderlands at the Symposium, but I didn't grow up in the Wilderlands like everyone else. I don't want to fall behind."

The Symposium was a set of courses that all apprentices of the Lore Keeper Guild were required to pass before they could sit for their licensing exam. It took place every year at the University of Al Faradh, the most famous school in all the Wilderlands.

Being an apprentice himself, Barclay had always known that he'd have to attend the Symposium, but he'd assumed that would be years and years away. Until four days ago, when their teacher, Runa Rasgar, had abruptly announced their travels to the Desert for the Symposium. And four days was *definitely* not enough time to prepare.

Viola shook her head. "You've been a Lore Keeper for a year and a half now, and you know as much about Beasts as Tadg and I do. You have nothing to worry about."

Tadg Murdock was their fellow apprentice, a hotheaded boy who always found something to be grumpy about. After complaining all afternoon about how boring and long their flight was, he'd fallen asleep on the cushions in the caravan's corner. His wavy light brown hair was matted from his pillow, and one of his Beasts, Toadles, had nestled himself into the crook of his arm.

Barclay hoped that Viola was right. Even if he ended up being the only student from the Elsewheres, which were the regions of the world without magical Beasts, he no longer felt like the scared mushroom farmer who'd accidentally wandered into the Woods. He'd faced not one but two Legendary Beasts. And after more than a year spent training at the Sea, he was smarter, stronger, and faster than he'd ever been.

Gurrrrrrrrrg. The floor tremored with Justine's latest stomach cramp.

The sound made Root wake with a start. Root was Barclay's Lufthund, a wolflike Beast with powerful wind Lore. Side by side, the pair of them looked similarly wild. Root had shaggy fur, hooked claws, and sharp teeth. He was all black except for the white bones that jutted out from the base of his spine. Meanwhile, Barclay had long, tangled dark hair to match, pale skin, and fingernails far too often caked with dirt.

Unlike Barclay, who was still as short as ever, Root had grown far bigger this past year. When he padded up to Barclay, he had to bend down to nudge his Keeper's head.

"I know," Barclay told him, scratching him beneath the chin. "I'm tired of being cooped up too. But we'll land soon."

Root huffed impatiently. Then he sat down and rested his head on Barclay's knees.

Barclay turned back to Viola. "Maybe you're right and I've been studying too much. But how come you're not?" That wasn't like Viola, who didn't deem a book finished until she'd read it three times over.

Viola shrugged. "Oh, I've been studying for the Symposium since I was seven, so I've spent the trip doing more important things. Like mapping out my to-do list for when I get home."

Mitzi and Root weren't the only ones to have grown this past year. When Viola stood to fetch her satchel, she towered over Barclay. She might've always been tall, but lately she seemed to stretch another inch every season, and her two hair buns of tight brown curls only added to her height. She was even taller than Runa now.

Viola sat down and flipped through the pages of her leather-bound notebook.

"Your mom lives in the Desert, right?" Barclay asked. "How long has it been since you last saw her?"

"Almost two years, since I first became an apprentice." Barclay was no expert on families, as his parents had died when he was small, but two years seemed like a long time to be apart. "Which is why the first thing I'm going to do when I get home is eat as much of my mom's cooking as possible."

Barclay agreed this task was very important. The food at the Sea left a lot to be desired.

"Second," Viola continued, "I'm going to meet Gamila Asfour. She's the new High Keeper of the Desert, now that Idir Ziani retired. I've heard she's very impressive, and I need her to like me if I'm going to be Grand Keeper one day."

Whereas High Keepers governed each Wilderland, the Grand Keeper was the leader of the Guild and the entire Lore Keeper world. Though the job was elected, not inherited, the Dumonts had been the Grand Keepers for three generations. And Viola was determined to follow in her family's footsteps. Barclay had no doubt she'd succeed. She'd already traveled to four of the six Wilderlands. She was an expert on languages. And she spent all her free time studying and preparing for a job that was years away.

"Last, I'm going to bond with a second Beast," Viola finished.

Barclay smirked. "Will Mitzi like that?"

Mitzi now creeped across the floor toward Toadles, her best friend—or, as Tadg referred to him, her partner in crime.

"Mitzi and I have had a lot of long talks," Viola replied. "And we agree that I'm more than ready for a second Beast."

Meanwhile, Mitzi tapped Toadles on the gemstone in the center of his forehead. The tiny Beast's bulging eyes flew open with surprise, and purple goo squirted out of his webbed hands. Tadg jolted awake, seething. Toadles's poison Lore had made his fair skin swell violet with an itchy rash.

"You're supposed to stay in your Mark!" Tadg snapped at Toadles, who only stared at him blankly.

Suddenly, the caravan lurched as Justine swooped to the right. Root howled. Viola collided with Barclay. And Mitzi frantically stretched out her long wings to take flight, smacking Tadg in the face.

"Whoa, girl! Steady!" the pilot hollered, tugging on Justine's reins.

In the span of a blink, Runa rose from her sleeping roll in the corner and darted toward the pilot's side. "What's going on?" she asked, her voice calm even as Justine plunged into a steep dive.

Runa Rasgar was never afraid of anything, because no matter where she was, *she* was always the scariest thing in the room. Her chain mail clothes looked fit for a warrior, and a jagged scar cleaved down the pale skin on the right side of her face. Her famous reputation as a Guardian and a Dooling champion had earned her the nickname the Fang of Dusk.

"I . . . Look! Over there!" The pilot pointed southward, and Barclay and Viola twisted around to peer out the windows.

In the distance, a dark, menacing pillar stretched up from ground to sky. It was as wide as a city or even a mountain, as though a vast hole had been torn through the world. It took Barclay several seconds to realize that the pillar was *moving*. Its surface swirled and billowed like plumes of smoke.

"What is that?" Barclay rasped. Beside him, Root sprang up to take in the sight as well, and he let out a low, threatening growl.

"It's a sandstorm," Runa answered gravely.

"But it's so small," said Viola, which made Barclay gape. The storm might've taken up only a sliver of the otherwise blue and sunny sky, but it still felt ridiculous to describe something so frightening as small. "If it was a sandstorm, it would be—"

"I don't think it's a normal one. Can you take us closer?" Runa asked the pilot.

"C-closer?" the pilot sputtered. "That's much too dangerous. You see how Justine reacts."

"We don't need to fly close enough to put us in harm's way. I just want to get a better look."

The pilot muttered something under his breath, then tapped his foot against Justine's long neck, steering her to the right. The caravan tilted, forcing Barclay and Viola to grasp onto the window frames to keep from falling, and Root's claws raked across the seat cushions. Along the back wall, a rack of pamphlets advertising *SKYBACK CARRIER DRAGONS, the #1 Keeper-recommended draconic flight service* toppled down with a crash.

Tadg pried Mitzi off him—she'd been clinging to his face—and stumbled toward Runa. "You told us that you didn't have any work to do in the Desert. You said that while we were studying, you'd be taking a vacation."

"Did I?" Runa said innocently, with a not-so-innocent twinkle in her icy blue gaze.

Runa was a Guardian, which was one of the four types of Lore Keepers licensed by the Guild, so it was her job to protect the Wilderlands from dangerous Beasts. Last year, Runa had been summoned to the Sea to investigate a carnivorous algae bloom called the weeping tide, which had been making Lochmordra, the Sea's Legendary Beast, attack islands and ships. But as it turned out, the seaweed wasn't to blame. The real culprits were a Lore Keeper named Audrian Keyes and his apprentice, Yasha Robinovich, who were trying to destroy the borders between the Wilderlands and the Elsewheres to let Lore consume the entire world. Even though Barclay and his friends had saved the Sea, Keyes and Yasha had escaped, and no one had seen them since.

"I *knew* there was a reason you were sticking us in the Symposium," Tadg said smugly. "You've been sent to investigate something in the Desert, haven't you?"

"High Keeper Asfour might've requested my presence," Runa admitted. "But the three of you don't need to concern yourselves with it. You should be focusing on your studies."

"No way! We'd rather help you than be stuck in some class." When Runa didn't respond, Tadg whipped his head toward Barclay and Viola. "Well? Don't you two agree with me?"

Barclay was only half paying attention. As they neared the sandstorm, he could make out huge, whirling currents of dust within it, twisting around one another like snakes. It looked as though the Desert was writhing. The sand that soared in the air was so thick that no light could break through from above, creating a deep, deep darkness.

"Is that what sandstorms usually look like?" Barclay asked Viola.

"No," she answered tightly.

Justine let out a fearful cry and lurched a second time, so strongly that Viola shrieked and Tadg was thrown to the floor.

"I'm sorry," the pilot told Runa. "She won't take us any closer."

Runa stared at the sandstorm through shrewd, narrowed eyes.

"Ma'am?" the pilot asked nervously.

"That's fine. Get us back on course to Menneset."

Justine swerved around, and Barclay breathed a sigh of relief. Just looking at the sandstorm had made goose bumps prickle across his skin. He wrapped his arm around Root's back, and after a few moments, Root relaxed and withdrew his claws from the shredded cushions.

As they soared away, something dark moved in the corner of Barclay's vision. He turned back to the window, and his heart stuttered to a stop.

One of the columns of sand had bent away from the storm and stretched out toward them, like a massive hand reaching for a candle flame.

No sooner did Barclay scream than the hand closed over them.

And the world snuffed out.

TWO

Sand exploded through the windows, smothering the entire caravan in a thick, prickly haze. Barclay coughed. It felt like he was breathing in pebbles. Even his eyes stung, forcing him to squeeze them shut.

Justine was wrenched backward, as if the storm was yanking her toward it. Barclay tumbled to the floor, and his shoulder slammed into something soft and shaggy, which he realized was Root. The Lufthund yelped, then nuzzled his head into his Keeper's side to block the harsh sand.

Barclay clung to Root tightly. He had to do something.

He drew himself to his knees, then stretched his arms in either direction and thought, *Wind!*

Gusts blasted from his palms at the windows, so powerful that any papers and loose trinkets were cast out with the sand and hurled into the sky. Barclay tried to gulp in a deep breath of clean air, but his chest only shuddered with more coughs.

As powerful as his wind Lore might've been, it wasn't enough to rip Justine from the sandstorm's grasp. The carrier dragon flailed, whipping the caravan this way and that. But it was no use. The storm dragged them backward as though trying to swallow them whole.

"Brace yourselves!" Runa shouted.

Their already dim surroundings went utterly black.

Then they were falling.

Everyone screamed as they were thrown upward. Barclay slammed into the ceiling, and his Lore abruptly died. Sand barged back into the caravan.

Sparing Root any more terror, Barclay returned him to the golden, tattoolike Mark on his shoulder, where he resided in stasis until Barclay was ready to summon him again. Immediately, it began to sting in warning, and he girded himself for impact—possibly, even, for doom.

A heartbeat before they crashed to the ground, Justine managed to spread her wings against the violent winds. They stopped free-falling with a jerk. Barclay smacked the floor face-first, and pain burst from his nose. He groaned and rolled over, tasting blood on his lips.

Seconds later, Justine clumsily landed, the blow softened by the cushioning dunes. They skidded for several seconds before finally coming to a halt.

At first, Barclay was too scared to move, certain he'd shattered all his bones. But the torrents of sand continued to rage, making it impossible to inhale. And so he had no choice but to raise his arms and muster his Lore again. The wind drove the debris outside, and he gasped for air.

A warm glow appeared. He opened his eyes to find Viola

lying beside him, an orb of light shimmering around her hands and illuminating the caravan. She looked as shaken as he felt, with several scrapes torn across her light brown skin.

Her eyes widened as she took him in. "Your *face!*"

Barclay was too busy using his Lore to find a mirror, but judging from the pain throbbing from his mouth to his forehead, he must've looked a mess.

Runa was in front of him in an instant. Her pale blond hair, normally braided, hung wild and loose, and sand was matted in her eyebrows. "Your nose is broken," she told him matter-of-factly. "I'm going to reset it with my bone Lore. Are you ready?"

Barclay was *not* ready, but Runa didn't give him a chance to say so. An invisible force yanked his nose back to the center with a loud, agonizing *snap!* Barclay screamed, and his wind Lore stuttered. But after a few strangled breaths, the pain lessened, and he regained his focus.

"Not my best work—it's still a little crooked. But it'll have to do." Runa patted Barclay on the shoulder. "That was quick thinking up there. Well done. How long do you think you can keep going?"

Barclay's wind Lore was far stronger than it used to be, but he'd never used this much longer than a few minutes at a time. "A while," he answered, determined not to prove his words a lie.

Viola woozily stood and gawked at the ruined caravan. "What are we going to do now?" Her voice was scratchy, as though a prickly pear had gotten lodged in her throat.

"Carrier dragons are all equipped with distress beacons, so once we find it, we can send a signal to the closest city to come help us," said Runa. "Now, where's Tadg?"

"I'm here," came a muffled voice from beneath a heap of carpets. Then Tadg crawled out from under them, like a dung beetle. He collapsed at their feet. "I want a better look. Fly a little closer. What could go wrong?" he mimicked Runa mockingly. Neither Barclay nor Viola was brave enough to make fun of the Fang of Dusk, but Tadg had known Runa his whole life. Before he died two years ago, Runa had been Tadg's father's best friend.

"Normal sandstorms don't just reach out and grab people," Viola said nervously. "What *is* this?"

"I don't know," Runa responded. "This doesn't seem as bad as what the High Keeper described in her letters."

"Doesn't seem as *bad*?" Tadg repeated. "Should it also be raining fire?"

"If there's been a sandstorm, why wouldn't Mom have told me in her letters?" asked Viola.

"I promise to answer your questions later," Runa assured them. "For now, let's just focus on getting out of here." She walked toward the pilot, who was slumped unconscious in the saddle. She shook his shoulder, but he didn't respond.

"Is he dead?" Barclay squeaked.

"No, but he's out cold. I'm gonna check on Justine. Tadg, would you search through these compartments for the distress beacon?"

With that, Runa slipped out one of the windows into the storm.

Tadg rummaged through the compartments in the walls on either side of the cockpit. Each drawer he thrust out was dusted in a thin layer of sand. "Is this the part where we all get eaten by a sand serpent? I heard they swim underneath the dunes."

"*Asperhayas*," Viola corrected, using their proper name, "are really rare. I'm more concerned with whatever Beast is causing this sandstorm."

"You think a Beast is doing this?" Barclay asked.

"Well, it's not a normal storm, is it? That means there's some Lore at work."

"Found it!" Tadg brandished a strange disk that looked like a smooshed beetle. He slid open two of its winglike slats, and the disk began to blink with red light. "Can a rescue team really reach us in here?"

"I don't know," Viola replied. "If they figure out we're in this storm, they'll probably send a team of Guardians to fetch us."

"How long do you think that'll take?" asked Barclay. He didn't want to admit it out loud, but his arms were already tiring.

GRRRRRRRRRRRRRLLLLLL!

A thunderous growl boomed in the distance, so loud it drowned out even the roaring of the storm.

The three apprentices froze.

"Are you *sure* Asperhayas are rare?" Barclay asked anxiously. His fingertips trembled, making his Lore stutter out in spurts.

Behind them, Runa climbed back inside. "The good news is that Justine is fine. She's just frightened, though I don't think the fall helped her stomachache. The bad news is that the winds are too strong for her to lift off again. Did you find the beacon?"

"Yeah, but are we just gonna pretend that there isn't some giant Beast out there?" Tadg demanded.

As always, Runa's tone was cool and measured. "I'm also

interested to see what made that noise. So come on—let's move outside. Barclay, Viola, you keep using your Lore. Tadg, you and I will grab the pilot."

"Outside?" Tadg echoed. "Is this for another *closer look*?"

Runa shrugged. "If you'd rather *not* see the possible monster hunting us, then by all means, go back to lying under your carpets."

Tadg had no argument for that. So the four of them—with the pilot limply in tow—shoved open the caravan's door and staggered outside onto the slope of a soft dune. Barclay had been looking forward to seeing the Desert up close, but it was so dark amid the storm that it might as well have been the dead of night. Even with Viola's makeshift lantern, the blustering sand obscured everything more than a few feet in front of them. It was also far hotter on the ground than it'd been in the sky, hotter and drier than even the longest Summer days in the Woods or at the Sea.

Gradually, Barclay shifted his Lore. Instead of blowing air in opposite directions, he shaped the wind into a sphere, with all of them protected inside.

The group walked along Justine's long red neck until they reached her head, which she'd half buried within the sand. Barclay widened his sphere to cover her face as well, and her green eyes gratefully met his own.

"Your control is improving," Runa told him, as though this was merely any other lesson and they weren't stranded in the center of a gigantic, terrifying dust storm.

"Thanks," Barclay managed. Beads of sweat dribbled down his temples.

GRRRRRRRRRRRRRLLLLLL!

At that, one of Runa's two Beasts—Goath—appeared at her side. Goath was a Haddisss, a large snake made only of skeleton. He slithered up his Keeper's back, and his bones rearranged themselves with eerie clicks until they bracketed Runa's upper body like armor. His tail stretched out over the top of her right hand into a long, lethal blade.

"What kind of Beast do you think it is?" Tadg asked, his voice cracking.

"It could be a Trickanis," Viola said, and the name alone made a shiver creep down Barclay's spine. "Or a Waramasa. Or an . . . Asperhaya."

"I knew it!"

"Quiet," Runa snapped, her voice unusually sharp with warning. Their bickering abruptly silenced.

In the distance, a sound rumbled. It reminded Barclay of an earthquake, and he immediately thought of Audrian Keyes, whose stone Lore had been powerful enough to shake the entire Isle of Munsey at the Sea. Barclay didn't know who he'd prefer to face—a genuine monster or the man who'd nearly destroyed an entire Wilderland to get what he wanted.

Runa must've been thinking the same thing, because for the first time, her expression betrayed a hint of fear. She dropped into a fighting stance.

Beside her, sparks of electric Lore sizzled at Tadg's fingertips.

"Is it going to attack—" Tadg started, but was cut off when something screeched overhead.

Three figures soared above them, and even from afar, Barclay could tell from the spindly shape of their wings that they were dragons. As they shot downward, the lashing against Barclay's sphere began to ease. The gales still blew as fast as ever, but the sand froze, floating in midair as though ignoring the wind entirely. Then, all at once, the sand hardened into a dome wide enough to shield them and Justine.

The rescue party had arrived.

Exhausted and relieved, Barclay lowered his arms and let his Lore release.

The three dragons landed in front of them. Dragons came in all sorts of varieties, and these looked far more elegant than Mitzi and not nearly so humongous as Justine. All three had long, slender necks and shimmering scales in brilliant hues of gold, ruby, and violet.

Barclay realized this was no average rescue party.

"Dad?" Viola asked, just as a man slid down from the golden dragon's saddle.

Barclay had never met the Grand Keeper before, and he couldn't imagine anyone with a more commanding presence. As he strode forward, his glossy cape billowed around his boots. He had blond hair and a matching neat beard, and he was so tall that Barclay had to crane his neck to look up at him. Embroidered over his heart gleamed the crest of a three-headed dragon.

"Viola," Leopold Dumont gasped, immediately seizing his only child in his arms.

A second person jumped from the ruby dragon and ran to Viola's side. Unlike the Grand Keeper, who donned leather riding gear, this woman wore a linen dress and dozens of gold bololanege bangles that clearly hadn't been chosen for flying. The second Leopold stepped away from Viola, the woman replaced him.

"Mom?" Viola sounded breathless from being squeezed so tight. "But you hate flying!"

"You think I wouldn't rush over here the moment we heard your distress beacon?" Viola's mom pulled away, but her hands still fretfully roamed over her daughter, from the scrapes on her cheeks to her torn sleeves. She kissed her on the forehead. "You're all right?"

"Yes, I'm fine."

"You're sure?" Leopold asked.

"Yes," Viola repeated, sounding embarrassed.

With the three of them side by side, it was impossible to tell which of Viola's parents she took after most. Viola's complexion was different from her mother's deep brown and Leopold's ruddy pink, but she and her mom shared the same slope of their nose and eyes, and she'd inherited Leopold's height and square jaw. Clearly, Viola had gotten her love of gold pieces from her mother. And there was even a mole on her father's chin that Viola had in the same spot.

Runa cleared her throat, interrupting the family reunion. "Kadia," Runa said warmly to Viola's mom. But when she turned to Leopold, her expression tightened. "Grand Keeper." Goath unlatched from her arms, but Runa had yet to relax her defensive stance.

"Runa." Leopold spoke her name far colder than he had Viola's.

A third figure dropped from the last dragon—a woman. She looked older than Leopold and Kadia by at least two decades, and she had broad, muscular shoulders, tan skin, and a stern expression. Perched on her raised arm was a falcon Beast whose beak and talons hooked like scythes. It spread its wings, which weren't made of feathers—but sand. It flapped them, spraying grit behind it, and between its strange form and glowing golden eyes, it looked more like a specter than a Beast.

"It's lucky our team wasn't far when we got your distress signal," the woman said. "I'm sorry your arrival was met with such unfortunate circumstances. But I suppose you can see why I asked you here."

"I have an idea, yes," Runa said.

"Now wait a moment," Leopold cut in. "I still think you're mistaken about the scale of—"

"Yes, I am aware of what you think," the woman said flatly, and Barclay's jaw dropped. Whoever this woman was, she had no problem spurning the Grand Keeper. "Though I'm surprised that witnessing your daughter's flight crash-land in the center of one of the storms has done nothing to change your mind."

Leopold's face reddened with fury. "I'm. Being. *Cautious*."

"It seems we have different understandings of what 'cautious' means." She turned back to Runa. "I take it these are your other apprentices?"

"Yes, this is Barclay Thorne and Tadg Murdock. And this is Gamila Asfour, the High Keeper of the Desert."

"Asfour?" Barclay repeated. Viola had mentioned the High Keeper's name earlier, but he realized he recognized it from another place as well—from his studying. "Like Faiza Asfour, the first Grand Keeper? The one who bonded with all six Legendary Beasts?"

The High Keeper's lips quirked into a smile. "That would be my ancestor, yes. Now, as happy as I am that you're all here and safe, I ask that we move out of the storm. It's strenuous to maintain the dome."

Barclay gaped. If it was Asfour's sand Lore holding up the dome, why didn't she have to use her hands? The High Keeper must've been strong enough to control her Lore with concentration alone.

"You told me the storm was a day southwest of the capital," Runa asked. "Has it moved?"

Asfour frowned. "No. I'm afraid this storm is a second one—it appeared early this morning. The three of us were accompanying a larger expedition studying it, which is how we reached you so quickly. From what we can tell, both storms show no signs of spreading or stopping. But this one isn't half as powerful as the first."

Barclay swallowed, trying to fathom what a storm twice as bad as this one must look like.

"What was that growl we heard in the storm?" Tadg asked.

Asfour's sharp gaze leveled on him. "You heard a Beast?"

Runa glanced at her apprentices warily. "We can discuss all of this later. For now, let's just get everyone safely to Menneset."

THREE

The next morning, Barclay awoke to a face looming inches over his own.

"Ahh!" he screamed.

"Ahh!" shrieked the person watching him, a young girl who looked about eight years old and had ears that stuck out wide. She lurched back, and the baby armadillo–like Beast in her arms whimpered and curled itself into a protective ball of sparkling diamond plates. "Sorry! I'm supposed to tell you that you gotta wake up or you'll sleep through Registration. I knocked a bunch of times. Didn't you hear?"

Barclay sat up, so groggy that he had no idea where he was. But as he studied the huge, bright windows and polished stone floors, he remembered arriving in Menneset— the Desert's capital city—late the night before. He'd been so exhausted that he'd barely paid attention to the house where Viola's mom had brought them, only sleepily rushed through a bath and mumbled good night.

"R-Registration?" Barclay repeated, yawning.

"For the Symposium," the girl answered. "You don't want to be late, do you?"

In a sudden panic, Barclay bolted out of bed. He hadn't unpacked last night, so he rummaged through his satchel for fresh clothes.

The girl peered at him curiously.

"Um," said Barclay. "Who are you?"

"I'm Pemba Tolo. Viola's my big sister." Barclay should've guessed this sooner. Pemba looked like a miniature version of Kadia, though she'd added wooden beads to the ends of her cornrows, which clicked and clacked as she bounced up and down. "And this is Bulu! He's a Mudarat."

Bulu the Mudarat did not unroll from his ball.

"Bulu isn't used to visitors," Pemba explained. "He's normally very friendly."

Viola appeared at the door, already dressed in her bauble-covered tunic. "Why are you still in your pajamas? We're going to miss it!"

Five minutes later, Barclay, Viola, and Tadg sprinted through the streets of Menneset.

"I can't believe all Runa did was leave a note," Viola said, panting. "Why didn't she wake us? What if we'd slept through Registration?"

"Probably because she knew we'd want to come with her," Tadg grumbled. "Would *you* rather be in school all day, or helping the Guardians study those sandstorms?"

As much as Barclay wished to help Runa, he wasn't surprised they hadn't been invited. They might've been another year older since Runa's mission at the Sea, but they were still only apprentices.

"How far is it to the University?" asked Barclay.

"You see that building up there?" Viola pointed to a giant obelisk in the distance that speared over the city skyline. "That's the University."

They quickened their pace and wove deeper into the Desert capital. The buildings reared high overhead, cloaking the narrow streets in cool shade. Though all the walls and roads were built of the same golden stone, the city burst with color. Columns with red and orange mosaics stretched up to aqueducts that crisscrossed Menneset in a massive knot. Vibrant embroidered awnings hung over the windows. Green-leaved palm and olive trees drooped over every alley.

Barclay had never visited a place so huge—or crowded. Countless people bustled past, many carrying armfuls of books for the University or baskets of wares for a market. As in other Wilderland cities, the people varied in features, but most wore light, long-sleeved clothing to protect their skin from the hot sun.

For as many people as he saw, Barclay counted twice as many Beasts. Large horse- and camel-like creatures plodded past, wearing elegant saddles decorated in beads. Flying Beasts swooped overhead or perched on clotheslines. The serpent Beast on the shoulder of a nearby man had scales like pure obsidian. The common Anthorns that scurried at their feet glinted as red as rubies.

Finally the alleys opened into a vast circular courtyard, where the University of Al Faradh stood like a palace in the city's heart. The tallest tower rose so high, Barclay had to crane his neck to glimpse the peak.

Viola led them past the gates onto the campus. Even outside, books lay scattered everywhere. Old books wedged beneath the legs of benches to hold them level. Books stacked tall enough to rival the stone columns. Books clutched in the hands of passing students. Books left aimlessly on tables. Books tucked like secret messages into empty slots within the walls.

The trio dashed between the buildings and skidded to a stop at the entrance of a hall with soaring ceilings and a stone floor so shiny, Barclay could see his sweaty reflection in it. Hundreds of Lore Keepers milled about, many of them young students. At the center, a folded card sat neatly on an empty desk.

Registration Closed.

"So much for that," Tadg muttered. "I say we go find Runa in Menneset's Guild House." Guild Houses were the headquarters of each Wilderland's chapter.

Barclay wasn't ready to give up just yet. "Maybe there's someone we can ask for help?"

The three apprentices gazed around the room, but Barclay had no clue who they were supposed to talk to. And he didn't recognize anyone.

"Let's split up," Viola suggested. "I'm sure someone will be willing to register us, even if we're a bit late."

"Fine," Tadg said bitterly. "But I'd still rather learn more about the storms."

The two of them strutted off, leaving Barclay alone by the empty desk. He wasn't as fond of splitting up as they were. After all, Barclay didn't have the Grand Keeper or a world-famous Surveyor for a parent. Maybe if he mentioned Runa, someone would be keen to hear him out. Runa was one of the most respected Guardians in the Guild. No, the best way to make a good impression was simply being polite.

Except when Barclay tried to take a step, he tripped and fell to the floor. Several of the nearby Lore Keepers turned to stare at him, and his face burned. So much for a good impression. When he rolled over, he saw that his shoelaces were tied together.

"How . . . ?" he started.

Then his shadow began to wiggle, even though he wasn't moving. It split into two halves, then one of them grew and grew until a girl took shape in front of him. She was scrawny and pale, with dark hair so short, it only brushed the tops of her ears.

Cecily Lloris smiled at Barclay mischievously. "You should pay better attention to where you're walking."

"Cecily! What are you doing here?" Barclay had last seen Cecily over a year ago, when her teacher, Cyril Harlow, had been sent to the Sea to investigate the weeping tide. At first, Barclay hadn't gotten along with Cecily and Cyril's two other apprentices, mainly because Runa and Cyril famously hated each other. But now Barclay considered the three girls his close friends.

"We're here for the Symposium. Shazi, Hasu, and I are all students," Cecily answered. "And Cyril is this year's Guardian Master resident or whatever it's called. It sounds boring to me, but he's awfully proud of it."

That didn't surprise Barclay, as Cyril cared more about status than anyone he'd ever met.

Then his heart lifted.

"Wait—that's perfect!" he said. "Cyril can help us register. Where is he?"

Cecily shrugged. "He had to leave this morning on official Guardian business. He wouldn't tell us what it was for."

Barclay retied his shoelaces properly, then stood up. "Probably the sandstorms, like Runa."

"Sandstorms?" Cecily tilted her head in confusion.

"You know, the sandstorms outside the city that are full of Lore and don't seem to ever stop and . . . You have no idea what I'm talking about, do you?"

Cecily smirked. "I'm pretty sure if that was true, *everyone* would be talking about it."

But not if no one knew. The Guild must've been keeping the storms a secret from the rest of the Desert, though Barclay couldn't guess why. However, now was not the time to get distracted.

"Never mind. I'll tell you about them later. What's more important right now is that Viola, Tadg, and I got here too late to register. Do you know someone who could help us?"

"Shazi's dad probably could. He's over there." Cecily grabbed Barclay by the wrist and yanked him with her across the hall toward a huge throng of people. After a dozen "Excuse mes" and at least five or six "Sorrys," the pair squeezed past the onlookers to the center.

The first person Barclay recognized was Shazi Essam, one of Cyril's other apprentices. Her clothes better suited a sparring match than Registration Day. A sheathed saber rested on each of her hips, and she wore leather practice gear across her forearms and right leg. On her other leg was her prosthetic, which measured from the knee down and which she controlled with her powerful metal Lore.

Beside her stood a man wearing gold robes with at least

a dozen twisted tassels adorning his shoulders. Barclay assumed he was Shazi's father, both because they shared the same light brown skin and straight dark hair, and because he beamed while patting Shazi's shoulder.

Barclay had forgotten that Shazi's father was Ata Essam, the Chancellor of the University.

"Has the University issued a statement about Younis's absence?" asked one of the crowd members, a handsome man dressed in a smart quilted vest. He held his quill poised over his notebook.

"Instructor Younis suffered an accident," Essam said. "It was very unfortunate, but he's recovering and will soon return to good health."

"He's taught the history course of the Symposium for almost five decades. Who will be replacing him?"

Essam shifted uncomfortably. "We . . . did succeed in finding a replacement on such short notice. Grusha Dudnik kindly accepted the position."

Murmurs swept through the crowd. Barclay was certain he'd heard that name before, but he couldn't recall from where.

"Isn't Dudnik known for being rather, um, unconventional?" the man asked.

"She's a Guild-licensed Scholar, which means she's qualified. And who are you again, sir?"

"Tristan Navarre, with the *Keeper's Khronicle*," the journalist answered smoothly, scribbling in his notebook. "And has the University altered its procedures in regard to student safety?"

"I—I don't know what you mean by that," Essam

stammered. "The students are perfectly safe, as they've always been."

"There have been reports of unusual weather patterns—"

"That is a question you should take to High Keeper Asfour. As always, all students of the University are safe, from those completing advanced degrees to the apprentices attending the Symposium. If I weren't confident, would I have permitted my daughter here?" He patted Shazi again on the shoulder, though he was no longer smiling. "That's all the questions I'll answer today."

With that, Essam strode away, and the crowd dispersed. Barclay hesitated, unsure if he should bother the Chancellor after such a scene.

Then he felt a light punch on his arm.

"I *knew* that was Tadg I spotted earlier skulking around," Shazi said smugly. "Are you all here for the Symposium too?"

"We would be, if we ever manage to register," said Barclay.

"Consider it done—I'll talk to my dad. Registration Day is barely for registering anyway."

"What's it for, then?"

"Scoping out the competition, of course." Shazi seized Barclay by the shoulders and spun him around to face the rest of the hall. "See that boy over there? The one with green hair?" Indeed, Barclay spotted a very good-looking teenager with hair dyed a vibrant shade of lime. "He's one of the only Apothecary apprentices I've ever heard of to come in first in his Exhibition. And those three over there, reading? They're the apprentices of the Chancellor of the Meridienne

College in Halois—that's Al Faradh's sister school. Or rival, the way Dad talks. And her?" Shazi pointed at a blond girl who roamed around carrying a giant map, as though she needed directions to find the building's single exit. "She's the apprentice to Yawen Li, who's the resident Surveyor Master this year."

"Does that mean everyone will be scoping *us* out because of Cyril?" Cecily asked nervously. Cyril was just as famous as Runa, and he even bore a nickname to match: the Horn of Dawn.

"Definitely," Shazi answered. "But not as much as Barclay, once they find out who he is."

"Me?" asked Barclay, stunned. "Why?"

"Because you're the Elsewheres kid who won first in his Exhibition. *And* you're the Fang of Dusk's apprentice. Obviously there are students way older than us here, but you're still one to beat."

All of Barclay's worst fears about the Symposium bubbled to the surface. He was already worried about being a miserable failure, and that would be twice as humiliating if all the other students expected greatness from him.

"Why would the Symposium be so competitive?" he choked. "I thought it was just school."

Shazi threw up her hands. "Don't you know about the Tourney?"

"The what?"

"Some people will tell you that you should spend the whole Symposium studying. Learning how the Guild works and all that. But would you rather *learn* history, or would you rather *make* it?"

Barclay couldn't tell if it was Shazi's words or the shifty gleam in her eyes, but a thrill fluttered inside him as though his stomach was full of moths. He might not dream of becoming the Grand Keeper like Viola, but he *did* have ambitions of his own. He wanted to help teach the Elsewheres that Beasts and Lore were nothing to be afraid of, so that one day the Elsewheres and Wilderlands could live in harmony.

"I guess," he admitted. "But I still don't know what you mean."

Shazi groaned. "Come on. Let's go find the others. Then we'll strategize."

After some searching, they spotted Viola and Tadg on the other side of the hall, deep in conversation with Hasu Mayani. Hasu was Cyril's third apprentice, a heavy girl with brown skin, dark hair she wore in a long, sleek braid down her back, and a dimpled smile.

Hasu threw her arms around Barclay as he approached. "I'm so glad you're here! Viola and I were just talking about being roommates."

"Hold up," Shazi said. "We agreed that you were going to try to spy on the enemy! If we're going to win, we need to know who we're up against."

Hasu pulled away and rolled her eyes. "I told you that all the two of them talk about is the Tourney." Her Beast, a Madhuchabee named Bitti, was fast asleep as usual on Hasu's nose. Her tiny wings twitched from her dream. "Not all of us are as obsessed as you two. Some of us want to make *friends* with the other students. Not enemies."

"I'd still like to know what the Tourney is," Barclay said, growing impatient.

"It's a prank competition the Symposium students do every year," Viola explained. "All the different apprentice tracks team up against one another. The Guardians normally win."

"They didn't last year," Shazi said quickly. "Last year the Surveyors won. And it's not just *pranks*. It's stunts!"

"The Tourney is against University rules," Hasu reminded her.

"Oh, the instructors don't care. It's not as if they didn't all compete when they were students. And the Guardians' chances have doubled now that you're all here. We should start planning right away, and—"

"That's not important," Tadg told them, earning affronted looks from Shazi and Cecily. "Hasu said she didn't know anything about the sandstorms, so listen to this." Then he lowered his voice so as not to be overheard, and he recounted the story of their arrival in the Desert, from the mysterious storm to their rescue party that included the High *and* Grand Keepers.

When he finished, Hasu's brown eyes were wide. "*That's* what Cyril's secret meeting must be about. But why wouldn't he tell us the truth?"

"I think Asfour must be trying to keep the storms quiet," Cecily said. "Otherwise, people might get scared, right?"

"Of weird sandstorms full of Lore?" said Shazi. "Yeah, I think people would get scared. There's a lot of cities in the Desert, and they have to trade with one another for food and things like that. This could make people too afraid to travel."

Between the rush of last night and this morning, Barclay hadn't gotten a chance to dwell on the sandstorm yet. But now that he did, his thoughts went nowhere good.

"What?" Viola asked, seeing his frown.

Barclay cast an anxious glance over his shoulder, but the other Lore Keepers were too busy intermingling to pay attention to a huddled group of apprentices.

"Runa and Cyril still hate each other, right?" he started.

"Yeah," Tadg said. "Runa still calls him 'the Pompous One' every time his name comes up."

"And last Spring, Cyril tried to make me throw out my champion card of Runa that she signed," Shazi said. "Which I didn't, obviously. It's worth at least twenty kritters."

"So there's only one reason they'd agree to work together again," Barclay said gravely.

Viola's expression darkened. "You think the sandstorms have something to do with Keyes?"

"No one knew what was causing the weeping tide at the Sea until we figured out it was him. Maybe Keyes is somehow behind this, too. Plus, he was their friend." Keyes had been even more than that—he'd been their fellow apprentice, back when he, Runa, and Cyril had all been Leopold's students. "They knew him better than anyone. And after they couldn't stop him at the Sea, don't you think they probably consider Keyes their responsibility?"

"I think you're right," Hasu said softly.

"All the more reason for us to be helping them and not be stuck *here*," Tadg said. "We know Keyes and Yasha too."

Barclay grimaced, remembering when their group of six had been truly a group of seven—Yasha among them. Barclay and Tadg had even lived with him. And Barclay didn't know what made him angrier: that Yasha had lied the whole time they'd been friends, or that their group felt strange without him, like an important piece was missing.

Viola shook her head. "Even if we know Keyes and Yasha, we're still just apprentices."

"So? We could help," said Tadg.

"Couldn't we do both?" Barclay suggested.

"The Symposium is *hard*, and you see the competition around here," Shazi said. "If we get distracted, we won't pass. And my dad is the University's *Chancellor*. If I fail, he'll be so embarrassed."

"Catching Keyes is more important," Tadg argued.

Shazi crossed her arms. "Yeah, but how can we be sure that Keyes is really behind this? You made the sandstorms seem *huge*, way too big for any one Lore Keeper to make. Maybe Runa and Cyril working together is just coincidence."

"Well, I know an easy way to find the answer," Viola said slyly. "I'll ask my parents."

FOUR

I can't believe the past day you've had," Kadia said while setting the table for dinner. "First the sandstorm, then nearly missing Registration. I'm just relieved that you're safe and everything worked out."

Viola lifted the lid on the pot simmering on the stove, then broke out into a broad smile. The whole room smelled delicious, like herbs and peanuts. "What time will everyone be here?"

Her question sounded innocent, but Barclay knew better. The Grand Keeper was joining them for dinner tonight, which made this the perfect chance to ask all the adults about whether the sandstorms were connected to Keyes.

"Any minute now," Kadia answered. "It's so nice to have everyone home. I can't remember the last time I didn't eat dinner in my office."

"Where do you work?" Barclay asked as he placed glasses of water around the table.

"I'm a Scholar at the University. I know you might not guess it from little Yaylay up there, but I specialize in studying Legendary Beasts."

Barclay looked up to where Kadia nodded, and it took him several moments to notice the very, very tiny owllike Beast perched atop the kitchen cabinets. It was smaller than most mice. Its huge yellow eyes were fixed frightfully on Root, who gnawed on an antelope bone in the room's corner.

"Why do you have to work so late?" Viola asked.

"It's the new High Keeper," responded Kadia. "She's brilliant, but I wonder if she ever rests. She's scheduled meetings between her, Chancellor Essam, and me before sunrise and after sundown. I know how dangerous that man is—and my ex-husband being who he is, I know better than most. But I still . . ." Seeing the interested looks on all their faces, Kadia paused, as though she'd said too much. "Enough talk about work. I'd rather talk about you. For one, I'd like to know who gave you permission to grow so much. You're taller than me now!"

Viola glanced at Barclay, and he could tell that she was itching to push her mother for answers. But seeming to decide better of it, she said, "I'm not the one who's grown the most. Last time I saw Pemba, she still called me Vola."

Pemba was currently peering over Tadg's shoulder as he shuffled his deck of champion cards. Each one depicted a famous Dooler. Dooling was the favorite sport of the Wilderlands, where Lore Keepers and Beasts battled head-to-head in a contest of strength.

"How many cards do you have?" Pemba asked Tadg eagerly. "A hundred? *Five* hundred?"

Barclay expected Tadg to roll his eyes, but instead he answered, "I have about sixty. Do you wanna see my signed copy of Runa's?"

Pemba nodded, and Tadg flashed the foiled hexagonal card with Runa's signature scrawled across it. In her illustration, she wielded an axe made entirely of bone.

Mitzi, catching sight of the shiny special edition, sprung out from beneath the table to snatch the card.

"Oh, no you don't," Tadg grumbled, yanking the deck out from her reach. "Go pester Toadles. He looks bored."

Toadles croaked from his puddle within the kitchen sink.

"Well! Look who it is!" a man bellowed as he stepped through the front door, and a small herd of Beasts skittered and soared in behind him. Barclay had never met the man before. He would've remembered someone with so many Marks—more than Barclay had ever seen. The golden tattoos covered his brown skin up and down his arms and neck, and one even curled up the crook of his cheek.

It was dangerous to bond with too many Beasts. If a Keeper couldn't contain all that power, the Lore consumed them, turning them into something like a Beast themselves. Barclay had witnessed it happen firsthand to Soren Reiker, who'd tried to bond with Gravaldor in the Woods a year and a half ago.

But nothing else about this man reminded him of Soren— especially not his cheerful smile.

While the dozen or so Beasts invaded the room, some clambering after Mitzi's half-finished food bowl or sniffing Root suspiciously, Viola bolted up from the table and threw her arms around the man. "I'm so glad you're here! I've been dying to talk to you about my plans—I'm ready to bond with a second Beast."

The man pouted. "Ah! So you just wanted to see me for my professional expertise. And here I thought you missed me for my wit and charm." He winked, then he held out a hand for Barclay and Tadg to shake. "I'm Mory Tolo, Viola's stepdad."

"Are you a Surveyor?" Tadg guessed. Surveyors were another one of the four types of Lore Keepers licensed by the Guild. They were explorers who ventured into new, unmapped parts of the Wilderlands or searched for undiscovered Beasts.

"No, I'm a Beast tamer. I find wild Beasts in need of a home and train them for young would-be Keepers to bond with. And"—Mory glanced down to where a Murrow ducked behind his legs and a Beast like a prairie dog clung to his sandal—"I've managed to collect quite a few myself over the years."

"That's not your way of warning me you're thinking of bonding with another, is it?" Kadia asked him. "Because you know what I think. You're far too close to reaching your limit—"

"Limit," Mory repeated dismissively. "You can never have too many friends. And that's what Beasts are, after all, right? They're our greatest friends."

He bent down in front of his daughter and tickled Bulu's glittery tail. Bulu uncurled from his ball in Pemba's arms and cooed.

Barclay instantly liked Mory. In fact, Mory seemed the sort of person who was impossible not to like. While Barclay and Viola helped Kadia put the finishing touches on dinner, Mory dazzled them all with the story of how he'd once wrestled a wounded Saladon, carried it to Menneset, and nursed it back to health.

"I hadn't been looking for a Saladon," Mory said dramatically. "And even if I was, I wouldn't have looked there. Saladons prefer to live atop the Lightning Plateaus not far from the city, where they can warm themselves out on the rocks. But there I was—just barely escaped from a colony of Arachadees—and fire blasts out from the sand beneath me! My beard never looked worse. Then the Saladon shook off the sand. She was bleeding bad—looked like she'd had a run-in with some Vultans. I pulled out some pricklefruit, hoping to calm her. She took it, and almost half my hand with it!"

Kadia clicked her tongue with disapproval. "You were too reckless."

"I think it's incredible," Tadg said. "My dad would've loved to find a Saladon on its own away from a herd."

"Your dad has good taste in Beasts," Mory said. "Has he seen many Beasts from the Desert?"

"Loads," Tadg told him. "The Sea, the Tundra, the Jungle, the Mountains . . . He traveled everywhere."

"Tadg's father is Conley Murdock," Viola explained. Conley was a Surveyor famous for his daring stunts. He'd written all about them in his popular book *A Traveler's Log of Dangerous Beasts*.

Mory's face lit up. "Conley! I met him a few times—we were even part of the same crew once following a flock of

Ostrellos. That was the only time in my life that I heard Shakulah's laugh."

"Enough of your stories. You know Shakulah's laugh is just a myth." Kadia might've been shaking her head, but she wore a teasing smile. "I, for one, would like to hear some stories from our guests. Barclay, Viola's told me in her letters that you're from the Elsewheres that border the Woods. I'd love to learn more about that region—I've heard those kingdoms are quite different from our neighbors here."

"What do you mean?" Barclay asked.

"The Desert has a friendly relationship with the nearby Elsewheres, as we trade with each other. They send us coffee and other goods, and we send them Lore items that they find useful."

Barclay had thought that all kingdoms of the Elsewheres feared the Wilderlands. Dullshire didn't trust anything to do with Beasts or Lore Keepers, and the Elsewheres that bordered the Sea was no different. This news filled him with hope. Dullshire might've cast him out, might not even miss him, yet maybe Barclay's dream wasn't as unlikely as he feared. Maybe one day Barclay *would* return, older and wiser and far more worldly, and he'd change Dullshire and the Woods forever. Just like a hero in an adventure novel.

The thought reminded him that a long time had passed since he'd last written to Master Pilzmann, his old teacher in Dullshire. The two had been exchanging letters for over a year now—secretly, of course. The sentries of Dullshire would never permit messages from a Lore Keeper into town. But it still felt great to talk to Master Pilzmann again. Barclay might not have a family like Viola's, but

Master Pilzmann was something close. And he'd love to hear all about Barclay's exciting crash-landing arrival at the Desert.

While Barclay told Kadia what it was like to grow up as an Elsie, the others fell into a heated discussion about which sort of Beast Viola should bond with.

"A Bilbot's sound Lore would be useful," Mory pointed out. "Or a Donkilisa. One rattle of their tails could put a grown man to sleep."

"But Bilbots are Familiar class, which isn't usually strong enough for battle. And Donkilisas are Prime class, and I already have the perfect Prime class Beast," Viola said, and Mitzi nodded approvingly. "We're ready for a Mythic class." Of the five levels Lore Keepers used to categorize Beasts, Mythic Beasts included the rarest and most powerful creatures, second only to the six Legendary ones.

"Skulkits make great companions," Mory said. "And their glass Lore would pair nicely with Mitzi's light Lore."

"That's true . . . ," said Viola thoughtfully.

"What about a *Raptura*?" Tadg suggested.

"Adult Rapturas are extraordinarily hard to tame," Mory explained. "And young Rapturas are also extraordinarily hard to find."

"High Keeper Asfour has one," Tadg pointed out.

"Look, if *I* say it's too dangerous, then it's too dangerous."

The front door swung open a second time, and Runa and Leopold entered. Both looked weary, but Leopold's expression brightened as he gazed around the room. He had a strange smile, a little too wide, as though he'd practiced it over and over again in front of the mirror.

"How'd it go?" Kadia asked warily.

"As well as could be expected," replied Leopold, his smile growing all the falser.

"Your meeting with Cyril?" Viola asked. "And the High Keeper?"

Leopold shot an angry look at Runa, who held up her hands and said, "I didn't tell them."

Leopold sighed and turned back to his daughter. "I'm not sure how you learned about that, but it's not important right now. It's been far too long since I've gotten to have dinner with my favorite child."

Viola rolled her eyes. "I'm your only child."

Leopold didn't seem to have heard her. "Kadia, Mory," he said, giving his ex-wife a hug and Mory a warm handshake. Then he bent low and grinned at Pemba. "You're a lot bigger than the last time I saw you."

Pemba lifted her Beast up. "This is Bulu," she said proudly, even while Bulu squeaked and rolled into a ball.

"A Mudarat!" Leopold gave Mory a conspiratorial glance. "The same one you told me you rescued last year?"

"The very one," Mory said happily.

Barclay hadn't known what to expect of this dinner. Since Leopold and Kadia weren't married anymore, he'd assumed that they wouldn't get along or that they'd act awkwardly around each other. Once or twice, Viola had alluded to as much. But whatever disagreements they'd had in the past must've been behind them, because even though Viola's family was shaped differently from most, they all still seemed like friends.

If Leopold was awkward to anyone, it was Runa. Even

after the meal was served, the former teacher and apprentice rarely spoke. Runa patiently told Pemba story after story about her time as a Dooling champion. And Leopold peppered Viola with questions about Mitzi, her training, and whether she'd liked her time at the Sea.

Viola answered them eagerly, but every chance she got, she snuck in questions of her own. "You never told me why you're in the Desert in the first place. You almost never leave Halois."

"I'm just here for a work matter," Leopold said smoothly. "I'm returning home in the morning. I've already stayed longer than I planned to—the *Khronicle* will twist some front-page headline out of that, I'm sure."

"When I talked to Cyril's apprentices today, they didn't know anything about the sandstorms," Viola said. "Are they being kept secret?"

"'Secret' is a strong word, but I've advised Asfour to wait until we understand them better before we inform the public. It's still possible they'll go away on their own."

Runa said nothing, only stabbed her fork into her stewed carrot.

"Do you think Audrian Keyes is behind them?" Tadg asked. Viola kicked Barclay hard in the shin—a kick he was sure was meant for Tadg. "What? I don't see the point in pretending it's not what we're thinking."

"No, we have no reason to believe that Keyes is behind them," Leopold said gruffly. "I would suggest you three remove Keyes from your mind. The best Guardians, Scholars, and Surveyors in the world are looking into the matter. You should focus on your studies."

If Leopold noticed Runa glaring at him, he ignored it.

No one brought up the sandstorms or Audrian Keyes again. Hours later, after a heaping dessert of sticky honey pastries from a local bakery in Menneset, the adults ushered all the kids upstairs. It was past Pemba's bedtime, and the apprentices had to wake early the next morning for the first day of the Symposium.

But after they'd said their good nights, Barclay didn't feel tired enough to go to bed yet. And Root wouldn't fall asleep until he finished the last nibbles of his tasty femur.

Barclay pulled out his stationery kit from his satchel.

Dear Master Pilzmann . . . , he scribbled.

His quill hovered over his parchment, dripping ink. In the last letter he'd received, Master Pilzmann had recounted nothing but happy news. Selby, Barclay's once fellow apprentice, was shaping up to be a great mushroom farmer, and Mrs. Havener and her wife had recently adopted a baby. Barclay wanted to share his own happy news. He knew Master Pilzmann would be amazed by his descriptions of the Desert and the huge city of Menneset.

Yet he couldn't shake his worries about Audrian Keyes. The Grand Keeper had assured them that Keyes had nothing to do with the sandstorms, but even though Runa hadn't argued, she'd looked so angry. . . . Something wasn't adding up.

"Barclay," Viola hissed from the doorway. She'd changed into her pajamas and tied her curls up in a silk scarf. "Hurry. Come listen."

Barclay abandoned his unwritten letter on the desk and followed after her. They tiptoed through the hallway to the steps, where Tadg crouched beside the banister.

Voices echoed from downstairs.

"I've made the offer before, and I will again," Leopold said. "We could have a Guardian stationed here and at your office around the clock."

"I don't want to be babysat," Kadia told him.

"But if it makes you feel more at ease . . . ," said Mory. "After what happened to Younis—"

"No, and there's never been any proof that he was responsible for Younis. I thought there was some sighting of him near Permafrosk, anyway?"

"That wasn't confirmed," said Runa.

"And neither is this. I think you're all smart to be prepared, but this is overreacting. I might not be a Guardian, but I'm perfectly capable of taking care of myself."

"Are they talking about Keyes?" Barclay whispered.

"I can't tell," Tadg said.

"But why would your mom need protecting?" asked Barclay.

Viola bit her lip. "I don't know."

For a few seconds, the conversation downstairs became too hard to catch, as several people spoke at once. Then Runa's voice rang out, cool and distinct.

"It's been nine years, and you still don't have anything to say to me?"

A pause, then: "Cyril and I are of one mind," Leopold snarled. "I don't see how anything has changed. In fact, I wonder how many of our present concerns would've been avoided if you hadn't chosen violence from the start."

Barclay sucked in his breath. Leopold was referring to

Runa and Cyril's confrontation with Keyes nine years ago. Keyes had tried to bond with the Legendary Beast of the Mountains, and after a battle, Runa had killed him—or so she'd thought. That was the moment when Runa and Cyril had begun to loathe each other. Their famous duel all those years ago would've been a fight to the death if Leopold hadn't put a stop to it.

"I *saved* the Mountains," Runa growled.

"You acted as a vigilante. You were all only eighteen, barely a year with your licenses. You should've never taken matters into your own hands. If you'd bothered to reflect afterward, you would understand that."

"Just because I don't agree with you, you think I haven't *reflected*? What do you think crosses my mind every time I look at my face in the mirror?"

Silence. Barclay squeezed the rails of the banister so hard that his knuckles whitened.

"Croak!"

Tadg cupped his hand around Toadles's mouth and shushed him. Toadles never stayed in his Mark for long, and he seemed to delight in appearing at the worst times.

For several heartbeats, the apprentices froze, certain they'd been exposed.

Then Leopold said curtly, "I think it's time I return to Halois. Kadia, Mory, thank you for having me. Dinner was delicious as always."

The door opened and closed, and footsteps thumped on the lower floor. The three apprentices scattered as Runa stormed upstairs and disappeared into one of the other guest rooms.

Barclay never finished his letter to Master Pilzmann. His thoughts were racing too fast, trying to connect the broken shreds of what they'd overheard. Who was Younis, and what had happened to him? What did he have to do with Kadia? And most importantly, if Keyes wasn't the one causing the mysterious sandstorms, then what was?

Barclay collapsed into bed, making Root jolt and look up from the edge of his mattress, the bone still clutched in his jaw. Barclay muttered a quiet, "Sorry," blew out his bedside lamp, and crawled under the linen sheets beside him.

Barclay wasn't a Guardian yet. He was still an apprentice, an apprentice from the Elsewheres who would probably have to study twice as hard as all the other students to pass the Symposium.

He might know Keyes and Yasha from the time they spent together at the Sea, but there was no proof that the two of them were involved in any of this. Runa, the High Keeper, and the other Guardians would fix the sandstorms in no time. And if Barclay got too distracted worrying about their problems, then he'd fail for sure.

Sensing that Barclay was brooding, Root paused his gnawing and nuzzled his Keeper's cheek. In the year and a half since Root had bonded with him, Barclay believed Root now knew him better than anyone in the world. Even Viola.

"Shazi said that all the other students will be paying attention to me," Barclay said while he rubbed Root's back. "I need to prove that I deserved to place first in the Exhibition. And that I deserve to be Runa's student."

Root's eyes glinted as he watched him in the darkness.

"Do you think I can?"

A breeze tore through the open window, making the skin on Barclay's arm prickle. Across the room, the papers on the desk rustled. The door creaked and closed with a click.

Barclay grinned and rolled over, and Root rested his head against his chest. "I guess I will, then, since I trust you."

FIVE

The next morning, on the first day of Autumn, the University of Al Faradh bustled with new students. They were a bumbling bunch, staggering as they hauled huge packs over their shoulders and dripping in sweat from the scorching sun. They crashed into one another. They tripped over steps. They halted midpath to squint at their campus maps, stalling all those behind them.

Everywhere, Beasts roamed wild, skittering and wrestling and swooping and prowling. They scurried up treetops, making fruit plunk down on the apprentices below. A flightless Bolikono sprinted circles around a quad. A Calamear waded in a nearby fountain, and the pool of water gurgled like a bubble bath.

"Come on. Come on," Kadia called, beckoning their group forward. "The Guardian dormitory is this way."

Pemba, who clutched Viola's hand, pointed at the obelisk

that rose over the campus. "Did you know that the tower's shadow makes a clock?"

"Yes. That's called a sundial," Viola told her.

"It's called a sundial," Pemba repeated for Barclay, Tadg, and Runa. Viola might've been right in front of them, but Pemba had appointed herself their official tour guide.

Barclay gaped in awe at the University's obelisk again. Dullshire also had a clocktower, which he'd accidentally destroyed the same day an angry mob had chased him into the Woods. But he doubted any tower in the world compared to this one.

A familiar thrill stirred in his stomach, one he hadn't felt in a long time. He was truly on a new adventure.

They zigzagged through the school's buildings until they arrived in a secluded, shady courtyard. A matching pair of dormitories stood on either side. Their gigantic wooden doors sprawled open, and scraggy Lore script covered them from top to bottom, reading, over and over:

In the University, history walks the halls beside you.

"This way," Kadia said.

Barclay and the others squeezed past a throng of students so they could slip into the building. Marble statues lined the atrium, so massive they nearly scraped the ceiling. Each depicted either a famous Lore Keeper or a Beast. Barclay's gaze skimmed over them until it landed on one he recognized: Gravaldor, his head raised skyward in an eternal roar.

"Is it just me, or are the statues creepy?" Barclay asked Tadg.

"It's not just you," he answered. "I feel like they're all staring at me no matter where I walk."

"Maybe that's because they do," Runa said, nodding at a small chipmunk Beast with bulging orange eyes that scuttled over Gravaldor's shoulders. It coughed, and a plume of fire flared from its mouth.

"This is Eldin Hall," Kadia told their group. "The Guardian dormitory is in the west wing"—she gestured at the set of open double doors to the left, then to the pair that mirrored it on the right—"and the Surveyor dormitory is in the east wing. The Apothecary and Scholar apprentices live in Hamdani Hall across the courtyard."

They strode through the left doorway and down a long, wide hallway. Barclay peered into each of the rooms they passed: miniature studies with cozy armchairs and giant bookshelves perfect for reading.

Beyond a grand, pointed arch, the hallway opened into a lounge with antique weapons displayed on the walls like pieces of art, and giant skylights cast golden pillars onto the plush, carpeted floor. Two Beasts—one pelican-like Fwisht and one that resembled a violet raven—squawked at each other in a battle for the top perch over the fireplace.

A line snaked in front of a desk in the room's corner. At the desk sat a wiry young man with bluntly chopped brown hair and posture so stiff and straight that he looked as though he was imitating the statues outside. Over a dozen medals gleamed on his vest, each one freshly polished.

Runa rolled her eyes. "The resident Guardian Master. He's dreamed about this since our Symposium."

In front of them in line, an apprentice who looked about seventeen swiveled his head between Cyril Harlow and

Runa Rasgar, not bothering to hide his gawking at the famous archrivals. He excitedly elbowed the student beside him, a pale, gloomy-looking girl with black-painted nails and eyes ringed with smudgy makeup.

"If you need me," Runa muttered to Barclay, Viola, and Tadg, "I'll be in the bathroom seeing if the jokes I wrote about Cyril are still on the walls."

Runa ducked down the right hallway. Cyril glanced at her, frowned, then forced his attention back on the apprentices at the front of the line. He handed them sets of brass keys.

"I don't blame her for leaving," Kadia said. "I'm still upset with Cyril myself."

"Mom, Cyril was my teacher *two years ago*," Viola said.

Before Barclay had met Viola, she'd been Cyril's apprentice, not Runa's. But after Viola struggled under the pressure and fell behind Shazi and Hasu, Cyril had quit being her teacher. He'd apologized last year at the Sea, but Viola was far happier with Runa as her instructor, anyway.

Kadia crossed her arms. "I know from Leo's letters that he gave Cyril more than a piece of his mind—as he should've! It was thanks to Cyril that you ran off to the Woods by yourself! I'm still upset with you about that too, you know."

Viola fiddled with her pins, looking embarrassed. "Again, two years ago."

"Moms have a long memory."

When their group reached the front of the line, Cyril beamed at them. "There you all are. I was very pleased to see your names on the list of this year's students. And Viola, you remember Tati."

A long tongue flicked out from beneath the desk. Barclay bent down and saw a huge, salamander-like Beast curled around Cyril's boots. The red, orange, and black of her scales rippled, and her eyes glowed with molten light. Of Cyril's two Beasts, Barclay had only ever glimpsed the other one, Codric, from afar, and Tati was much larger than he expected.

"As the resident Guardian Master," Cyril continued, "I live in the dormitory with you—my suite is there." He puffed out his chest and nodded toward the set of doors at the back of the lounge. "I'm here to provide any necessary guidance in your studies, to help you with your training outside of class, as well as to make sure the students are behaving appropriately. Down *those* two hallways are your own rooms. Beasts are permitted out of their Marks so long as they don't attack other students or Beasts. Lights-out every night is at ten o'clock."

Cyril sounded rather giddy as he rattled off each rule.

"Now, Viola," Cyril said, peering at his neatly organized list. "Hasu told me you're rooming with her. You're down the right hallway, room nine. Barclay and Tadg, you'll be down the left hallway, room two."

He slid them each their keys.

"Unpack and get settled. Your books and supplies are already in your rooms. The opening ceremony will begin at six."

While Viola, Kadia, and Pemba veered down the right hallway, Barclay and Tadg explored theirs. Their room waited for them at the end of the corridor, directly across from the set of teenagers whom Barclay had noticed earlier.

Tadg unlocked their door and swung it open. His face fell. "It's . . . small."

He was right. The room barely squeezed in more than two

beds and two wardrobes. As Tadg stepped inside, Toadles appeared on his shoulder with a loud, throaty *"Croak!"* He leapt onto one of the beds and—not a moment later— vomited purple sludge on the pillow.

Barclay snickered. "Guess that one's yours."

He set his satchel on the floor and summoned Root from his Mark. Root took up an enormous amount of space in the tiny room, and even more so as he planted his front paws on the ground and stretched out his back.

"There's no way Root is going to fit with you on that bed," Tadg said.

Root huffed indignantly. Root always slept beside him, and neither of them was about to change that just for a little extra wiggle room.

Barclay scratched Root's chin. "Don't listen to Tadg. We'll manage."

Satisfied, Root climbed atop their bed, which groaned as though it might collapse. He padded in a circle before settling himself in the corner. Then he peered at Tadg and tilted his head to the side, as if to say *See?*

While Root made himself comfortable and Tadg unpacked his belongings, Barclay swung open the doors of his wardrobe. A set of leather-bound books was already stacked on the top shelf. The first several all belonged to the same collection, called *The Lore Keeper Histories*, volumes 1–4. The next was a glossy new edition called *The Wilderlands: Around the World in One Thousand Pages*. He picked up the final book gingerly; its ancient yellow paper barely clung to its spine, and mysterious splotches stained its corners. The faded text on the front read *Guildocracy*, and even

Barclay, who loved books, thought it looked dreadfully dull.

"Watch out!" someone shouted, and Barclay ducked just in time as a slimy silver cannonball shot into their room. It landed on the far window with a wet *splat*. Root bolted off the bed and barked at it loudly.

The first teenager from earlier poked his head in their doorway. Whatever the slime was, the boy was absolutely covered in it. Shimmering strings dangled from his black ponytail and clung to his clothes.

"Sorry! Sorry! That wasn't supposed to go off yet." Then his eyes fell on Root. "Whoa. That's a mighty big Beast for someone so small. Tell me—how do you feel about tiny spaces? I found a secret passage underneath my bed, but it's too tight for me. I think it goes to Hamdani Hall—"

"You found a secret passage?" asked Barclay. He'd only ever heard of secret passages in castles from adventures books.

"I've found six since this morning. The school is full of them."

Tadg poked the stringy ball of slime on the window and grimaced. "What *is* this stuff?"

"It's Chimpachipa web. Slime Lore," he explained. "I'm setting booby traps up and down the hallways. Even if the Horn of Dawn is this year's resident Guardian Master, I don't trust the Surveyors being just across the building. And with the opening ceremony tonight, we have to be ready for anything."

"Rohan!" a girl's voice shouted. "Did you booby-trap my wardrobe?"

"Why would you open it?" the boy—Rohan—shouted back.

"Why would I open it? *Why would you booby-trap it?*"

Rohan winced. "One moment please," he told them, then he slipped back into room 1 across the hall. Barclay watched through the open door as Rohan burst into laughter. Then something roared, so powerful that the strings of web in Rohan's hair were whipped back and splattered across the wall behind him. Root jolted in alarm and stepped protectively between Barclay and the door.

Then the girl with the smudgy makeup stormed out of the room. A tiny, fluffy white seal Beast sat in her arms, and both were covered in slime.

Barclay and Tadg glanced at each other in confusion. It didn't seem possible that either the girl or her Beast had made that roar.

"Anyway," Rohan slurred, stumbling dizzily back into the hallway, "as I was saying. Small spaces. Little wolf boy. D-do you . . ."

His voice wobbled then died as Runa strode toward them. She brushed past a starstruck Rohan and studied Barclay and Tadg's room with a frown. "Room two? Is this the one with the crack in the floor in the corner?"

Barclay turned. Sure enough, beneath his bed, a crack wove across the checkered tiles.

"How'd you know that?" he asked her.

"This was Cyril and Audrian's room during our Symposium."

Barclay recoiled. The crack in the floor must've been from Keyes's stone Lore.

"Let me guess," Tadg said snidely. "You need to leave because you have some supersecret meeting with Asfour."

Runa didn't bother rising to Tadg's taunt, but her smirk was answer enough. "A word of advice: if you want to sneak out after dark, the second study down the first hallway has a false bookcase. The passage will lead you straight into the courtyard. If Cyril asks, you absolutely tell him you heard so from me."

With that, Runa left. Barclay stared again at the crack in the floor, disturbed at the idea of sharing the same old dormitory room—maybe even the same bed—with the most dangerous Lore Keeper in the Wilderlands. Root must've agreed, as he sniffed the broken floor tile suspiciously.

Barclay was so lost in his thoughts that he'd forgotten Rohan was still in their room, until Rohan burst out, "If the Fang of Dusk is your Lore Master, there's no way the Guardians won't win the Tourney this year. Did you know that when she was in the Symposium, she rang the bell at the top of the University tower? Only the Chancellor knows how to get in—there are no doors in or out of there. She's legendary. To this day, no one has any idea how she did it."

Barclay had a feeling that Rohan would get along well with Shazi and Cecily. "So is the Tourney some kind of stunt war?" Even after Shazi's explanation, Barclay still didn't understand how it worked. Not that it mattered. He cared too much about his schoolwork to join in something so ridiculous.

"Stunts, pranks, mayhem." Rohan's smile stretched wider with each word.

"And how do you know who wins?"

"Oh, believe me, you know." He rubbed his hands together. "And this year, it's going to be us."

The opening ceremony of the Symposium took place in a vast outdoor amphitheater. The sunset painted the sky deep orange and scarlet, and torches burned in a ring around the stage. As Barclay filed into one of the rows, he counted the other apprentices around him and estimated that the Symposium had about one hundred students. They sat divided according to their Guild track, and it was clear that not every track was the same size. The Apothecaries and Scholars had the most apprentices, while the Surveyors had the fewest.

On the stage waited five adults. Barclay recognized two of them: Cyril, who wore twice as many medals as usual, and Chancellor Essam, whose chair was draped in golden tassels.

Barclay sat between Hasu and Viola. Behind them, Shazi, Cecily, and Rohan—who'd met on the walk here—debated over the best way to sneak into the Surveyors' lounge, which Rohan hoped to decorate with slimy spiderweb before morning.

Once the apprentices had all taken their seats, Chancellor Essam stood. A hush fell over the students.

"Welcome to the eight hundred and sixty-first Symposium," he said. "Every year, the University of Al Faradh is given the honor of instructing the next generation of Guild-licensed Lore Keepers, which means that a great number of others have sat where you are right now. As the local wisdom goes, in the University, history walks the halls beside you."

Though Barclay knew Essam's words were meant as inspiration, he couldn't help but think of his room once belonging to Audrian Keyes. A shiver prickled down his back.

"Among this year's resident Lore Masters, I'm pleased to welcome the Scholar Joshna Oza, whose work studying the effect of seasons on the Wilderlands was nominated for last year's Foxtail Prize. Beside her is Otto Drager, the Apothecary who invented Scare Sap, which is so effective at curing hiccups that it is sold across all six Wilderlands and even in multiple nations of the Elsewheres."

Both Lore Keepers were met with polite applause. It wasn't until Essam mentioned Cyril's name that the cheers grew raucous. It seemed the Guardians were already in a competitive spirit. Loudest among them hollered Shazi and Rohan.

"Cyril Harlow holds the office of Deputy Administrator of the Grand Keeper. Among his many awards, he has received two gold medals for exceptional service to the Guild, for his single-handed reconstruction of the Tundra's Guild House after a Midwinter blizzard and for quelling a volcanic eruption that would've destroyed an Elsewheres town."

Barclay must not have heard right. There was no way one Keeper could stop an entire volcano from erupting.

"And lastly, the resident Surveyor Master is Yawen Li, who has discovered forty new species of Beasts, not including the Nitwitt bird, which was long believed to be extinct."

The Surveyor students erupted into applause. Barclay couldn't tell if it was out of excitement for Li or to upstage the Guardians. Regardless, Li seemed pleased. She wore thick hiking boots and a thicker pair of goggles over her head, as though she intended to go straight from the opening ceremony to exploring a cave for diamonds.

"Some of you are near the end of your apprenticeships and will sit for your licensing exams as soon as you graduate from the Symposium. For others, your exam remains years away. However, I want to impress upon you that what you learn here is not simply for the purpose of obtaining your license—indeed, many of you will ultimately not obtain a license at all. The primary goal of the Symposium is to make you informed Lore Keepers, capable of solving complex problems thanks to a greater understanding of the world. So I urge you to use your time here wisely."

Though Essam never looked at Barclay directly, Barclay felt as though his words were for him and him alone. Barclay *would* use his time at the University wisely. Because he was going to pass his classes, no matter what it took. Because he was going to be one of the few Lore Keepers to earn a Guild license. And because, one day a long, long time from now, he was going to help change the Elsewheres for the better.

Behind him, Shazi's whispers were anything but quiet. "You're right. We have to strike the Surveyors first. Otherwise, they'll definitely make the first move."

"There's a secret entrance into their lounge behind the statue of the phoenix in the central hall," Cecily said. "What? I heard their lounge has a chandelier made out of petrified dragon fangs, and I wanted to see it."

"You've already been inside?" Rohan asked, sounding impressed.

Chancellor Essam cleared his throat—the mischievous trio behind Barclay weren't the only students chattering. "Lastly, I wish to advise that any suspicious behavior should be reported directly to either the visiting Masters or myself. I am aware of certain . . . traditions that take place here every year, and though I have given up on dissuading students from participating, safety remains my chief priority. If you see any strange activity from someone who is clearly not a student, please inform us at once."

"What do you think he means by that?" Barclay murmured to Viola. Essam was probably referring to the Tourney, but Barclay had never heard anyone claim it might be dangerous.

Except Viola wasn't looking at Barclay. She wasn't even looking at the Chancellor. Instead, she stared at the building to their right with a funny, disbelieving expression.

"What?" Barclay asked.

"I swore for a moment I saw . . ." She shook her head. "Never mind. It's too dark to see anything anyway."

Essam continued his final remarks. "Remember, classes begin tomorrow at nine o'clock. Please be punctual. No running or using Lore in the courtyards. You're the future of the Guild and the next generation of Lore Keepers. We expect the best from you and won't tolerate any less." Then, with a wave of dismissal, he said, "Welcome to the Symposium."

Dear Master Pilzmann . . .

Barclay scooted to try to give himself more space on the bed, as Root was hogging most of the mattress. A meager flame burned in a sconce above him on the wall, the only light in the otherwise dark room. Across from him, Tadg snored, his arms hugged around his pillow and his feet flung out from beneath his sheets.

Barclay knew he should sleep as well. He'd need his energy for their first day of classes tomorrow. But he wanted to write his letter to Master Pilzmann so he could tell him about their latest adventure.

As he put the finishing touches on his description of the Symposium's opening ceremony, several muffled thuds sounded—footsteps.

Beside him, Root stirred and lifted his head, and Tadg's voice rasped through the darkness.

"Did you hear something?"

"I don't know," Barclay answered nervously. He slid down from his bed and crept toward the door. Then he inspected the empty hallway. "It's nothing. Go back to sleep."

But even as he curled up next to Root, his skin was prickled, and he had the eerie feeling of being watched.

And so he whispered, "Do you ever think about Yasha?"

"Why?" Tadg asked sharply. Despite the year they'd lived above the Planty Shanty at the Sea, they never talked about when their group of two roommates had actually been three.

"I don't know. He was our friend, wasn't he?" Barclay wasn't sure why he spoke it like a question—of course Yasha had been. Yasha was the one who'd helped Barclay figure out how to control his Lore. And if things were different, maybe Yasha would be here at the Symposium with them. "And it's weird being in Keyes's old room."

"Well, you know what I think? He was never really our friend, and this is just a room."

Tadg rolled over and left it at that.

Barclay sighed, but he pushed thoughts of Yasha out of his mind. As he returned to his letter, he remembered

Kadia's words from last night, and the revelation that not all regions of the Elsewheres feared the Wilderlands like Dullshire did.

Do you think Dullshire could ever change its mind about the Woods? he wrote.

Master Pilzmann would give him his honest opinion, even if Barclay so badly wanted the answer to be yes.

By the time he sealed the envelope, midnight had long since passed. Exhausted, he squished himself beside Root, and it felt as though he had barely closed his eyes when . . .

Barclay awoke to the foulest reek he'd ever smelled. It reminded him of mold and old fish and garbage left outside to bake on a hot day. He sat up and clamped his hand over his nose. Root buried his head beneath the blankets.

Across the room, Tadg muffled a groan into his pillow.

"What *is* that?" Barclay asked.

The sounds of doors opening thumped outside. Barclay slipped out of bed, creaked open their own door, and peered once again down the hallway. Several students in their nightclothes blinked at one another blearily, handkerchiefs pressed over their noses.

A green haze hovered near the ceiling, growing denser and smellier toward the lounge.

Barclay, Root, and the other students and Beasts followed the putrid trail. In the lounge, the smelly fog was so thick that it looked as though the room had sunk to the bottom of a scummy lake. On the table by the fireplace, a large copper-colored feather rested beside a piece of parchment.

Your move.

—The Surveyors

Several of the Guardian apprentices bickered around it.

"I knew I should've laid my booby traps!" complained Rohan, whose Chimpachipa clung to his shoulders like a backpack. "We were defenseless!"

"No one expected the Tourney to begin the first night," said someone else.

Shazi paced to and fro, waving her arms wildly. "How are we going to upstage this?" Beside her, Saif, her Scormoddin, stretched out his metal scorpion tail as though still waking up. A silk nightcap rested crookedly on his head, and slippers fit onto each of his eight feet.

"Upstage it?" echoed Hasu. "If everyone goes pulling pranks like this, it'll be mayhem by the end of the week."

The doors to the center of Eldin Hall burst open, and Cyril stormed into the lounge. He looked oddly unlike himself without his medals and with his hair messy from bed.

"Well," he huffed. "I just spoke to Li, and it seems that, despite her duties as resident Surveyor Master, she has no intention of punishing her students for their actions. And she denied the fact that the feather of the Badachidia clearly belongs to one of her students."

"How are we supposed to sleep with all the stink Lore floating about?" Viola asked.

Cyril sighed. "Open your windows. Let's hope it airs out."

The students groaned. Their windows were already open. They'd be lucky if their dormitory stopped reeking by next week.

"Now to bed, all of you," Cyril said. "You'll need to be alert for classes tomorrow."

With that, Cyril disappeared into his suite.

"A lot of help he was," Rohan muttered.

"Barclay can get rid of the smell," Cecily suggested, and all eyes in the room swiveled to him and Root eagerly.

"I don't think I can. . . ." But Barclay's voice trailed off as Root nudged him forward, and Barclay glared at him—he was making it awfully hard to lie. They *could* do it. He knew they could. He just wasn't so sure he liked the Tourney and all the havoc it caused. And he didn't want to get in trouble the first night of the Symposium. "Won't Cyril be upset with me?"

"Do you want the Guardians to be a laughingstock for the rest of term?" Shazi demanded.

"Well, no, but—"

"Go on, then!" Cecily said. "Give it a whirl!"

The other apprentices nodded, and Barclay didn't want to disappoint so many people he'd only just met. Nor did he want to lose sleep the night before classes because of the rotten odor. So, begrudgingly, he asked, "Can someone open the doors to the atrium?" Beside him, Root's chest swelled in satisfaction.

Stealthily, Shazi, Rohan, Viola, and Hasu opened the two sets of double doors that led from the the Guardians' dormitory into the entrance hall of statues.

Then, as Barclay and Root readied their stances, Cecily said, "Wait. Wait. I have the perfect idea."

Before Barclay could object, she summoned her Tenepie, Oudie, a black-and-white magpie Beast who was even sneakier than her. With Oudie roosted in her hair, Cecily crept down the hallway, and the image of them grew smaller and darker with every step. By the time they reached the doors across the atrium, they'd faded entirely into shadow.

"What's she doing?" Hasu hissed.

"She's opening the doors to the Surveyors' dormitory," Shazi said, grinning wickedly. "She swiped one of their keys this morning, and I made a copy."

Everyone held their breath as Cecily inserted the counterfeit key into the set of double doors to the Surveyors' dormitory. Then she shot a devious smile at her classmates behind her and pushed the doors open wide.

"This is brilliant!" Rohan breathed. "We're gonna send the stench right back to them."

Barclay hesitated, locking eyes warily with Root. He hadn't agreed to that. "But I—"

"Go on!" one of the other apprentices said eagerly. "What are you waiting for? Do it!"

Barclay wanted to argue. Saving their dormitory was one thing, but pranking the surveyors was another. But with the doors already open, it seemed too late to chicken out now.

The other apprentices backed away while Barclay readied himself in a wide stance to match Root's. He focused on the foul green haze that wafted below the ceiling, then he raised his arms.

Wind!

Instead of blowing the wind away, Barclay pulled it toward them. It was a technique he hadn't fully mastered on his own, but his Lore was always more powerful when he and Root worked together. To his pleasant surprise, the green haze began to seep from the left and right hallways into the lounge. It swirled around them in a noxious whirl-wind. One of the other apprentices watching, a boy who looked no older than eleven, had been holding his breath so long, he fainted.

When all the green stink Lore had been sucked out of the hallways, Barclay and Root blasted it across Eldin Hall into the east wing. After they'd gotten rid of the last of it, Cecily shut the doors and sprinted back to the Guardians' lounge, Oudie soaring above her. Her short hair had been swept upward, and her clothes reeked, but she was laughing too hard to care.

Rohan slapped Barclay's shoulder. "That was *amazing!*"

"You've gotten so much stronger, Barclay," Hasu told him, while scratching Root appreciatively behind the ears.

By the time everyone crawled back to their beds, Barclay and Root had accidentally become Eldin Hall's local heroes.

Maybe, just maybe, he was starting to understand the excitement of the Tourney.

SIX

Barclay's first class, Guild Studies, took place in a domed building halfway across campus, with sunlight streaming into the lecture hall through the glass ceiling. Three banners draped on either side of the chalkboard, each in a different color, and each bearing the coat of arms of one of the Wilderlands. On the left hung the Desert, the Tundra, and the Woods. And on the right: the Jungle, the Sea, and the Mountains.

As Barclay entered, a pair of Scholar students strode past down the aisle, whispering to each other. He caught phrases like "huge tornado" and "the Fang of Dusk's apprentice." One of them glanced at Barclay over her shoulder.

"Everyone is staring," Barclay said nervously to his friends.

"Just ignore them," Viola told him.

"Oh, it's not so bad to be a celebrity," said Cecily brightly.

Maybe Cecily was right. After all, with Runa Rasgar

as a Lore Master and the kids of the Grand Keeper and a world-famous Surveyor as fellow apprentices, Barclay was used to being the one everyone overlooked. But he still wasn't sure he wanted to be a celebrity. The Tourney might be fun, but he couldn't afford a distraction.

And judging from the prickly glares around the room, he suspected being famous in the Tourney also made you a target. He gulped and slumped into an empty seat.

The chattering died as the teacher swept into the classroom. He was a clever-looking man with brown skin and large, copper-rimmed glasses shaped like hexagons. Barclay recognized him instantly: Mandeep Acharya, one of the Lore Masters who'd helped Barclay in the Woods during his Exhibition. Mandeep had mentioned that he worked at the University, but Barclay hadn't realized that he was one of the instructors of the Symposium.

"Welcome to Guild Studies," Mandeep began as he wrote his name in Lore script on the chalkboard. "I'm Instructor Acharya, and for the next two seasons, we'll be studying the structure of the Guild. . . ." His roaming gaze found Barclay's. He smiled warmly, but he didn't interrupt his lecture. "As apprentices, all of you are training to one day pass the licensing exam and become members of the Guild, and that means you need to understand why the Guild was created and how it works. Now, before we turn to the opening chapter of *Guildocracy*, who can tell me what the original capital of the Guild was?"

Several hands rose into the air—most of them from the Scholar students, as well as Viola and Hasu. Mandeep called on one of the Scholars.

"It was here in Menneset," she answered matter-of-factly.

"Correct," said Mandeep. "The Desert was the first Wilderland to establish a Guild chapter, and the charter was written here, at the University. Over the next fifty years, the other Wilderlands created chapters of their own. Eventually, the capital was moved to Halois, in the Mountains, to be more centrally located."

Barclay tried very hard to write each of Mandeep's words into his notebook, but it was tricky to concentrate. His skin still burned under the heat of stares from around the room.

"And can anyone tell me how many High Keepers there are?" Mandeep asked.

This time, far more hands shot up, and he called on Rohan's roommate and fellow apprentice—who Barclay had learned at breakfast was named Deirdre Gaffney.

"There's five," Deirdre answered.

"That's correct, but it's only correct in a very special circumstance. Who knows what that is?"

This time, only Viola's hand lifted.

"Yes, Viola?" Mandeep asked.

Viola beamed, seeming pleased that Mandeep remembered her name from a year and a half ago. "When the Grand Keeper is from the Mountains, they work as both a Grand Keeper *and* a High Keeper, since they're already in Halois. But when the Grand Keeper is from a different Wilderland, the Mountains elects a local High Keeper."

"Isn't her *dad* the Grand Keeper?" someone whispered behind them. Embarrassed, Viola fiddled with a gold button on her sleeve.

"That's absolutely right," Mandeep said. "For the past

seventy years, there have been only five High Keepers, but throughout most of the Guild's history, there have been six. And who elects Grand and High Keepers?"

This time, even Barclay knew the answer, and Mandeep called on him when he raised his hand.

"High Keepers are appointed by the Grand Keeper. . . ." Barclay paused, realizing everyone had twisted in their seats to look at him. "A-a-and the Grand Keeper is elected by all residents of the Wilderlands."

"Correct. An election is held every five years. And in the case of the Grand Keeper's sudden resignation or death, their interim replacement is elected by the Guild, of which there are currently about fifteen hundred active members."

Gradually, the class faded from back-and-forth questions into a proper lecture. Mandeep recited so many facts that Barclay scribbled nearly eight pages of notes. At this rate, he would need a new notebook by the end of Autumn.

Their next course was called Lore Keeper History, and their classroom couldn't have been more different from the one they'd left. It was dark and dusty and so filled with books that everyone struggled to find a place to sit. Barclay had to rearrange the tower of tomes on his desk so as not to block his view of the chalkboard.

At the front of the room, the instructor silently watched the Guardian and Apothecary apprentices enter. She had pale skin and frizzy gray hair tied back beneath a colorful, fraying scarf. None of her clothing seemed to match or fit right, and she'd bundled herself within a heavy wool jacket despite the hot day.

"Hello, hello," she spoke in a throaty voice. "My name is Instructor Dudnik. As many of you heard, Instructor Younis is unable to join us this year, as a horrible accident befell him. Such dreadful, dreadful luck."

She bowed her head gravely, as though in mourning.

"Isn't that the Scholar your parents mentioned the other night?" Tadg whispered to Viola.

"Yeah," she answered. "But I couldn't ask Mom what happened to him without giving away that we were eavesdropping."

"Since I joined the staff last minute," Dudnik continued, "I've been asked to keep with the old teacher's curriculum. That means we'll be using his textbooks and quizzes. So make sure to study the textbook on your own time. And now . . . today's lecture."

She ambled toward the chalkboard, tripping twice on the long train of her skirt.

One of the Apothecary students raised his hand—the handsome boy with the lime-green hair Shazi had pointed out at Registration. But Dudnik didn't notice, so he called out, "Does this mean you won't be teaching what's on the quizzes?"

When Dudnik didn't respond, he repeated himself louder.

Dudnik startled and peered at him. "Mm-hmm, yes? Your name is?"

"Fen Zhong," he said, ignoring the three fellow Apothecaries to his left, who looked scandalized Dudnik didn't know who he was. "I asked whether or not you'll be teaching what's on the quizzes."

"No, no, Mr. Zhong. I have much more important topics to cover. . . ." She batted away the cobwebs clinging to the board. Then she wrote in huge, loopy letters:

THE GREAT CAPAMOO WAR

"Is this a joke?" Tadg hissed.

"I don't think so," Barclay answered, because suddenly, he realized he knew who this instructor was. He'd read her textbook *The Nine Most Crucial Events of Lore Keeper History (They Really Did Happen!)* at the Sea when Runa mistakenly assigned it to him. The Great Capamoo War was one of the many conspiracy theories that Dudnik loved to ramble about. "Runa told me that she and Dudnik are cousins."

Dudnik sneezed, making the dust around her plume into the air.

"Yeah," Tadg said sarcastically. "I can really see the resemblance."

"The Great Capamoo War happened here at the Desert along the southeastern coastline," Dudnik explained. "Capamoos are large, flightless avian Beasts. There are some Scholars who will claim that these events were insignificant, but I disagree. It's estimated that between six and three thousand people lost their lives thanks to the Capamoo general's ruthless guerrilla tactics. . . ."

Tuning her out, Barclay turned to the first page in *The Lore Keeper Histories*, volume 1. The print was so tiny, he had to hunch closer to read it right, and he wondered miserably how he'd learn so much for the exams if Dudnik taught totally different lessons in class.

"Capamoos are Prime class Beasts," Viola grumbled after they left. "There's no way they could defeat an entire Lore Keeper army."

"Plus, their brains are the size of strawberries," added Tadg.

After their second class was a break for lunch and free

time. Barclay wolfed down a meal of eggplant stuffed with rice and hurried with Root to the edge of campus. He needed to deliver his letter to Master Pilzmann to the post office, and according to Viola, the closest one was over a mile from the University.

"We'll have to run so I can make it to my next class," Barclay told Root.

Root wagged his tail eagerly. Then, before Barclay had even taken his first step, he shot off. Barclay grinned and sprinted after him.

Barclay had always loved running, even back when he'd lived in Dullshire. He liked the feeling of the wind whipping through his hair. He liked how it felt as though adventure awaited him just around the corner. He liked to feel a little bit wild.

Most importantly, he liked to run *fast*. Which made Root the perfect Beast for him, as Lufthunds were the fastest creatures in the world.

In the heat of the afternoon, Menneset's streets were nearly deserted. And so Barclay and Root wove through the narrow alleys, veering side to side to dodge the pillars of the aqueducts that vaulted above. Soon they gained speed. Faster and faster, until the ruffles of Root's coat began to look less like fur and more like smoke. Until Barclay's fingers and clothes blurred, and he felt the Autumn breeze course through his bones.

They had become the wind.

No matter how many times they ran together, Barclay never grew tired of it. And so he was disappointed when they quickly reached the post office, skidding to a halt outside its front door. Beads of sweat dribbled down his temples, and Root panted, his tongue lolling out.

Inside, a middle-aged man slumped over the counter, idly scratching his pencil in the crossword of today's edition of the *Keeper's Khronicle*. He scowled as Barclay approached. "What do you want?"

"I'd like to send a letter to the Elsewheres, sir," Barclay said politely.

"Which kingdom?" The man turned around to the wall of cubbies behind him, where fifteen small postal dragons roosted. Wrinkles drooped over their eyes, and each wore a brown uniform with a red scarf tied around their neck.

"Humdrum," Barclay answered. Technically, Dullshire was squished between the borders of two kingdoms, Humdrum and Diddlystadt, but Barclay had sent Master Pilzmann many letters from the Sea, and Humdrum had worked just fine.

"Never heard of it," the man grumbled.

"It's near the Woods."

"The Woods? That'll be ten kritters. No—twelve."

"*Twelve?* But it cost only six in Munsey."

"Well, the Woods is a bit farther from here than it is from the Sea, isn't it?" The man held out his hand, and Barclay bitterly passed him twelve brass coins along with the letter. Runa paid her three apprentices an allowance, but it was small. "I'm sorry, Root. It looks like we'll be buying less treats for a while."

Root, who'd been drinking from the water bowl by the entrance, shot the postman a dirty look.

Barclay was still in a sour mood by the time he returned to

the University, making him forget that he'd been dreading his final class the most: the Wilderlands, which the Guardians shared with the Surveyors. As soon as he stepped foot in the lecture hall, the Surveyor apprentices glared at him. They all smelled faintly of rotten fish.

Behind him, Rohan crinkled his nose. "Why are you so sweaty?"

"Running," Barclay said dismissively. He didn't care about that. "I don't get it. *They* filled our dorm with stink Lore first. It's their own fault."

"Maybe. But it's probably a good idea to watch your back."

Barclay was so anxious that he barely paid attention to where he was walking, and he collided with another student. The girl clearly hadn't been paying attention either, as she'd been bent over a map so large, its edges grazed the floor.

Barclay reddened. He'd noticed the girl at Registration, and she was quite pretty up close. Her map, however, made little sense—it was more covered in scribbles and ink splotches than actual places.

"Sorry," he said hastily. He suddenly cared far more about being sweaty than he had a moment ago.

Before he could flee back to his friends, the girl grinned. "So *you're* the reason we all woke up smelling like Badachidias." Then she lowered her voice. "I'd be careful if I were you. I'm pretty sure some of the Surveyors are already planning revenge."

"B-but you're all the ones who started it," he stammered.

She shrugged. "So? Guardians always get all the glory, even when they don't deserve it. Just trust me and stay away from the courtyard this evening."

Barclay probably should've been offended on behalf of his fellow students, but he was oddly pleased that she'd been willing to give him advice. "Um, thanks."

She walked off, once again studying her map. He tried not to stare too long. Maybe being a local celebrity wasn't so bad after all.

Shazi swatted Barclay when he sat down. "Why were you fraternizing with the competition? Zenzi Kipping is Li's apprentice! You know . . . the *resident Surveyor Master*?"

Before Barclay could defend himself, the instructor sauntered into the classroom. Unlike the other teachers, he didn't dress like a Scholar, with any ropes or tassels. Instead, he wore casual, loose-fitting trousers and leather gloves, similar to the pilot of their carrier dragon. He even looked windswept. His coily gray hair had been blown back, and droplets of sweat gleamed on his dark brown skin. In his hand, he clutched a steaming cup of coffee.

"Don't mind my appearance," he told them. "I just returned from doing some research in the Ironwood Forest. It had a remarkable growing season this past Summer, and I . . . Well, I ought to save the exciting stuff for a future lesson. Today is for introductions, after all."

Rather than move toward the chalkboard, he sat cross-legged on his desk, set his coffee to the side, and leaned back on his hands.

"My name is Instructor Dia, and this class is called the Wilderlands. Very descriptive, isn't it? We'll be talking about the six regions of the world where Lore Keepers live, from their cities and natural landmarks to a few of their common and most distinctive types of Beasts. I say talking—not studying—because that's truly what we'll be doing. I have lessons and homework to give you, of course, but we'll also be learning from one another. Now, by a show of hands, how many of you are from the Sea?"

Several hands rose, including Tadg's and Deirdre's.

"The Tundra?" A few more shot into the air. "The Desert?" This time, Instructor Dia lifted his own hand, along with Viola, Shazi, and three other students.

A lump lodged in Barclay's throat. He had no idea what to answer.

"The Jungle? . . . The Mountains?" Viola lifted her hand a second time. "The Woods?"

His face flushing, Barclay stretched up his arm. Across the room, he noticed Zenzi do the same.

"The Elsewheres?" Dia asked last, and Barclay froze. He hadn't expected the Elsewheres to be included. Not wanting to be singled out, he didn't move, but then Tadg elbowed him in the side, and Barclay awkwardly held up his hand. Several Surveyor apprentices whispered behind him, and he slouched lower in his seat.

Thankfully, Dia didn't remark on the lone Elsie student. He only grinned, took a sip of his coffee, and slid off the desk. "Excellent. We'll have plenty of knowledge to share with one another. Most of our time will be spent in this classroom, but throughout the term, we'll be taking field trips to admire the natural wonders of the Desert up close. But for our first unit, we'll be discussing . . ."

He reached above the chalkboard and yanked down a map that Barclay instantly recognized.

"The Woods," Dia finished. Like most maps of the

Wilderlands, it had huge chunks that weren't filled in, as they still had yet to be explored.

Dia rubbed his hands together eagerly, and though Barclay considered Mandeep a friend, he had a feeling that Dia would be his favorite instructor. And he wasn't alone. All across the classroom, the apprentices leaned forward in their seats, keen to hear what Dia would say next.

They were all disappointed.

"I thought we could start with a pop quiz," Dia suggested. At the students' groans, he chuckled and said, "I've been teaching this class for twenty years, and the response is always the same. But don't worry—it's just for practice. I only want to learn how much you already know."

He passed around the quizzes, which were each only a single page. Barclay's heart pounded as he remembered all too well the last Lore Keeper test he'd taken—the written exam of the Exhibition, where he'd known barely any of the answers.

Yet as he scanned the questions, his grouchy mood from earlier vanished. Thanks to the studying he'd done over the past year and a half, he didn't know just some of the answers. He knew *all* of them.

He was still beaming an hour later when he and his friends walked across the courtyard.

"Why do you look so happy?" Cecily asked accusingly. "That was impossible. I've never even heard of the Stingur Caves or the Hasifuss Orchards."

"I did better than I thought I would, is all," Barclay told her.

"I knew that would happen," Viola said. "You know more

than you think you do. You should tell Runa when she comes back from her mission."

Beside her, Hasu picked at her fingernails.

"What are you nervous about?" Shazi asked her. "All you've done for the past year is study, and that quiz didn't even count."

"I'm worried I forgot to write my name on mine—"

"Hey! Guardians!" someone shouted, and the six of them whipped around in time to glimpse what looked like colorful cannonballs soaring straight for them.

Hasu was the only one to react fast enough. A golden hexagon of light flashed in front of her, like a shining honeycomb, and she vanished a split second before the cannonballs splatted them all in the face.

Barclay sputtered and wiped the liquid out of his eyes. It was just water—or so he first thought. Then he saw that Cecily's eyebrows were dyed a vibrant candy pink. Tadg's hair was a flaming orange, and Shazi's shirt had gone from beige to sunflower yellow.

"What is this stuff?" Tadg grunted. Behind them, a throng of Scholar students burst into laughter.

"It's inkyfruit juice," Viola answered, scrunching the purple liquid from her curls. "Don't worry—it comes out with water."

Across the courtyard, a group of Surveyors cackled. One of them wielded a strange wooden contraption like a slingshot, while Zenzi loaded juice balloons inside. Seeing them glaring, Zenzi waved, and Barclay felt foolish for forgetting her warning about the courtyard. He didn't guess that she'd been warning him about herself, though.

"It's only the first day of classes," Barclay grumbled, "and I'm already tired of the Tourney."

Light shimmered beside them, and Hasu reappeared, giggling. "You look like an Agmor," she told Barclay, who'd been dowsed in splotches of peacock blue.

"You couldn't have used your spatial Lore to save one of us, too?" Shazi asked, and Hasu shrugged sheepishly.

Turning away from the Surveyors was a mistake, because a second later, another juice-filled balloon splattered across Barclay's backside.

"Run!" Shazi yelled, and the six of them sprinted across the courtyard. They dove for cover inside Eldin Hall, but not before getting drenched in sticky inkyfruit juice—and laughed at by half of the Symposium.

"Don't worry," Cecily said fiercely, "we'll plan our revenge. Rohan already has a hundred ideas."

"Great, but count me out of them," Barclay muttered.

He might've been sweaty, and his pants might've looked as though he'd sat in a puddle of raspberry jam, but the day had one silver lining. If the rest of his classes went as smoothly as his first pop quiz, then maybe Barclay wouldn't be as miserable of a student as he'd feared.

Maybe he could even be a good one.

SEVEN

D o we really have to wear this?" Barclay cringed as he sniffed his training gear. The leather padding on his chest, shoulders, and legs reeked of body odor, a memento from the likely hundreds of students who'd worn it before him. On his left, Root pawed at his oversized helmet as it wobbled side to side.

"It's University policy," Cyril told him.

"But it's heavy. How are we supposed to run in this?"

"The added weight will help you get stronger." Cyril flipped through his notebook until he reached a fresh page. "Now, it's been a long time since we last saw each other in Munsey. Why don't you show me what you can do?"

Readying himself, Barclay faced the practice dummies on the other side of the arena. Training sessions with the resident Guardian Master took place in a gymnasium filled with all kinds of equipment: hurdles, ropes, climbing walls, and even a pool. Two weeks had passed since the Symposium's move-in day, so most of the other students had already finished their first one-on-one session with Cyril. And Hasu, Tadg, and Rohan had warned Barclay about what to expect.

"I spent over an hour throwing a disk to myself back and forth across the arena," Hasu had complained last week with a yawn—using too much of her Lore always made her tired. "My arms feel like pudding now."

"Cyril wants me to build up a tolerance to Toadles's poison Lore," Tadg had told him one night, rolling up his sleeves to reveal arms covered in itchy hives. "Toadles loved it. Cyril basically let him torture me."

"Have you ever climbed a rope of slime all the way to the ceiling?" Rohan had asked yesterday, shuddering. "It's so stretchy that you climb and climb and end up right back on the floor."

The twelve wooden practice dummies were riddled with holes from the many students who'd whacked, shot, and stabbed them. Half of them looked human shaped. The rest were Beasts, some looming twenty feet in the air or crouched low to the ground, some on four legs, others two— and one even had fourteen.

Barclay glanced at Root, who'd already dropped into a fighting stance, and he nodded at Barclay seriously. They could do this. This was no harder than anything they'd faced before.

Barclay widened his legs and stretched his arms out in front of him.

Wind!

A gale tore across the arena at the targets. All of them, from the humongous dragon to the stooping Jackawa, fell backward with a loud, collective thud.

When Barclay faced Cyril once more, Cyril was no longer alone. A black ramlike Beast stood tall beside him, its majestic, curved horns made of coarse tree bark. Thin twigs sprouted from it, with leaves that still held on to their Summertime green.

"You've met Codric, I believe," Cyril said, though Barclay had only ever glimpsed Cyril's first Beast from afar. Barclay had always thought the nickname the Horn of Dawn a bit silly, but it certainly suited Codric. His amber eyes glowed with the warmth of sunrise, and he bent low into a stately bow.

Cyril flicked his wrist, and in an instant, each dummy rose back to standing.

"This time," Cyril said, "strike only the Lore Keepers."

Barclay chewed his lip. His Lore was stronger when Root was out of his Mark, but he still wasn't sure if he could aim like that. And if the Guardian Master had been anyone different, Barclay would've told them so. But Cyril and Runa were still rivals. If Barclay failed, Cyril would blame it on Runa's teaching methods.

He steeled his nerves and summoned the wind a second time.

All the targets clunked down.

"Again," Cyril commanded, and the targets sprang back to standing.

The third time, Barclay managed to keep one target up, but it was one of the Lore Keepers.

"Again . . .

"Again . . .

"Again . . ."

By the thirty-fourth attempt, Barclay barely managed

to knock down any targets, let alone aim. His shoulders heaved. Beside him, Root panted. He'd concentrated so hard that he'd raked claw marks beneath him in the dirt.

By the fortieth round, Barclay swallowed his pride and asked, "Is there something I should be doing differently? I could try one at a time."

"One at a time is too slow. In the height of battle, you won't have any seconds to spare," answered Cyril, while Codric nodded vigorously beside him. "I'm afraid it'll just take practice. Here."

Cyril handed Barclay a cup of water. Barclay eagerly gulped half of it down, then offered the rest to Root.

"You're far stronger than you were at the Sea," Cyril told him.

Barclay was flattered; he knew Cyril didn't toss around compliments lightly. And as of late, Barclay's confidence kept soaring. His first grades hadn't been nearly as miserable as he'd feared. Instead, they'd been stellar. Viola had proven right all along; Barclay might've started off behind the other apprentices because he was an Elsie, but in the year and a half of studying and training since then, he hadn't just caught up—he'd earned a place among the top of his class.

It reminded him of when he was Master Pilzmann's apprentice. Thanks to his hard work, he never doubted that he was a good mushroom farmer—not once. He'd forgotten how good that felt.

But Barclay couldn't thank Cyril for the compliment. He was too loyal to Runa.

So he nodded and said, "Runa is a good teacher."

A muscle in Cyril's jaw clenched. But when he replied, his voice was level. "I had far less mastery of my wood Lore when I started my Symposium, and I was a year older than you. Then when I bonded with Tati, lava Lore came naturally. But wood was always a challenge, no matter how patient Codric was with me."

Beside him, Codric puffed out his chest proudly.

"How did you get better?"

"I worked hard. While *other* students focused on the Tourney, I came here every day to practice in between classes." His clipped tone made it clear he was talking about Runa and Keyes, even if he didn't say so. "All these years later and I still don't see the appeal of that particular tradition."

Barclay didn't admit it to Cyril, but he didn't either. The glimmer of thrill he'd felt the first night of the Symposium had long since snuffed out, as the Tourney had quickly descended into havoc. Rohan had succeeded in setting all his booby traps, scoring facefuls of slime for two Scholar students who'd tried to sneak into Eldin Hall. (As well as six Guardians who'd accidentally sprung them.) Outside the Guild Studies classroom, Fen had painted a huge mural of each of the resident Masters doing something very un-Master-like. (Cyril was picking his nose.) Cecily had snuck into the Surveyor dormitory and rearranged all their furniture.

Barclay paid it no mind. He spent nearly all his time studying—he was far too proud of his high grades to let them slip.

Cyril glanced at the hourglass resting on a nearby stool. The few fallen targets sprang upright. "Halfway done. Let's try a few more, shall we?"

Barclay and Root were so exhausted after their training session that they *walked* all the way to the post office. Perhaps it was too soon to expect a reply from Master Pilzmann, but after failing Cyril's assignment a hundred times over, Barclay decided to check anyway. He needed good news.

To his delight, Master Pilzmann's letter was indeed waiting for him. He excitedly tore it open at the counter, ignoring the glares of the postman trying to focus on his crossword.

Dear Barclay,

I had to sit down while reading your last letter because I was so frightened. A fall out of the sky! An unending storm! It all reminds me of the adventure books you used to borrow from the library. I can still hardly believe that you're on the other side of the world.

There is very little news to share from here. The leaves are beginning to change. Of course, Selby and I are very busy with the peak of mushroom season. Yesterday we filled a whole wheelbarrow with oysters and black trumpets.

In response to your question, I can't say that Dullshire will ever change its mind about the Woods. But I do believe that if anyone can manage that, it will be you, Barclay. I've never known you to fail at anything when you set your mind to it!

Sincerely,
Niclaus Pilzmann

Barclay's heart swelled like a loaf of pumpernickel. "Master Pilzmann says he thinks I can do it," he told Root. "That I can change Dullshire's mind about Beasts."

Between this and all his success lately, Barclay was starting to believe he could too.

Though Root didn't know Dullshire well enough to share Barclay's happiness, his tail flicked eagerly from side to side.

"Quiet down," the postman barked. "I'm trying to think. Eight letters . . . eight letters . . . Dinglebug? No, that's nine. . . ."

With a newfound burst of energy, Barclay and Root raced back to the campus. As they slowed outside its ancient stone walls, the tolls of a bell pealed through the evening air. The pebbles on the ground rattled with each low and heavy knell.

Barclay stared up at the University tower. "That's strange. I've never heard the bell ring before."

His confusion morphed into unease as he and Root entered the central courtyard. Hundreds of students and Beasts thronged below the steps outside the Chancellor's office, unusually quiet. The air seemed to sizzle as though it were moments before a lightning strike.

"What's going on?" Barclay asked the person in front of him, who carried a giant, leafy plant. It wasn't until the person poked their head out from behind the fuzzy stalk that Barclay realized it was Fen.

"No idea," Fen told him. "I heard someone say that the bell only rings when the Chancellor is going to make an announcement."

As he spoke, the plant's vines slithered up his arm and between his fingers, but Fen didn't seem to mind. Root's fur stood on end, and a growl of warning rumbled in his throat. Barclay rested his hand against Root's side to calm him.

To their left, Fen's fan club eyed Barclay and Root suspiciously. They'd grown in number since the first day of classes, now including three girls and two boys.

"Ignore them," Fen muttered. "They don't bother me when I've got Chuji with me. She's basically my bodyguard."

Barclay didn't quite hear him right away, as he'd been staring a little too long at the smudge of paint on Fen's cheek. He was starting to understand why Fen had so many admirers. With his art, his green hair, and even a silver piercing in his eyebrow . . . he was very cool.

Then the stalk twisted, and a gigantic thorny mouth loomed over Fen's shoulder. Barclay replayed Fen's words and realized that Chuji was the plant, and the plant was actually a Beast—a *monstrous* Beast. Though she had no eyes, Barclay swore she was leering at him.

"Huh, she likes you," Fen said.

"How can you tell?" Barclay asked nervously.

"Well, otherwise, she'd eat you."

Barclay didn't know whether to be terrified or flattered.

Suddenly self-conscious, Barclay tried to think of something clever to say, when someone called his name. He turned and spotted Viola waving at him in the distance. Relieved, he returned Root to his Mark and slipped through the crowd to his friends.

"Maybe someone got in trouble because of the Tourney," Hasu said.

"No way," said Shazi. "Dad only makes announcements if it's something important."

Tadg tugged on Barclay's sleeve. "Look who's here." He pointed toward the shade of a nearby dormitory, where Runa and Cyril stood side by side. Both wore grim expressions.

When Runa sighted them, she jerked her head for them to join her. But before the six of them could squeeze past the crowd, the doors at the top of the steps opened, and Chancellor Essam strode out and peered somberly over the courtyard.

"As some of you may have heard," started Essam, "there have been recent reports of sandstorms throughout the Desert. The first one originated near Dakmana, the second only a few hours from Menneset, and now there is a third at our northern border with the Elsewheres."

Though the third sandstorm was news to Barclay, this was the first time that the rest of the students were learning about sandstorms at all. Whispers and gasps ricocheted throughout the crowd, and several apprentices looked up at the clear sky with wide, frightened eyes.

"Though sandstorms are common in the Desert and normally no reason for extra alarm, these have been behaving irregularly," Essam continued. "It's the belief of High Keeper Asfour, as well as the University's Scholars, that the sandstorms are fueled not by typical weather patterns, but by Lore. They've remained confined to small areas, but once they appear, they do not subside. They're being called the Ever Storms. The first of them is the most severe. The last expedition sent inside has yet to return after three days."

Chills crept up Barclay's back. He still couldn't imagine a storm worse than the one they'd been rescued from when they first arrived. If the expedition still had yet to return, it probably wouldn't return at all.

"Rest assured that the Guild has its best Guardians, Surveyors, and Scholars working around the clock to understand these phenomena. But until this matter is resolved, it's my responsibility to inform you that the University has instituted procedures should a similar sandstorm occur in Menneset. In the event of an evacuation, students will be transported by carrier dragon to the Meridienne College in Halois, where you'll be able to complete your courses. The chances of this happening are extremely low, but nonetheless, it's a precaution we must put in place. If any of you have additional questions or concerns, please seek out your resident Masters. Thank you."

Essam vanished back through the double doors to his office.

"I'm gonna go talk to him," Shazi said. "You all hear what Cyril and Runa have to say."

She slipped away, and the rest of the group squirmed through the tangles of students to Runa and Cyril. Cyril stood tall and stiff, gnawing his lip with obvious irritation. Beside him, Runa slumped against the wall, her arms folded lazily across her chest.

"I thought you told us not to worry about the storms," Hasu said fretfully. Bitti, who was usually napping, buzzed and jittered beside her ear. "You told us to focus on schoolwork."

"I still think that," Cyril grumbled. "And if Asfour hadn't

gone behind Leopold's back and leaked the story to the *Khronicle*, this announcement wouldn't have happened at all."

"What do you mean?" Viola asked sharply. "Why would she do that?"

"Never mind that. It's not important," Runa told them, though Barclay suspected otherwise. The Grand Keeper was Asfour's boss—she wasn't supposed to disobey him. But then again, why didn't Leopold want the Wilderlands to find out about the Ever Storms? The Desert had a right to know. "I came to tell you that I'm going to be in Dakmana for a while." Runa's voice was oddly cheery. "If you need anything, you can ask Cyril."

"How long is a while?" Tadg asked.

"I'm not sure. A few days, possibly weeks."

Cyril scowled.

Runa elbowed him in the side. "Oh, don't sulk. I might be studying the Ever Storms, but you'll be *babysitting*. I'm sure that will be just as exciting. It's what you've always wanted, isn't it?"

"Studying the Ever Storms?" Barclay repeated tightly. "Won't that be dangerous?"

"As always, your maturity makes a great example for your students," Cyril muttered.

Runa ignored Cyril and answered, "There's no need to sweat over me. You know I can take care of myself."

That might've been true—Runa was the most powerful Lore Keeper Barclay had ever met. But the Ever Storms were perilous for anyone, even the famous Fang of Dusk.

"I don't suppose Asfour is concerned that my invitations

to all these recent Guild meetings keep getting misplaced?" Cyril asked dryly.

"No, I don't believe she is," Runa quipped.

"Why can't we come with you?" Tadg demanded. "We faced Keyes at the Sea. We could help!"

Runa tensed. "Who said anything about Audrian?"

Barclay stepped on Tadg's foot. He was going to give away that they'd eavesdropped on Viola's family that night.

But Tadg didn't back down. "First the weeping tide, now the Ever Storms. It fits the pattern."

"We have no evidence that Audrian is connected to any of this," Cyril said hotly. "The Ever Storms are clearly caused by some type of sand or wind Lore. Audrian only possesses stone and healing Lore."

Runa opened her mouth like she wanted to argue, then, seeming to think better of it, clamped it shut.

"If Keyes isn't causing the Ever Storms," Barclay asked, "then what *is*?"

"I have no idea, but I'm going to find out." Runa tossed them a wave and stalked away. "Don't do anything I wouldn't do while I'm gone."

As Cyril watched her leave, his Adam's apple bobbed. Suddenly, he blurted, "Good luck."

Runa cast him an odd look over her shoulder, then continued off.

One of the other Guardian students hovered behind them awkwardly, clearly hoping to ask Cyril a question. So Barclay and the others shuffled back toward Eldin Hall. Barclay's thoughts raced in a hundred different directions: what the Ever Storms meant, whether Runa would be all right, why Asfour wouldn't obey the Grand Keeper. It was a lot to make sense of.

Tadg scratched at his arms anxiously. "Did Runa seem a little off to you?"

"I'd be, if I was about to go into an Ever Storm," Cecily said.

"Runa is, well, Runa," Barclay added, as much to soothe himself as Tadg. "She'll be fine."

"Well, I've known Runa my whole life," Tadg snapped. "I think I'd know better than you."

Barclay winced. Maybe Tadg and Runa were basically family, but he cared about her too.

Before the five of them reached their dormitory, Shazi dashed up behind them—colliding with Barclay and Hasu, who both grunted out low, surprised "oofs."

"You all need . . ." Shazi panted for breath. "To come look at this."

The others stared at her, boggled.

"Didn't you hear me?" she pressed. "Hurry. It's important."

Then Shazi broke out in a run across the courtyard. Bewildered, they raced after her to the eastern section of campus, which was mainly home to Scholars attending lectures or conducting research. Shazi expertly led them through a maze of twists and turns and narrow alleys until they skidded to a halt at a dead end.

"See?" Shazi said, her voice unusually frazzled.

"Are you feeling all right, Shazi?" asked Hasu.

"You don't—you don't see it?"

Barclay squinted. "See what?"

Shazi gestured at the empty, dusty wall. "The door? The massive door? All covered in gold?"

"Are you pranking *us* now?" Tadg asked. "There isn't any-thing—"

"I see it," Viola said softly.

The others gawked at her.

"You do?" Cecily asked.

Viola fiddled with her pins. "Yeah, and this isn't the first time. I saw it the opening night of the Symposium."

"Why didn't you say anything?" Shazi demanded.

But Barclay realized Viola *did* say something—she'd mentioned seeing something strange, but she'd never told him what it was. That must've been the same thing Shazi was talking about.

"Because I thought it was a mistake," answered Viola. "It seemed impossible. We're only apprentices, and we're not even Scholars."

"I'm still not convinced this isn't some elaborate prank you're both pulling on us," Tadg muttered.

"What we can see and you all can't, apparently," Shazi said, sounding oddly pleased, "is the entrance to the Library of Asfour."

Shazi obviously expected this news to have an effect on them. Hasu squinted, as though trying to guess if she'd heard of such a place before. Cecily glanced at Barclay, looking as stupefied as he was.

"Lower your voice," Viola hissed. "What if someone heard you?"

"I thought the Library of Asfour was a myth," Tadg said. "Like everyone thought the Isle of Roane was." The Isle of Roane was Lochmordra's home at the Sea, which Barclay, Tadg, and Viola rediscovered last year after the island had been lost for centuries.

"Not at all," Viola told him. "Lore Keepers—usually Scholars—have been exploring the Library for its whole history."

"Slow down," Barclay said. "The Library of Asfour . . . like High Keeper Asfour?"

"More like Faiza Asfour," Shazi replied. "Before she retired as the first Grand Keeper, she built a gigantic library deep underneath the University. Dad said she did it both to 'preserve' knowledge, so that it was never lost, but also to 'protect' it, so it couldn't fall into the wrong hands. The Library is full of Lore. The entrance moves, and it only shows itself to people the Library deems as worthy." She hiked up her chin, clearly proud to be counted among the chosen few. "I can't wait to explore it."

"Explore it? The Library is dangerous," Viola said. "It's a labyrinth, and it's supposed to be full of puzzles, making it easier to get lost. Most of the people who go into the Library never come out."

"That's what makes it exciting!"

"I don't know . . . ," said Hasu, Bitti buzzing loudly on the tip of her nose. "I think we should tell Cyril about this."

Shazi frowned. "Why? This doesn't have anything to do with him."

"Then promise us you won't go in alone," Viola said.

"You won't go with me?" Shazi pouted.

"No. I don't want to get hurt. And our classes are more important."

Viola's words were the first shred of sense Barclay had heard all evening. He was finally feeling confident about his life at the Symposium—where he studied each night, how to dodge Rohan's booby traps in their dormitory, how to sleep crammed beside Root in their tiny bed. Now they might one day need to evacuate. Now mysterious doors to a deadly, underground Library were appearing to his friends. Now he didn't know what to think.

Shazi glowered and kicked a pebble across the ground. "Fine. It wouldn't be as fun to explore it alone anyway. But I hope you know you're wasting a *once-in-a-lifetime* opportunity. This door will move before long, and we might never find it again."

"And if we go down there, we might never *walk out* again," Viola told her. "I say we listen to Cyril and focus on what's important. Besides, Runa and Asfour are brilliant. They'll figure out what's causing the Ever Storms before long."

EIGHT

Six weeks after Shazi had stumbled upon the door to the Library of Asfour, she still hadn't given up hope of exploring it. She pestered Viola in between every class and through every meal, reciting names of famous Lore Keepers throughout history who'd entered the Library, or quotes from poems or stories about all the wonders it contained.

"I bet all the knowledge in the *world* is down there."

"At least half of those people became Grand Keeper one day. Don't you want to follow in their footsteps?"

"The Library chose us! *Us!*"

None of Shazi's tactics wore Viola down, and now Viola had begun avoiding her. She rose early to eat her breakfast before anyone else and studied in her room rather than the lounge. If it wasn't for classes, Barclay would've rarely seen her.

Which was why he jolted one Saturday morning when Viola plopped into the seat beside him in the cafeteria. His bowls of fruit and mashed beans rattled on the table.

"What's going on? What happened?" he mumbled, yawning. Before he could react, Mitzi reached from beneath the table and snatched his fork.

"We're going to—were you asleep?" Viola asked.

Barclay fought to wrench his utensil from Mitzi's grasp. "I—Mitzi . . ." With a grunt, Mitzi tore the fork away and scampered off with her shiny trophy. He sighed and turned to Viola. "No, I was just resting my head."

No matter how tired he was, it was impossible to sleep in the University's noisy cafeteria. Students chattered at each of the round tables, their Beasts nibbling or munching their own meals beside them or amid the rafters crisscrossing the ceiling. Plates clattered. Food sizzled. Though the cooks always offered delicious dishes from the various regions of the Desert, they also rotated options from other Wilderlands. Last night, Barclay had devoured a spiced bratwurst that tasted almost—*almost*—as juicy as the ones in Dullshire. And he was looking forward to the braised pork belly they were serving tonight from the Mountains.

"Well, liven up, because today we're going to Menneset Market," Viola said brightly.

As much as Barclay would've liked to explore the city, his expensive letters to Master Pilzmann had left him few kritters to spend. "I was going to train today with Root."

Behind him, Root perked up from his cushion on the floor, the bone of a half-eaten roast chicken leg jutting out between his fangs.

Viola groaned. "Come *on*. It's no wonder you're tired—all

you do is train or study. And I refuse to let you leave Menneset without visiting the Market. It's a landmark!"

"I don't only train or study," he grumbled.

But his coin purse wasn't the only thing holding him back. Shopping excursions with Viola were not for the faint of heart, as she could spend hours combing through stores and haggling with merchants for a good bargain.

"Runa promised to meet us there," Viola added.

Barclay perked up. "She's returned from her last mission?"

"Yep. Mom passed along her message this morning."

Barclay tore into his pita bread and shoveled down the rest of his breakfast. "You could've led with that, you know."

An hour later, the two of them and Tadg set off for the center of Menneset. The closer they got to the Market, the more familiar shops they passed. A Draconis Emporium, seller of all dragon-related goodies, still advertised their Midautumn sale. Red and yellow streamers fluttered outside the door of a Fillitot's Gourmet Beast Treats. Viola and Tadg made a quick detour to the Argentisaurus Bank to withdraw some kritters.

Soon the spindly alleys opened into a huge plaza. Hundreds of stores ringed the perimeter, their windows displaying everything from basic Beast-keeping supplies to rare fossils to designer-brand saddles and traveling gear. Within the square wove rows and rows of sloping tents. Some beckoned customers with the delicious aromas of food, like fresh prickly pear and grilled chicken and dibi speared on large skewers. Others flaunted handblown glassware or tapestries woven with beautiful designs of wild Beasts.

Viola whipped out *A Traveler's Log of Dangerous Beasts*. Her copy was so beloved that cracks webbed down its binding and notes were scribbled throughout the margins.

"These are the six items to build a Skulkit's lure." She traced her finger across the page as she read. "One jar of bubbling aloe jelly, a salt crystal, and a pebble of Desert sea glass. Those seem easy enough. And then . . . the shed cocoon of a Buzzardfly. I *think* I can manage that. But I've never even heard of a breathing cactus, and a *Bellflower*. Ugh. That one's going to be almost impossible to find."

"So Mory convinced you about a Skulkit, did he?" asked a voice behind them.

The trio whipped around to face Runa. Dark circles rimmed her eyes, and bandages wrapped around her left wrist. Despite all that, she grinned broadly. Goath, whose skeletal head perched on her shoulder, must've been happy to see them, as his tail rattled.

"What happened to you?" asked Barclay, stunned. He'd never seen Runa hurt before.

"Oh, this? It's just a scrape." Runa waved her good hand dismissively. "I'm more interested in hearing about these plans to bond with a new Beast. Most would say you're too young for a second Beast, but you and Mitzi already work in tandem. I'd say you're more than ready."

"Did you learn anything about the Ever Storms?" Tadg blurted at the same time that Viola asked, "When did you bond with Goath?"

Even though Goath more often kept Runa company, he was actually her second Beast. Her first, Klava, the saber-toothed Dolkaris who'd earned Runa her nickname, was aggressive and wary of humans. She roamed free only in private.

"Goath and I teamed up near the end of my apprenticeship," Runa answered, seemingly ignoring Tadg. "As you can guess, Klava was a lot for me to handle. But then Cyril bonded with Tati during our fifth year—he was tired of being in our shadows, apparently. And I wasn't about to let him outmatch me." Runa's face darkened, as it always seemed to when she spoke about their time as apprentices with Keyes. "Come on. Let's get you your ingredients."

They swept past a tasseled curtain and ducked inside the inner maze of Menneset Market. The largest tents rose high, balloons and ribbons waving at the tip-top of their poles. Other stalls squeezed themselves into the tightest corners, so tiny and narrow that Barclay might've missed them if he wasn't staring around everywhere with bug-wide eyes.

For half an hour, they explored. Barclay wandered into a hat shop and tried on over ten varieties: Flat hats and pointy hats. One with a dragon feather that drooped over its brim. A pair of furry earmuffs whose tag claimed they were 100 percent soundproof. (YOUR SNUGGLIEST, QUIETEST SLEEP GUARANTEED!) An iron helm whose breathing holes made it look like a cheese grater. A sheep-wool beret that promised to make the wearer smarter. (NO REFUNDS ALLOWED.)

Next he roamed a very pricey store called Artisan Apothecaries, with elixirs bubbling in crystal vials and beakers.

A Beast toy shop that sold everything from squeaky fake mice to scratching posts made of indestructible Hookshark skin.

A stall that offered a little bit of everything: spiral candle-sticks and dried herbs, woven palm baskets and crisp white parchment.

Barclay *could* use more stationery. "How much for this?" he asked the merchant, a kind-looking man with freckles smattering his light brown skin.

The man shrugged and answered in a language Barclay didn't understand. He wasn't a Lore Keeper, which meant they heard each other in their native tongues instead of Lore-speak. When Barclay finished the Symposium, he should really ask Viola to help him learn more languages, but besides small children, he wasn't used to meeting people in the Wilderlands who hadn't bonded with a Beast.

A nearby woman wearing an elegant crimson headscarf gave Barclay a smile and asked the merchant, "How much for the parchment?" When the man responded, she told Barclay, "It's two kritters for a hundred sheets. He says it's the best-made paper in Tepejuq."

Barclay had never heard of that place before. "Is that in the Elsewheres?"

She nodded. "It's one of our northern neighbors. The people there are excellent craftsmen."

Barclay eagerly made a mental note to learn more about Tepejuq so he could write about it to Master Pilzmann. "I'm from the Elsewheres too," he told the merchant brightly.

The woman translated, and the merchant beamed. Then he grabbed a parchment bundle and handed it to Barclay.

"F-for free? No, this is good parchment. . . ." Barclay fished in his satchel for his coin purse.

The man shook his head insistently. Barclay didn't need the woman to translate to know the man was giving him a gift.

"Thank you very much," he said, hoping the man could tell how much he meant it. Judging by his grin, he did. "And thank you," he told the woman, who waved as he left the stall.

After some searching, Barclay spotted Tadg and Runa hovering next to a tent while Viola haggled for a Buzzardfly cocoon inside.

"There you are," said Runa. "Tadg was just telling me how *interesting* and *enriching* your classes are. Especially my dear cousin's."

"Ha, ha," Tadg said sarcastically. "I still don't see why we can't study the Ever Storms with you."

Runa patted them both on the shoulder—which, as usual, felt rather like being bludgeoned. "Oh, it can't be that boring with the Tourney going on."

Tadg smirked. "Funny you mention that. During my last training session with Cyril, he said that during your Symposium, you froze all the water in the toilets and accidentally flooded Eldin Hall. How come you never mention *that* when you talk about the glory days?"

Runa frowned. "I'm not old enough to have glory days."

"So you don't deny it?"

"Don't test me, Murdock. I still remember the names of all your stuffed animals, which I'm sure Barclay would love to hear about."

Normally, Barclay would be gleeful to learn embarrassing stories from Tadg's childhood, yet he couldn't help but remember Tadg's comment from a few weeks ago, that he and Runa knew each other far better than Barclay did. And he was right. Not even Master Pilzmann knew such stories from when Barclay was small. He had no family left to tell them.

Tadg's ears reddened. "Maybe you should ask Barclay about the Tourney. He has *loads* to tell you."

As far as Barclay was concerned, his famous stink Lore incident was old news, and he'd happily put his stardom behind him. He had more important things to focus on, like the hours of homework Mandeep assigned every night, or the new Wilderland unit they'd started: the Jungle.

But Runa's expression was curious, so Barclay recounted the smelly events of the first night of the Symposium.

"It was miserable for days after that," Barclay finished. "I wish everyone would just focus on classes."

"The Tourney is an important part of the Symposium," she said. "Without it, apprentices would barely interact with anyone outside their dormitories. And it's a good idea to get to know the other students. You might be working with them someday. Take Kamil Okasha, for instance. When we were students together, he lived three rooms down the hall from me. And if it weren't for his homing Lore in battle, our team might've never made it far enough to recover the last expedition sent into one of the Ever Storms."

Kamil Okasha was Rohan and Deirdre's Guardian Master. Barclay had never met him, but Rohan idolized him. Even Deirdre, who'd once told Barclay her two favorite things were graveyards and thunderstorms, spoke of Kamil like he was a hero from an adventure novel.

"So the expedition made it out all right?" Barclay prodded.

"They'll live," Runa said flatly. "I'm not sure the first expedition was so lucky."

Barclay had once witnessed Runa battle face-to-face with Lochmordra at the Sea, and even after that loss, Runa hadn't sounded so grim. It unnerved him. If she was worried, then he should be worried too.

"How did you injure your wrist?" he asked.

Runa stuffed her hand in her pocket, hiding the bandage. "Arm-wrestling an Asperhaya. I won, of course."

Tadg shot Barclay a pointed look. It wasn't like Runa to lie, especially when the apprentices could easily guess that she'd injured herself in an Ever Storm.

Tadg squeezed his fists. "I'm going to look in that stall." He stalked to a squat little store the size of a sleeping tent, where the merchant sat cross-legged among stacks of yellowed, dusty books. That was odd. Tadg kept up with his schoolwork, but Barclay had never seen him read for fun.

"So what do you think of the Symposium, Barclay?" Runa asked him. "Is Cyril having his fun enforcing curfews and doing room inspections?"

Cyril definitely enjoyed rules—almost as much as Dullshire did. But Barclay suspected he hadn't become resident Master to keep students in line. He'd clearly accepted the position because he loved school. He loved it so much that he brought desserts to all his nightly tutoring sessions, even if none of the Guardian apprentices showed, and Barclay had once even caught him reading *Guildocracy* for fun. So far, the only students he'd actually scolded had been Shazi and Cecily, whose room was so messy, they couldn't close the door.

"Cyril's been fine," Barclay answered. "And I like the Symposium. I'm doing better in my classes than I thought I would."

"Of course you are. You're my apprentice, aren't you?"

She grinned. "And let me guess, knowing you, you're kicking your feet up and relaxing the rest of the Symposium. After all, you have no reason to work yourself so hard now."

Runa was only teasing, but Barclay wasn't in the mood for jokes. His gaze snagged once again on her bandages. On the bags beneath her eyes you could only get from nights and nights of bad sleep.

Before he thought better of it, he burst out, "I'll relax once *you* do."

He braced himself for Runa to scold him. Instead, she chuckled, but there was no mirth in it. "Fair point."

Tadg was right—Runa wasn't herself. No one would be if their job was battling the Ever Storms. But Runa Rasgar wasn't just anyone, and the weeping tide had been every bit as scary without fazing her at all. Something must be different now.

Maybe the thought shouldn't have terrified him like it did. He liked Runa, but they weren't as close as her and Tadg. They weren't family. And yet the thought of anything happening to her made his heart clench painfully—hard enough to break.

"Well, is there anything you've been doing that *isn't* just studying and training this whole time?" asked Runa. "Because if you say no, I'm going to be disappointed."

Barclay considered telling her about Viola and Shazi finding the Library of Asfour. But since both girls had sworn never to go inside, he needn't bother Runa with it. She had enough on her mind.

"No," he answered, looking away to hide the telltale flush on his cheeks.

"Mm-hmm," Runa said, then she barked out a laugh. It sounded real this time. "Well, if you can squeeze it into your busy schedule, I do have a request: please make Cyril's life miserable for me. The University never discovered the culprit of the Great Sewage Incident from our Symposium, and I'd rather the whole Guild didn't find out it was me."

On the return journey from the Market, the three apprentices stopped by the post office so Barclay could pick up his latest letter from Master Pilzmann, and he waited until he was alone in his room to read it. Tadg had slipped out for Mar-Mar's evening bath time, the hour between five and six when he let his one-hundred-and-twenty-foot-long, bloodthirsty electric Nathermara have free rein of the boys' bathroom. Rohan had complained to Barclay more than once about needing to sneak into the Apothecaries' lounge to secretly use their toilets. ("There's a man-eating *plant* napping in there!" Rohan had told him, which could only have been Chuji.)

> *Dear Barclay,*
> *I'm afraid this letter won't be like my regular ones: Beasts have infiltrated Dullshire. They have destroyed so many pumpkins and squash. Frau Petersheim even said they smashed her entire season's worth of turnips! They're living in our pantries and barns. In packs. Their eyes glow in the dark, and they make all these terrifying noises— squeaks, chitters, and squeals. I will admit,*

*even with all the incredible tales you tell
me, Selby and I are too terrified to leave
the house! And we're not the only ones. Our
streets are quiet day and night.*

*I was wondering if you had any advice
for us. I think I could convince the town to
do something if we had a plan of action in
place.*

*Sincerely,
Niclaus Pilzmann*

Barclay's throat squeezed tight. The Beasts Master
Pilzmann described sounded like Miskreats. They were
Familiar class, tricky, yet not much scarier than pests. But
a couple of years ago, Barclay would've been terrified of
them. Though now he did find them quite cute.

Two days later, once his Guild Studies class had finished, Barclay lingered afterward to recount the problem
to Mandeep.

"Do you think there's a way we could get a message to the
Woods' Guild chapter?" Barclay asked. "They could send
help."

"That's a good idea," Mandeep told him, "though Erhart
keeps things so disorganized there that it might not be any
use." Erhart was the greedy, bumbling High Keeper of the
Woods. "But it's still worth a try. Why don't you write a
letter explaining Dullshire's problem, and I'll sign it with
you?"

Barclay nodded hopefully. Mandeep was a member of the

Guild—the Lore Keepers in Sycomore would listen to him. "Great, thank you! I'll do that right now, if that's all right."

He leapt into one of the desks, pulled out a fresh piece of the parchment he'd been gifted at Menneset Market, and got to work. Barely five minutes later, he thrust the letter into Mandeep's hands. The pair of them both signed it with Mandeep's peacock feather quill, then Mandeep pressed his wax seal onto the envelope.

When he lifted the stamp, he revealed one of the most striking seals Barclay had ever seen. The dark orange wax gleamed, smooth and glossy, and the image of a quetzal-like bird was emblazoned in the center, with the initials *M.A.* in scratchy Lore script underneath.

"Runa has a stamp like that," Barclay said. Except Runa's silvery, icy-blue seal said *R. R.*, with Klava above it.

"All members of the Guild have a distinctive one. You receive yours when you graduate from the Symposium, with the color wax of your choice," Mandeep explained. "That's when you're granted correspondence privileges and can sign onto contracted missions. The stamp is meant to signify that."

Barclay hadn't realized that graduating from the Symposium was that momentous. Intrigued, he thanked Mandeep for his help and strolled to the door, debating what color he would choose for his own seal one day. Dark blue was one of his favorite colors. Maybe yellow . . .

But before he left the classroom, Mandeep said, "You're doing exceptionally well, by the way. You should be very proud of yourself. You and your friends are making it hard for the Scholar apprentices to compete."

Barclay beamed. He'd come a long way from the scared Elsie in Sycomore.

Afterward, Barclay wasted no time claiming one of the study rooms so he could write his response to Master Pilzmann. If this had been a normal letter, Barclay would've described his latest classes and the Elsie merchant. He might've even asked if Master Pilzmann remembered anything from Barclay's childhood—he'd known Barclay's parents a little before they died. But he didn't have time for that.

He'd scribbled only a few sentences when he noticed Cecily lurking outside the door, looking oddly fiendish in the dim light of the hallway, Oudie nestled in her hair.

"You can come in, you know," Barclay told her.

Cecily creeped inside and slid into the seat across from him. She pushed him a pack of papers facedown, and Barclay peeked at it. It was her last Lore Keeper History quiz. The grade wasn't very good.

"So . . . ," she said awkwardly, scratching Oudie's head. "Do you think you could, um, help me at all? Your grade was way better than mine."

"How do you know that?" Barclay hadn't shown it to anyone.

"I looked over your shoulder."

He pursed his lips. "This isn't really a good time, but I can help later."

Cecily gave a panicked glance down at his parchment. "There's not an essay due for one of our classes, is there?"

"No, this is something else."

"Then you *can* help me," she said brightly. "So this early

Guild history stuff, there are so many names to remember. And I don't—"

"I said this wasn't a good time," Barclay snapped. He needed to hurry to reach the post office before it closed. He wanted to warn Master Pilzmann before a bunch of Lore Keepers barged into Dullshire; otherwise, the Dullshire sentries would probably attack them before they could help. "This is really important. More important than the Tourney meetings you have with Rohan and Shazi every day. You could study more then, you know."

"I didn't mean . . ." She stood up, and her shadow shrunk in embarassment. "Never mind. I didn't mean to bother you." Then she slinked out of the room. Oudie flew off after her.

Barclay felt a pinch of guilt—his words sounded meaner now that he replayed them in his head. But this *was* important.

Pushing thoughts of his friend aside, he raced to finish the letter, then—much to the postman's irritation—he dashed into the post office moments before it closed. He returned to Eldin Hall exceptionally proud of himself. Maybe Barclay Thorne, outcast of Dullshire, had just saved it.

Three days later, a clump of students bottlenecked outside the entrance of Instructor Dia's classroom. It took Barclay several moments of squishing past to sight the cause: nine of the stone statues in Eldin and Hamdani Halls now stood in between the desks, including one of Gravaldor and several famous Lore Keepers. He had no clue who could've moved them. Each of the statues had to weigh over a thousand pounds.

Dia must've been thinking the same thing, because he asked, "Which one of you is responsible for this?" None of the students responded. "You won't get in trouble, but I *will* ask you to move them back."

The Guardian and Surveyor apprentices appraised one another with reluctant admiration. Still, no one came forward to claim the prank.

"Maybe it was one of the Scholars or Apothecaries," Hasu said.

Shazi scoffed. "Who pulled off a stunt like this? No way. Someone isn't coming forward."

"But why not? Wouldn't they want to claim it?"

While they spoke, goose bumps crept up Barclay's skin. He glanced over his shoulder, wondering if he was being watched. But only the wall stretched behind him.

Rohan elbowed Barclay in the side, pulling him away from his thoughts. "Did you do this, Barks?"

"Him? No way!" Cecily said, making Barclay wince. She'd been avoiding him since he hadn't been able to help her with her schoolwork, which he probably deserved.

But she was right. Even if Runa thought the Tourney brought students together, Barclay had no desire to reclaim the spotlight.

With no other recourse, the students sat around the statues—which forced several to share desks. It was hard to concentrate on Dia's description of Celestial Peak, the highest point of altitude in the Mountains, while the marble wings of a humongous three-headed dragon blocked Barclay's view of the chalkboard.

By the end of that day, all anyone could talk about was

the anonymous Tourney competitor. Rumors ricocheted through the Guardian dormitory.

"I bet it was Fen," one apprentice said. "Maybe the statues were an art statement."

Barclay didn't want to encourage them, yet he couldn't help but point out, "He paints, not sculpts."

"Whoever they are, we have to do something even bigger now," Cecily said.

Hasu sighed dramatically. "Don't you all ever grow tired?"

NINE

I think I'd rather ride Root, if that's all right," Barclay said. The large Beast in front of him—a Sanamhisan—huffed, offended. It wasn't that Barclay didn't like the Beast, or any of the others in the stable, but the enormous humps on its back didn't look comfortable for sitting, and its gigantic neck—nearly twice as long as Barclay stood tall—unnerved him.

"Sanamhisans' water Lore helps them conserve their energy in the heat," Mory told him. "The Lightning Plateaus aren't too far, but that's a tough journey for Root to make midday."

In the stall across from them, Tadg heaved himself into his Sanamhisan's saddle. The Sanamhisan's head twisted around so that it stared at Tadg eye to eye.

"What are you looking at?" Tadg demanded.

The Sanamhisan spat in his face.

Viola, however, already sat atop her Sanamhisan and waited for them at the stable's entrance. Mitzi perched on the hump behind her.

"Come on!" she called impatiently. "It's not like a Skulkit is going to be easy to find."

Mory beamed. "I wouldn't worry about that. You have me with you, don't you?"

Barclay squeezed the saddle's handle and hoisted himself onto the Beast's lumpy back. Thankfully, the Sanamhisan didn't spit on him, and it began plodding toward Viola. Every step made Barclay jostle to and fro.

"How long is this going to take again?" he asked.

"About two hours each way," Mory answered.

Barclay braced himself for an extremely sore backside, then squinted as he emerged into the bright daylight. They were in one of Menneset's outer neighborhoods, close to the towering walls that surrounded the city and protected it from sandy winds. Overhead, water roared through the aqueducts with a steady rush.

While they waited for Tadg, Viola flipped through the compartments attached to her Sanamhisan's saddle. Stuffed within each one were glass jars filled with the lure ingredients she'd bought last week at Menneset Market.

She held up a particular one containing what looked like a brass tulip. She rattled it, her eyes wide, as though making sure it was real. "Where did you even find a Bellflower? The Apothecary I asked said they only grow deep in the Death Corridor."

Mory grinned, a mischievous twinkle in his eye. "I'll never spill my secrets. Besides, it's a gift." While she repeated more thank-yous, he ushered his Sanamhisan closer to Viola so he could give her a fatherly pat on the shoulder. "No need to thank me. Today is an exciting day! Your second Beast! It doesn't seem that long ago that you were boasting to me about your ferocious vegetarian baby dragon."

Viola fiddled with the pins on her shirt. "Don't jinx me! I really want this to work."

She might've been embarrassed, but the exchange made a painful lump lodge in Barclay's throat. It didn't make sense. He was doing better in his classes than he'd ever hoped—he should've been happy. But seeing Viola spend time with her parents, hearing Runa tease Tadg, listening to Shazi talk about her dad . . . it all reminded him that he didn't have a family of his own.

When Tadg emerged from the stable, one of his ears burned bright purple, and Toadles was nestled in his lap. Despite that, he hardly looked grumpy at all.

"What are you so happy about?" Barclay asked. "Hoping we see another Ever Storm up close?"

"Unsure you should be wishing for that, buddy," Mory said darkly. "And lucky for us that the three Ever Storms are all far away from where we're traveling."

"It's not that," said Tadg. "I just think it'll be interesting, is all."

Barclay hoped so, because as much as he wanted to support Viola, he worried the ride was going to be far from easy. He shifted uncomfortably, and his Sanamhisan huffed again at his squirming.

With that, they started off.

While studying in their carrier dragon and crash-landing

in the Ever Storm, Barclay hadn't had the chance to appreciate the Desert's beauty for what it was. Before long, the skyline of Menneset disappeared behind them, and the uneven dunes rippled in all directions. The sand here looked nothing like the gray beaches of the Sea. Vibrant copper and gold and diamond white eddied across the landscape like the strokes of a paintbrush.

But beautiful or not, the Desert was a Wilderland—and that meant it was a little bit frightening, too.

Blurry forms swayed in the distance, but it was impossible to tell if they were mirages or Beasts. The sheets of sand that blew off the dunes whirled around his Sanamhisan's hoofs and occassionally grazed a prickly caress across Barclay's cheeks. Noises carried in the breeze—whispers, caws, chitters, and even a quiet scream.

But it was very hard to be afraid with Mory as a tour guide.

"This area around us is called an erg," he explained. "That means a place with lots of wind and dunes like these. There are several ergs in the Desert, and Menneset is located in the largest one."

"What does the rest of the Desert look like?" Barclay asked.

"Haven't you been learning that in your Wilderlands class?"

"We're not on the Desert unit yet," Tadg told him. "So far we've only studied the Woods and the Jungle."

"Ah, well, there are many different types of terrain in the Desert," Mory said, "just like there are in any of the Wilderlands. What the Desert regions all have in common is that they're very dry. But did you know that the Tundra also has regions that are deserts?"

"It does?" Barclay asked.

"Yep! We don't call them that, of course, and the Desert and the Tundra aren't exactly close to each other. But even though the Tundra is cold, it's also very dry. Not all deserts have to be hot."

After over an hour and a half of riding, the flat tops of humongous plateaus rose on the horizon like pillars lifting up to the sky. It became clearer just *how* humongous they were the more the group neared—like tables that only giants could eat at. Gold veins zigzagged up their sides like streaks of lightning. Barclay counted seven plateaus stretching across the landscape, casting the ground between them in cool shade.

"Not bad, right?" Mory said proudly, as though he'd built the Lightning Plateaus himself. "Skulkits live throughout most of the northern Desert, but I've come across some here twice before, just at the edge of the erg."

Below them, the sandy dunes had begun to thin and give way to coarse, graveled dirt. Plants sprouted in patches, most of them stubby, prickly shrubs.

They parked their Sanamhisans, and Barclay wasted no time sliding off his saddle and stretching out his sore muscles. Sitting through classes on Monday wasn't going to be pleasant.

Viola's hands trembled as she fumbled through her compartments for the jars. Barclay could guess why she was so nervous: Skulkits were Mythic class Beasts. Mitzi was Prime class, and though Prime was still strong, Viola had once confessed to Barclay that she felt like the odd one out among her friends, who all had Mythic class Beasts.

While Viola arranged the jars in a line, creating a lure, Barclay was reminded of the last time he'd watched her do so—the first day they'd met near the edge of the Woods. She'd meant to summon Gravaldor, but she'd mistaken one of the ingredients. So she'd summoned Root, a Lufthund, instead. Then Root had accidentally bonded with Barclay, and so Barclay's adventure as a Lore Keeper had begun.

Before Viola set down the final jar, Mory said, "Hold up. Hopefully, this only summons one Skulkit, but on the slight chance that more show up, we should be prepared." He opened the compartments of his own saddle and pulled out leather gear similar to what they wore in their training sessions. He handed a vest to each of them.

"What are these for?" Tadg asked.

"Glass shards," answered Mory.

Barclay swallowed and slipped his vest over his shoulders.

Once the four of them were fully armored, Viola lowered the final jar.

For several minutes, the only sound was the scratching of brittle grass against the cacti. Barclay braced both his hands in front of him, palms out, ready to blast away anything shiny and sharp that flew toward him.

But nothing came.

Eventually, he lowered his tired arms and glanced at the others. Viola's focus was trained on her surroundings, but her fingers fiddled fretfully with her pins. Tadg met Barclay's eyes and shrugged, as though he had no idea what was taking so long either.

"Maybe the lure isn't in range," said Viola grimly.

"Hold on a moment," Mory told her. "Have a little patience."

Something jingled behind them, and the group swiveled around.

A tiny four-legged creature like a fennec fox prowled on a rock in the distance, its light fur the same color as the sand. Its ears were huge, and clear, shiny objects glimmered from both of them, as though it wore several sets of piercings. Of its two ears, its right stood high and pointy, while its left folded at the top, a little lopsided.

"Is that a Skulkit?" Tadg whispered.

Mory hushed him. "Skulkits have very good hearing."

Instantly, the Beast froze and stared at them.

Then something else jangled to Barclay's right, and he spotted two more Skulkits. They stalked across the sand toward the Lore Keepers, and his Mark stung in warning. They might've been small and cute, but they were still Mythic class Beasts.

"It seems we've summoned a whole pack," Mory said, and when Barclay spun to where he was looking, he caught sight of another six Skulkits.

"What do I do?" Viola asked anxiously.

"Don't panic. This isn't what we prepared for, but Skulkits normally only attack if they feel threatened. So—"

"Mitzi, no!" Viola called just as Mitzi leapt off her Keeper's shoulder and soared straight toward the group of wild Beasts and their treasure trove of glinting glass jewelry.

"Look out!" Mory shouted.

The pack of Skulkits turned their tails to them. Their paws dug at the sand, sending shards of glass whizzing behind them like a rainstorm of needles.

Barclay threw his hands into the air and thought, *Wind!* The glass flew out of their path and clattered onto the dirt.

But the Skulkits weren't finished. Several darted together in a row. As they ran—and they ran *fast*—glass reared from the ground behind them, and a clear wall of it sprung up toward the sky. Sweat soon poured from Barclay's forehead. It felt as though they were ants trapped beneath the world's biggest magnifying glass.

Mitzi, not noticing the glass, flew straight into it with a loud *bonk!* She crumpled to the gravel.

"Mitzi!" Viola cried out.

"Viola," Mory said. Despite all the commotion, his voice was surprisingly level. "Mitzi will be fine. Put her back in her Mark and be patient. The lure will coax one of them close enough to trap, and once you touch it, the bond will form."

As he spoke, the first Skulkit with the lopsided ear drew closer apprehensively, and each of the six jars of the lure began to shine with a warm golden light.

"That's it! That's it!" Barclay urged under his breath. He was so distracted cheering on the tiny Beast that he didn't notice another barrage of needles soar in his direction. He yelped as several stabbed into his arm, making him look like a human cactus. Tiny droplets of blood oozed out of his wounds.

When he looked up, the Skulkit was walking into the light of the lure, and its body began to glow a matching gold. Barclay watched in awe. He'd never seen a bond made the proper way before. The closest he'd come to it was when Keyes had tried to bond with Lochmordra, during which

Barclay had felt far more terrified than fascinated. Several paces away, Tadg stood with his mouth agape as he also marveled at the sight.

Cautiously, Viola stepped in front of the lure, her arm outstretched.

At the light, the other Skulkits sprinted away—many disappearing into burrows in the sand.

The Skulkit with the lopsided ear lifted its head to study Viola. Then, seemingly deciding that it liked what it saw, it wagged its tail twice. The snare might've trapped it in its light, but the Skulkit wasn't afraid—if anything, it was eager.

Barclay's chest swelled. The bond was going to work.

Viola knelt on the ground in front of it. Carefully, she rested two fingers against its forehead.

The golden light flashed twice as bright. Then, all at once, it vanished, and the Skulkit vanished with it.

When Viola stood and turned around, a wide, triumphant grin split across her face. Then she bent down and bunched up the bottom of her right pant leg. Above her ankle, the golden Mark of the Skulkit padded across her skin.

When Barclay, Viola, and Tadg returned to Eldin Hall— each of them exhausted but cheery—they were greeted by blares of paper horns and a ruckus of applause.

"Surprise!" the other Guardian apprentices chorused— Shazi and Hasu loudest among them. Crinkly gold streamers hung from the lounge's ceiling, and plates were heaped with snacks and pastries on all the tables.

Viola gaped. "What . . . ?"

"We threw you a party!" Hasu said. "It was Shazi's idea."

"But Hasu did most of the work," said Shazi, her mouth already crammed full of pastry. She gave Viola a friendly punch on the shoulder. "Well? We want to hear all about your new Beast!"

Viola smiled slyly. "How do you know it went well?"

"Because you're you," Hasu told her. "There's no way it didn't go well."

"You didn't have to do all this," Viola said, but she wrapped them both in a hug anyway, all their arguments about the Library of Asfour forgotten. Then, per Shazi's request, she launched into the story of the day's events. Barclay tried to listen, but he was distracted when Rohan motioned him over to the room's corner.

Rohan sniffed the air suspiciously. "Do you hear or smell anything funny?"

"No, why?" Barclay asked, alarmed. "Do you think there will be another stink attack?"

"What about a strange buzzing noise?"

All he heard was Viola describing the Lightning Plateaus. "No."

Rohan cast shifty glances around them. "I've got a feeling, is all. A loud, happy party in the Guardians' lounge? It's the perfect time for someone to strike."

"What if you're just being paranoid?"

"I don't know. There haven't been any more pranks since Mischievius's." Mischievius was the nickname everyone had taken to calling the student who'd moved all the statues into Instructor Dia's classroom. The statues had since been returned to where they belonged, but the perpetrator had yet to come forward. "Eventually, someone is going to try to show them up."

Maybe that was true, but if Barclay spent all his days at the University bracing for someone to pull another stunt, he'd barely get any studying done. And so he left Rohan to his snooping and inspected the snack tables, which had been picked halfway through by the throng of Beasts lurking beneath them, nibbling—including Root, who'd devoured a whole plate of peanut butter biscuits, and Mitzi and Toadles, who were wrestling over a treat. But before Barclay could dig into a gooey jelly pastry, the doors to the atrium burst open.

Barclay jumped. Rohan's words must've gotten into his head, because he clamped his hands over his nose, bracing himself for another smelly prank. Instead, it was Cyril, looking frustrated and weary.

"She can't honestly turn me away forever," he muttered to himself as he strode toward the lounge. "I'm the Horn of Dawn, for . . ." His voice trailed off as he finally noticed the party. "What's going on here? It's past lights-out."

All the laughter and storytelling abruptly died. No one wanted to get in trouble with the Horn of Dawn, especially when he was in a foul mood.

"Viola bonded with a Skulkit!" Hasu said happily.

At first, Cyril looked like he wanted to argue—Cyril never let them break the rules. Then he sighed. "Congratulations," he told Viola, and he trudged toward his own quarters. But before he made it, he paused in front of a platter of pastries that resembled jam-filled unicorn horns. "Are those alicornettes?"

"Yep!" Shazi answered. "From the Piebrary."

Still looking disgruntled, Cyril stacked three onto a napkin and disappeared into his room.

Viola resumed her story. The Guardian apprentices made a rapt audience, as they oohed and aahed at all the right times. Once she finished, everyone gave another round of cheers.

"Can we meet it?" Hasu asked eagerly.

"All right, but try to keep quiet," Viola said. "He hasn't socialized with very many people yet."

The room fell into a hush as Viola summoned the Skulkit.

At first, the tiny Beast looked around the room with wide eyes. His gaze ricocheted from the curious Lore Keepers to the tables of food to the colorful carpets, and his tail rose and poofed out in fright. Then Viola crouched and smiled at him, and he huddled close to her and nuzzled his cheek against her knee.

The students cooed.

"He's so cute!" Hasu said.

Deirdre brushed her hair aside to show off her own piercings. "Look—we match."

Viola scratched the Skulkit beside his lopsided ear. "You're very friendly, aren't you?" she asked, and the Skulkit reached up its front paws onto her leg. Then he climbed higher, as though Viola was a rock he could scale. He sniffed her nose.

"Will he grow bigger?" Shazi asked.

"Nope, this is his full size," Viola answered.

Then the Skulkit tripped, and Viola quickly caught him before he smacked the floor. She scooped him into her arm, cradling him like a baby. At first, Barclay thought he'd squirm away, but he clearly liked it.

"What will you name him?" asked Hasu.

"I don't know yet."

"You should try to use glass Lore," Shazi said.

Viola hesitated. But at the hopeful eyes of the other apprentices, she said weakly, "I'll give it a try, but it will probably take a while before I . . ." Her voice trailed off. With her free hand, she snapped, and a needle of glass shot from her fingers toward the ceiling. A balloon burst with a loud *pop!*

Everyone hollered, and Viola beamed all the brighter.

The only one who didn't join the party was Cecily, who was curled on a sofa in the corner of the room with her heavy copy of *Guildocracy* in her lap. In front of her, Oudie pecked the fallen pastry crumbs from the floor.

Barclay approached her nervously. "Aren't you going to take a break and have some fun?"

"I can't," she grunted, not looking at him. "I have to study." She turned the page of her notebook, only to reveal one covered in doodles instead of notes. She muttered angrily under her breath and flipped to the next section.

"I'm sorry I snapped at you the other day. I shouldn't have done that."

Cecily sighed. "It's okay. I'm just embarrassed. What do you think will happen if Shazi and Hasu pass the Symposium and I don't? Will I have to come back next year alone?"

"That's not going to happen. It's just one bad grade. You'll do better on the next test."

"But what if I don't?" She looked as though she'd swallowed a hair ball. "School isn't easy for me the way it is for all of you, and Cyril doesn't know that because he let me be his student even though I'd never been in an Exhibition.

What will he do when he finds out that I'm stupid?"

Barclay grimaced. She was being awfully mean to herself, and Cecily wasn't usually mean to anyone. "Cyril won't think that because that isn't true."

"It is, though." Her shadow, normally long and slithering about, was small and shriveled, and her leg jittered restlessly. "I try so hard to pay attention, but then class is over and I realize that I missed half of it because I was thinking about something useless. I lost my Lore Keeper History textbook and looked everywhere and still can't find it. I didn't even finish our last test. And I feel like I can't remember *anything*. Yesterday I told Shazi the same story twice in the same hour."

"Everyone feels like that sometimes," Barclay said.

"Yeah, but if this was just sometimes, I wouldn't be failing two of my classes."

She had a good point. "You can borrow my notes, then, and we can study together. You're plenty smart, Cecily. You've found secret passages that no one else has noticed, come up with all sorts of pranks for the Tourney, *and* your Lore would never be as strong as it is if you didn't give it tons of practice and concentration. If what you're doing isn't working, then we'll just find another way for you to do it, one that works for you."

Cecily smiled feebly. "Yeah, that sounds like it would be a lot better." She closed her textbook and eyed the pastries across the room longingly.

"I'm still sorry for snapping at you."

"It's fine. You're right about the Tourney, anyway. It's a waste of time."

"No, I was being mean." He still wasn't sure he believed Runa's claim that the Tourney brought students together, but the thought gave him an idea. "How about this, to make it up to you, I'll help you and the others with whatever stunt you're planning next."

"You don't have to do that. You're already helping me study."

"No, really. I want to." He didn't, but it felt like the right thing to do.

Cecily's eyes lit up, and she rubbed her hands together slyly. "This is so exciting! Your wind Lore opens up so many new possibilities. . . ."

Barclay hoped he hadn't just made a grievous mistake.

After that, the festivities lasted late into the night. They didn't have classes the next day, so no one was in a hurry to go to sleep.

Then, shortly after a few students trickled to bed, a scream rang out from the left wing of dormitories. Everyone stopped their conversations and peered down the corridor. A hole had been cut in the ceiling, and out of it poured a cloud of loud, buzzing insects. Their bulging red eyes took up most of their heads, and they had long stingers on either side of their fuzzy bodies.

"Dungwasps!" Deirdre screeched, sprinting back toward the lounge while the Beasts swarmed after her.

The party descended into chaos. Students shrieked and careened for the exit, except the double doors that led to the atrium were locked, as though they'd been melded shut. Panicked, the apprentices lunged in any other direction, many colliding with each other or toppling over their confused Beasts. The Dungwasps swooped and stabbed. Pastries skidded across the carpet.

Barclay's and Root's gazes found each other from across the room, and the two dove for cover together behind a couch. Beside them, Shazi whacked at the bugs with a pillow, while Saif jabbed at them with his spearlike tail.

"Everyone calm down!" Hasu called, always the voice of reason in a crisis. "I can get us out of here two at a time if you just . . ." But it was no use, as the buzzing of the Dungwasps drowned out her voice. Frustrated, she seized the closest apprentices—two eleven-year-olds—and disappeared with them in a flash of light.

Cyril's door burst open. "What's going . . ."

Barclay didn't catch what Cyril said next, because a Dungwasp stinger sank into his leg. Barclay grunted and wrenched it out of his skin, wishing he'd asked Mory if he could keep the protective vest from earlier. He'd been stung and stabbed so many times today that he felt like a pincushion. Beside him, Root snapped his jaws at bug after bug—always missing.

All types of Lore surged through the air: a slime lasso from Rohan, a cannon of juice Tadg had siphoned from the punch bowl, a stray sizzle of fire or puff of smoke. The only one who was happy was Oudie, who chased after the Dungwasps for a nighttime feast.

By the time Cyril reached the other side of the long hallway toward the atrium, several Dungwasps stuck out of his skin where they'd stung him. He ignored them and placed both his hands on the doors. Instantly, the wood crumpled as though as flimsy as paper. He thrust them open, and everyone raced through the atrium toward the exit.

To Barclay's shock, similar sounds of chaos echoed from the Surveyors' lounge. He skidded to a halt beside the statue of Navrashtya, the Legendary Beast of the Tundra. Several feet away, Cyril pried a Dungwasp from his forearm.

"They're in the Surveyors' lounge too!" Barclay told him.

Cyril scowled and dashed toward their doors. But before he could open them, a hole erupted from the ground, and Li and several of the Surveyor students poked their heads out, each covered in dirt. They'd tunneled out like meerkats.

"You too?" Li asked deliriously as she grasped Cyril's offered hand and climbed out.

"Whoever did this took the Tourney too far," Cyril fumed.

Barclay and Root followed the last of the students outside. Across the courtyard, more students poured out of Hamdani Hall—the Apothecaries and Scholars. Every single lounge had been hit.

"Who'd prank their own classmates like *that*?" Cecily asked.

"I don't know how they did it," Rohan said, "but I bet you five kritters it was Mischievius."

Though no student came forward to claim the prank, the mystery of how it was accomplished was solved a half hour later, when large lumps of Voxen droppings were found in the ceilings of all four dormitories.

"This took planning," Rohan said bitterly. "Mischievius had to collect the droppings and wait long enough for the hives to be built. And *then* they had to carve holes in all the ceilings."

"At the same time?" Barclay asked. That sounded impossible.

"Well, it couldn't have happened by chance," Shazi said

fiercely. "And we can't let Mischievius get away with this. We need to figure out who they are, and we need to strike back."

"Your last plan was to glue mustaches made from Codric's wool on all the statues," Cecily pointed out.

Tadg snorted. "That'll show them."

Shazi's nostrils flared. "*Obviously* we'll think of something better."

"Barclay said he'd help us," Cecily said.

Root wagged his tail eagerly, but Barclay gulped. He could already tell he was going to regret this.

Even with his face swollen from so many stings, Rohan beamed. "Excellent. We'll meet in the lounge tomorrow at seven o'clock, and come with ideas—this needs to be our best prank yet."

TEN

A long-awaited day had finally arrived: the Symposium's first field trip.

It'd taken six carrier dragons to transport the whole Symposium, and they soared through the sky in a giant V. Students leaned out the windows to wave at their classmates in other caravans or marvel at dazzling views. Others passed the hours trading champion cards. Some napped. Several more caught up on homework, which Barclay might've liked to do, but instead he found himself concocting plans for the Tourney.

"It has to be Thursday," Rohan said. He, Cecily, Shazi, and Barclay huddled together in the prized seats at the back of their caravan. "Right before everyone moves back into their rooms."

After Mischievius had turned Eldin and Hamdani Halls into buzzy, Dungwasp-infested chaos, the Symposium students had spent over four weeks in spare dormitories across campus while exterminators transported the hives to a safer location. Chancellor Essam had furiously reminded everyone that the Tourney existed for friendly sport, not to distract from their studies.

"Cecily, you'll help us sneak into each lounge using your shadow Lore to slip past the doors and unlock them from the inside," Rohan told her. "Barclay will help me lift the furniture in the air, then I'll use my slime Lore to glue them upside-down on the ceiling."

"What about me?" Shazi asked.

"You'll be keeping watch."

She crossed her arms. "That's the most boring job."

"Not if there are still any Dungwasps to battle," Barclay pointed out.

This seemed to please Shazi, as she leaned back into the cushions and returned to polishing her swords.

"Look! Look!" one Apothecary student called, pointing out the window. Barclay and the others twisted around and peered outside.

At first, Barclay thought his eyes were playing tricks on him. A vast forest stretched below them to the edge of the horizon, as though they'd flown all the way to the Woods. But this forest couldn't be more different from the one Barclay called home. It was utterly lifeless. The trees bore no leaves, and their briary gray branches made the landscape resemble a sea of barbed wire.

"What is this place?" he asked.

"It's the Ironwood Forest," Shazi said eagerly. "I've wanted to visit since I was little, but Mom and Dad have always been too busy to take me."

The carrier dragons landed beside the tree line, and up close, the strange trees were even spookier to behold. They didn't look to be made of wood at all. Instead, their trunks and branches were pure iron, glinting in the sunlight. Every twig looked sharp enough to cut.

Instructor Dia beckoned the wary students closer. He slumped more than usual—they'd gotten up early for their travel—and he clutched his coffee dearly. "This is the Iron-wood Forest, the driest part of the Desert. It's rained here only twice in all of recorded history, which makes it the perfect place for these Lore plants to thrive. Can anyone guess why?"

Several hands shot into the air.

"Yes, Viola?" Dia said.

"Because water makes iron rust," she answered.

"That's right. This forest is home to many kinds of rare Beasts and phenomena. Now, does everyone have their worksheets? Good, good. Each of you is to explore these surroundings and see if you can answer the questions. Don't rely on your fellow classmates. The trees have all the answers you need."

Barclay found that hard to believe, as the questions looked very complicated. *Why do all the trees grow the same distance apart? How can you tell how old a tree is? If it doesn't use water to grow, what does it use?* He met eyes with Hasu, who looked as baffled as he did.

Despite Dia assuring them all that the forest was harmless, the apprentices tiptoed as they ventured inside. Wherever Barclay walked, dozens of his reflections crept after him, distorted from every curve and knob in the tree trunks.

Dia might've forbidden them from consulting other students, but that didn't mean Barclay had to complete the assignment alone. He summoned Root from his Mark, and Root's ears immediately perked up, suspicious of this strange new place. He padded closer to one of his engorged reflections. As with all the other trees, the branches pointed straight up to the sky like the bristles of a broom.

Root sniffed the metallic bark, then placed his paw against the trunk and scratched. The sound was so grating that Barclay covered his ears with his hands. A Scholar student to their right shot them a dirty look.

"Maybe don't do that again," Barclay told Root, whose nostrils flared indignantly.

While they worked, Barclay stole glances at the other students. Shazi placed her palm flat against one of the tree trunks, using her metal Lore to make it wiggle. Fen poked a needlelike root jutting out from the ground and wrenched his finger away, muttering angrily. Tadg paid no attention to his worksheet and was instead yelling at Toadles and furiously scratching his rashy arms.

Even Viola had made little progress. She chased after her Skulkit, who'd stolen her paper and was attempting to bury it in the gravel.

The only apprentices making any sense of the assignment were the Surveyors. They each strutted through the forest with purpose. Some knocked against the tree trunks, their ears pressed to the bark. Others wielded clever gadgets to climb to the treetops or drill into the ground.

Barclay tried to mimic them. He squatted and dug through the dirt. It was oddly colored—more red than brown, and very pebbly. But he didn't discover anything interesting. All he managed was to cake grit underneath his fingernails.

"Looking for treasure?" a voice asked, and Barclay peered up to see Zenzi standing over him, smirking.

His face went hot, and he hurriedly stood up and wiped his hands on his pants. "I thought I'd—I don't know." He glanced at Root, too embarrassed to meet Zenzi's eyes. Root was busy tracking a large, mothlike Beast that flitted through the air behind Zenzi, its wings crinkled like yellowed parchment. It wasn't until it landed on Zenzi's arm that Barclay realized it must be her Beast. "I'm not sure what I'm doing. You and the other Surveyors make it look easy."

"Surveyors are trained to pay attention to nature. The dirt is red because there's iron in it. And the gaps between the trees, well . . ." While she fished around in her pocket, Barclay considered telling her that he didn't want to cheat. But he liked talking to her, and despite the class they shared, they didn't speak often.

Zenzi held a kritter up at eye level.

"What's that for?" he asked.

"Just watch."

Then she threw it into the distance.

Rather than flying in a straight line, the coin zigzagged around the trees. Finally, it plunked into the dirt.

"Are the trees magnetic?" he guessed. "That explains why they grow far apart. They repel each other."

Zenzi nodded, looking impressed. "Not bad for a Guardian apprentice."

His face heated again, but it wasn't so bad this time. "Thanks. And thanks for helping me too."

After Zenzi left to explore more of the forest, Barclay felt Root staring at him. His tail flicked back and forth teasingly.

"Don't look at me like that," he grumbled.

Over the next twenty minutes, Barclay did his best job at pretending to be a Surveyor. He closely inspected the spear-like branches. He pressed his ear against the tree trunks—even though they were *scalding* hot—and tapped, only to realize the trunks were hollow. He even tried climbing one, but jumped down when a twig jabbed him in the leg.

When he'd finally filled in as much of the worksheet as he could, he strolled over to Viola, who'd attracted the attention of a small crowd. With one arm, she cradled her Skulkit. In the other hand, she held a glass disk in front of her eye like a monocle and closely inspected a tree trunk.

"I want to see!" one of the Surveyors exclaimed.

"Me first," Cecily said.

Viola handed the glass disk to Cecily, and Barclay squeezed through to Viola's side.

"What is it?" he asked.

"I made a magnifying glass with my Skulkit's Lore," Viola said happily, which Barclay had to admit was impressive. It'd taken him ages to learn how to use his wind Lore after he bonded with Root, and Viola had mastered several tricks in a matter of days.

While Viola introduced her Skulkit to a nearby student, Cecily spun around, the glass still perched in front of her eye. She laughed as she stared at Barclay. "I can see the pimple on your forehead close up!"

Barclay frowned and brushed his hair down to cover it. He glanced hurriedly behind him, but thankfully, no one seemed to have overheard.

"Don't worry." Cecily smiled slyly. "Fen looks busy. And Zenzi is way over there."

Barclay was so stunned by her words that he tripped over Root's hind leg, earning him an annoyed flick in the face from Root's tail. He spat a strand of Root's fur out his mouth. "Wh-what are you talking about?"

"I haven't been spying on you, if that's what you're wondering." Cecily brandished her finished worksheet. "I was spying on Zenzi, since she's the one with all the answers."

Barclay's embarrassment squirmed through him like a worm. The only person he'd ever spoken to about Fen or Zenzi was Root, and even then, only about normal things. Like that he was curious why Fen became an Apothecary when he had a Mythic class Beast. Or that he wondered how Zenzi ever got anywhere when she was always walking with a map in her hands. *Normal* things. Not at all what Cecily was suggesting.

Root snorted, as though Barclay wasn't fooling anybody.

"Relax," Cecily said. "I'm only teasing."

"You won't be able to sneak around like that during a real exam," he told her.

"Oh, I know, which is why I'm making sure to do it as much as possible while I can."

He rolled his eyes. There was no getting through to her. But he was pleasantly surprised on the flight home when Cecily asked to borrow his notes. While he read an adventure novel—*The Canyons of Doom*—Cecily neatly copied down his writing onto flash cards. Then she quizzed herself for a whole hour. By the time they landed in Menneset, she knew each of them by heart.

The next evening, Viola talked Barclay and Tadg into attending her mother's lecture.

"Different Scholars give presentations on their research

every week at the University," Viola told them. "Mom has been preparing for hers since last Winter. It would mean a lot to her if we all went."

Barclay didn't need much convincing—he thought a Scholarly lecture sounded fascinating. The only one who complained was Tadg.

"We just sat in class *all day*," he grumbled. "Do we really need to go to another?"

But Viola wouldn't take no for an answer, and so the trio returned to the breezy outdoor amphitheater where Essam had given his speech at the Symposium's opening ceremony. Apart from Pemba, who waved at them from the back row with Mory, the three of them were the youngest members of the audience. Everyone else donned Scholar robes, including Kadia, who smiled in their direction as she began her lecture.

"Many consider the Legendary Beasts to be the most powerful class of Beasts in the world," she said. "But to list the Legendary class among the others is akin to comparing an entire ocean to lakes, ponds, and puddles, as the six Legendary Beasts are unique from any other creature on the planet. They do not age. In normal circumstances, most of them sleep all but two days of the year. Their mood and behavior affect the entire Wilderland over which they reign, making it impossible to determine whether the Wilderlands as we know them would exist if the Legendary Beasts did not."

Kadia's lecture proved even more captivating than Barclay had hoped, and she pointed out similarities and differences between the Legendary Beasts that he'd never considered. For instance, all but one of them—Raajnavar, the Legendary Beast of the Jungle—lived in a single place they called home. Navrashtya, of the Tundra, hadn't been sighted in over two centuries. Of the six, Gravaldor was the most destructive, which was why so few settlements had grown into cities in the Woods. Lochmordra's sleep cycles flowed in tandem with the weeping tide. Shakulah was associated with the most myths, as Lore Keepers throughout history had claimed to have spotted her wandering the Desert at unusual times or heard her famous laugh, rumored to foretell death. Dimondaise was the only one who laid eggs, which she hid each Midsummer in secret places in the Mountains. None of the ones found had ever hatched.

By the time the lecture ended, even Tadg was impressed.

"I never understood why Dad was so obsessed with studying the Legendary Beasts until now." He stood up from their stone bench and stretched. "They rule the Wilderlands, yet we barely know anything about them."

"Can you believe that sixteen people have bonded with them?" Barclay asked. "I know that's in all of history, but that still seems like so many. How can a Keeper's body contain all that Lore without being ripped to shreds?"

"Oh, I'm pretty sure bonding with a Legendary Beast *can* rip you to shreds," Viola told them. "I read about it back when I wanted to bond with Gravaldor."

"And that didn't change your mind about trying?" asked Barclay, horrified.

She shrugged. "If Faiza Asfour bonded with *six*, then I figured I'd be okay with one."

Below them, Kadia intermingled with her colleagues, who looked like a flock of birds with their many colors and tassels. Leaving her to her conversation, Mory and Pemba descended the stairs toward the three apprentices.

"I took notes," Pemba told them, showing off her note-book. Inside were messy doodles of the six Legendary Beasts. Barclay guessed the largest one must've been Shakulah, as it had whiskers and a long tail.

"You draw a lot better than I do," Tadg told her, which was probably true, as Barclay had seen Tadg's handwriting—besides Tadg, only a professional code breaker could decipher it.

"It was good of you each to come," said Mory. "Kadia was nervous about this lecture. She couldn't prepare for it as much as her last one, since she's been working so many hours for the High Keeper."

"I thought the presentation was amazing," Barclay said.

Mory chuckled. "Make sure to tell her that. For some reason, she never believes me when I do. Apparently I'm biased and love her too much to be trusted."

While they waited for Kadia, Mory invited Viola, Tadg, and Barclay over for dinner, and an hour later, they all sat at the dining table at the Tolo house while Mory served them his grandfather's secret recipe for a lemony chicken and rice.

"So how is your Skulkit adjusting?" Mory asked Viola.

On the other side of the room, over fifteen Beasts—including Bulu, Yaylay, Root, Toadles, Mitzi, and the Skulkit—devoured a feast of their own. The others all belonged to Mory, and Barclay noticed that many of them were injured in some way. One Beast was missing its hind leg. Another had a clipped wing, and a line of stitches crawled up the smoldering, serpentine tail of a Tasumabasa, clearly from a recent medical procedure. It was no wonder that Mory had so many Beasts when he worked with ones who most dearly needed a home.

"He's doing well, though he isn't used to sleeping at night," Viola answered. "I've also been testing out my new glass Lore, and I've managed a few tricks."

She pulled the miniature magnifying glass from her pocket and passed it to her mother, who peered through it at her caramelized onions.

"This is very clever, Viola," Kadia said. "Maybe you could talk Shazi into making a rim for it so you can actually wear it."

While they debated whether Viola would or wouldn't look good with a monocle, Barclay picked at his food, frustrated with himself. Because even though he was having fun and the meal was delicious, he felt a familiar pinch of sadness in his chest. It didn't make sense to miss his parents after so long—he'd been too little to really know them. But maybe grief didn't disappear one day like a growing pain. Maybe its soreness came and went.

He was feeling sore a lot lately.

"I can't believe you haven't *named* your Beast yet," Pemba said, sounding scandalized.

"I still haven't come up with anything good," said Viola.

Pemba's eyes widened with glee. "I already made a list." Then she lurched from the table and fled the dining room.

"Not until you've finished your dinner!" Kadia called, but it was no use. Pemba's footsteps were already thumping up the stairs toward her bedroom. Kadia sighed, then turned back to Viola. "Have you heard from your father recently? I wouldn't be surprised if he returns to Menneset soon. The *Keeper's Khronicle* has begun a daily column about the Ever Storms, and the picture it paints of him is far from flattering."

Viola shook her head. "The last letter he sent me, he mostly talked about how all three of his dragons are molting and the house is covered in feathers."

"What do you mean, far from flattering?" Barclay asked Kadia.

"Take a look for yourself." Kadia stood and handed Barclay that day's edition of the newspaper from where it rested on the counter. The headline read, in bold letters, THE STORMS THAT NEVER CEASE. Barclay skimmed the lengthy article, which claimed that the Grand Keeper was doing nothing to help the Desert's three Ever Storms. It even used the phrase "It's easy to look down your nose when you're high up (and safe) in the Mountains."

"This isn't fair," said Viola, who read over Barclay's shoulder. "Dad has been doing a lot to help High Keeper Asfour. He's sent over sixty Guardians—that's practically half of them!"

"But he's only come himself once," Kadia said.

"So why doesn't he just travel down here again?" Barclay asked.

"Because he feels it'll look worse for him if even *he* can't solve the problem. He gets nervous about these things when there's an election coming up, and there's one next year."

"But he won't really have a problem, right?" asked Tadg. "Hasn't the Dumont family been the Grand Keepers for over seventy years?"

"Yes, but that's also the reason he's nervous. A lot of people, like this reporter, Tristan Navarre, think it's time for some change."

"Maybe he's right," Mory said, earning a pointed look from

Kadia. "No offense to Leopold—I like him well enough, and I know how hard he works. But seventy years is a long—"

"Does that mean that people won't want me to become Grand Keeper?" Viola asked, sounding distressed.

"Of course not," Kadia said quickly. "Navarre just has strong opinions, and his words have a way of catching people's attention."

Before she could finish, Pemba returned, brandishing a paper that looked as though she'd torn it from her notebook. She slapped it onto the table beside Viola. "These are all my favorite names. Do you like them?"

Viola studied the paper with raised brows. "Thank you for all these ideas, Pemba, but I don't think I'm going to name my Beast Sparklestar."

As though realizing he was the topic of the conversation, the Skulkit abandoned the rest of his meal—to the delight of Root, who'd scarfed down his own supper in seconds—and leapt onto the kitchen table.

"Manners," Viola scolded him, despite smiling and shaking her head. Then she picked him up and set him on her lap. He examined her glass of water curiously, then he reached his paw out. The glass contorted, twisting up into a strange, curvy carafe. "Hey! That isn't ours!"

"Looks like you have a second troublemaker," Mory said, grinning mischievously at Mitzi, who kept poking Toadles's warts.

The Skulkit glanced up at Viola, his glass hoops rattling.

Viola laughed and flicked his lopsided ear. "You're lucky you're cute, you know." Then she looked at him thoughtfully. "I think his name is Kulo."

Kadia smiled. "Welcome to the family, Kulo."

Kulo reached again for the water glass, and Viola hastily moved it out of his reach. "Not again, you don't." The table laughed.

Barclay raised both of his hands and blasted an arc of wind at the practice dummies. The force struck down over half of them, but several of the human targets remained upright.

"You're improving," Cyril offered kindly. Beside him, Codric nodded in approval, making his fading red and orange leaves rustle atop his horns.

Barclay stifled a groan. What Cyril and Codric didn't know was that Barclay had mastered this challenge when he'd last practiced alone. He was distracted. Today was the first day of Winter, which meant he had to help Rohan, Cecily, and Shazi with their grand stunt that evening.

"Let me try again," Barclay said, and with a flick of Cyril's wrist, each of the targets lifted from the floor. Barclay did his best to shove thoughts of the Tourney from his mind. He focused only on the targets.

Wind!

This time, the human dummies plunked over. *Thunk! Thunk! Thunk!* Each of the Beasts stayed standing.

Root barked and leapt to his feet. But when Barclay glanced behind him, Cyril was glaring furiously at today's edition of the *Keeper's Khronicle*. Codric peered nosily over his shoulder.

"Um . . . Cyril?" Barclay asked awkwardly. When Cyril still didn't respond, Barclay said louder, "Cyril?"

Cyril snapped the newspaper closed, making Codric jolt. "Sorry. Rude of me, I know." It might've been, but Barclay had never known Cyril to be distracted or apologize before. He took his work far too seriously for that. "Well done. I suppose we'll move on to flying targets next."

"On to wh—?"

The Beast targets launched into the air, fifty feet above their heads. Barclay rushed to fire pellets of wind at each of them, but all of them missed.

"Just a little more," Rohan said, and Barclay blew the upside-down armchair higher. Its legs set into the slime on the ceiling with an audible *squish*.

"Are you almost done in there?" Shazi called from down the corridor.

"Just about!" Barclay answered. But the truth was, Barclay was having *fun*. It was exciting, sneaking under the noses of the other students and resident Masters. Maybe Runa and his friends were right, and he'd been working himself too hard. One day, he would go down in history as the Lore Keeper who'd changed the Elsewheres, but maybe he could go down in Tourney history first.

And the best part: they got to explore the other dormitories. The Surveyors' lounge was amazing, with a map of the constellations painted on the—now slimy—ceiling. The hallways resembled underground tunnels more than typical corridors, with coarse stone walls and colorful glass lanterns dangling overhead.

The Apothecaries' lounge was very smelly, though not in a bad way. Cauldrons hovered over the six fireplaces. Ferns and flowers bent toward the windows. And a whole laboratory's worth of vials and beakers were scattered across the tables, abandoned midexperiment. Rohan and Barclay made quicker work of their furniture, as their ceiling was oddly lower than all the others. It wasn't until Barclay climbed the mysterious ladder in the room's corner that he realized all the Apothecary students slept beneath a greenhouse of exotic Lore plants and the Trite class Beasts who helped pollinate them.

Their last target, the Scholars' lounge, could've been mistaken for the world's coziest library. Bookshelves lined every inch of the walls, and there was no surface that lacked a soft cushion or knitted blanket.

"Here, you take that end. I'll take this one," Rohan said. Then the two boys groaned and gently turned the table onto its back. They each panted. Barclay's muscles ached from his training session with Cyril that morning. "You know, when I planned this out in my head, I didn't realize it would involve so much manual labor."

"What were you expecting?"

"Excitement. It's for glory, isn't it?" Rohan tapped his fingers together, and strings of webby slime stretched taut between them. He pulled and pulled until he'd formed enough to make a ball, then he threw it against the ceiling with a wet *splat*. He frowned and shook his hands. "Muskrats. I glued my fingers together again—"

"What are you doing?" a muffled voice asked, and the four of them spun around to face several Scholar students staring at them through the windows.

They'd been caught.

"Run!" Rohan shouted. They scrambled down the corridor where Cecily and Shazi lazily sat on the floor. The boys hoisted them to their feet and shoved them ahead into the atrium, where the Scholar students came bursting in.

"Hey! Stop!" one of them shouted.

"You're not supposed to be here!"

Stricken, the four of them dashed out the opposite doors, and the Scholars followed in close pursuit.

"Let's split up," Shazi huffed. "You two go that way. Barclay and I will go this way."

Before Barclay could argue, Shazi seized him by the wrist and yanked him to the left. They bolted across the courtyard into one of the academic buildings. They might've been fast, but their steps weren't exactly quiet. Every thud of their shoes echoed off the stone floor.

"Get back here!" one of the Scholars called after them.

The pair turned a corner—only to come skidding to a halt. They'd reached a dead end.

The footsteps behind them grew louder, and Barclay looked around frantically, his Mark stinging in warning. His gaze fell on a strange door in the corner, one he swore he hadn't noticed the moment before. And it would've been hard to miss. It was hugely tall, and its top came to a point. An intricate lattice of gold covered the wood, as though the door was draped in metallic lace. And the doorknob wasn't a knob at all; it was a giant, glittering ruby.

Barclay pointed at the door. "In there! Hurry!"

Shazi's eyes widened, but then she nodded and tore after him. Barclay twisted the gemstone knob, and together, the two of them thrust the heavy door open just as the Scholar apprentices rounded the corner behind them. They slipped inside and slammed the door closed.

Barclay braced his hands on his knees to catch his breath. Strangely, his Mark still stung, but he ignored it, letting out a wild laugh. "That was close. Do you think they saw us?" When Shazi didn't respond, Barclay turned to face her. "Do you think they . . ."

His voice died, all his breath leaving him in a single, shocked rush.

They stood at the landing of a stairwell. Sconces lined the walls, and they flared to life one at a time, illuminating a descent as far down as he could see. A luxurious carpet draped over the steps. It was woven with colorful bazen designs in thousands of shapes and patterns, making it almost too beautiful to walk upon. Stacked along the edges of the steps were dusty books, so old they looked like little more than dust themselves. The air smelled of ancient paper.

"Shazi," Barclay said nervously. "What is this place?"

It was a useless question because he already knew the answer. They were in the entrance to the Library of Asfour.

Without answering, Shazi slipped off her shoes and began walking down the steps.

"Wait," he said, his voice hitched in panic. "We can't be here! It's too dangerous! We should go back to—"

"Are you telling me that you don't want to see it?" Shazi had a razor-edge glint to her eyes that scared Barclay, because he could already tell there would be no dissuading her. "Do you know how rare it is to find a door to the Library? No matter how much I begged Viola, she refused to go inside. But now you can see the door too, and . . . don't you want to *know*?"

Barclay held his breath because he didn't trust himself to answer. In his head, he knew the right decision. It was no wonder Root kept trying to warn him—this was far, far more dangerous than a Tourney prank. They should wait here until the Scholar students left. Then they could sneak back to Eldin Hall and never speak of this again.

But his heart yearned for a different choice. To explore the wonder and mystery that awaited them down these steps.

Barclay had a hard time saying no to adventure.

He wasn't even sure if he said yes, but a moment later, he reluctantly let Shazi lead their way downstairs. While they walked, his Mark stung worse with every step, and he promised himself and Root that they'd only venture down to *look*. They wouldn't touch anything. They wouldn't search for other rooms or passageways. They'd only stay long enough to make a memory of it. Then they'd flee back upstairs and pretend this had never happened.

The steps went on and on. Shivers crawled up Barclay's spine as he wondered how deep they were underground. The sconces on their either side burned without any oil. Whatever Lore was within the Library was very old—and *very* powerful.

Finally, the stairwell opened into a grand chamber whose every wall, from floor to ceiling, was filled with books and scrolls. And the ceilings were *tall*. So tall that Barclay saw only blackness when he stared up. If he didn't know better, he'd guess he was staring into a starless night sky.

A large golden statue of a woman stood in the hall's center. Her extremely long hair draped around her like a shroud, and her pleated robes reminded Barclay of the sort that Scholars wore. In one arm, she lifted a lantern, and like the sconces in the stairwell, it burned with magical flame.

"'Faiza Asfour,'" Barclay read on the plaque at the statue's feet. The woman didn't look much like the High Keeper, but Barclay supposed that no one closely resembled their ancestor from eight hundred years ago.

"This place is amazing," Shazi said, so loudly that her words echoed, and each reverberation sounded deeper and eerier than the last. "Sorry. I forgot you're supposed to be quiet in libraries."

Barclay took it all in—the statue, the endless shelves, the smell of old books. Then he swiveled on his heels and started back toward the stairs.

"You can't want to leave already," Shazi protested. "Don't you want to read any of those scrolls? There could be all sorts of forgotten secrets in them."

"We've already risked enough coming down here. What will we do if Cyril notices we're gone?"

"Fine. Leave if you want. But I want to read." She walked toward the far wall and began scanning the titles.

Barclay scowled and stalked to the stairs. Then he hesitated. The Library of Asfour was supposedly a deadly labyrinth—what if he woke up the next morning and Shazi still hadn't returned? And the next day? And the day after that? He couldn't abandon her down here. No matter how much he disagreed with her, she was still his friend.

So he swallowed his frustration and trudged to Shazi's side. Mites skittered across the shelves, and upon closer inspection, he realized the mites were *words*. Fragments of Lore script marched across the wood like regiments of ants, and when Shazi slid a leather-bound tome from a shelf and blew away the dust, tiny, scraggly characters puffed into the air. Barclay sneezed.

"There are sketches of Beasts in here," Shazi breathed. "I think some of them are extinct now." She pointed to an illustration that could've been either a dragon or a rooster— it was hard to tell. "Dad won't admit it, but he'd love to see this place. He's told me stories about it for as long as I can remember."

"Hasn't he found a door?" If anyone should be allowed to enter the Library of Asfour, it was the Chancellor of the University.

"Yeah, but he won't go in. Some Chancellor a hundred years ago made it against the rules, and Dad says she made the right decision."

Shazi slid the book back into place, and Barclay let out a sigh of relief. Finally, they could leave. But Shazi didn't turn toward the stairs. Instead, she strode straight for the humongous set of double doors on the far wall. As with the door on the surface, a gold lattice was splayed over the wood.

In front of the doors was a podium.

Barclay's heart quickened. Beyond those doors must be the labyrinth—and the danger.

On the podium was a book, open to a page that read:

I have spoken every story ever told,
From the ones of fable to the histories of old.
Though I may bleed or fade away, I can never die.
Look upon me as I ask of you—what am I?

"What do you think that means?" Shazi asked.

"It means we should get out of here."

She sighed. "You're right. It's not like a bunch of students are ever going to figure out the riddles anyway. But I just wanted to try."

Barclay wasn't used to Shazi sounding so disappointed. But he was too jittery to console her. High above in the ceiling he swore he caught a pair of red eyes staring down at them. But when he blinked, they were gone.

The climb to the surface was long and exhausting, but even after they'd snuck into Eldin Hall, a strange buzz tingled like static at his fingertips. He didn't sleep a wink that night. His mind was too restless, reciting the phrases from the riddle over and over in his thoughts, trying to guess the answer.

ELEVEN

The more Barclay tried to forget about his and Shazi's adventure in the Library of Asfour, the more he dwelled on it. No matter where he went or what he did—be it sitting in class, running with Root, or training at the gymnasium—the words of the riddle haunted him.

It wasn't that he *wanted* to explore more of the deadly, mysterious library. But he'd always liked books and puzzles, and so it was hard to stop pondering it, like an itch he couldn't help but scratch. He knew it was pointless to crack the riddle of a door he never planned on opening, yet he still wanted to solve it—very, very badly.

Shazi did nothing to help matters. Though she never brought up the subject of the Library again, Barclay often felt the heat of her stare. Sometimes in class. At the cafeteria. In the campus courtyards. He didn't think Shazi was following him, exactly, but whenever the hair on his arms suddenly stood on end, he'd cast a glance over his shoulder, and there she was, lurking behind a column or palm tree. Her gaze was as sharp as her swords.

So Barclay bided his time until her next training session with Cyril, then he snuck into the University's library after dinner. This library might not have been as magnificent as the Library of Asfour, but it still housed an impressive collection.

"Historians, histories," Barclay mumbled under his breath, scanning the titles.

The Oral Histories of the Sea
Bygone Eras: The Four Great Lore Keeper Ages
Extinct Beasts: Creatures Lost to History

"What are you doing?" a voice asked.

Barclay yelped, and several of the Scholars at nearby desks cast him stern looks. Viola stood behind him, her arms crossed.

His face flushed. "N-nothing."

"I *knew* you've been sneaking around." She peered at the books around them. "History? Did Dudnik assign homework I don't know about?"

"I like to read. What's so weird about that?"

"You like to read adventure stories, not . . . whatever this is." Viola slid *Extinct Beasts* from the shelf, whose cover depicted some kind of frightening, seven-headed fish.

Knowing he was caught in a lie, Barclay sighed and recited the riddle.

Viola must've thought that he'd put in one hour of

studying too many, because she gawked at him as though he'd uttered nonsense. Then she gasped. "A riddle? Is that—is that from the Library of Asfour?"

"Shazi and I went in by accident. That was the riddle written on—"

"You went *inside*? Don't you realize how dangerous that was? Dozens of Scholars have gone missing in there. Not to mention it breaks the University's rules."

Barclay glanced around to make sure no one was close enough to overhear them, but the Scholars were too busy scrutinizing their books and documents. Then he whispered, "I told you it was an accident. And I don't plan on going back."

"Then why are you trying to solve the riddle?"

"Because I can't get it out of my head, all right? That's the only reason, I swear."

He could tell from her pursed lips that she didn't believe him. Which was exactly why her words surprised him.

"I don't understand. It's extremely rare for the Library to show itself to anyone, let alone a bunch of Guardian apprentices. First me, then Shazi, then you. It's almost like . . . No, that doesn't make sense."

"What?"

Viola fiddled with her pins. "It's almost like it *wants* us to go inside. That it wants us to learn something."

"*It* is just a library. It's not alive. It doesn't have thoughts or feelings."

"I know. It's just strange. Maybe we should tell Runa about it."

At first, Barclay wanted to argue. Runa was so busy working for the High Keeper that she rarely left the Guild House, yet they'd still made no progress in understanding the Ever Storms. He and Viola shouldn't add to her worries.

But this wasn't like before, when the Library of Asfour had merely felt like a legend. He and Shazi had gone *inside*, and Runa would want to know about it. He knew she would.

Before Barclay could agree, Tadg's voice called out through the library. "Viola! Bar—don't tell me to be quiet! This is important. Barclay! Viola . . ." He skidded to a stop at the end of their aisle, spotting them, then raced in their direction, panting. He looked shaken. "Viola, you have to come quick."

"What? Why?" she asked.

"It's your mom. She was attacked. Hurry. Runa is waiting for us at Eldin Hall."

The three of them bolted through the library back to their dormitory, where Runa was arguing with Chancellor Essam on the outside steps. Several other members of the University staff thronged behind them, including the instructors, Cyril, and the other resident Lore Masters.

"Why shouldn't we interview the students?" Runa demanded. "If it happened on campus, then one of them might've seen something."

"I want answers as much as you do," Essam assured her, "but questioning students would start a panic. And this is a matter for the Desert law enforcement, not the University."

"A Scholar was attacked on University grounds, and it's not a matter for the University?"

Barclay, Viola, and Tadg pushed through the surrounding teachers.

"Runa?" Viola choked out, close to tears and hugging Kulo in her arms. Mitzi nuzzled her leg, looking more serious and protective than Barclay had ever seen her. "What's going on? Is Mom all right? What happened?"

Runa tore away from Essam and placed her hands on Viola's shoulders. "Don't worry. Kadia is fine, and Mory and Pemba are already with her at the hospital."

"At the hospital?" Viola squeaked.

"Someone broke into her office earlier today. She was found an hour ago, with moderate but treatable injuries. We're going to leave right away to go be with her. Are you ready?"

"I—I guess so."

Runa steered Viola around, and the staff members parted so they could leave. But before they moved, Viola asked frantically, "Wait! What about Barclay and Tadg? Are they coming too?"

"Only if you'd like them there with you," Runa said gently.

Barclay was relieved when Viola nodded, wiping the tears from her eyes. He wanted to be there as Viola's friend, but he liked her whole family—a lot. And though he was trying to be strong for Viola, he felt close to tears himself.

Before they started off, Cyril peeled himself away from the other teachers. "I'd also like to come with you, if I may." His voice was unusually tight, though Barclay wasn't sure why. Maybe he wanted to support Viola as her old instructor. Or maybe he was another friend worried about Kadia. "I should—"

"Don't bother," Runa snapped at him, and he froze, stricken. Then Runa turned to the boys and jerked her head toward the campus gates. "Come on. Let's get moving."

It was a short walk to Menneset Hospital, so short that Barclay was still barely processing Runa's words by the time they walked through the doors. Why would Kadia have been attacked? And *who* would've attacked her? Kadia was so kind, and she gave so much of her time to the University and to the Guild. He couldn't imagine anyone wanting to hurt her.

In Dullshire, the local doctor made visits to each patient's house, so Barclay had never been inside a proper hospital before. But he'd heard about ones in large Elsewheres cities.

Obviously, those hospitals looked nothing like the one in Menneset, which roamed full of Beasts. He spotted a Turtletot burrowing its head into its Keeper's lap in the waiting room. An Ostrello was being wheeled away on a gurney, one of its legs bandaged. Others walked or flew side by side with the doctors and Apothecaries. One dragon even wore a tiny stethoscope.

After Runa spoke to the Lore Keeper at the visitors' desk, they climbed to the third floor, where Mory, Pemba, and many of the Tolo family Beasts waited in the hallway. Mory held Pemba even though she was far too big to be carried, and she buried her face in his shoulder.

Immediately, Viola ran and hugged them both.

"How is she?" she asked fretfully.

"She's awake," Mory answered, his eyes bloodshot, "and Dr. Essam said she's going to be fine." Shazi had once mentioned that her mother worked at the hospital; she must be Kadia's doctor. "We got to talk to her for a little while, but Asfour is speaking with her now. Apparently

it's confidential, and it can't wait, not even for her family."
Mory clearly wasn't happy to be kicked out of the room.
"She assured me she'd be quick, so we should be able to see
her again soon."

Viola sniffled. "But I don't understand. What happened?"

Mitzi snatched a wad of tissues from a nearby box and
handed one to Viola. She took it and blew her nose.

Mory gratefully accepted one as well. "This morning,
someone broke into her office to interrogate her on the Legendary Beasts—namely, on Shakulah's lure items."

Barclay and Tadg exchanged a dark look.

"Obviously, Kadia doesn't know what the items are—no
one does. But she's the University's leading Scholar on
Legendary Beasts. She knows more about Shakulah than
anyone in the world. So this person assumed she knew the
lure items too. Thankfully, they didn't hurt her, but truth
elixirs have side effects. She was woozy and knocked her
head hard while untying herself from her chair." He shook
his head, his expression pained. "We were all scared something like this would happen, and now that it has, I'm . . .
I'm so angry. Your mother loves her work. No one should be
allowed to ruin that or scare her the way they did."

Before Viola could respond, the door to Kadia's room
swung open and the High Keeper strode into the hallway,
looking disgruntled. After Viola and her family hurried in
to see Kadia, Asfour marched to Runa, Barclay, and Tadg.

"I'm calling a meeting at the Guild House," she grunted.
"Tonight. We need to discuss this, the Phantom Roar,
Midwinter—everything."

"It was him, wasn't it?" asked Runa darkly.

Even if Barclay had already been thinking so, hearing Runa's words made his dread harden in his gut like a stone.

"We can't know for certain. Kadia wasn't able to identify any details about the assailant, other than they seemed to be working alone. Whoever they were, they wore a mask, and they used tools to mask the sound of their voice."

"But this is still a pattern," Runa said. "First Younis. Now Kadia."

Asfour nodded. "Yes, so it seems, and I plan to take it seriously. Come by later when you can."

Once Asfour left, Tadg asked, "Younis? The teacher who Dudnik replaced last minute?"

Runa nodded grimly.

"You think Keyes is behind this, don't you?" Barclay asked. "You think he's behind everything. The Ever Storms too." He didn't know how to feel now: angry that Runa and Cyril had lied to them before, or foolish for not realizing the truth anyway.

"Of course we do. Every Wilderland has been on high alert since what happened at the Sea." Runa cracked her knuckles one by one, each popping with a loud *snap!* "Unfortunately, we have no evidence, as Leopold and Cyril keep reminding us. Maybe this is what it'll take for them to come to their senses." Judging by the flatness of her tone, she didn't seem optimistic.

"If you thought it was Keyes this whole time," Tadg growled, "why did you stick us in the Symposium?"

"No shouting," warned a nearby doctor, one who looked very much like a taller version of Shazi wearing a surgical cap.

Runa hastily ducked around the corner to the waiting room,

and the boys followed. "I know that you all want to help, and you did help at the Sea. But you shouldn't have had to."

"But we—" Barclay cut in.

"No," Runa snapped, so fierce that both boys recoiled. "You're still apprentices, and this has never been your problem. It's *mine*." Her voice was so icy that Barclay was surprised her breath didn't fog in the air. "Now, I have a meeting to organize with the High Keeper."

She stormed away, and Barclay considered calling after her. Amid all the commotion, he'd forgotten to tell her about the Library of Asfour. But she had work to do, and even though the Fang of Dusk was supposed to be invincible, she'd sounded so angry and upset.

So he stayed silent. He didn't want to burden her more than she already was.

After midnight passed, Mory told Barclay and Tadg that they could return to their dormitory, and Viola would stay at her family's house for the next few days. And so the two boys retraced their steps back to the University.

The streets of Menneset were peaceful and quiet— nothing at all like how Barclay felt inside. He kept picturing how Kadia had looked when they visited her, a bandage plastered across her forehead, her family gathered anxiously around her bedside. It scared him. And all his worst memories from the Midsummer his parents had died felt sharper than ever.

"I don't understand." Barclay's fury quivered in his throat, a scream he forced himself to swallow down. "Keyes *knew* Kadia. How could he do that to her?"

"Is it any worse than nearly destroying the entire Sea?" Tadg asked flatly. "Or nearly killing Runa and Cyril in the Mountains?"

Barclay supposed that it wasn't, but it did nothing to make him feel better. The worst part about dwelling on Keyes and Yasha's crimes wasn't all the damage they'd caused, but that Barclay had *liked* them before he realized who they really were.

The man named Edwyn Lusk had been funny and good natured. He'd been everyone's favorite teacher, and he'd proven to Barclay that Elsies could make great Lore Keepers too.

And even though Tadg had claimed that Yasha had never been their friend, he'd felt like one to Barclay. A real one.

"What do you think Runa meant when she said that Keyes was *her* problem?" Tadg asked.

"He was her friend," said Barclay.

"That doesn't mean it's her fault that he's a monster."

"No, but maybe that's not how she sees it. Or maybe . . ."

"Maybe what?" Tadg prodded.

Barclay shuddered at his own thought. But just because it was horrible didn't mean it wasn't true. "Maybe Runa blames herself for not killing him years ago, when she thought she had."

Ever since Runa had told them the story of what had happened between her, Cyril, and Keyes in the Mountains, Barclay had tried to imagine it so many times that now it almost felt like *his* memory. He could see Cyril unconscious in the snow. He could hear Dimondaise roaring in the sky. And he'd seen the old, faded scars on Keyes's abdomen with his own eyes: two of them, for each of Klava's fangs.

Barclay and Tadg returned to Eldin Hall expecting to find it silent at this time of night, but as they approached the steps, the front doors burst open. Tristan Navarre, the reporter Barclay recognized from the Symposium's Registration Day, stalked past. When he sighted the two boys, his eyes widened.

"You're Viola Dumont's fellow apprentices, aren't you? Murdock and Thorne?" Navarre asked. He spoke almost twice as fast as a regular person. "Were you with the family just now? What was Viola and her family's perspective on what happened to Kadia Tolo?"

The scream that Barclay had swallowed down came spewing back up his throat. "Do we look like we want to answer—"

"I already told you, the University is closed to visitors at this hour," someone barked behind them, and the boys whipped around. Cyril stood in the doorway, his fists clenched at his sides. "And I suggest you think carefully before pestering these students with questions, unless you'd like to have the Fang of Dusk to reckon with." After a pause, glancing between Barclay and Tadg, he added, "Or me."

"Denying interviews won't keep the story out of the *Khronicle*," Navarre warned. "Tolo is the Grand Keeper's ex-wife, after all."

"What happened has nothing to do with the Grand Keeper," Cyril growled.

"But people still have a right to be informed of negligence, don't they?" When Cyril didn't answer, Navarre jutted up his chin. "Well, good night to all of you."

Then he strode away toward the campus gates.

"That man is worse than a Serpensala," Cyril grumbled. His expression softened as he took in Barclay and Tadg. "How *is* the family doing?"

Barclay might've been grateful that Cyril had spared them from Navarre's prodding questions, but truthfully, he wasn't all that happy to see Cyril right now. He should've been helping Runa and Asfour investigate Keyes's whereabouts, not clinging to a grudge over a murder that had never truly happened.

"They're all right," Barclay said tightly. "Kadia is recovering."

"Shouldn't you be at the meeting at the Guild House?" Tadg asked.

A muscle in Cyril's jaw twitched. "The Chancellor and High Keeper both thought it better that I remain at the school to watch over the students. And that's probably for the best with journalists like Navarre skulking about. Leopold isn't without fault, but he is still the Grand Keeper, which means he deserves respect. I shudder to imagine the article that'll be published about this whole affair." Then he sighed and motioned for the boys to come inside. "You should try to get some rest. I'm sure it's been a long night."

Barclay, however, doubted he'd get any sleep. He'd be too preoccupied thinking about what happened to Kadia. Or picturing Keyes creeping across the campus at night.

Tadg must've been as angry as Barclay, because he spat out, "Actually, I'm going to the gymnasium. I want to swim."

Then, without bothering to wait for Cyril to argue that it was past curfew, he stalked into the darkness. If Barclay wasn't so exhausted, he might've joined him. Or gone running with Root. Anything to clear his head.

"Would you like any tea, Barclay?" Cyril asked.

Barclay frowned. Cyril's expression looked honest, but over his shoulder, in the atrium, the statue of Dimondaise seemed to watch. Her six eyes were knowing and sharp.

"I understand if you'd rather sleep," Cyril added. "It's been a hard day."

Angry or not, Master Pilzmann had taught Barclay never to decline an invitation to tea. And so, despite himself, Barclay muttered, "Sure."

Ten minutes later, Cyril brought a tray of hibiscus iced tea into the Guardians' lounge with three glasses—one for him, one for Barclay, and one for Codric, who lapped at his daintily. Tati had no interest in them and had instead snuggled into the fireplace, using the smoldering embers as a bed, her scales glowing with molten light.

The pair sipped in awkward silence until Barclay worked up the nerve to ask a question. "Will the Grand Keeper come back to the Desert because of this?"

"I don't know. I'm sure he wants to."

"But he might not?"

Cyril seemed to consider his words before answering, "He's very concerned about perception at the moment—about what the Wilderlands think of him."

Barclay grimaced, remembering Viola's tears. She could use her father right now. "But won't it look stranger if he doesn't? He and Kadia were married. Doesn't he care?"

"Of course he cares. And to some it would look strange, I'm sure. But to others, he would be abandoning his post for a personal matter."

"I don't see how it's personal if all the Guardians in the Desert are having an emergency meeting right now, in the middle of the night. Or if Keyes is the prime suspect."

Instead of scolding Barclay for mentioning Keyes, Cyril scrutinized him carefully. "I think you and I agree about what should be done, but he doesn't, and I'm afraid it's not my place to tell him otherwise."

Barclay hadn't expected Cyril to say that. "Aren't you his assistant, though?"

"Something like that. I've worked for him ever since I obtained my license."

"Why?"

"I think it's the right thing to do. I owe him a lot." Cyril stared into his glass. "I don't know if Runa ever speaks about the past, but maybe she once told you that she, Audrian, and I placed at the top of our Exhibition. And Runa and Audrian . . . they had their pick of Guardian Masters who offered to teach them."

"But you didn't?" Barclay asked, surprised. He couldn't imagine Cyril ever being anything less than the famous Horn of Dawn.

"I earned my placement because I got the top score on the written exam—Runa certainly didn't come close, and Audrian all but failed his. And I skirted by in the practical. But it took me a long time to learn how to control my wood Lore, and so I was quickly eliminated in the tournament matches. It was humiliating, as I was one of the few with a Mythic class Beast. And you know how Guardians care about those things."

Codric must've cared about those things too, because he lifted his curled horns high. Barclay used to think *Cyril* was pretentious, but Codric acted as though he was the Prince Charming of a fairy tale.

"I could've pursued a different type of license, of course," Cyril continued. "But I didn't want to—I wanted to be a Guardian. So after the Exhibition finished, I cornered Leopold and begged him to pick me as his student."

"Because his mom was the Grand Keeper?"

"Yes, and because he was respected and admired. My family are all Lore Keepers, but we've never had much, and my parents were so nervous about me leaving home to join the Guild—my aunt never passed her exam, no matter how many times she tried. They said I was doomed to fail, and I thought I could change their minds if I had a good teacher."

Because Cyril's three original students—Shazi, Hasu, and Viola—were all the children of such prestigious people, Barclay had assumed that Cyril must've been as well. He never would've guessed that Cyril came from so little, and though their backgrounds weren't the same, Barclay understood all too well how that felt. Maybe that was why Cyril cared so much about status now. He'd always had something to prove.

"Anyway." Cyril cleared his throat. "I'm very grateful to him, and he's much cleverer than people give him credit for lately. Kadia is also wonderful, but Viola doesn't get it *all* from her mother."

"So you're loyal to him." Just like Barclay was to Runa.

Cyril smiled weakly. "I've always been, hence why I'm the only Guardian in the Desert not invited to Asfour's meetings. And maybe that's for the best. Audrian was my best friend. I used to believe that he could be saved from the path he'd taken, but I don't know anymore. If it came down to it, I don't know if I could . . ." He never finished his thought. Instead, he stood up, leaving his empty glass on the table. "I'm going to try to get some sleep, but if you ever need anything or want to talk again, I hope you know that you can always find me. Tadg, too."

After that, Barclay returned to his room. He didn't know if it was the conversation or the tea, but all the anger had drained out of him, replaced by exhaustion. He drifted off seconds after his head hit the pillow.

TWELVE

Nightmares prowled through Barclay's dreams. In one, his parents were still alive, but they didn't know who he was. His mother threw apples at him, and his father forced him out of their home, his pitchfork pressed against Barclay's throat. In the next, Barclay was at the Symposium, and Yasha sat beside him in class. They were friends—good friends. Until Yasha's Smynx, Motya, lit the Guild Studies classroom on fire with all of them in it.

Barclay jolted awake. Out the window, dawn bloomed pink across the sky. He tried to fall back asleep, but the memories of last night swept over him like a heat wave. He tossed and turned—Root grunting beside him with displeasure. At last he gave up, crept quietly out of bed so as not to wake Tadg, changed, and headed toward the gymnasium.

He shivered as he walked. It was cool in the mornings, especially now that Autumn had begun to fade into Winter. Root, who padded sleepily beside him, had grown a thicker coat for the season, making him look larger and fluffier by the day.

To Barclay's surprise, the gymnasium wasn't empty. Shazi practiced her footwork on the balance beam. Her sabers arced through the air so gracefully that she looked more like she was dancing than training. Her feet were bare, making the differences between her two legs more pronounced— how she leaned more weight on her right side, how her prosthetic flexed from her metal Lore, remolding its shape over and over with her every step.

Barclay froze at the gymnasium's entrance. He didn't want to interrupt her, nor did he want to argue about the Library of Asfour when he had so much else on his mind.

But Shazi caught sight of him. "You never come this early," she called.

"You do?" he called back.

"Every morning." Then she returned to her drills, leaving him be.

Maybe company wouldn't be so bad. Barclay and Root walked past her to the infantry of dummies lining the far wall. Without Cyril's wood Lore, they didn't move, but he was used to practicing on his own. He struck them down one at a time, counting the seconds under his breath. Faster. Faster. Each round, Root prowled behind the targets and blew them back to standing. Until Barclay tired, and they switched places. Root always got the better score.

Barclay had hoped that training would clear his head, but it did the opposite.

Keyes could make earthquakes that reached as deep as the seafloor, he chided himself. It didn't matter how much progress he'd made. He was strong, but not strong enough. He was fast, but not fast enough.

Clang! Clack!

Behind him, Shazi sparred Saif, his long tail whipping to and fro to parry each of her swords. Sparks sizzled off their blades.

They were admittedly distracting, but only because it was hard not to watch their match. Shazi looked like a hero in one of his adventure novels.

An hour later, when it was time for the cafeteria to open for breakfast, Barclay approached her while she stretched.

"Cyril told us last night about Viola's mom," Shazi said grimly. "Is she all right?"

"She's frightened, and she'll probably have some headaches for a while. But I think she'll be okay."

Shazi nodded. "That's good. My mom's a great doctor, so she's in good hands." She tilted her head curiously. "Did you get to meet her at all?"

"Not really. She was busy. Well, she did tell Tadg to be quiet."

Shazi laughed. "Better her than her Scormoddin—trust me."

"You and your mom have the same Beast?"

"Yep. My mom uses metal Lore as a surgeon. I use it for swords."

Beside them, Root neared the metallic scorpion hesitantly. Saif wasn't as friendly as Bitti or Oudie, and his eight spindly legs had unnerved Root at the Sea. But now they seemed used to each other's company. Saif didn't even snap his pincers as Root sniffed his butt.

"I, um, wanted to tell you that I'm sorry," Shazi said.

Barclay blinked. "For what?"

"After that Tourney prank, when you pointed out the door to the Library, I knew what it was, but I didn't tell you. I feel like I tricked you into going inside." Shazi stood up, grimacing, then continued stretching. She braced herself on the balance beam while swinging each leg side to side. "It all feels ridiculous now anyway. Cyril told us that the High Keeper thinks Keyes and Yasha are in the Desert. That they might've been who attacked Viola's mom. And I spent all Autumn gluing furniture onto ceilings and trying to sneak into the Library."

"I feel like that too," Barclay admitted. "But the Library was never ridiculous. Just dangerous."

"I know. It's just—I've always wanted to see it. Dad used to tell me stories about it when I was little. Now he'd be so mad at me if he found out I went inside, and he's already been mad at me about a lot lately."

Barclay wasn't in the mood to talk about someone else's family problems right now, but Shazi had no way of knowing that. So, trying to be a good friend, he asked, "You and your dad don't get along?"

"We do, I guess, but we argue a lot. That's all we've ever done since I got home." She sighed. "Mom and Dad weren't happy I decided to become a Guardian, even though it's what I've wanted my whole life. After my accident, they got scared about everything, like I might get hurt again. And being a Guardian isn't exactly safe."

Barclay could understand why her parents were so protective, but it must've been hard to feel like your family didn't want what *you* wanted. "But you became Cyril's apprentice over two and a half years ago. Haven't they come around?"

"Mom has, but Dad doesn't understand why I picked something so dangerous. He loves his job, and I think he secretly wishes I'd become a Scholar like him." Hard as Barclay tried, he couldn't picture Shazi in the frilly robes and tassels. "When we argue, he makes it seem like I don't care at all about his work or the University, but I have no idea why he thinks that. I practically grew up on this campus. I know almost all the secret passages. I've been planning my Tourney pranks since I was five. Just because I'm not the same as him doesn't mean I don't love it here, you know?"

Barclay did know. He might never have belonged in Dullshire, but it would always mean something to him.

"I'm sorry. I hope he changes his mind," Barclay told her.

"Me too." Then she grinned. "You should train early more often. Maybe we can spar together."

Sparring with Shazi sounded like a good way to earn some painful bruises, but getting stronger wasn't supposed to be easy.

"Yeah," he answered. "I'd like that."

"The Ickypox Plague is more commonly—and mistakenly—known as the Kankerous Plague," Instructor Dudnik droned from the front of the classroom, white-knuckling the podium as though she'd teeter over in excitement if she let go. "After originating in the Tundra five centuries ago, it spread to the Jungle, the Mountains, and across the rest of the Wilderlands. It causes large pustules to form on the skin, filled with a gooey green liquid that has a terrible odor—"

Dudnik yelped as the doors swung open and whacked against the walls. All the students napping or doodling jolted. Rohan even tumbled out of his seat.

"I'm sorry to interrupt, Grusha," Cyril said, "but the Guardian apprentices have all been summoned to the Guild House."

The Guardian students perked up. Barclay and Tadg met each other's eyes curiously.

"Why?" Cecily asked. "What are we doing?"

"You'll see when we arrive," Cyril answered. "And we better hurry. Asfour doesn't like to waste time."

Each of them hastily collected their books and dashed out the door. Cyril led them off campus onto the busy streets of Menneset.

"Do you know what's going on?" Barclay whispered to Shazi.

"No," she replied. "But if it's just the Guardian apprentices, that must mean it's something exciting."

Barclay had visited two Guild Houses before. In the Woods, the Guild House had been little more than an oversized, crumbling cabin, with a gigantic tree that jutted right out of its center. In the Sea, it'd been a lighthouse.

The Guild House of the Desert resembled a fortress, with huge walls and columns, all engraved and painted with designs of Beasts. Inside, the vaulted ceiling was covered in so many patterned tiles that it looked like the world's largest kaleidoscope.

The apprentices shuffled into a central courtyard, where at least a hundred Lore Keepers gathered on stone benches, all arranged in a circle. In the middle stood High Keeper

Asfour, Runa, and several people Barclay didn't recognize. Asfour's Raptura perched on her shoulder, and between the two of them, it was hard to tell who had the sharper gaze.

"Thank you for fetching them, Harlow," Asfour said. "Apprentices, take a seat and listen closely."

Asfour nodded to the first row, roped off and empty except for a single person: Viola. She didn't say anything as Barclay sat beside her, only nodded at him seriously.

"A fourth Ever Storm appeared last night, this time near the Salt Plains," Asfour told the apprentices, making Barclay's stomach roil with panic. A fourth Ever Storm? How many more would it take before the Desert was thrown into peril? "Apparently the Grand Keeper has no more Guardians at his disposal to send to our aid."

From the irritated clip of her voice, Asfour clearly believed otherwise. Barclay glanced at Cyril, and he was far from the only Lore Keeper to do so. If Cyril noticed everyone's stares, he gave no sign of it, only stood stiffly at the edge of the courtyard.

"Because our personnel has been spread thin," continued Asfour, "we've decided to evaluate each of you to determine if any of you can lend extra support to our teams."

Barclay's breath hitched. After weeks sitting around in class, they were finally being given the chance to join a mission.

"We'll only be taking students whose Lore is suitable for the task," Asfour said. "So don't compare these evaluations to licensing exams. It doesn't matter how skilled you are if your abilities are incompatible with the needs of the mission. Now, I'm going to call off each of your names, and when it's your turn, a Guardian will accompany you to your test."

Then Asfour announced the first list of names, including Viola, Tadg, Deirdre, Shazi, and several of the other students. After they left, Rohan scooted closer to Barclay and whispered, "I'll bet three kritters that the little one gets picked."

Barclay peered at the smallest Guardian apprentice, a boy named Georgy Ekel. He was sitting by himself, nibbling his fingernails.

"But he's the youngest one here," Barclay said.

"Yeah, but he has tracking Lore. That's dead useful."

"You're not going to bet on yourself?" Cecily asked from Rohan's other side.

"Slime Lore? In a giant sandstorm? No way."

While Rohan and Cecily agreed to the bet, Viola emerged at the edge of the courtyard. Her face was so somber that Barclay couldn't tell whether or not her test had gone well until she sat down and whispered, "I got picked."

"That's great," he told her. "But, um, are you sure you want to be here? Wouldn't you rather be with your mom?"

"I'm still going to stay with my family for a little while, but when Runa told me about this meeting, I decided it was too important to miss. I'm glad I get to go. I want to make sure Keyes doesn't get away with this."

Shazi, Tadg, and Deirdre weren't so lucky. When Shazi returned, she collapsed onto the bench, her arms crossed. "This is the worst. I wanted to be chosen so bad."

"What were you going to do to the sand?" Tadg grumbled. "Swat at it with your swords?"

"I heard they've fought some powerful Beasts in the storms. We could've helped with that."

"Not better than sixty licensed Guardians, we can't," Deirdre said.

Barclay, Cecily, and Georgy were called next. Barclay gulped as he walked toward the edge of the courtyard, where a tall, brown-skinned man was waiting for him with a bow and arrows strapped to his back.

"I'm Kamil Okasha," the Guardian told him. Barclay recognized the name. He was Rohan and Deirdre's Master. "What sort of Lore and Beast do you have?"

"A Lufthund, and we use wind Lore," Barclay answered.

"Good, good. Runa mentioned you quelled some of the winds of the Ever Storm you got caught in at the end of Summer. When we step into the barracks, do you think you can show me what you did?"

"Definitely," Barclay said, trying to sound confident. He followed Kamil into a training facility much like the one at school. Across the room, Cecily was demonstrating her shadow Lore to an old woman wearing a horned warrior's helmet.

Barclay wove between a set of familiar target dummies arranged in a circle. At the center, he widened his stance the same way he'd done a thousand times before. Then he took a deep breath and raised both of his hands out.

Wind! he thought.

A gust spun around him. It widened and widened until it formed a vortex, whipping so fast that Barclay's hair was blown over his eyes.

In a flash, Kamil grabbed his bow from his back, aimed an arrow, and fired it—directly at Barclay.

Barclay yelped, but he didn't stop using his Lore. The

arrow struck the funnel of wind and zipped in a new direction. It plunged into one of the targets, directly in the heart.

"Great work," Kamil said. "I'll mark you down as a yes. You'll probably get a lot of practice out there. Mishra and Nass are our only other wind users, and Nass is in the hospital right now, so we could use a replacement."

Barclay might've been more excited if Kamil hadn't told him that. But regardless, he walked out with a smile.

"That makes three of us," Viola said brightly. The third of them was Georgy—Cecily bitterly paid Rohan his three kritters when she returned.

But the exams weren't finished just yet. Hasu came out last, looking anxious.

"It's all right," Shazi said mournfully. "Obviously, Asfour meant it when she said it was more about compatibility than strength."

"I passed," Hasu told her. "They said they could really use my spatial Lore, so I'm going with Viola and Barclay."

Shazi punched her in the arm. "That's great! What are you upset about?"

"What happens if I mess up and someone gets hurt because of me?"

"Don't be silly. The Guardians are lucky to have you. And your mom will be so excited."

Hasu buried her face in her hands. "*Ugh.* Don't remind me."

The High Keeper cleared her throat. "Excellent. Dumont, Mayani, Thorne, and Ekel—you stay here. The expedition team to scope out the newest Ever Storm will depart in a few minutes. All other students, you can return with Harlow to the University."

Viola's eyes widened. "We're leaving now?"

Barclay suddenly wished he'd tried harder to fall back asleep that morning. Or hadn't eaten so much fried food at lunch.

While the apprentices and Guardians chattered, Asfour spoke to the Lore Keepers at her side. Of the six of them, Runa stood the closest—and interrupted her the most. Each time, Asfour shook her head, until finally, she held up her hand, silencing Runa's argument completely.

Barclay had been so focused on Runa that he hadn't noticed Cyril move toward the High Keeper until Viola nudged him. Asfour's circle stopped their conversation, making it just quiet enough for Barclay to listen.

"I'd like permission to join the team," Cyril said. "I'm sure I could be of use."

Runa's glare was so piercing, it could've drawn blood.

"I don't doubt you would be, and I appreciate you coming to speak with me this morning. Again," said Asfour. "But the team for this mission has already been prepared. For now, I ask that you escort the other apprentices back to the University. I promise to alert you when your services are needed in the future."

Cyril nodded. "Thank you. That's all that I can ask." Then he strode away, motioning for the curious, ogling apprentices to follow him.

"Good luck," Cecily told Barclay, Viola, and Hasu cheerily. The others offered them goodbyes—Rohan ruffled Barclay's already messy hair—and trailed Cyril out of the Guild House.

Asfour addressed the remaining students: "A team of twenty-eight Keepers, plus you four, will be entering the

Ever Storm. Our objective is to determine the cause of these storms, but the four of you will be focusing primarily on supporting the Guardians. There will also be a medic proficient in healing Lore, as well as three Surveyors who have a better understanding of the terrain and navigating Lore phenomena. Any questions?"

Barclay had a million questions, but he was far too scared to ask them. The others didn't utter a peep either.

"Good," finished Asfour. "The carrier dragons are waiting out back."

The pair of carrier dragons touched down half a mile from the edge of the Ever Storm. Evening had fallen, making the temperature plummet, and Barclay shivered as he emerged from the caravan. The dark sandstorm raged in front of them from earth to sky. Even at a distance, the howling winds whirled shrilly in his ears.

"Where are we?" Hasu asked, examining the ground. It didn't look like the sandy dunes outside Menneset, nor the rocky landscape near the Lightning Plateaus or the Ironwood Forest. If Barclay didn't know better, he would've guessed they were standing on snow. The ground was pure white, except for the web of cracks that splintered through it as far as the eye could see.

"These are the Salt Plains," Viola explained. "This land used to be a salt lake thousands of years ago, but it's dry most of the year now."

It was one of the most incredible places Barclay had ever visited. But it was hard to appreciate it with the storm looming ahead of them.

Once everyone had disembarked from the carrier dragons, one of the Surveyors handed out leather backpacks. Inside were useful supplies, including goggles with a strange scarf attached to the bottom. Barclay slipped them on, and the cloth draped over his nose, mouth, and neck. The fabric was fine enough to breathe through without inhaling mouthfuls of sand.

Next were a set of gloves. A Saladon scale, which the Surveyor explained would glow like a lantern once shaken. Buried at the bottom lay a notebook, a rope, basic healing tinctures, and one of the same scarab distress beacons they'd used on their crashed carrier dragon flight.

"Everyone is to report back to this location in three hours," Asfour called from the front. "Like before, we'll split up in smaller groups to cover more ground. And as a reminder, we'd like to keep injuries at a minimum, so don't summon your Beasts unless you have to. We don't need to repeat the incident with the Waramasa."

Barclay, Viola, and Hasu exchanged a nervous look.

While the group set off toward the storm, Asfour's Raptura flying at the lead, Runa trailed behind to walk beside the three apprentices. "The Ekel kid is going to accompany the medic team, and I'd like the three of you to stick with us." She nodded toward the trio of other Guardians with her, including Kamil. "And don't get any ideas about wandering off."

There was nothing Barclay wanted to do *less* than leave Runa's side.

"Our goal is to find the source of the Phantom Roar," Kamil explained. "That's what we've named the Beast some of our expedition teams have heard in the Ever Storms. So far, we've recorded it in the first three storms, but no one has found the source of it yet."

Barclay remembered Asfour mentioning the Phantom Roar in passing last night, but he'd been too worried about Keyes and Kadia to dwell on it.

"You mean it could be anything?" he asked, stricken.

"Or any*one*," Runa answered pointedly.

Kamil raised his brows. "Keyes doesn't have the power to create a storm like this. His two Lore are—"

"Stone and healing. I'm aware," she muttered. "But that was over a year ago. We can't assume he hasn't bonded with another Beast—or more."

The thought of Keyes growing even *more* powerful made Barclay shudder down to his toes.

"We've heard the Phantom Roar already, haven't we?" Viola asked. "We heard it in the Ever Storm when we first arrived."

Amid the arrival of Leopold, Kadia, and Asfour, Barclay had nearly forgotten about the thunderous growl outside their caravan. It'd sounded as though a Beast was hunting them, yet none had ever shown.

"That's right," Runa said. "And hopefully, we'll hear it again today."

"What about regular Beasts?" Hasu asked. "Haven't the teams had to battle wild Beasts in the storms?"

Kamil nodded. "We've seen some in the other storms, but not a lot of Beasts live in the Salt Plains. So don't worry—I doubt we'll encounter any. But it's better to be safe than sorry."

Soon the team reached the edge of the storm. The sandy winds were so dense that Barclay couldn't glimpse anything inside, and a breeze blew around their ankles, as though dragging them within.

Runa moved first, and she vanished before even taking a second step. Kamil and the other Guardians went next, gone in an instant.

"Here we go," Barclay said tightly.

"Here we go," Viola and Hasu repeated.

The moment they stepped inside, the orange glow of sunset disappeared. Sand pelted Barclay's skin, stinging even through his clothes. The overwhelming roar of the storm thundered in his ears, and he had to hunch and spread his legs so as not to be thrown sideways.

"Viola, we'll take some light," came Runa's voice. She sounded close, but it was too dark to see her. "Barclay, can you settle some of the wind?"

While Viola shone a beacon of light from her palms, Barclay raised his arms, the same way he'd shown Kamil. He focused, and the winds around them slowed into a steady, protective circle around their group.

In front of them, Kamil readied his bow. Runa poured a canteen over her hands, and the dripping water froze below each of her fingers, forming icicle throwing knives that clacked together with her every move.

They trekked forward. After several minutes, Barclay's nerves began to relax. The storm might've been fierce, but they hadn't encountered any danger.

Then a silhouette emerged in the distance, racing toward them.

Kamil aimed an arrow.

"Wait," one of the other Guardians said sharply. "Don't shoot yet."

Suddenly, a tall Beast like a skinny, long-necked llama appeared through the sandy winds. It sprinted forward, and everyone dove out of its path. Then, as though it hadn't noticed the Lore Keepers at all, it galloped off into the darkness.

"It's just a lost Alcuna," Kamil said.

GRRRRRRRRRRRRRRLLLLLL!

A terrible, tremendous roar ripped through their surroundings, so loud that it rumbled in Barclay's stomach. It sounded every bit as frightening as the one from their first day in the Desert.

"What was that?" Hasu squeaked, though Barclay and Viola already knew the answer.

"*That* is what we're looking for." Runa faced the apprentices. Her tightly woven braid had come undone, making her hair whip over her face. "Hasu, if we find Keyes, I want you to get all three of you out."

"All right," Hasu said, at the same time Barclay and Viola argued, "No! We're staying."

"You're not, and you won't change my mind. Now come on. Let's get moving."

As they walked in the direction of the roar, Barclay tried to picture what kind of Beast could create a storm of this size. Like Runa, he knew in his gut that Keyes was connected to the Ever Storms somehow, but even a Mythic class Beast couldn't make something like *this*.

Which was how a horrible thought occurred to him.

"Could Shakulah be making the storms?" he asked Viola.

"Shakulah lives in the Arid Oasis," she answered. "And she's asleep at this time of year, just like Gravaldor and Lochmordra."

Barclay glowered, frustrated. None of this made any sense.

GRRRRRRRRRRRRLLLLLL!

The roar echoed a second time. It was still violently loud, but it sounded no closer than it had before.

"Keep moving," Runa said.

Barclay's knees trembled with every step. He envisioned a monster as tall as a building waiting for them up ahead, with glowing red eyes and razored teeth. He wished he could summon Root.

Suddenly, his Mark began to sting, and a new noise cut through the wind.

Thump! Thump! Thump!

"That sounded close," one of the Guardians said.

Beside them, Kamil aimed an arrow once more.

"Can you shine the light forward, Viola?" Runa asked.

Viola focused her Lore ahead of them in a spotlight, and a huge creature came into view. It wasn't the monster Barclay had pictured, but it was no less petrifying to behold. It looked like a giant, stumpy lizard, at least twenty feet long and six feet high. Two huge horns jutted out from either side of its head, and sharp brown scales studded its body, like a monstrous pine cone.

"What *is* that?" Hasu asked.

"It's a Shayika," Kamil said. "Watch out!"

Sighting them, the Beast charged forward. Both Barclay and Viola had to stop their Lore to dodge out of its path, plunging the group into windy darkness.

A moment later, Viola's light flickered on—just in time for Barclay to spot the Shayika's spiky tail whipping toward him.

Hasu seized his shoulder from behind, and a golden light shimmered around them. For several heartbeats, Barclay's world went dizzy. He felt like he was falling *up* instead of down. Then his shoes struck land, and after he caught his balance, he realized they had portaled to the other side of the Beast.

Runa pressed her hand against the ground, and ice seeped across the salt beneath the Shayika's feet. It slipped and skidded. Its tail thrashed in all directions. Kamil ducked out of the way a split second before he would've been struck.

"Can you subdue it?" Runa asked one of the other Guardians.

"Not when it's worked up like this," he answered. "Can you trap it?"

"Definitely," the other Guardian replied. She lifted both her arms into the air as though heaving up a bulky weight, then the salty ground around the Shayika rumbled. Large stone walls erupted from the earth, trapping the Shayika on all sides.

The Shayika roared, and though it wasn't as loud as the noise they'd heard earlier, Barclay still gulped.

The Beast rammed itself against the walls. A small, ominous crack split through the stone.

"Hurry," Runa urged.

The first Guardian pulled a flute from his backpack and lifted it to his lips. Barclay had no idea how music could help, and the Guardian managed to blow only a single note before the Shayika stretched its tail into the air.

"Duck!" Kamil called.

Sharp, scaly daggers shot from the end of the tail in all directions. Barclay spotted the worst of them aiming right for the Guardian with the flute, so he sent a gust of wind toward him. The man blew over like one of Barclay's practice targets, safely out of range from the scales.

Unfortunately, Barclay didn't have time to dodge himself, and he cried out when one buried itself in his left arm. Pain coursed through him so fiercely that he stumbled, and all the breath burst out of his chest.

"Barclay!" Runa rushed to his side. "Are you all right?"

Barclay didn't know how to answer. He wasn't dead, but his arm throbbed. "I—I think I'm fine."

"Hasu," Runa said. "Take him back to the carrier—"

"The wind is too loud!" the Guardian called. "I'm playing, but it can't hear me!"

The Beast threw itself at its cage again. The stone cracked deeper.

Runa muttered something under her breath that Barclay couldn't make out. "Barclay, do you think you can calm the wind, just for a little longer?"

Barclay had never mastered using such a difficult move with one arm, and when he tried to raise both, the sharp end of the scale dug painfully into his muscle. He winced and lowered it.

But when he tried to quell the wind with one hand, it was no use. The wind sputtered but didn't stop.

The Shayika slammed into the wall a third time, and the stone crumbled into a heap of rubble. For a second, the Beast swayed, dizzy from striking its head.

"Rasgar!" the Guardian shouted.

Runa cast a final, wary look at Barclay, then her Dolkaris, Klava, appeared beside her. Runa never summoned Klava unless the situation was dire, and Klava instantly dropped into a low, predatory crouch and bared her saberlike fangs. As her icy blue gaze swiveled between the Lore Keepers, Barclay felt the air drop several degrees.

Sighting the Shayika, Klava let out a bloodthirsty growl. She sprinted toward it, and Barclay's breath hitched. The Shayika was only scared. It wasn't its fault it'd been caught in the storm, and Klava could hurt it—or worse.

Barclay reacted without thinking. With his right hand, he grabbed the scale in his other arm and wrenched it out. The pain made his whole body jerk back, but he was too focused on the Beast to feel the worst of it. He tossed the scale aside and raised both his arms.

Wind!

The winds around them slowed into a soft, steady current.

The Guardian blew into his flute. The notes drifted out slow and soothing, like a lullaby.

Both Klava and the Shayika stumbled, growing woozy. Then their eyes drooped, and they crashed to the ground, fast asleep.

After several seconds passed and the Shayika didn't rise, Barclay let his Lore relax, and he lowered his arms to his sides. Runa sighed with relief and returned Klava to her Mark.

"That was impressive, kid," the other Guardian told him, and the Keeper with the flute also flashed him a smile. Barclay would've felt prouder if he hadn't caught sight of the red splotch bleeding through his shirtsleeve. His throat shrunk to the size of a papyrus reed. He'd never bled so much before.

"Shayikas have spike Lore," Kamil said. "There's no way it made the Ever Storm."

"Which means whatever Beast makes the Phantom Roar is still out there," said Runa, staring out into the void. At first, Barclay thought Runa would urge them to press on, but instead she sighed. "Come on. Let's get Barclay patched up, and we'll meet back with the others at the carrier dragon."

THIRTEEN

Two weeks after Kadia was discharged from the hospital, Viola returned to school.

"I can't believe we've already started the Sea unit," she groaned while they gathered their books after their Wilderlands class. "I have so much to catch up on. And final exams are getting closer. . . ."

"My older brother told me that last year's Guild Studies exam was over six hours," Hasu said fretfully.

Cecily blanched. "*Six* hours? That can't be right."

"I heard it was eight," said Barclay gravely.

Shazi slung her backpack over her shoulder. "I don't get why any of you are worrying. We're not training to be Scholars, so as long as we pass, it doesn't matter what grades we get. And we're all going to pass."

"You don't know that," Cecily muttered.

"Yeah, the three of us have missed a lot of class helping

the Guardians," Barclay reminded her. Thanks to the medic team and daily doses of Mendijuice, Barclay had quickly recovered from his battle with the Shayika. Which was good, because Asfour kept summoning the apprentices for more and more missions. His lack of free time had made Root very mopey—he couldn't remember the last time they'd gone running.

"And my grades *do* matter when I run for Grand Keeper one day," added Viola.

Shazi rolled her eyes, then she caught sight of Tadg at the front of the classroom, talking to Instructor Dia. "Since when did Tadg become a teacher's pet?"

At first, Barclay thought Tadg must've had a question for Dia about their homework, but the book Tadg was showing him didn't look like their textbook.

"Viola," Hasu asked curiously, "isn't that your mom?" She pointed out the window, where Kadia was strolling a campus path, dressed in her Scholar robes.

Viola knitted her brow. "What's she doing here? She's not supposed to go back to work for another two weeks, at least."

She rushed through the rest of her packing and dashed outside. Barclay and their friends followed.

"Mom!" Viola waved, making all her pins and buttons clack together.

Kadia turned as Viola and the others caught up with her. "Hi, sweetie. How was your first day back at class?"

"Fine, but I thought you told the Chancellor you were going to relax more at home? Are you sure you want to be . . ." Viola trailed off, chewing on her upper lip.

"To tell you the truth, I *would* rather be home. But Asfour asked me if I'd look into something for her, and it's too important to put off, I'm afraid." Kadia sighed. "I did ask Ata to switch my office. I'll be happier if I never step foot in that room again." Then she smiled warmly at the group of apprentices lingering behind her daughter. "It's nice to see you again, Shazi—you're a lot bigger than when you used to sit on Ata's lap at meetings. And, Hasu, you're the spitting image of your older siblings. I sent a letter to Makara only a few weeks ago about an exhibit she's putting together at the Meridienne College's museum. And you must be Cecily. Viola's told me a lot about you."

Cecily's shadow squirmed shyly on the ground. "It's nice to meet you."

"What does the High Keeper want you to research?" Viola asked.

"Well, Midwinter is only a little more than four weeks away, which is when Shakulah is next due to wake up," Kadia explained. "It's far from certain, but there's a chance that Shakulah will be able to end the Ever Storms. Scholars have been monitoring her constantly since the storms began, but she's slept undisturbed. However, it's her nature to maintain the balance of the Wilderland. We're hoping that when she rises, she'll sense the chaos that the Ever Storms have created and put a stop to them."

"Even if she's not the one causing them?" asked Viola.

"Yes. There's precedent—Dimondaise prevented an avalanche two centuries ago, and Raajnavar has stopped several fires. There haven't been any recorded instances of Shakulah doing the same, but I think we could all use something to hope for, don't you?"

The idea that the Ever Storms could cease before the

end of the Symposium was very welcome indeed. But the mention of Midwinter reminded Barclay of the holiday two years ago when he, Viola, and Tadg had stopped Soren from bonding with Gravaldor. And a dreadful thought occurred to him.

"I—if Audrian Keyes is in the Desert," he stammered, "doesn't that mean Midwinter would be the perfect time for him to try to bond with Shakulah?"

The smiles faded on everyone's faces, including Kadia's.

"The Guardians are preparing for that possibility, yes," she said seriously. "But should Keyes arrive, he'll be confronted by a team of some of the most powerful Guardians in the world. So do your best not to worry about it, and focus on your schoolwork. Besides . . ." She brightened. "I imagine finals mustn't be so far away now. I'm sure studying will keep you very busy."

As much as Barclay tried to heed Kadia's advice, the normally cheerful holiday looming in their future filled him with nothing but dread. Almost certainly, Runa would be among the Guardians protecting Shakulah for the solstice, but he didn't have a chance to ask her about it until three days later, when the apprentices joined her on another mission.

"The original Ever Storm?" Barclay repeated fearfully as they boarded the carrier dragon with Viola, Hasu, and Georgy Ekel. "Won't that be dangerous?"

"We won't be going inside," Runa told them. "This is just a routine patrol."

Barclay had never seen the original Ever Storm, but from

the tales he'd heard, it made the other three storms seem like pleasant breezes in comparison.

During the flight, Barclay worked on his Guild Studies essay about Archivists, the Scholars specially licensed to guard the highest-classified documents of the Guild. Every few sentences, he peeked at Runa across the caravan. Despite the open book resting in her hands—a romance novel, judging from the heart-shaped flourishes around the title—her attention was fixed thoughtfully out the window.

Barclay strode toward her and cleared his throat. "Runa? Could I ask you something?"

She turned to him, then patted the cushion beside her. Goath slithered away to make room. "Of course. Homework?"

He'd forgotten that he was still clutching his essay. He sat down and set it aside. "No, but Kadia told us about Midwinter. You're going to be on the team, aren't you?"

"We all will be—Cyril, Leopold . . . about another thirty Guardians, at least—Asfour included. Audrian would be a fool to try anything."

"So you don't think he'll show?"

"Oh, I think he'll show. He could never resist a challenge."

A smile played at the corners of her lips, and Barclay realized that Runa *wanted* Audrian to attack on Midwinter. This was her chance to confront him, a chance she'd never had at the Sea.

Noticing Barclay's horrified expression, she playfully whacked his shoulder. "Cheer up. With any luck, after Midwinter, Shakulah will have stopped the Ever Storms, and

Audrian and Yasha will be in Guild custody."

Barclay hoped that would be true, but he realized he'd never considered what would happen to Keyes and Yasha once they were stopped. "What will the Guild do to them, once they're captured?"

"I can't say for Yasha—he's barely older than you. Maybe his punishment will be less severe." Barclay ignored the prickle of relief he felt—it didn't make sense. Yasha deserved whatever punishment he got. "But for Audrian, his bonds with his Beasts will be removed, and he'll be sent to Wrathengate, which is the Lore Keeper prison in the Jungle." Her expression darkened. "Even after everything, it's a hard fate to imagine. I still remember the day we met at our Exhibition. He came in dead last in the written exam. He knew almost nothing about the Wilderlands."

Barclay wasn't surprised. If Mandeep hadn't awarded him extra points for not cheating, then he would've placed last too. "But he still got one of the top ranks, didn't he?"

"Yep—second overall, since he came in first in both the other tests. Knocked me flat out during the tournament finale. It took me weeks to forgive him after that." Runa laughed softly. "Hard to believe how long ago that was, and how different everything is now."

A low hum coursed through the air, like the buzzing of a hornet's nest. Runa's head whipped toward the window.

"What is that?" asked Barclay.

"We're here. Look."

She pointed into the distance. At first, Barclay didn't see anything—only the shadow of a plateau on the horizon. But as they flew toward it, he realized that was no plateau.

It was an Ever Storm.

It must've been the size of ten Mennesets, and its swirling currents writhed like a viper pit. Even from a distance, sand and dust plumed into the air. Every inhale sent fragments needling down his throat, and the hum of it rattled him all the way to his bones. Soon Viola, Hasu, and Georgy set aside their schoolbooks and joined them at the window, and they all gasped.

"People went in *there*?" Barclay asked.

"That mistake won't be made again," Runa said darkly.

Even as his eyes watered from the coarse winds, Barclay couldn't bring himself to look away. If this force of nature was what the Guardians were up against, then they had no chance of stopping it. Shakulah was their only hope.

In the commotion of the past few weeks, Dullshire's problem with the Miskreats had all but slipped Barclay's mind. But as more and more days passed without a response from Master Pilzmann or the Guild chapter of the Woods, he began to worry. What if a more dangerous Beast had invaded Dullshire? What if Master Pilzmann had admitted to sending letters to Barclay, and he'd been exiled from town? He wasn't as spry as he used to be, and he'd be lost without tending to his mushroom caves.

The post office was near its closing hours when Barclay and Root arrived, and they found the usual cranky postman hunched in front of its door, fiddling with a ring of brass keys.

"Excuse me," Barclay said. "I was hoping to check if there's a letter for me?"

"Nothing has arrived from the Elsewheres," said the man gruffly. "If you want me to check again, you'll have to come back tomorrow. I'm closing up for the night."

"Please. We came all the way from the University, and I'm really worried. How long would it take to check?"

"A while."

Root huffed indignantly.

"What about a letter from the Woods?" asked Barclay. "It's been weeks since we wrote to the High Keeper, and—"

"A High Keeper, eh?" The man inspected Barclay's and Root's matching messy hair and fur. "What would you be writing to a High Keeper for?"

"Guild business—I'm an apprentice." When the man only narrowed his eyes in suspicion, Barclay added, "Asfour thought we'd hear from Erhart *weeks* ago. But you know how he is—always late. It's just that this is really important."

Barclay hoped the postman didn't notice his face flush scarlet from the lie.

The postman seemed to chew on his words before grunting, "Fine. I'll check. What's the name?" Barclay suspected he was only asking to be difficult—he'd given him his name many times before.

"Barclay Thorne."

"Mm-hmm. Right." The man swung open the door, rousing the postal dragons asleep in their cubbies. While they blinked at Barclay and Root blearily, the man lumbered into the back and rummaged through one of the mail sacks. "I don't see anything for a Barclay Thorne."

Barclay's heart clenched. If something had happened

to Master Pilzmann, surely Selby would write to him? Wouldn't he?

"Oh—there *is* a letter for you," the postman said. "Not from the Elsewheres, though. Or the Woods."

He handed Barclay a rather dusty, crinkled envelope, which bore no writing other than Barclay's name. No address. No sender.

On its back gleamed a large seal. The wax was a dark color between gray and brown, like a shadow cast on stone. Subtle hints of gold shimmered within it.

It looked like an official Guild seal, but all the distinguishing shapes on it, from the image of the Beast to the Lore Keeper's initials, had been scratched out. As though the owner had dragged a knife across their stamp, over and over.

Barclay tore it open, but before he could remove the parchment inside, the postman snapped, "Shoo, shoo. You got what you came for. Now I'm closing for the evening."

Barclay and Root scampered onto the street then, with Root peeking over his shoulder, he snatched out his mysterious letter. Written on it was a single word.

Ink

He flipped it over, hoping to find something else on the other side. But it was blank.

Confused, he studied the lone word again. Then he gasped.

"This is the answer to the riddle from the Library," he hissed at Root. "It has to be. Think about it! 'I have spoken every story ever told.' All stories are penned in ink."

Root cocked his head to the side—he didn't believe him.

"I mean it," Barclay pressed. "'Though I may bleed or fade away'—well, ink bleeds, right? And . . . and . . . the last clue! 'Look upon me as I ask of you.' It meant the writing itself. We were literally reading the ink upon the page." He felt foolish for not realizing it before.

Finally, he must've convinced him, because Root leaned down and sniffed the envelope.

"Can you tell who sent it to me?" Barclay asked.

Root shook his head, but his ears now perked up in alarm. He cast shifty glances down the street in either direction, as though expecting someone to be watching them.

Chills prickled up Barclay's neck. "This is weird, right? I mean, why would a stranger give this to me and not even sign their name?"

Root's expression darkened, then his head whipped to the left. In the distance, the postman disappeared around the corner.

He bolted, Barclay scrambling after him. The pair ran so fast that when they caught up to the postman, a wind swept through the alleyway.

The man angrily smoothed down the hair he'd combed over his bald spot. "What is it now? Can't you let me go home in peace?"

"Do you know who dropped this off for me?"

"Of course not. There's a mailbox slot on the front door. Anyone could've slipped it in as they passed by. Now, if you *don't* mind, I've got dinner waiting for me."

Barclay let the man go, then he leaned against the wall behind him, his palm on his forehead.

"Maybe we're just being paranoid," Barclay breathed. "Maybe this is all some prank." A very strange, mysterious prank.

Root shook his head.

"You're right—that doesn't make sense. I *know* that this is the answer to the riddle, but entering the Library is supposed to be forbidden! Which means whoever sent this went inside it anyway, and they know that I did too." Other than Viola, Barclay hadn't told a soul about his and Shazi's secret adventure.

An anxious breeze rustled around Root, ruffling his fur and making Barclay's hair fall into his eyes. Root *definitely* didn't think it was all in Barclay's head.

The two of them raced back to Eldin Hall. They burst through his door, making a gust flutter the curtains and blow aside the mess on Tadg's half of the room. Tadg jolted atop his bed, where he'd been sitting and slipping his most valuable champion cards into protective sleeves.

Panting, Barclay thrust the envelope into his hands. "Look at this."

"What is it?" Tadg asked, flattening his windswept waves.

"Just look!"

"All right, all right." Tadg slid out the letter, Toadles peering nosily from atop his knee. "'Ink'? That's all it says? What's that supposed to mean?"

"It's the answer to the first riddle in the Library of Asfour. I know because Shazi and I went down there, and we read it. But no one except Viola knows."

Tadg cocked a brow and muttered, "Wow. Thanks for including me in all your adventures." Then he flipped the envelope over and frowned at the seal. "Let me get this straight. You got this letter at the post office? And this was all that was in it?"

"That's it." Barclay paced beside Root across their cramped floor. "That's weird, right? We both think it's weird."

"And you're *sure* you didn't tell anyone about the Library?"

"I swear, and I don't think Shazi did, either. And Shazi and I were alone. I mean, I think we were." He swallowed. What if someone else *had* been lurking down there, spying on them?

"The Library is forbidden for a reason, right? Viola said it's dangerous, that people *die* down there. So if someone went in anyway, that can't be good." Tadg returned Toadles to his Mark and jumped to the floor. "We need to talk to Runa. *Now.*"

Though Barclay had already been worried, Tadg's reaction made panic seize him in a choke hold. "No—she's all the way at the Guild House. We should tell Cyril."

Tadg scoffed. "Why?"

"I trust him," Barclay said, which was the truth.

"Ugh. Fine."

The two boys and Root sprinted down their hallway to the lounge. They banged on Cyril's door.

It swung open, revealing a small sitting room. Tati lifted her head up from where she slept in the hearth, the warm glow of the fire splayed across her scales. Codric stood in the room's corner, his ears perked in alarm from their knocking.

Cyril scrunched his forehead in confusion. "Barclay? Tadg? Is everything all right?" Then his gaze lowered to the envelope clutched in Tadg's hands, and the color seeped from his face. "Where did you get that letter?"

"It was waiting for me at the post office," Barclay told him. "I don't know who sent it."

Cyril snatched the envelope and traced his finger over the wax. "This is Audrian's seal."

FOURTEEN

yril's shock transformed into action in an instant. He seized Barclay and Tadg by their wrists and yanked them into his sitting room. While the boys and Root still stumbled across the carpets, Cyril closed his door and drew the curtains over all his windows. At his desk, he wrenched out drawers and shoved his paperwork and copy of *Guildocracy* aside, letting loose documents flutter to the floor. Hurriedly, he scratched a message onto a piece of parchment and stuffed it in an envelope.

"Tati," he spoke. "I need you to bring Viola, Shazi, and Cecily here at once."

With a flick of his wrist, the door hurled open. Tati bolted outside, and it slammed closed behind her the moment the tip of her tail crossed the threshold.

Cyril dropped three pellets of emerald-green wax into a melting bowl, then he closed his fist around it. Tendrils of smoke wisped from the crevices between his fingers. After several seconds, he let go and poured the melted wax onto the envelope.

"Find Hasu," he told Codric. "She needs to deliver this letter directly to the High Keeper. Go with her—even if it's the Guild House, I don't want her anywhere alone."

Codric nodded seriously, then he bent low in a knightly bow as Cyril fastened the letter by string around one of his horns, where it dangled amidst the withered brown leaves.

After closing the door once again, Cyril finally turned to the boys. "You're going to be asked a lot of questions tonight, Barclay. I'll do my best to spare you the worst of it, but that means you need to help me understand. Can you do that?"

"I—I think so," Barclay stammered. He knew that the letter was serious. It confirmed that Keyes was in the Desert. That he'd somehow entered the Library of Asfour. And most alarmingly, he'd reached out to Barclay, of all people. That was a lot to process in only a few moments.

Shakily, Barclay lowered himself into an armchair. Tadg paced behind him, while Root protectively stood guard at the door.

"Where did you receive this letter?" Cyril asked.

"At a post office in Menneset," he answered. "I've been there a bunch of times to send and pick up messages from home."

"Do you know how the letter arrived at the post office? When it was delivered?"

"I'm not sure. The postman said it was dropped off in

the flap in the door—it could've been anyone. But it wasn't there the last time I visited a few days ago."

"Then the message. 'Ink.' Does that mean anything to you?"

"It's the answer to the first riddle in the Library of Asfour. It opens the doors in the entrance chamber."

Cyril's expression didn't change, but he inhaled sharply through his nose. "And how did you come to know that?"

Barclay dug his nails into the armrests. "I went inside with Shazi. Shazi and Viola discovered the entrance first—after the Symposium's opening ceremony. Then Shazi and I accidentally went into it a few weeks ago. I don't know for sure if that's the answer to the riddle, but I think it is."

"So you're telling me that the six of you have known where to find the entrance to the Library of Asfour since early Autumn, and you never told anyone about it?" Though Cyril never raised his voice, his frustration was obvious all the same.

At that, the door opened, and Cecily strolled inside, looking confused. Oudie flew in after her. "What's going on? Tati scared the cafeteria half to death when—what are you doing here?" Her gaze darted between Barclay and Tadg.

"Just sit," Cyril told her. "I'll explain everything soon."

He turned back to Barclay, his brows raised expectantly.

Barclay's chest felt tight. Cecily's arrival had made the situation feel far more real—and far more terrifying. "We didn't tell you or Runa because we didn't want to worry anyone. Well, we were going to tell Runa, but then Kadia was attacked, and . . . it didn't seem to matter, not like the Ever Storms matter. And we swore we'd never go back inside."

As Barclay blinked panicked tears from his eyes, Root padded toward him. With his ears and tail perked up, he looked far from calm himself, but he still lowered to the ground and rested his chin on Barclay's knees. Barclay petted his head appreciatively.

Cyril's face softened, and he dragged a nearby footstool beside them and sat. "When you went into the Library," he asked gently, "did you ever see anyone? Or evidence that someone else was there?"

"No."

"What about on campus? Have you ever noticed someone you didn't recognize? Anyone watching you?"

"No," Barclay choked out, horrified.

The door opened again, and Viola staggered inside. Her eyes were bloodshot from crying. "What's going on? Is Mom all right?"

"Your mom is fine," Tadg told her. "Barclay got a letter from Keyes. Keyes has been in the Library of Asfour."

Cecily gasped, and Viola gaped in shock. *"What?* Why would Keyes send a letter to Barclay?"

"That's a very good question," Cyril said. "Barclay, can you think of any reason why Keyes would try to reach out to you?"

"I . . ." Barclay's mouth went dry. "I suppose he knows us, right?"

"He knows all of us," Tadg said. "That doesn't explain why you're the one he singled out."

"Could it have been Yasha?" Barclay had been closer to Yasha than the others had. Maybe Yasha had realized how wrong he'd been to help Keyes. Maybe he'd reached out to Barclay so that he could join them again.

Cyril shook his head. "This is Audrian's handwriting."

Disappointment burned inside Barclay—he should've known better than to get his hopes up.

As he racked his brain for a true answer, a memory

returned to him from the Sea. Keyes had just revealed the truth of who he was and his aspirations to change the world—the Wilderlands *and* the Elsewheres. Then he had held out his hand to Barclay, like a friend.

What do you say, Barclay? Will you help me, one Elsie to another?

"It's because I'm an Elsie," Barclay rasped. "Just like he is."

Cyril's expression tightened. "I see."

The next few minutes passed in uneasy silence, until finally, Shazi entered the room. Viola quickly filled her in on what had happened, their whispers grating, putting Barclay more and more on edge.

When they finished, Cyril stood. "All right, now that you're all here, we're going to the Chancellor's office. Hasu will know from my letter to meet us there."

"We're telling my dad about the Library?" Shazi asked tensely.

"Yes. This situation couldn't be more serious. Let's go— hurry."

Barclay returned Root to his Mark, and the six of them rushed through Eldin Hall to Chancellor Essam's office in the center of campus. The gigantic obelisk loomed over them as they dashed up the stone steps. With a wave of Cyril's hand, the entrance burst open, and they swerved around the hallway's corner to a door with a golden plaque.

Ata Essam
One Hundred and Sixteenth Chancellor of the
University of Al Faradh

Thud! Thud! Thud! Each of Cyril's heavy knocks made Barclay flinch.

The next hour passed in a frenzied blur. Essam ushered them inside what was an entire spacious wing of the building. While the apprentices waited in Essam's personal library, he and Cyril spoke in a private room. The walls muffled their voices too much to make out what they were saying, but they were loud—louder still when the door opened, and Hasu and Bitti slipped out.

"I brought Asfour and Runa here, like Cyril asked." She threw her arms around Barclay. "I made Asfour read me the letter Cyril wrote, and I'm so sorry, Barclay. That's so scary. Are you all right?"

"I'm fine," he mumbled, even though he wasn't. His thoughts raced so fast that he felt light headed.

Keyes must've known that both Runa and Cyril would instantly recognize his seal. So why would he risk exposing himself all to give Barclay the answer to the first riddle? Maybe he hoped that Barclay would test out the answer alone. Maybe he was lurking in the Library at this very moment, hoping for Barclay to open the first door and find him waiting behind it.

Maybe this was their chance to finally catch him.

"What are you doing?" Viola asked as Barclay lurched up from his seat. Without bothering to knock, he threw open the door to Essam's office. The conversation inside cut off abruptly, but the tension in the room left a charge like static. Asfour removed her palms from where she'd flattened them, leaning across the Chancellor's desk. Essam anxiously straightened the stacks of parchment between them. Across the room, Cyril stopped his pacing by the acacia bookcases, and Runa straightened from where she leaned against the wall, her arms crossed.

"We need to go into the Library of Asfour," Barclay said fiercely. "If Keyes is down there, we need to find him."

"It seems Thorne and I are of one mind," said Asfour.

"Absolutely not," Cyril argued. "It has to be a trap."

"Keyes is an immensely powerful Lore Keeper. If he wanted to harm Thorne, then Thorne would already be dead." Asfour advanced on Barclay, her hands clasped rigidly behind her back. "Are you quite sure that this is your first communication from Keyes?"

"You can't be serious," Runa said. "Cyril already—"

Asfour held up her hand. "I want to hear it from Thorne. So?"

"Th-this is the first time I heard from him, yeah," Barclay stuttered.

"Are we expected to take you at your word? Keyes took a calculated risk sending this to you, which means he must've believed there was a chance that he would coax you into the Library. Why would he think that you would help him?"

Barclay stiffened. She thought he was on Keyes's side.

Behind Asfour, Runa's shoulders trembled with anger, and frost sparkled on her breath. "That is *enough*, Gamila. Barclay is my student."

"And it is my home at risk. I have a right to my questions," Asfour told her coolly. Then she leveled her gaze on Barclay once more. "Well?"

"I told you—I don't know why he thought I'd help him. Because I *wouldn't*."

Seeming satisfied, she straightened. "Fine. Since you're helping us, I need you to take us to the entrance to the Library of Asfour."

Barclay swallowed. "I'm not sure if I remember where it is. I'd never been in that building before."

"I can take us," Shazi said, stepping ahead of the cluster of apprentices huddled, eavesdropping, at the door. Her father shot her a furious look, which she ignored.

"I thought the door moved locations?" Cyril asked.

"Not once you've opened it," Shazi told him.

"Excellent," Asfour said. "Lead the way."

Campus was quieter at this hour. Students, now finished with their supper, had returned to their dormitories to study, and a bitter chill clung to the night air. However, Barclay was far too on edge to feel it. He kept picturing Keyes and Yasha waiting for him beyond that grand first door to the Library, their hands outstretched, as though expecting him to join them.

As they walked, Runa wove past Tadg and Viola to Barclay's side. "It was good of you to go to Cyril," she said, "but why didn't you tell me about the Library on any of our missions? When we went to the Market?"

Barclay hesitated. "We didn't want to worry you." When a muscle in Runa's jaw tightened, he quickly added, "You've been so busy with the Ever Storms. And the way you've talked about Keyes . . . we can tell you've been stressed."

Runa stopped and took Barclay's shoulders. The others continued on, unaware of the pair stalling behind them.

"Barclay, the three of you are family to me," Runa said, and Barclay sucked in his breath. Her tone was matter-of-fact, but he didn't think she'd throw around such words lightly. "You know that, don't you?"

Barclay stared at the ground. "R-really?"

"What, did you think you'd be rid of me the second you'd earned your license?" She laughed. "I'm sorry to break this to you, but I care about you all very much—and I don't have a lot of people I care about left. Which means you're stuck with me, forever."

Runa made it all sound so simple that Barclay felt foolish for not realizing it before. It was true that he, Viola, Tadg, and Runa didn't share any blood, and he'd known them for only a small piece of their lives. But he'd never once doubted that they'd do anything for one another. And that made them family.

"And if there's ever *anything* you're worried about," Runa continued, "I want you to worry me, too. Got it?"

Barclay sniffled, embarrassed but very touched. "And what if we worry about *you*?"

She flicked his temple. "Then you've been studying yourself too hard. I'm invincible. Doesn't make sense to worry about me."

A year ago, Barclay would've believed that, but he wasn't so sure he did anymore.

They hurried to catch up with the group, who hadn't seemed to notice their absence. The building Shazi led them inside didn't look familiar until they turned into that final, dead-end hallway. The Library of Asfour's gigantic golden door stood exactly where the pair of them had left it. Warm light poured out from its crevices, casting it in an otherworldly glow, and Barclay's Mark stung at the sight of it.

Hasu gasped. "I see it."

"So do I," Tadg said.

Cecily balked and traced her finger down the lattice. "It's beautiful."

"So all six of you can see the door." Asfour examined Cyril shrewdly from the corner of her eye. "But you cannot."

Color flushed across Cyril's cheeks. "N-no."

"And you?" Asfour asked Runa.

Runa clenched her fists and shook her head.

"I can't believe you didn't tell me about this straight-away," Essam hissed at Shazi. "You're lucky you weren't killed. And you should know better than anyone that going inside is a breach of University rules."

Before Shazi could argue, Asfour said, "There will be time for parenting later. Ata, you and I will be the ones to venture inside. You will solve whatever puzzles we find, and when it comes time for it, I'll confront Keyes."

Essam stiffened, and Shazi cast him a worried look. "Oh. Of course." He reached forward and twisted the ruby doorknob, then frowned. "It's locked." He shook it, even seized it with both hands. But it didn't budge. "I—I don't understand. I can see the door. And I'm the Chancellor of the University. If it should open to anyone, it should be me."

After he stepped aside, Asfour tried it herself. Then she backed away, her brow knitted in irritation. "It seems the High Keeper is not welcome either." The High Keeper descended from the Library's founder, no less.

"But that doesn't make sense," Viola said nervously. "Everyone who sees the door is worthy."

"Which means something isn't right," Asfour said. "Essam, will you try it for us?"

"But I . . ." Essam's shoulders slumped in failure.

"Not you, Ata. Your daughter."

Shazi's eyes widened at being addressed by the High Keeper. Then she straightened. "All right," she said confidently. She grasped the knob and turned it with an audible *click*. The door creaked open, pouring the Library's torchlight into the darkened corridor.

The Chancellor gaped. "That shouldn't be possible."

"The school is my home, Dad," Shazi told him. "Just as much as it's yours."

Asfour strode forward, but her foot knocked against an invisible barrier that stretched over the threshold. She rested her palm against it. "As I suspected, the Library won't allow for loopholes." She turned to face the apprentices. "The rest of you—you try."

With their hands braced in front of them, just in case, the six apprentices crossed the open door into the stairwell. The Library of Asfour had welcomed them.

Nerves stirred in Barclay's stomach. This wasn't right.

"It seems the six of you are the only ones allowed to enter the Library," Asfour said. "The six of you . . . and Keyes."

"Could it be Keyes's doing?" Runa asked.

"I don't think so," Essam said. "The Library is maintained by very ancient, very powerful Lore. It's as much a part of the Desert as the Lightning Plateaus or the Salt Plains. Even a Keeper as strong as Keyes couldn't meddle with it."

"And we've established that it's Thorne who Keyes is interested in; otherwise, the other five would've been contacted as well," Asfour said, making Barclay shift uncomfortably. "Whatever the reason, all we know for certain is that they're the only ones who have the capability of testing whether 'ink' is indeed the answer to the riddle."

"You're not seriously suggesting that we send them down there?" asked Cyril.

"I'll do it," Barclay said—and not just to prove himself to the High Keeper. "I want to stop him."

"We'll all do it," Tadg agreed, and the others nodded.

Runa and Cyril both barked out a laugh at the same time.

"That's out of the question," Cyril said.

"Don't even think about it," snapped Essam.

"And if you try to fight us on this," Runa said scathingly, "I'll pull you out of the Symposium, pack you on a carrier dragon, and send you straight back to the Sea, where Orla can babysit you."

Rage coursed through Barclay. Runa and Cyril weren't the only ones who wanted to stop Keyes, and if this was their one chance, then they should take it. But his nerve deflated at the furious looks on each of the adults' faces. In a choice between a fight with Keyes and a fight with Runa, Barclay wasn't so sure he'd pick Runa. Nor was he eager to be baby-sat by the unnerving High Keeper of the Sea.

"It seems there are matters you *can* agree on," Asfour said dryly, tossing a glance between Runa and Cyril. Neither graced the comment with a response. "And I promise that so long as I'm High Keeper, no thirteen-year-olds will be sent on a mission to their death. Come out of there, all of you."

Reluctantly, the six students stepped back into the

corridor, and the door to the Library closed behind them.

"I shudder to imagine what it is that Keyes seeks in the Library of Asfour or how he's entered when we cannot, but our plans remain unchanged," the High Keeper said firmly. "If Audrian Keyes attempts to bond with Shakulah at Midwinter, then we will be there to stop him."

FIFTEEN

The day before Midwinter, the Grand Keeper invited Viola, Barclay, and Tadg to tea.

Leopold awaited them in one of the Chancellor's private conference chambers. He wore his usual regal cloak and wide smile, as though posing for a portrait.

Viola threw her arms around him. "Dad! It's so good to see you. But I thought you weren't going to visit? You said in your last letter that the *Khronicle* keeps accusing you of putting family matters ahead of your job."

"I did, but after what happened to your mother, I've decided I care less about what the *Khronicle* writes and far more about spending time with the people important to me." Leopold poured them each a cup of tea. The tea set was almost too beautiful to touch, with delicate designs of Desert Beasts painted onto the shiny porcelain. "Tadg, Barclay, I'm glad you could join us. Viola's told me a lot about you both in her letters, and we haven't had as much of a chance to get to know each other as I would've liked."

He gestured at the silk floor cushions, and Barclay nervously took a seat beside Leopold. He knew Leopold was Viola's dad, but it was hard to see him as anything other than the Grand Keeper.

"So, Tadg," Leopold started, "I respected your father's work very much, and I was saddened to hear of his passing. I'm curious—did you ever consider becoming a Surveyor to follow in his footsteps?"

"I thought about it," Tadg said awkwardly. "But then . . . well, I changed my mind."

Though Tadg didn't elaborate, Barclay already knew the full story. After Conley Murdock was killed by Lochmordra, Tadg chose to become a Guardian to prevent the same accidents from happening to others.

"Sometimes we follow our families," Leopold said, nodding. "And sometimes we're meant to forge our own paths."

Viola smirked. "You literally have the same job as Grandma."

Leopold laughed. He had a surprisingly carefree, bellowing laugh, and his smile no longer looked so practiced. "I miss having you at home to keep me on my toes. And you're quite right: I give advice better than I take it."

Before, Barclay hadn't been sure he liked Leopold, as Leopold definitely didn't like Runa. But if Barclay could forgive Cyril, maybe he could forgive the Grand Keeper, too.

"What would you have done if you hadn't become Grand Keeper?" Barclay asked curiously.

"I have no idea. I've always wanted to follow my mother's

path, who in turn followed my grandfather's. I was even named after him. It always felt like my destiny to carry on the Dumont legacy."

When Barclay had first met Viola, he'd thought she must be a princess. He'd been wrong, of course, but Leopold did speak of the Dumonts as though they were a noble family, with all their traditions and history and being named after one another. If he remembered correctly, Viola was named after a great-aunt.

Since Barclay's talk with Runa, his woes about his own family had faded. But they hadn't gone away, not completely. He wished he knew why.

"Now, Barclay." Leopold narrowed his eyes, as though scrutinizing him, and Barclay shifted uncomfortably. Leopold hadn't looked that way at Tadg. "Viola told me the story of how you met. A boy from the Elsewheres bonding with a Lufthund, winning a top rank in his Exhibition a mere few weeks later. That's not a story you hear very often."

Now Barclay understood the sharpness in Leopold's gaze. It *was* like a story he'd heard before—once before.

Barclay hastily reached for his cup to have something to fiddle with. "I guess," he said blandly.

Viola cleared her throat. "I almost forgot, Dad. You haven't met Kulo yet!"

In the next instant, Kulo appeared in Viola's arms.

Leopold's face brightened. "Well, you're even cuter than Viola described in her letters."

"He *is* very cute." Kulo nuzzled his head against Viola's chest, and Viola obediently scratched him behind his lopsided ear. "And needy."

"Have you practiced using your glass Lore yet?"

"Yeah. Cyril has been helping me in our training sessions. And look at this." Viola pulled her monocle from her pocket and held it to her eye. She looked around the room, then grinned and handed it to her father. "When I use my Lore, I can make it zoom in even more, like an adjustable magnifying glass."

He examined the contraption. "Very clever. You know, I still remember the day when I bonded with Fifi—she was my second dragon," Leopold explained to Barclay and Tadg. "It wasn't long after my Symposium. Not long after I met your mother, actually . . ."

For the next twenty minutes, Leopold spoke fondly of his own days as an apprentice and the pressures he faced as the son of the Grand Keeper. Though he sounded cheerful, it was hard not to notice how he skirted around the topic of his own time as a Lore Master. The way he made it sound, he'd gone straight from freshly licensed Guardian to Grand Keeper, skipping all the years in between.

It wasn't until their tea had long gone cold that Viola asked—quietly, as Kulo had drifted asleep—"Do you really think Keyes will show tomorrow?"

A shadow darkened Leopold's face. "I do."

In the weeks since he'd received the letter from Keyes, Barclay had tried hard not to think about Midwinter. But that was easier said than done. He glanced over his shoulder whenever he walked on campus, certain that someone was watching him. He kept having frightening dreams: Earthquakes. The glowing red eyes of Keyes's Tarmacedon. Runa being swallowed by an Ever Storm and never coming out.

"There's no way he can bond with Shakulah," Viola said firmly. "Not with you and so many Guardians there to stop him."

"I agree with you," Leopold said. "And Shakulah's lure ingredients have never been recorded. He can try, but he won't succeed."

Tadg shook his head. "No one knew Lochmordra's lure ingredients either. Then he discovered them."

Barclay agreed with Tadg. Underestimating Keyes was a dangerous mistake.

"The Sea didn't know he was coming. When I consider that it was three apprentices who had to stop him, my own daughter included, I . . ." Leopold closed his eyes. "This ends tomorrow. I'll make sure of it."

No matter how much Barclay had been dreading it, Midwinter arrived all the same. Candles decorated the Guardians' lounge, and the cafeteria served a heaping breakfast of specialties from all six Wilderlands, the perfect comfort for any homesick students. But Barclay didn't eat a bite. He hadn't slept, either. It was hard to do either when he knew that Runa, Cyril, Leopold, Asfour, and all the Guardians now awaited Keyes in the Arid Oasis.

For all Barclay knew, the battle had already begun.

He was hardly the only one of his friends to worry. Dark circles rimmed Tadg's eyes from a poor night of sleep. Shazi and Hasu were both grouchy, and Cecily's shadow had grown to three times its normal size, dimming the light of every room she entered.

Altogether, it was a bad day for the Symposium's final field trip.

Excited chatter buzzed around the caravan as the carrier dragons touched ground, and Barclay shuddered as he stepped out onto the golden sand. In front of him stretched a haunting sight: shipwrecks, miles and miles of them, as far as the eye could see.

It didn't make any sense. They were standing in the Desert, not on one of the isles of the Sea. But there was no mistaking the rotten wooden masts and fraying sails. These were definitely boats, and unless Lore Keepers used to ride them across the ergs, Barclay had no idea how they ended up here.

"This is Shipwreck Coast," Instructor Dia said as the last of the students disembarked from the dragons. "Not to be confused with Shipwreck Stretch, of the Sea."

They approached one of the closest ships, barely more than a heap of broken beams in the sand.

"I know it's hard to see, but about three miles south of here is ocean," continued Dia. "This strip of land used to be part of it, but the wind here blows from land to sea. That means that, over hundreds and hundreds of years, the land slowly swallows more of the ocean. And when you combine that with heavy fogs out on the water, you get, well, beached shipwrecks. Let's take a closer look, why don't we?"

Dia climbed into the gaping hull of the ship, and the students filed in after him. Barclay and his friends, however, lingered sullenly behind.

"We don't need to worry," Viola reassured them. "Dad is the *Grand Keeper*. He's the most—"

"Your dad is the Grand Keeper?" Shazi asked sarcastically. "I never knew that!"

Viola pursed her lips. "All I'm saying is that he's powerful—the most powerful Lore Keeper in the world. There's no way that he won't be able to stop Keyes."

"You can't know that," Barclay said. "Not for certain."

"Actually, I can," Viola said brazenly, then she strutted after the other students into the ship.

Barclay stared out at the horizon. Keyes wasn't the only danger on their mission. Barclay had seen firsthand the destruction that Legendary Beasts could wreak. And the Arid Oasis, where Shakulah lived, was near the center of Death Corridor, the deadliest part of the Desert. There, the heat scorched no matter the season, and only the most monstrous Beasts called it their home.

Gradually, Barclay followed after his friends into the wreck. The inside smelled stale, as though not even a breeze had disturbed the ship for decades. The wood was prickly with splinters and crusted in salt. He peered at the darkest corners suspiciously, half expecting to spot a skeleton clutching an empty treasure chest.

"Occasionally, a very rare species of Beast can be found in these empty ships," Dia told the class. "Does anyone know what it is?"

None of the students responded. Barclay couldn't guess what creature would dwell in a place so lifeless and frightening.

"As a hint, it can also be found within caves, catacombs, and graveyards," Dia continued.

"A Rithis?" one student guessed.

"No. Any other takers?"

"A Kabusoon," Tadg answered.

"That's exactly right. Beasts that inhabit so-called haunted places. They're very rare and dangerous. Mythic class. And they possess a Lore that falls into an unusual category: fear Lore. They can make their homes feel far scarier than they actually are. Adult ones can even scare you to death."

"Then why did we come in here?" one of the Apothecaries asked anxiously.

Dia laughed. "Well, I scoped out this ship yesterday to make sure it was safe, and the worst I encountered was a few Anthorns." Still, many of the students didn't look convinced. Several crept closer to their friends. "Let's climb up to the deck. Two at a time, please—it's not the strongest of structures."

While the students each waited their turn, Barclay muttered to Tadg, "Maybe that's why I feel like this. It's a Kabusoon hiding under the floorboards."

"Don't you think we should've gone with them?" Tadg asked. "We could help."

"I'm pretty sure we'd just get in their way."

"Says *you*."

Barclay rolled his eyes.

"Fine, I guess we would," Tadg grumbled. "But I can't just wait around all day. It's still morning and I already feel like I might explode."

Barclay grabbed ahold of the ladder next, squinting up into the bright, cloudless sky. "What other choice do we have?"

The field trip returned from the Shipwreck Coast early that evening. It being the shortest day of the year, the sun had already set, and Barclay miserably rolled over in bed and buried his face in Root's side.

"What if they don't come back?" he whispered.

Root whined.

"I'm sorry. I'm just scared. Maybe everything will go to Asfour's plan. And Keyes will be caught. And Shakulah will stop the Ever Storms."

Root lifted his head from the pillow, and his tail swished— only once. It was a happier thought, but Root wasn't sure if he believed it.

Barclay wasn't sure either.

"Maybe we should eat something. Tadg said that the cafeteria is serving potato dumplings. And stollen." But all his worrying had ruined his appetite, even for his favorite fruitcake.

A scream sounded from the hallway.

Barclay's pulse quickened to rapid-fire. He leapt from his bed and raced out of his room, Root dashing behind him. They followed the noise to the boys' bathroom, but no sooner did they barge through the door than they collided with Rohan.

"There is . . . a giant . . . eel thing . . . in the bath," Rohan panted, grasping at the towel around his waist.

Around the corner, Mar-Mar roared gleefully. Or maybe it was angrily. It was hard to tell Mar-Mar's joy and blood-lust apart.

"That's Tadg's Nathermara," Barclay said.

"*That's* Mar-Mar? When Tadg said he needed bathtime, I was picturing something small! And cute!" Rohan clutched at his heart dramatically. His hands, much like his face and neck, were covered in dirt. "He almost took a chunk out of me."

"I think Tadg assumed everyone would be at dinner. Why aren't you? And how did you get so dirty?"

"I was exploring the secret passages under Eldin Hall. There's only two weeks of classes left—I need to plan something *big*. Something that will go down in Tourney history. At this rate, Mischievius will claim the crown."

Barclay had stopped paying much attention to the Tourney since joining the Guardians' missions.

"Why aren't *you* at dinner?" Rohan asked.

"Oh, I . . ." The Midwinter mission was a secret; otherwise, Keyes might find out he was heading into an ambush. "I'm homesick, I guess." It wasn't entirely a lie. The more time that passed without a letter from Master Pilzmann, the more Dullshire weighed on Barclay's mind.

Rohan's face lit up. "Do you want to see the passages? I can show you them."

"I don't . . . I mean . . ." Barclay couldn't come up with a good reason to say no. The Guardians would remain in the Arid Oasis until midnight, so they wouldn't likely return to Menneset until the early hours of the morning. "All right."

"Excellent. I'll just—"

Mar-Mar roared again, and sparks sizzled across the floor. Rohan yelped and barreled out of the bathroom.

Several minutes later, after Rohan had changed back into his filthy clothes, he led Barclay and Root into Eldin Hall's atrium. They crept behind the statue of Piliba Cagney, who, according to the plaque, was a Lore Keeper famous for being eaten by a Silberwal and living to tell the tale (only to be eaten later, regretfully, by a Jawbask). Rohan flattened his palm against the wall and pushed. The stone slid to the side.

"It's a bit narrow," Rohan said, which was an understatement. The squeeze was so tight that by the time Barclay squirmed into the passage, he felt as though he'd been pressed two inches taller. Behind him, Root's paw scraped at the wall, but he couldn't fit through the crevice.

"Sorry, buddy," Barclay told him, then returned him to his Mark.

The hallway was as dark and dusty as a tomb. They stumbled blindly down a slippery set of stairs until they reached a lower level. Thin slivers of light shone from the ceiling—the cracks between tiles above.

"Aren't these passages amazing?" Rohan asked. "They travel underneath the entire University."

Barclay wondered how that was possible when the Library of Asfour was also underneath the University, but the Library's stairwell had been long—far longer than this. The Library must've burrowed even deeper in the earth.

"Come on," Rohan said. "This leads right underneath the Guardians' lounge." Then he pointed at the narrower offshooting hallways. "That leads up to one of the study rooms—there's a secret panel in the bookcase. That one leads outside. That one—I don't know where that one goes. It still smells a little of Dungwasp, though."

They walked what must've been half the campus, happening upon a mischief of Rattles, a seemingly bottomless pit, and what looked to be a long-forgotten, very cluttered storage room.

"I like it down here," Rohan said. "It's peaceful."

"It's a bit grimy."

"That adds to the charm." Then he sighed. "I didn't really come here for fun—I wanted to think. Kamil told us about the Midwinter mission. He's on it too."

Barclay felt foolish for not realizing that earlier. "Why didn't you say so?"

"What's the point? Our Masters are off on a potentially deadly assignment. Talking about it won't change anything." Rohan retraced their steps toward Eldin Hall. "You know what does make me feel better? Knowing that next year, I'll be with them. Deirdre and I test for our licenses this Spring."

"Are you nervous?" Barclay was already nervous for his licensing exam, though it was years and years away.

"Nah. Kamil's a good teacher. If he thinks we'll pass, we will."

They turned down a hallway littered with rubble. Already familiar with the path, Rohan scaled the beams easily, while Barclay struggled to keep up behind him.

"Runa told Kamil that the three of you faced Keyes at the Sea—you, Viola, and Tadg," Rohan said. "What was he like?"

Barclay didn't know how to answer. As Edwyn Lusk, he'd been easygoing and charming. As Audrian Keyes, he'd been ruthless and terrifying.

"I liked him at first," Barclay admitted. "We all did."

"Well, that's not too surprising. He wouldn't have been Runa and Cyril's friend otherwise." Rohan whistled. "The Horn of Dawn and the Fang of Dusk fighting side by side. That's a battle I'd want to watch."

A light appeared down a crooked hallway to their right, flickering like a torch. Then it flared and split into two flames, each cupped over a pale hand.

Above the flames, a face watched Barclay in the distance. Though he couldn't make out the features, he recognized fire Lore when he saw it.

Yasha.

Memories tugged at him. Barclay spying on Yasha while he trained. Motya, Yasha's Smynx, peering down at the boys from atop the attic's wardrobe. Yasha laughing with Barclay and Tadg. Yasha helping Barclay master his Lore after he'd struggled for weeks.

Yasha betraying them.

Barclay took off down the hallway.

"Where are you going?" Rohan called, but Barclay didn't answer. He was too focused on ducking around the hallway's slants and curves.

Before Barclay could reach the light, the flames snuffed out, draping his surroundings in darkness. He held his breath, but he didn't even hear the thuds of footsteps.

"Have you gone barking mad?" Rohan shouted. "Get it, Barks? Barking mad?"

But Barclay didn't crack a smile. He *swore* he'd seen Yasha, but the more he staggered around in the dark, the more he wondered if his mind was playing tricks on him. He'd gone too long without sleep.

He slinked back to Rohan. "Sorry. I thought I saw something. Do you know what's down that hallway?"

"Not sure. Judging from where we are, I'd say it goes right under our rooms."

Great—now Barclay wouldn't sleep tonight, either.

When he and Rohan returned to the Guardians' lounge, they found their friends gathered in the corner. Tadg silently shuffled through his champion cards. Shazi and Viola huddled together while Shazi built some kind of contraption, a metal tube stretching and warping between her hands. Kulo snuggled on Viola's lap. On the floor below them, Deirdre painted Cecily's, Hasu's, and Mitzi's nails black. Saif, his metal plates looking freshly polished, paraded proudly around them.

"What cave did you both crawl out of?" Hasu asked, eyeing Barclay's and Rohan's filthy clothes.

"In my defense," Rohan said, "there's a gigantic monster in the boys' bathroom."

"Oh, right," Tadg muttered. "He'll probably be wanting dinner." He reached into his backpack and pulled out a giant hunk of raw meat wrapped in butcher paper. It dripped pink juice as he walked down the hallway.

Viola scrunched her nose. "Doesn't he carry his textbooks in that?"

"That reminds me," Hasu said, handing Barclay a container. "I brought you some of that fruitcake. You mentioned you liked it."

Rohan pouted. "Did anyone bring free food for *me*?"

For the rest of the evening, the eight of them remained in the lounge, laughing and tearing off pieces to share of the enormous slice of stollen. It was the closest thing to celebrating they would have this Midwinter. Soon Barclay's mysterious encounter in the tunnels was all but forgotten.

The best part of the night was when Viola jumped to her

feet and triumphantly declared, "It's done! It's done!" On the cushion behind her, Kulo perked his head up eagerly.

"What's done?" Hasu asked.

"Shazi helped me make a telescope. Look." Viola handed the metal contraption to Hasu, who raised it to her eye. While Hasu peered into it, Viola traced a circle in the air with her finger, and Hasu gasped.

"It can zoom in and out! This is amazing, Viola."

She handed it next to Barclay, who stared wondrously at the beautiful lacework on the metal. "You made this?" he asked Shazi.

Shazi grinned. "I can do more than just stab things, you know."

Hours later, a voice woke Barclay from sleep. He stirred from where he lay next to Root on the floor. Cecily snored beside him.

"Hasu," the voice said. "Shazi. All of you, wake up. You should be in bed."

Barclay's eyes fluttered open. Cyril leaned over them, gently shaking each of their shoulders. Barclay instantly sat up.

"You're back," he breathed. "What happened? Are the Ever Storms gone?"

Cyril shook his head. "The mission was a failure. Shakulah woke up, shifted position, then fell right back asleep."

"And Keyes?" Viola pressed, now awake as well.

"He didn't show."

SIXTEEN

During the Symposium's final week of classes, the University of Al Faradh appeared eerily deserted. Apprentices rarely scuttled out of their dormitories or study nooks except for lessons or meals. Loose papers and empty cups had cluttered the Guardians' lounge. Beasts, bored while their Keepers buried themselves in books, freely roamed around Eldin Hall, startling students by charging around corners, swinging from the statues, and transforming the bathrooms into rowdy watering holes.

"This is our final session," Cyril told Barclay and Root in the gymnasium. "So let's make the most of it. Show me everything you've got."

With that, Cyril pointed both of his palms at the targets, and Codric bowed his head in concentration. A moment later, the targets reared to life. The Lore Keepers began to walk, their wooden limbs creaking with each step. The flying Beasts soared into the air, while those on the ground scattered—galloping, sprinting, hopping, and prowling.

Barclay had no time to be awed by Cyril and Codric's amazing control, as every target was racing toward *him*.

He and Root tore into two opposite directions—Barclay faced the dummies on the left, while Root took to the right. It was far harder to aim his Lore at moving targets while running himself. Nearly every gust of wind missed. Those that didn't landed off-center, slowing the targets down but not knocking them over.

One of the Lore Keepers barreled into Barclay's back, sending him sprawling onto his hands and knees. He rolled away a moment before the Karkadann could trample him beneath its hooves.

"Careful!" Cyril called, despite making no effort to slow the targets down.

Across the arena, Root was faring much better than Barclay. He moved in a blur, little more than a streak of black fur weaving between the dummies. Every arrow of wind he fired hit its mark.

Barclay wished he could ask him how he did it, but he didn't have the chance. Root barked at him in warning, and Barclay whipped around. Behind him, a wooden dragon swooped overhead. He raised his hands, and a powerful gust of air burst toward it with the force of a cannonball. The target toppled to the floor.

It was one victory, but he wasn't proud of himself yet. The targets swarmed him on all sides. He was so busy dodging or getting whacked that it was very hard to look at Root. The few times he did, Root danced around the targets. Whenever they moved toward him, whether from behind or from above or head-on, Root had already changed his direction.

While he was staring, a lionlike Waramasa slammed into Barclay's side, its spiky wooden mane jabbing against his ribs. He grunted and collapsed onto the ground. More targets advanced toward him. Out of options, he threw his arms over his head and squeezed his eyes shut.

Nothing happened.

When he peeled open his eyes, the targets all loomed over him, frozen still.

"That was very good." Cyril strode over and offered Barclay his hand. Barclay grasped it and climbed to his feet. "You've made a lot of progress."

"I nearly got pummeled."

"Back in Autumn, you couldn't hit one target without hitting all of them. You should be proud of yourself and how hard you've worked."

Barclay smiled weakly. He would've preferred a proper victory.

As he and Root walked toward the exit, he heard a distant *clunk*, as though a pebble had been kicked across a stone floor. He turned, confused.

"Something the matter, Barclay?" Cyril asked.

"I-it's nothing." Barclay rubbed away the chills on his arms. The stress of exams was getting to him. And as Cyril stared at him with concern, Barclay realized that, apart from graduation, he had no idea when he'd see Cyril again. This was goodbye.

"Are you going back to the Mountains, once exams are over?" Barclay asked.

Codric slumped his shoulders, looking extra dour now that the leaves had all fallen from his horns.

Cyril sighed. "It seems so. As much as I'd like to help the Desert, I think it'd be easier for everyone if I left."

Easier for everyone? Barclay wanted to ask. *Or easier for you and Runa?*

Barclay knew he had no business saying anything. Runa was his family, but he liked Cyril. And Shazi, Hasu, and Cecily felt like family too.

"Maybe, but it'd probably be easier for Keyes, too," said Barclay. "If I were Keyes, I'd be happy that the two people who knew me best hated each other."

Cyril stiffened. Then, as he turned to leave, he said curtly, "Good luck with your exams, Barclay."

So much for a warm farewell.

But Barclay didn't care if he'd meddled somewhere he didn't belong. Deep down, he knew he was right.

That evening, Barclay and Tadg went straight from dinner to their room. Oil lamps and candles burned on every surface, and the only sounds were Root's yawns and the scratching of quills against parchment.

"I've tried to re-create this map of the Jungle five times, and I *still* can't get it right." Seething, Tadg tore the page from his notebook and crumpled it in his fist. Poisonous purple acid bled through the paper, and it wilted like a dying flower. He tossed the wet clump onto the floor.

"Your poison Lore is getting better," Barclay said.

"Yeah, barely." He rolled up his right sleeve, where Toadles's Mark glimmered above his wrist. Surrounding it swelled red hives.

Barclay cringed and changed the subject. "I'm sure your

map isn't that bad. Isn't the Wilderlands your favorite class?"

Tadg scoffed and slammed his textbook shut. "What do you mean?"

"You've stayed late talking to Dia before. And you know the answers to almost all of his questions."

Red crept across Tadg's cheeks. "Well, I . . ."

Before he could finish, an envelope slid beneath their door. Barclay shot up. Since the letter from Keyes, Essam had arranged for all the students' mail to be delivered directly to their dormitories. And Barclay recognized the handwriting.

"That's from Master Pilzmann." He lunged out of bed and ripped it open.

He'd skimmed only the first few words before Tadg asked, "Well? What does it say?"

Surprised Tadg was interested in the goings-on of Dullshire, Barclay cleared his throat and read. "'Dear Barclay, I'm sorry for how long it took me to respond to your last letter. As you can imagine, since the Miscarrots' invasion—I think he means Miskreats—'Dullshire had been living a nightmare. Until a pair of Lore Keepers from the Woods showed up to help. At first, the mayor thought we were under siege, and he recruited every young person in town to take up arms to defend Dullshire, including Selby.'" Try as he might, Barclay couldn't picture his once-weepy, bumbling fellow apprentice wielding a sword or pitchfork. "'Then I showed the mayor your letter, and eventually—once the Miscarrots had lain waste to our pumpkin fields and moved on to the turnips—he met with the Lore Keepers, who used some kind of magic contraption to draw all the Beasts out of Dullshire. I will admit, not everyone in town was grateful, but I gave the Lore Keepers the last of this year's Mourningtide Morels as thanks. They were very appreciative. Clearly, even Lore Keepers recognize the value of a good mushroom! I will write again soon after we rebuild the clocktower a third time. Several people in Dullshire send along their well wishes. Sincerely, Niclaus Pilzmann.'"

Tadg scrutinized him. "No offense, but your hometown sounds nuttier that Dudnik."

That might've been true, but Barclay's heart fluttered with happiness all the same. Dullshire and Lore Keepers had gotten along for once, no pitchforks or torches involved. Because of him.

He collapsed back onto his bed, making Root open one eye with annoyance. Clearly, Barclay had interrupted a very pleasant nap.

After Barclay basked in his success for a few moments longer, he said to Tadg, "Sorry. What were you saying earlier about the Wilderlands class?"

"Never mind," Tadg said quickly. "It doesn't matter."

"Why? I want to hear it."

"Fine, but you have to promise not to laugh."

"I won't," Barclay said solemnly, now twice as curious.

"I've been researching Beast bonds. I want to learn more about them. Especially the kind that the Beast forges with the Keeper, not the other way around. Take Toadles, for instance."

Tadg hoisted up his covers, revealing Toadles, burrowed within the sheets.

"Croak!" Toadles uttered, then he leapt into Tadg's lap.

Tadg peered at his Beast closely. "I notice things about

Toadles that I don't with Mar-Mar. Like we're similar or something."

"Really? Because you and Mar-Mar have very similar personalities." Then Barclay snapped his fingers. "Oh, I get it! It's the warts."

Tadg scowled. "I'm being serious. Sometimes, I feel like Toadles can read my thoughts. He always leaves his Mark when I'm angry or annoyed or something."

"So . . . all the time."

Barclay ducked out of the way of another projectile of sludgy paper.

"Do you have any idea what I'm talking about?" Tadg grumbled.

Barclay forced himself to be serious. "I think so. I know all Lore Keepers have a connection to their Beast, but when I met Root, it was like he already knew me. He still knows me better than anyone."

Tadg nodded. "Yeah. And Dad always thought that only Mythic class Beasts could forge bonds on their own, but I'm not sure he was right. Toadles isn't as powerful as Root or Mar-Mar or Kulo. I've been doing some research in the University libraries, and I found some interesting books at Menneset Market. Dia has been helping me." Barclay was about to ask some more questions, but Tadg kept talking excitedly. "If we ever go to Halois, I'd like to look at the libraries in the Meridienne College. Dad used to go there a lot to examine its rare-book collection. There are some libraries that only Scholars have permission to visit because the books are so valuable and fragile, but if I submit a formal request to . . . What?"

"I'm just impressed. I had no idea you were so interested in this stuff."

"I wasn't sure I was, at first. But it reminds me of Dad. Not in a sad way. Just a good way."

Barclay cleared his throat. "Do you ever . . . do you ever think of him in a sad way, sometimes?"

Tadg's smile fell.

"Sorry," Barclay said hastily. "I didn't mean—"

"No, it's fine. Of course I do." He set Toadles back on the sheets and covered him with the quilt. The Toadles-shaped bulge roamed around before snuggling in the bed's corner. "Not as often as before, but sometimes. Why?"

"I've been thinking about my parents lately. I know it doesn't make sense—they've been gone a long time, and I don't remember them that well. Plus, I've got Root now, and you and Viola and Runa. And I've been doing better at the Symposium than I ever thought I would. . . ."

Without opening his eyes, Root scooted closer to Barclay, and Barclay stroked his fur.

"I guess I just wish I knew if they'd be proud of me," Barclay finished.

"Of course they would," Tadg said without hesitation.

"You say that like you know for sure."

"I do know for sure. You're brilliant, and you always do the right thing, and you just saved Dullshire, didn't you? Not to mention the Woods and the Sea. Are you proud of yourself?"

"Yes," Barclay said meekly.

"Then so are they. Because even though they're gone, they're still a part of you, no matter how much you remember. So if you're proud of yourself, they are too."

Barclay blinked away tears. He hadn't realized how much he'd needed to hear that.

"At least, that's what Orla told me once," Tadg added. "And she's, what, a million years old? She probably knows what she's talking about."

Their studying forgotten, the two talked for hours and hours, until nearly all their candles had burned out. Barclay told Tadg some of his funniest stories from Dullshire, like the one about the stray cat the entire town was convinced had magical powers, and only after hanging up over a hundred wanted posters did they discover it was a regular tabby. Tadg recounted all the ridiculous gifts that Conley had gotten him for various birthdays, from the twelve-foot-long fishing spear when Tadg was three to the lava lamp that oozed real lava when he was nine.

"Why do you think Keyes never showed up at Midwinter?" Barclay asked. "Do you think he was scared of the ambush?"

"I don't know, but whenever I ask Runa about it or what Asfour plans to do next, she won't say anything."

"Maybe she doesn't have a plan."

"Or maybe she does." Tadg's voice was more ominous in the dark. "And she doesn't want us to find out."

Instructor Dudnik rapped her wooden poker against the chalkboard. "Pay attention, pay attention. Shame on you all for sleeping through the last day of class. It's terrible luck to disrespect your teachers, you know."

Barclay jolted, lifting his head from his arm. Beside him, Tadg kept on snoring.

"What was I talking about?" Dudnik muttered. "Oh, yes—the Arid Oasis. What would you say if I told you that it wasn't an oasis at all?"

"What is it, then?" Fen asked sarcastically. "Another fallen piece of a meteorite? Or the hiding place of some ancient prophecy?"

Dudnik ignored him and the laughter of his fan club. "Consider this: Why do all oases have water beneath their ground, yet the Arid Oasis is completely dry? It's the only oasis in the world—both in the Wilderlands *and* other deserts—not to have a source of freshwater."

The class fell into silence. Barclay drowsily glanced around the desks for Viola, who usually answered Dudnik's questions out of politeness. But strangely, Viola was nowhere to be found.

Cecily flipped through the notes she'd copied from Barclay. "Well, Shakulah lives in the Arid Oasis, doesn't she? It's probably just special."

"Maybe, maybe," said Dudnik, "but the homes of the other Legendary Beasts aren't so special. Gravaldor doesn't cause the trees of his grove to grow. Dimondaise didn't carve out her cave in her mountain. So is it that Shakulah is truly unique, or that there's something we aren't seeing?"

Dudnik let her words hang in the air, clearly believing them more menacing than they actually were. Even Barclay barely paid attention. He'd been in the midst of an unnerving dream: Keyes and Yasha had been chasing him through the secret passages beneath the school, and the tunnels were covered in glowing, bulbous mushrooms.

Then loud, deep tolls rang out.

The students looked between one another curiously. Dudnik smiled, as though she'd planned the noise for dramatic effect.

"Is that . . . ?" Rohan asked.

"Dad didn't tell me about any announcement," Shazi breathed.

Ignoring Dudnik's protests, the students dashed outside. The peals of the bell thundered across campus, and the Surveyors and Scholars also abandoned their class to cluster in the courtyard, gaping at the obelisk in the distance. Whispers of "the Tourney" and "impossible" flitted through the crowd.

"No fair," Cecily whined. "I was nearly finished planning my last prank—and this is way better!"

"But who is it?" Rohan asked.

Barclay peered at the other apprentices. He spotted Zenzi among the Surveyors, and Fen with the Apothecaries. He had no idea who it could be.

But one person was missing.

He gasped. "Viola."

Shazi's eyes widened. "No way!" She took off running, and the throngs of students followed. They stopped in the center of campus beneath the bell tower.

"There's a Beast up there!" Cecily pointed at a small flying figure that circled the tower.

"That's definitely Mitzi," Barclay said.

"Do you know how Viola got in there?" Tadg asked Barclay.

"I have no idea," he answered honestly—though he had his suspicions. They'd been inside the Chancellor's private wing twice now, and when Tadg and Barclay had met Leopold, they'd been nervous. Viola could've easily spotted a secret passage they didn't, especially using her magnifying glass.

After a few minutes, Fen stalked over. "Barclay! Did Runa Rasgar tell you all how to do it?" he demanded. "That was her famous stunt, and she's your Lore Master!"

Despite Barclay's few days of Tourney fame, he hadn't realized that Fen knew who he was. "Sh-she didn't," Barclay swore to him, flushing. But Fen only narrowed his eyes.

Then Tadg said, "It's the truth. Runa refused to tell us how she got up there."

At that, Fen sighed. "Then it's over, I guess. I don't think even Mischievius could top that."

"But who is Mischievius?" Shazi asked. "The Symposium is basically over now. They don't have to stay secret anymore."

The question swept through the students. It seemed that all the apprentices were eager to unmask the mysterious figure.

"I think it's Deirdre!" Rohan declared.

Deirdre stared at him blankly. "Of course it's not me. Why would you think that?"

Rohan shrugged. "Spite."

"I thought it was you," Cecily told Rohan.

After ten minutes had passed and no one had come forward, Rohan climbed onto the nearest set of steps. He raised his hands to his mouth to shout. "The Symposium is over and . . . Yes, yes." He waited as the crowd cheered. "So will Mischievius please step forward and reveal yourself? You have unanimously won second place."

No one moved.

"I don't get it," Tadg said. "This is *all* of the students."

Hasu's brow furrowed. "How do we know Mischievius is a student at all?"

Before any of them could dwell on that, the doors to the Chancellor's office swung open. The apprentices applauded as Viola emerged—and all the louder when Rohan seized her hand and raised it triumphantly into the air.

"I don't know why everyone is so surprised," Barclay heard a Scholar student whisper behind him. "She's the daughter of the Grand Keeper, isn't she?"

"I bet *she'll* be Grand Keeper one day," the student's friend replied.

Viola's eyes searched the crowd, and Barclay waved at her, knowing she was looking for them. When their gazes met, Viola beamed proudly, and Barclay grinned. He bet Viola would be Grand Keeper one day too.

SEVENTEEN

The desks are organized in alphabetical order." Mandeep's voice carried across the large academic hall, echoing throughout the vaulted ceiling. "You'll find your names written on your booklets."

Barclay cast a final fearful look at Viola and Tadg before they each shuffled through the jittery crowd of Symposium students to their seats. He found his in the back row, between Aaliyah Tellier and Lias Vinter, who were both Scholar apprentices, neither of whom he knew well. He studied the thick stack of papers and swallowed.

"Your exams are inside your booklets," Mandeep told them. "You won't be permitted to look until the bell rings."

In the corner of the hall, the resident Apothecary Master—Otto Drager—stood beside a massive bronze bell. He clutched a mallet in his hand.

"And . . ." Mandeep flipped over an hourglass. "Begin."

The bell tolled, and the deep sound rattled in the air while students tore into their booklets. Barclay's quill trembled in his hand. Portraits of previous University Chancellors lined the walls, gazing sternly at him as though he'd personally offend them if he failed.

He squinted at the tiny text of the first question.

What are the six capitals of the Wilderlands?

Relieved he knew the answer, he scratched each of their names into the first clean page of the booklet.

The next hour slipped past, and Barclay was pleased that the Guild Studies exam didn't prove half so dreadful as the rumors had claimed. He'd just flipped to the essay section when a shadow dipped over his paper and his Mark twinged with pain.

He glanced up at the window to his right. The clear blue sky from moments before now churned with dense clouds. The daylight dimmed further and further by the second, and a shrieking wind sent many students floundering out of their seats.

"What's happening?" an apprentice behind him gasped.

"Is that rain?" asked Aaliyah Tellier to his left.

At the front of the hall, Mandeep rose from his desk and cautiously approached the nearest window.

All at once, the last of the daylight snuffed out, plunging the hall into darkness.

The windows exploded. Barclay dove beneath his desk as shattered glass rained from above. For several heartbeats, his mind went blank with shock. He squeezed his eyes shut and shielded his head with his hands as sand pelted his cheeks. Screams rang out in all directions, overpowered only by the crashes of desks toppling over and the clatters of portraits being ripped from the walls.

When Barclay peeled his eyes open, he caught a glimpse of Lias Vinter, who'd curled himself into a fetal position, cupping a flame no brighter than a candle. Exam booklets blew past. Chairs skidded across the floor. On the closest wall, a long gash tore through one of the portraits, making the Chancellor look as though she'd been sliced in two.

Only when bursts of light and fire Lore flared through the chamber did Barclay realize what was happening.

Menneset had been consumed by an Ever Storm.

A moment later, the double doors in the back of the hall barged open. More sand and dust swarmed into the air, making Barclay choke.

Cyril and Li strode inside. "Students!" Cyril bellowed. "A sandstorm has fallen over the city. We'll escort you back to your dormitories, where you'll stay until we receive word from Chancellor Essam or High Keeper Asfour. Hamdani Hall, you'll be with Li. Eldin Hall, come with me!"

The apprentices stampeded toward the exit. Barclay had barely managed to stand before being knocked in the shoulder, and students crushed him at either side as everyone tried to cram out the doors at once.

When he finally wedged himself outside, a sickening sight greeted him. The great University of Al Faradh was in chaos. Palm trees bent sideways. Dirt and shards of glass coated the stone paths, and the buildings looked like little more than shadows looming overhead.

"Hasu!" Cyril yelled, pushing past the terrified students. He spotted her pressed against the door. "Go to Chancellor

Essam's office and bring him to Eldin Hall as soon as he is able."

Hasu nodded, then disappeared in a golden honeycomb of light.

"Barclay? Barclay?" Cyril called next.

"I'm here!" he answered, his voice strangled.

Cyril whipped around to face him. "How much can you help?"

Barclay looked dismally at the huge throng of students. He could calm the winds enough to form a protective sphere, the same as he'd done in the other Ever Storms. But he'd never attempted it in so wide a space with so many people.

"I-I'm not sure," he stammered, but that didn't stop him from trying anyway. He raised both of his arms and thought, *Wind!*

The gusts around them changed direction. They swirled in a vortex, and Barclay grimaced as he struggled to stretch it bigger and bigger to squeeze in as many students as possible. That amount of power made pain throb at his temples, and he wheezed. His Lore was tearing the air out of his own body.

"I . . ." He tried to speak, but he didn't have the breath.

Clearly realizing that Barclay couldn't keep this up for long, Cyril shouted, "Eldin Hall—move! Move!"

As the Scholar and Apothecary apprentices separated from his group, Barclay let his sphere shrink, and he gasped as air rushed back into his chest. With the light of Viola's and one of the Surveyors' Lore to guide them, they raced back to their dormitory.

As soon as they'd scrambled through the doors, the exhausted students collapsed onto the floor beneath the statues. Several sported scrapes and cuts. More than one cried.

"All of you, go pack your bags as best you can," Cyril told them. "When you're finished, come back here. The Chancellor should give us instructions any minute."

They dashed to their rooms, and Barclay and Tadg found theirs even more of a mess than usual. One of their two small windows had shattered, and sand was strewn all over their beds and nightstands. They each flung open their wardrobes, and Barclay stuffed whatever clothes and belongings he could into his satchel.

"Where do you think we're going?" Barclay asked.

"I don't know," Tadg answered. "Dakmana, probably. It's the next-biggest city in the Desert."

"But what about exams?"

"*That's* what you're worried about? What about Menneset? The entire city will have to evacuate."

The havoc reminded Barclay of when the isles of the Sea were destroyed, but this was even worse—the Desert had lost its capital, and now thousands of people would have to flee their homes for someplace safe. But was anywhere in the Desert safe, if an Ever Storm could appear at any moment?

Once they'd collected everything that mattered and abandoned what didn't, the two boys bolted back to the atrium. The returning students sat on the floor, scratched up and exhausted, including Georgy Ekel, who hugged his backpack to his chest, and Zenzi, who sadly whispered to her mothlike Beast perched on her hand. The storm roared behind the doors, whose bolts rattled but didn't budge.

In the corner, Chancellor Essam argued with Cyril.

"—to the Meridienne College?" Cyril asked, aghast. "That's across the continent! Won't it be easier for the apprentices to finish out the Symposium in Dakmana?"

"Asfour has already made the order," Essam said. "And she wants Mayani to take you to the Guild House at once."

Cyril gaped. "B-but the students. Will we really be sending them on the carrier dragons alone—"

"She's made up her mind. And she said to tell you . . ." Essam lowered his voice, and Barclay and Tadg crept closer to listen. "She's gathering the team for the mission you discussed after Midwinter. She said you would know what that meant."

The color seeped from Cyril's face. Then, stiffly, he nodded. "I see."

Essam rested a hand on Cyril's shoulder. "Don't worry. I'll make sure the students all board safely."

"You won't be leaving as well?"

"There are centuries' worth of documents and artifacts here at the University that have to be protected. I can't just—"

"You're not coming with us?" a frazzled voice cried out behind them, and Shazi shoved past Barclay and Tadg to her father's side, a backpack strapped over her shoulders.

"I have to make sure the school's property is transported safely to Dakmana," Essam said. "I'll be fine. I have your mother to take care of me, don't I? And I'll feel better knowing you're safe at—"

Shazi threw her arms around him and buried her face in his chest. "I'm sorry about the Library. I didn't—"

He shushed her. "You have nothing to be sorry for."

As Cyril left the father and daughter to their goodbyes, he

spotted Barclay and Tadg hovering by the door. He moved toward them, sighing. "The Symposium is going to be completed at the Meridienne College in Halois. They're rounding up carrier dragons to leave within the hour."

"Within the hour?" Tadg repeated. "But where's Runa? We're not leaving without—"

"She's at the Guild House with Asfour. If there's a message you want to get to her, I suppose I can . . ." He cleared his throat awkwardly. "I'll tell her when I arrive."

"Why can't we come with you?" Barclay asked. "Hasu is taking you there, isn't she?"

"Yes, but—"

"We're not leaving until we see Runa," Tadg argued. "After that, we'll go with Hasu straight to our carrier dragon."

Cyril rubbed his temples. "Fine. You can go with us if you must, but we have to hurry. There's no time to waste."

They found Hasu in her and Viola's room, packing. Both of their windows had shattered, and now the art and garlands that had once decorated their walls littered the floor. Viola grunted, trying to shove far more books into her backpack than would fit.

"I'm sorry to rush you," Cyril told Hasu, "but Asfour needs you to take me to the Guild House."

Hasu's hands slipped as she fumbled to close her bag. "The High Keeper asked for my help specifically?"

"Yes, and if you're not too tired, these two have requested a trip as well."

"You're both going?" Viola asked. "What about the carrier dragons?"

"We'll meet you there," Barclay assured her.

"No way," said Viola. "If you're going to see Runa, I want to come too."

"All five of us? Across half the city?" Hasu squeaked.

She glanced at Cyril, who shook his head. "Don't look at me. You know best what you're capable of."

At first, Hasu looked uncertain, then a steely expression hardened on her face. "All right." She sealed her bag and summoned Bitti, who had to cling to a strand of Hasu's hair so as not to be blown away by the wind. The five of them linked arms, and a golden hexagon of light appeared before them, as large as a door. Hasu took the first step inside, dragging the others with her.

After so many Guardian missions with Hasu, Barclay should've been used to the feeling of her spatial Lore by now. But the falling up still disoriented him, and he stumbled as he took in the mayhem of the Guild House. Lore Keepers and Beasts rushed past, many of them shouting or screeching at one another. In the courtyard, a humongous carrier dragon was being prepped for flight. It wore leather battle armor over its wings and tail, and a large pair of goggles shielded its eyes from the thrashing sand.

To the right, Asfour bellowed orders into the frenzy. "The medical supplies still need to be loaded! Evacuation teams, what have we heard from Dakmana?"

"They're sending twenty carrier dragons, ma'am," a Lore Keeper beside her answered.

"Only twenty?"

"It's dragon breeding season. They're too hard to control, and most have already flown back to the Mountains. Even in Menneset, we can fly only about half of the ones we have."

Asfour cursed in frustration. Then she spotted Cyril and waved him over. "Good. You're here. It looks like you'll be seeing some action after all."

"Who else will be coming?" Cyril asked.

"Of the Guardians, Okasha, Sami, Lynch, Chen, and Runa, assuming you both can manage a mission without tearing at each other's throats."

Cyril nodded grimly. "Of course."

As though summoned, Runa emerged from the caravan. She braced her hand in front of her face as she ducked for cover within the Guild House, then she frowned at her apprentices. "What are you doing here? The University is evacuating to Halois—"

"We wanted to see you," Barclay said. "What mission are you going on? What was Essam talking about?"

Runa grasped Viola and Barclay by the arms and steered the three of them out of the way of the bustling Lore Keepers. Past the doorway to their right, more Beasts prepared for battle. Barclay spotted both Klava and Codric being fitted with fighting gear. Klava clawed at her helmet, while Codric pranced gleefully in a circle, his head flung back, as though he was a knight in shining armor.

Runa cleared her throat. "After Shakulah did nothing to fix the Ever Storms, Asfour planned a mission should one ever hit one of the Desert's cities. A team of us are going into the original Ever Storm to see if we can discover what's causing it."

Barclay's heart felt as though it'd turned to lead. "The first Ever Storm? The one an entire team *died* in?"

"This team includes the most powerful Guardians and

Surveyors currently in the Desert," said Runa. "We're more than capable, and we knew what we were getting into when we volunteered."

"It's a suicide mission," Tadg snapped, and Barclay agreed. He knew as a Guardian that Runa had dedicated her life to protecting the Wilderlands, and he was proud of her for that. But this was one mission he wished she wouldn't risk, for all their sakes.

Runa shook her head. "You three shouldn't worry about me. Go to Halois with the other students. I'll meet up with you before Midspring."

"Midspring?" Viola echoed incredulously.

"'Don't worry about me,'" Tadg choked out. "That's the last thing Dad said to me too."

Pain flashed across Runa's face. Then she forced out a smile. "This isn't like that. You think I plan on dying with that one over there?" She jerked her head toward Cyril, who, by the looks of it, was having a similarly fraught conversation with Hasu. "I don't think so."

But Barclay wasn't in the mood for jokes. "We could come with you. Viola and I have been in—"

"It's noble of you to volunteer, but no. Like it or not, you're still just apprentices, and you have your Symposium to finish."

Something as trivial as school seemed a poor reason to split up the only family Barclay had left. But the other Guardians in Runa's squad had already begun to board, awaiting takeoff. And so Runa hugged them goodbye and followed Cyril and Asfour into the caravan, and Barclay watched them disappear through the door with a dread churning inside him. He hadn't felt this scared since the day he accidentally followed Selby into the Woods.

As the carrier dragon readied its mighty wings, Barclay heard a quiet sound, distinct even amid the howls of the wind and the shouts of the remaining Lore Keepers. No matter which direction he turned, it was always behind him, as though coming from just over his shoulder.

A laugh, high pitched and grating.

Ei-ah-ah-ah-ah-ah!

Goose bumps prickled across his skin. He had the urge to break away from the others and call after Runa and Cyril again, but the carrier dragon lifted off and soared into the storm. In seconds, the shadow of the great Beast disappeared, and they were gone.

"Come on." Viola tugged at Barclay's sleeve. "We need to get to the station before the rest of the students leave."

He nodded numbly, certain the noise had been a figment of his imagination. A minute later, Hasu transported all four of them to the carrier dragon station, which was more crowded than a termite's nest. Citizens of Menneset shoved their way through the masses, so desperate to flee the city that they swarmed around every departure gate, regardless of where in the world the flights were headed. Parents clutched children in their arms. The carrier dragons roared, rowdy, even violent. A pack of flight attendants dove out of the path of a whipping tail, while others offered armfuls of food to calm the Beasts down.

"Where is the rest of the Symposium?" Barclay asked, sandwiched painfully between Tadg's elbow and Hasu's shoulder blade.

Viola reached into her pocket and pulled out her telescope. She lifted it to her eye and turned it clockwise, zooming in as she scanned the room. "There!" She pointed to the opposite side of the station.

Rather than cram their way through the crowds, Hasu portaled them to the other students. Shazi yelped when they appeared. "Ow! You couldn't have landed on my other foot?"

"There you are," Cecily said. "We've been looking for you for ages. The dragon takes off any minute!"

To their right, the resident Apothecary and Scholar Masters, Drager and Oza, counted each of the students as they boarded the caravans.

Ei-ah-ah-ah-ah-ah!

The laugh sounded again, this time so loudly that Barclay jolted. "Did you hear that?" he asked frantically.

Tadg furrowed his brow. "Hear what?"

"I swear I heard a . . ." He hesitated, knowing how absurd his words would sound. "A laugh."

Viola scowled. "Now isn't the time to joke—"

"I'm not joking," he insisted. "Something's wrong. I don't have a good feeling about this. And I—"

Ei-ah-ah-ah-ah-ah!

"All right," Shazi croaked. "I definitely heard that." And judging by the looks of terror on his other friends' faces, so had they.

"Didn't Mory say something once about Shakulah's laugh?" Tadg asked Viola nervously.

"But that's not . . ." Viola shook her head, looking unsure. "It's not real. It's supposed to be a myth."

"What does her laugh mean?" Barclay asked.

"It means that doom is coming."

Shazi gestured at the wailing crowds. "Yeah, well, doom is already here."

"Why doesn't anyone else seem to care about it?" Cecily glanced over her shoulder at Rohan and Deirdre, who waited in line to board one of the caravans. "Can't they hear it?"

"I don't know if they can," Barclay breathed. He caught Viola's eye, and he could tell from her face that they were thinking the same thing. "First the Library, and now this. It almost feels like—"

"Like the Desert is trying to tell us something," Viola said.

Shazi frowned. "If that's Shakulah's laugh, does that mean that Shakulah's awake?"

The apprentices quieted as they considered this. Legendary Beasts were only supposed to rise on Midsummer and Midwinter, and according to the Guild, Shakulah had been sleeping soundly since the Ever Storms began, and had barely even roused during the solstice. Clearly, the Lore Keepers were missing something.

Barclay sucked in his breath. "If Shakulah's awake, then Keyes could bond with her. And the Guardians . . ." He could barely choke the words out.

Viola's eyes widened with horror as she realized what he meant. "The Guardians are leaving. They're flying into the first Ever Storm, and all the ones who aren't are helping evacuate the city."

"Which means this is Keyes's perfect chance to bond with Shakulah," Barclay finished. "*This* is why he didn't show at Midwinter. This is the chance that he's been waiting for."

EIGHTEEN

ymposium students!" Drager bellowed over the ruckus of the station. "Our flights depart in ten minutes! If you aren't already in line to board, please do so now!"

Viola cast an uneasy glance at their classmates as they shuffled toward their carrier dragons. "We could tell one of the instructors about Shakulah's laugh, then maybe they—"

"Dad gave them the order to evacuate," Shazi said. "They can't abandon the students."

"And what are they going to do?" Tadg asked. "They're not Guardians. And all the Guardians are either flying into the first Ever Storm or helping people flee the city."

"Which means no one can stop Keyes," Barclay said, his voice hitched with panic.

"Last call!" Drager shouted. "Last call!"

For several seconds, no one spoke. It felt as though a veil

had draped over the six of them, separating them from everyone else in the station. None of the other Lore Keepers knew that the Legendary Beast was in danger. None of them knew that the Desert's already dire problems were about to grow far, far worse.

And as Barclay looked between his friends, he could tell they were all thinking the same thing.

If no one else could stop Audrian Keyes, then they would have to try themselves.

"So," he said hoarsely. "How will we get to the Arid Oasis?"

"Even if it was closer," said Hasu, "Bitti and I can't portal to a place we've never been."

"Can we take a carrier dragon?" Shazi suggested.

Viola shook her head. "They're all flying people to other cities or Wilderlands."

"Didn't someone tell Asfour earlier that not all the dragons in Menneset can be used?" Barclay asked. "That means there must be others."

"Yeah, but it's breeding season," Viola said. "They'll be aggressive, even dangerous."

"It's the best chance we have," Tadg said.

"Fine," Viola let out. "But how do we get one?"

Cecily rubbed her hands together. "I can take care of that."

Fifteen minutes later, after the Symposium's flights had already departed, the six apprentices who'd stayed behind took advantage of the mayhem and slipped through an empty gate into the hangar. If the station was loud, then the hangar was raucous. Over two dozen dragons were in the massive warehouse, and all of them were angry.

They stretched their necks and roared at the ceiling. They stomped their gigantic feet, raking their claws across the walls. Pilots struggled to separate the calmer ones from the vicious.

"Are you sure you can do this, Cecily?" Barclay asked fretfully.

"Of course," Cecily said. "We just need to find the right one."

At that, her body began to fade, then slinked to the ground until there was nothing left of her but shadow. The others watched as she crept across the floor, unnoticed by the rowdy dragons or desperate pilots.

After she'd scoured the entire hangar, she returned to their side.

"I found one," she said. "They already suited her for flight, but she's grumpy. I think they gave up. But I know how to sweet-talk her."

"Really? How?" asked Viola.

Cecily drew what looked like a black marble from her pocket. Then she crushed it in her fist, and a raw, dripping steak appeared in her hand. They all recoiled. "Because I stole this from the food storage, and I could tell she's interested. She sniffed me even though I was a shadow." Then she pointed at the other side of the hangar. "You five go outside and wait for my signal."

That order was more easily said than done. Even with the use of Barclay's Lore protecting them from the worst of the Ever Storm, the runways were a dangerous place to simply stand and wait. The light beaming from Viola's hands barely cut through the darkness, and the ground rumbled with the thunderous footsteps of carrier dragons breaking into a run. If the apprentices weren't careful, they'd all be trampled.

Then an enormous shape loomed in the distance, barreling closer and closer. Its head burst through the vortex of Barclay's Lore, and its front leg came crashing down above them. The five apprentices flung themselves out of its path to escape being pulverized.

On the dragon's neck, Cecily waved from the saddle. "Come on! Come on!"

"She can't mean . . . ," Tadg started, but she *did*. A rope ladder to the caravan's door dragged on the ground, waiting for them to grab on.

The carrier dragon spread its wings, preparing for liftoff. The apprentices bolted after her. Without Barclay's Lore as a shield, the winds of the Ever Storm tore at them. His hair whipped into his eyes. In the darkness, he could barely make out more than Viola sprinting in front of him and the dragon's giant red tail at his side.

Tadg snatched the ladder first, followed by Shazi and Hasu. The three swung helplessly as the dragon gained speed, the ladder flailing in all directions. Then Shazi— clinging to the rope with her right hand—unsheathed one of her swords. The metal blade rippled as it transformed into a massive hook. She swung it down and scooped Viola up by the strap of her satchel. Viola screamed as she was wrenched into the air.

"Come on!" Tadg called to Barclay, extending his hand. Barclay grasped for it, but before he could, the carrier dragon flapped its wings and took off into the air. The ladder rose out of reach.

He was going to be left behind.

And so he set his hopes on the only thing he could—the dragon's tail. He threw himself onto it, landing on his chest with a grunt. The tail was wider than a tree trunk, and Barclay wrapped his arms and legs around it, clinging for everything he was worth. His stomach plummeted as the carrier dragon soared into the air, and the ground disappeared beneath him, swallowed by the storm.

This is how I die, he thought in terror, his cheek pressed against the scales, his eyes squeezed shut to block the prickly sand. He'd fall from the sky and land impaled on the University tower.

Then the carrier dragon broke through the edge of the Ever Storm, and the world brightened in a sudden burst of daylight. Barclay twisted his head back to stare at the storm clouds writhing behind him. A tendril of dusty wind reached for the dragon, but it'd already flown beyond its grasp.

"Barclay!" Viola screamed from the back window of the caravan. "Hold on!"

"Already doing that!" he shouted.

Cecily appeared beside her, then a long, thin shadow stretched out the window. It slithered toward Barclay and spiraled around his wrist. Then, before he could brace himself, it *yanked*. He hurtled over the hump of the dragon's tailbone and crashed through the back window of the caravan.

He rolled over on the floor and barked out a delirious laugh.

Viola smacked the top of his head. "You could've died!" she snapped at the same time Cecily burst out, "That was awesome!"

"Um, do any of you know how to fly a dragon?" Shazi called from the pilot's saddle. "Because I don't think I'm doing this right!"

The carrier dragon swerved suddenly to the left, and a gurgle grumbled under their feet.

Tadg frowned out the window. "You have *got* to be kidding me."

Shimmering red scales. An angry stomachache. This was the same carrier dragon that Barclay, Viola, and Tadg had first ridden to the Desert: Justine.

As though in greeting, Justine uttered the loudest belch Barclay had ever heard.

"How far is it to the Arid Oasis?" Barclay asked.

"A little over an hour probably," Viola said. "Let's just hope Justine makes it that long."

And it seemed like she would. The hour trickled past, silent except for the rumbles of each stomach cramp. While Shazi tried her best to comfort Justine from the pilot's saddle, the others braced themselves for what lay ahead. They'd had only a split second at the station to decide to try to stop Keyes and Yasha, but now they could dwell on it, and dwelling didn't feel good.

Barclay would be lying if he claimed he wasn't scared. Keyes and Yasha were powerful Lore Keepers, so powerful that on Midwinter, an entire team of Guardians had gone to the Arid Oasis to stave them off, including the Grand Keeper, the High Keeper, Runa, Cyril, and more. And the six of them were a bunch of second- and third-year apprentices. The only reason they'd stopped him at the Sea was because they'd gotten lucky.

At least, he hoped, they had the element of surprise.

Below them, the barren wasteland of dirt gradually gave way to dunes, much like the kind surrounding Menneset. But unlike in Menneset, Barclay couldn't spot so much as a palm tree or a cactus on the ground. Only red sand stretching on and on, a scarlet sea. The weather, pleasantly chill that morning, began to warm. Until not even the breeze wafting through the windows could stop the sweat from beading on Barclay's forehead.

Justine writhed with the pain of her latest stomach cramp, jostling the caravan. Viola, who'd been petting Kulo, caught him just before he toppled to the floor.

Another cramp. Justine let out a low moan.

"Is she all right?" Hasu asked with concern.

"I'm not sure." Shazi leaned forward and ran her hand along Justine's neck. "You're doing amazing, girl. I know it's getting hotter, but we're almost there, and—"

Justine heaved several times, retching. Her wings faltered, and she swooped from side to side in a bumpy descent.

After one final cry of discomfort, they were falling.

"Hold on!" Shazi shouted.

Barclay scrambled to grasp onto the windowsill. Outside, the erg rose up to meet them. Then Justine's hind legs slammed into the sand, and everyone screamed as the carrier dragon skidded down the sharp slope of a dune. Only when they'd finally slowed to a stop did Justine lean forward and puke what was clearly *far* more food than Cecily had given her onto the ground.

"Are we alive?" Cecily asked from where she was splayed upside down across the opposite window seat.

Everyone else dizzily clambered to their feet. Tadg rammed the door open with his shoulder, and a small pile of sand spilled into the caravan. He clambered out onto the dune. "If the oasis is close, I can't see it."

Viola followed after him, her telescope at the ready. "I don't see it either," she called, and Barclay's chest tightened. They couldn't afford delays, not when the whole Desert was depending on them. "But we can't be far."

"That explains why it's so hot," Hasu grumbled.

As soon as Barclay stepped outside, the heat wafted against his face, as though he'd opened the door to a furnace. It smothered him at all sides. Raising his hand to block out the glare of the sun, he took in their surroundings. A wavy haze smeared the horizon, and up close, the red sand glinted like bits of rubies.

A restless feeling stirred in his gut, one he recognized from the Woods and the Sea. They were deep within the wilds.

"Is Justine all right?" Viola asked.

Shazi trekked around the carrier dragon's shoulder, stumbling from the uneven ground. "I think she ate something that didn't sit well. I'm not sure she's going to fly again anytime soon."

"Then what are we supposed to *do*?" Tadg growled, kicking at the sand.

"The oasis can't be far," Viola said.

"You're suggesting we walk there?" said Hasu, aghast. "This is the Death Corridor."

Thanks to Dia's class, the six of them were very familiar with this stretch of the Desert. Hundreds of miles of nothing but sand in every direction. Scorching hot at all times of the year. And home to some of the Wilderland's most dangerous . . .

Barclay winced, clutching his shoulder as his Mark began to sting.

To their right, a nearby dune shifted. A small avalanche of sand poured down its hill.

"What was that?" Cecily asked nervously.

Another dune moved. Something golden glinted at its peak, but a moment after Barclay caught sight of it, it vanished.

"Maybe it's a Kabusoon," he suggested, hoping it wasn't. He lowered himself into a defensive stance. Beside him, Shazi drew both her swords.

"Maybe it's an Asperhaya," said Tadg.

Viola scoffed. "How many times do I have to tell you? Asperhayas are extremely rare. They don't . . ."

She trailed off as one of the dunes began to rise. A brown head broke through, followed by a slender body of coarse, gravellike scales. Higher and higher it reared, so tall that when Barclay gaped up at it, it blocked out the sun. For several heartbeats, the giant serpent didn't move, only watched them through slitted golden eyes.

"Don't tell me . . . ," Barclay started.

"An Asperhaya," Viola breathed.

The Asperhaya's mouth opened, baring hundreds of razored fangs. A forked tongue stretched out into the air, as though it was whetting its appetite for a six-course dinner.

"Run!" Cecily screamed, and they scrambled out of the Beast's path as its jaws took a gigantic bite of the dune where they'd just been standing. While the apprentices scattered in all directions, the Asperhaya straightened once more, sand leaking out from its gums.

Immediately, the fight began. Barclay summoned Root, just like Shazi did Saif and Cecily did Oudie. The Asperhaya lunged at Shazi, and a clang rang out as her swords parried its fangs. Saif stabbed at it with his tail, puncturing the side of its face. Annoyed, the serpent jerked its head, and Shazi screamed as she and Saif were thrown fifteen feet through the air. They landed on the side of a dune and rolled down its hill.

The Beast lowered to the ground and slithered toward them, shockingly fast for its massive size.

"Look out!" Barclay yelled.

"Hey! Sandy!" Tadg shouted.

Boom!

A crack of electricity bolted from Tadg's fingertips. It struck the Asperhaya in the neck, and it lurched backward with a shriek. Its head shook from side to side, then it righted itself and fixed its gaze on Tadg.

"Bad move, bad move," Tadg breathed as he took off running in the opposite direction. His arms flailed out as his balance slipped.

Barclay's heart leapt into his throat. He raised his hand and aimed a blast of wind at the Asperhaya, hoping he could distract it.

But it was no use. The giant serpent opened its mouth wide, its body shooting across the sand. Its jaw snapped closed over Tadg with a dreadful *thud*.

Viola screamed. Barclay staggered and lowered his hands. Beside him, Root let out a low, terrible whimper.

Then a light flashed, and Hasu and Tadg appeared not far

from Viola, Hasu's arms still wrapped around Tadg's waist, midtackle. They fell and skittered across the sand.

With the sun beating down on them, the apprentices aimed everything they could at the Beast. Barclay and Root pelted it with wind. Viola disoriented it with blinding bursts of light. With Oudie's help, Cecily's shadow lashed against it like the cracks of a whip, then coiled around the Beast's neck.

The Asperhaya heaved back, caught in the grip of the leash. Seizing the opportunity, Shazi leapt upon its tail and sprinted up its spine. Only when the climb became too steep to continue did she stab one of her sabers into the serpent's scales. It did little to truly harm it—no more than a needle to a creature of that size—but it still shrieked in surprise. It whipped back and forth wildly, while Shazi dangled, still clutching her sword's hilt.

It all felt like little use. Try as they might, none of them were strong enough to defeat the Beast, not even together. It was only a matter of time before the Asperhaya and the heat exhausted them.

Then Justine lurched toward the serpent and sank a bite into the Beast's throat.

For a moment, the Asperhaya stilled in shock. Then it squirmed in Justine's grasp. Its tail thrashed against her, and the wooden caravan split into pieces and crashed into a heap below them. But despite the battering, Justine hung on. Shazi tumbled onto the sand below and crawled beneath the protection of Justine's stomach.

The carrier dragon straightened, lifting the serpent higher off the ground. Cecily cheered, and the others joined in. Then Justine tossed the Asperhaya through the air. Rethinking its meal, the Beast dove into the closest dune and slithered off.

Barclay was so relieved, his knees buckled, and he leaned into Root to steady himself. "Is everyone all right?" he called.

"All right?" Shazi repeated, sprinting out from beneath Justine with a whooping victory cry. Then she stumbled and face-planted onto the sand. "Asfour should've never had me sit out on those Guardian missions. Did you *see* the way I sparred with its fangs?" Then she stood, shaking her head. "Lost a good sword to it, though."

"Oh, um, thanks for saving my life," Tadg muttered to Hasu.

Hasu smiled nervously and fidgeted from side to side. "You're welcome."

Behind them, Justine's stomach let out a violent rumble, and she drooped her head.

Shazi turned and stroked her snout sympathetically. "I know, I know. You were the real champion, girl."

"So we still can't fly," Barclay said. "And if we don't get moving soon, who knows what other Beasts will show up next."

"Plus, any longer and we'll all be cooked through," Tadg grumbled. He wiped off his forehead, and the drops that hit the sand sizzled with a hiss.

"But what are we supposed to do?" Hasu asked, examining the broken mess that was once the caravan. "Justine's still sick, and the caravan was destroyed."

Viola trudged over the wooden beams. "I don't know. . . ."

Then she crouched and thoughtfully ran her hand along the edge of the carpet. "Barclay, Cecily, if you're not too tired, I have an idea."

An hour later, their makeshift skiff glided across the sand.

Barclay's shoulders heaved from the effort of using so much Lore. A powerful wind spiraled out of his hands and Root's mouth against the carpet, which stretched up into the air like a sail, tethered to the skiff by the ropes that had once tied the caravan to Justine's back. Now the carrier dragon rode with them, the caravan's floor and roof combined into a single deck. Cecily stood at the center, one foot on either half, as her and Oudie's shadow Lore held the massive structure together.

They soared over the crest of a dune and thudded into the dip below.

"I don't know how much longer I can keep this up," Cecily grunted.

"Me either," Barclay echoed. His hair was plastered to his neck with sweat.

"We've got to be getting close." Viola peered into the distance through her telescope.

"You have water Lore," Shazi snapped at Tadg. "What do you mean you can't make water?"

"Where am I supposed to get water from?" Tadg shot back.

"I don't know, the air?"

"We're in the middle of a desert. How much water do *you* think is in the air?"

Shazi groaned. "Great. So we're all going to die of thirst."

"There!" Viola said excitedly. "There! I see it!"

Green appeared in the distance, so lush and vibrant that Barclay swore it had to be a mirage. Immediately, images of cool, refreshing pools of water filled his mind. His mouth was horribly dry, and Root panted beside him, his tongue hanging out.

Then his heart skipped, remembering that they weren't racing to the Arid Oasis for a drink.

Echoing his thoughts, Viola ordered the others, "Get up. Keyes could already be there, which means we need to be ready for a fight."

Their skiff slowed to a halt at the edge of a grove of palm trees and tall saguaro cacti. It was nearly as dense as a forest, with an underbrush of succulents and scraggy grass.

Leaving Justine to recover with the skiff, the apprentices returned their Beasts to their Marks and crept into the Arid Oasis, separated into pairs: Barclay with Tadg, Viola with Hasu, and Shazi with Cecily. The two boys walked shoulder to shoulder. For a place so seemingly full of life, it was gravely quiet.

Until a soft noise rumbled through the silence.

"Ow!" Barclay bit out. Root's Mark stung so hard it throbbed.

Tadg shushed him. "I think I heard something."

Then, at the oasis's center, a huge creature came into view. Jagged black stripes streaked down her light brown fur, and a matching black mane rose from the back of her neck to the tip of her tail, making her look twice her true size. Her hyena-like head had large ears and long, protruding fangs. Swirl patterns traced over her brow and down the slope of her snout.

Shakulah.

Barclay and Tadg froze. Several paces to their right, the others stilled as well.

"B-but that's impossible," Viola stammered. "We heard her laugh. She can't be—"

"Asleep?" a voice finished for her. "But, so it seems, she is."

Behind the Legendary Beast, two figures emerged—the first a man, and the second a boy. With each of the man's steps, the earth rattled beneath Barclay's feet, as though the very land trembled at his presence.

"My friends' apprentices," Audrian Keyes greeted them, his voice charming, his smile sinister. "How dearly I've looked forward to our reunion."

NINETEEN

Keyes looked far different from what Barclay remembered.

Though his appearance had always been haggard, the dark circles beneath his eyes had sunk into hollow pits. His fair skin was ashen, his hair a color not quite brown but not quite gray. Several of the veins on his face bulged, like worms had burrowed beneath his forehead, his jaw, and his left cheek. It was impossible to fathom that he was truly a young man, the same age as Runa and Cyril.

Despite these changes, he seemed to stand taller, broader, no longer hunching like someone in need of sleep. The amber of his eyes had never gleamed so bright.

Yasha, too, had changed. A growth spurt had stretched him lanky, and he'd shorn off the sides of his blond curls to a harsh, short buzz. Barclay barely recognized the boy he'd once considered a close friend. But as Barclay looked at him, stunned, Yasha never once looked back.

Keyes barked out a laugh. "You've all come alone, haven't you? How very much you take after Runa and Cyril, so stubbornly noble."

Barclay, like the others, had frozen at the edge of the tree line. They'd lost the element of surprise, and without it, he didn't know what their odds were in such a match. Zero, probably.

But that wouldn't stop him from fighting. Ignoring the stinging of his Mark, he lifted his arm, prepared to summon a gale of wind. Then Tadg seized his wrist and shook his head. This wasn't the time to strike—not yet.

Frustrated, Barclay called out to Keyes, "Someone had to stop you after you started the Ever Storm in Menneset. People have died, thanks to you. Is that really what you wanted?"

Keyes laughed again. "I didn't make the Ever Storms."

"You expect us to believe that?" Shazi snapped. "If you didn't, then who did?"

Keyes turned to face Shakulah, and Barclay's breath hitched. His back was to them—this could be their chance. But Tadg hadn't let go of his wrist.

However, Viola must've been thinking the same thing, because the sand beneath her launched into the air and hardened into glass needles. Dozens of them rained down over Keyes's and Yasha's heads.

Before any could meet their marks, Keyes lazily flicked his wrist, and a wall of stone jutted out from the earth. The needles smacked against it and shattered. The wall crumbled into a heap of gravel, which crunched beneath

Yasha's shoes as he advanced toward the other apprentices.

"Try that again," he growled, fire Lore erupting over his fingertips, "and you'll regret it."

"Yasha," Keyes scolded, his voice slightly teasing. "Play nicer with your friends."

Yasha's glare made it clear that the six of them were not his friends. "They came here to stop us."

"They came to try. I doubt even they believe they'll succeed." Barclay shuddered at Keyes's words, unable to deny the truth in them. "Fetch the ingredients. It's already taken us this long to save the Desert—let's not keep them waiting any longer."

"*Save* the Desert?" Viola repeated. "You're the one who attacked my mom! You're the one who—"

"I didn't harm her, only questioned her. I have no quarrel with Kadia. In fact, I was pleased when I heard she'd left your coward of a father. He must've been relieved when I never showed on Midwinter, that he still didn't have to face me. He'll regret that when our duel finally comes to pass and I have Shakulah at my side."

With that, as though the six apprentices were no threat to him at all, Keyes ignored them and stalked closer to the Legendary Beast. Barclay's heart lurched with panic, and he hissed, "He's going to wake—"

"Summon Root," Tadg said, finally letting Barclay's hand fall. "We need to wait to attack once he begins the bond, just like we did with Lochmordra. He'll be distracted. It's our only chance."

Tadg was right, and so Barclay called to Root. The Lufthund appeared several feet behind him, and he bent low, prowling through the grass. To their right, Mitzi and Oudie crept through the treetops, and Saif waited in the shade, his tail pointed and ready to strike.

Their friends, too, had braced themselves for battle. Viola and Hasu inched toward cover behind a cactus, and Shazi unsheathed her lone remaining sword. Cecily . . .

Barclay's eyes widened. Cecily was gone.

Then he spotted a shadow snaking across the gravel. Not toward Keyes—toward Yasha. Apparently she and Tadg had different plans.

"You said that you didn't make the Ever Storms," Barclay blurted, hoping to distract Keyes. "What did you mean?"

Keyes shot an amused glance at him over his shoulder. "Did anyone really believe I'm capable of that? How flattering. Maybe Asfour isn't as clever as I feared." He took another step closer to Shakulah, so close that his hair billowed from the breath puffing out of her nostrils. "Shakulah caused the Ever Storms. It seems she doesn't take kindly to intruders in her old Keeper's Library. After I had to use my stone Lore to tunnel our way in, the first storm appeared. I'll admit—the Library was trickier than I expected. It took me almost two seasons to explore a fraction of its rooms and uncover the six snare items that the Guild claimed were never recorded. But there's no piece of knowledge about the Desert missing from the Library's shelves."

Then, to Barclay's horror, Keyes lifted Shakulah's eyelid, exposing not white but solid gold. Still, the Legendary Beast didn't stir.

"You've been at the University," Shazi said, her voice shaking. "You're the reason the Library is locked to—"

"Everyone but the six of you?" Keyes swiveled around and grinned at them. "I'll admit, I'm curious about that. What do you each make of it? Destiny?"

"Justice," Viola shot back. "Because the six of us will be the ones to stop you."

Barclay cringed—that was the wrong thing to say. Now Keyes scanned each of them, counting one of them absent.

"Yasha," he spoke softly. "You have a companion."

Yasha, who'd been rummaging through their bags heaped beneath a palm tree, froze. Cecily's shadow hovered in the center of the clearing, obviously out of place.

All at once, light flashed in every direction.

First, Hasu vanished through a portal and reappeared at Cecily's side.

Viola beamed a laser of light at Keyes.

Yasha blasted fire toward Hasu and Cecily.

The battle had begun.

Keyes stomped his foot onto the ground, and the gravel rose from its pile into a new wall, so tall that it cast the five of them in shade. Then it fell like a crashing wave, forcing them to flee so as not to be crushed.

Barclay and Root tore through the grass. While Tadg shot a bolt of lightning at Keyes, Barclay hurled a powerful wind from the opposite direction. But both attacks died as they met stone. They'd barely fazed him. The most Barclay had managed was blowing some sand into the air.

Shazi charged at Keyes next. In the fraction of a second it took for her to swing her sword, a matching blade formed in Keyes's hand. Metal clanged against rock. Then the earth rumbled beneath them, and Shazi screamed as she was thrown into the air. Her sword skittered across the ground.

In an instant, Hasu was at her side, and Barclay was relieved to see that she'd portaled herself and Cecily away from Yasha's fire just in time—but it seemed they'd taken the fire with them. Flames smoldered in the grass, and Barclay's heart stuttered in horror. In a place this dry, the entire oasis could be engulfed in minutes.

Then the fire disappeared. Barclay blinked, unsure he'd seen right. The flames hadn't simply snuffed out—they'd vanished. As though they'd never been there at all.

In his distraction, Barclay didn't notice Yasha make it to Keyes's side. If it'd been hard to reach Keyes before, it was impossible now. As he and Viola tried to advance, Yasha launched cannonballs of fire in all directions, and Barclay and Root dove to the side to avoid being burned.

"If you don't stop this now," Keyes warned, "one of you will get hurt, you know."

"Not a chance," Tadg spat. Then he cast another bolt of lightning, not at them, but into Hasu's portal. A moment later, the electricity reappeared behind Yasha. Yasha ducked out of the way, but Keyes was even quicker. With a punch through the air, a stone tore from the earth and flew through the portal. It shot out of the second one and struck Hasu on the side of the head. She crumpled.

"Hasu!" Viola shouted, but Hasu didn't move.

"What did I tell you?" Keyes taunted. Then the gravel swept up Cecily's, Viola's, and Tadg's ankles and yanked them down. They crashed to the ground, and more rocks snapped over their wrists like shackles. Above them, Mitzi and Oudie dropped, their legs encased in stone. They both squirmed and flapped their wings, but the weights were too heavy for them to move.

Which left Shazi and Saif, and Barclay and Root.

Shazi charged at Yasha. Motya appeared beside him, her fur so shiny and white beneath the sun that she looked like a trick of the light. She hissed, and flames danced at the points of her lynxlike ears. While the pairs of Keepers and Beasts began to duel, Keyes turned his attention on Barclay.

"Well?" he goaded. "Let's see all that Runa and Cyril have taught you."

Pillars of gravel surged from the earth, all of different size, all hurtling toward him. Targets, just like in Barclay's training sessions at the gymnasium.

"How did you know about that?" Barclay rasped. In tandem, he and Root hurled shots of wind at each pillar, and they crumbled, pebbles scattering across the ground.

"Because I was there, obviously. How do you think I knew which post office you visited every week?" With a loud groan of shifting rock, the targets righted themselves. Keyes was toying with him. "Who do you think moved the statues in your dormitories? Who released the Dungwasps in the middle of your little party?"

Wind after wind after wind—it was no use. The targets shielded Keyes from their attacks, and the pillars reformed with every new strike.

Sweat poured down Barclay's forehead. "*You* were Mischievius?"

"Of course. We spent ages living in the Library and the underground tunnels. What else was there to entertain us? Though I'm a bit bitter about my loss, to tell the truth.

Imagine my frustration, losing to Runa's same prank all over again . . ."

Barclay felt sick. All term he and his friends had worried about Keyes, and he'd been lurking under their very bedrooms. When Barclay had spotted Yasha in the tunnels, he'd thought he'd imagined him. But it *had* been him. All those times he'd heard mysterious noises or felt someone staring, they'd been there, listening and watching and *laughing* at them.

With a cry of fury, Barclay blasted all the power he had at Keyes. But it was useless. He might as well have been trying to blow down a mountain. He bent over, his hands braced on his knees, huffing. He'd never been so thirsty.

"Tell me, did you even consider my invitation? Even for a moment?" Keyes asked him. "Wouldn't you have liked to speak one on one, Elsie to Elsie?"

Barclay had been right. Keyes had singled him out because he believed that they were the same. That he could still convince Barclay to join him.

"I have nothing to say to you," Barclay said.

The charm in Keyes's expression faded, and only rage remained. "So be it, then."

Crack!

Barclay's balance veered as the ground shifted beneath his feet, then began to sink. He took off in a run, but it was no use. The sand dragged him down with every step. He fell to his chest. It felt as though a riptide had seized him in its grasp, and when he looked over his shoulder, he realized it wasn't simply that the ground was moving. The earth had split in two, a chasm spreading like a gash through the oasis.

And now the sand was pouring in—and Barclay with it.

"Root!" he screamed, his hand reaching out to him. Root sprinted after Barclay, but the sand only swept him up too, and Root howled out in terror.

Heart breaking, Barclay returned him to his Mark. If they were about to be buried, he didn't want Root to feel it.

Then a hand did reach for him—Yasha's. He must've overpowered Shazi and Saif. And now he was the only thing stopping Barclay from plunging into the abyss.

Memories flashed in Barclay's mind. The rare times he'd ever glimpsed Yasha smile. The lessons together, the nights the two of them and Tadg had stayed up late talking in the attic above the Planty Shanty. The first time they'd met, when Yasha had saved Barclay from being skewered by a Sleábeak.

Maybe all his hoping hadn't been for nothing. Maybe the Yasha he'd once known wasn't truly gone.

Barclay grasped Yasha's hand a moment before slipping over the edge. Relief washed over Yasha's face.

Until the ground gave way beneath them.

They fell for a split second before hitting sand, and they didn't have the chance to take a breath before more sand piled overtop them, entombing them. In the moments before Barclay was crushed to death, his world was black, and all he felt was the pain of Yasha's nails stabbing into his hand and the *weight* of so much sand pouring onto them.

Then they were falling again—falling *up*. The earth beneath them surged up, and the sand spat them like a geyser into the air. Both apprentices gasped as they tumbled back onto solid ground.

Before Barclay could collect his bearings, Yasha lunged for him and punched him in the stomach.

"You tricked me," Yasha said, seething.

Barclay hadn't, but he couldn't defend himself. He was too busy groaning.

Then a shadow stretched over him, blocking out the sun.

"That was surprisingly cunning, Barclay," Keyes told him. "You knew I'd have to save you to save him."

"That wasn't what I meant," Barclay wheezed.

Keyes glanced at Yasha. "And what did *you* mean?"

Yasha stiffened, then glared at his shoes. "I don't know. I wasn't thinking."

Barclay winced, and Keyes leaned lower over him. Barclay couldn't help but stare at the veins threaded across his face. He wondered what it'd taken for Keyes to survive after Runa almost killed him. What it'd taken to change his appearance into a new person altogether.

"It hurts when your friends betray you, doesn't it?" Keyes asked.

"He's not my friend," Yasha snapped. Barclay would've said the same if he'd had any breath.

Stone drew up from the ground, encasing Barclay's wrists and abdomen. He grunted. They were hot enough to burn.

"You have a choice," Keyes told Barclay while he struggled, a mouse caught in a trap. "You can either join me while I make history, or you can witness it."

Barclay lifted his head up. Behind Keyes, a line of six jars waited for him so he could bond with Shakulah.

"After I succeed, the borders of the Desert will lift, and Lore will spread into the surrounding Wilderlands. This part of the world will be remade—the first of many," Keyes said. "Soon there will be no divides between Wilderlands and the Elsewheres, and Lore will be more powerful than it has been in almost a thousand years. There will be no limits to what we can accomplish."

Barclay didn't think Keyes was trying to trick him—he meant every word he said.

"Why me?" Barclay asked. The two of them weren't the only Lore Keepers who'd once been Elsies.

"Isn't it obvious? Because you and I are the same. Well, you may not see it yet, but there will come a time when you realize how different you are from your friends. What it means to be born for the wilds." Keyes let his words linger, as sinister as a promise. "And because of all the uncanny ways our stories cross. One day I will slay my old Master, your friend's father. I will show Runa how it feels to lie dying on a mountain peak and watch the vultures circle overhead. And I will make Cyril regret the day he swore that he could save me. How arrogant he's grown over the years. He's the one who will beg to be saved."

Barclay couldn't answer, so terrified that a scream had lodged in his throat.

"So what will it be?" Keyes asked. "Now or later?"

"Never," he choked out.

Keyes shrugged and stood up. "Then watch."

He strode toward the jars, and with one final, scathing look at Barclay, Yasha followed.

Barclay writhed under the grip of the stone shackles, but it was no use. And so he could do nothing but gaze in horror as Keyes approached the snare. He laid one hand on a center jar, and light seeped across the ground. It spread and spread until it covered Shakulah's body in a dazzling golden glow.

"At last," Keyes said triumphantly. "A Legendary Beast will be mine."

Barclay forced himself not to close his eyes. He didn't deserve to look away. If he was stronger, he could've stopped them.

But the longer he watched, holding his breath, the more doubt crept into his mind. Nothing was happening.

"I don't understand," said Keyes. "If it wasn't right, it wouldn't glow. Something is wrong. Something isn't what—"

To Barclay's shock, Shazi let out a howl of *laughter*.

Keyes whipped around, his face red with fury. She silenced in an instant.

"Did you tamper with it?" he bellowed, stalking toward her. Barclay craned his neck, desperate to catch a glimpse of his friend. But she was too far away. "What did you *do*?"

"Nothing," Shazi squeaked. "I didn't do anything."

"You're lying." Seething, Keyes looked to Viola and Tadg, lying nearby. "Do you know as well?"

He squeezed his hand into a fist, and the shackles around all their wrists constricted. Barclay groaned in pain—any tighter and his bones would break.

"Well?" Keyes shouted. "I don't want to hurt you, but I will if you don't talk." When no one said anything, he continued, "More specifically, I'll hurt *him* if you don't talk."

With a stomp of his foot, Keyes sent a boulder soaring into the air to hover above Tadg. Tadg froze.

"Fine! Fine, I'll tell you!" Shazi said frantically.

"Don't—" Tadg started, but Shazi cut him off.

"That isn't Shakulah," she said. "It never has been."

Barclay's mind raced. He had no idea what she meant—she must've been trying to fool him somehow.

Yasha scoffed. "You're lying. That's obviously her. It looks exactly—"

"But of course," Keyes said, sounding awestruck. "It *looks* exactly like her. I should've realized it before." He paused. "Yasha, load the supplies back onto the carrier dragon. I know where she is."

"But what about—" Yasha protested.

"*Hurry.* We need to move before Asfour and the others return."

Yasha stiffened, and briefly, his eyes flickered to Barclay. Even if he'd claimed confusion, he *had* saved Barclay only minutes before. Maybe he would save them now.

Then he shook his head and sped off to gather the jars, and Barclay knew that when it came to Yasha, he'd never bother to hope again.

Keyes looked between the apprentices lying trapped beneath the scorching sun. "If you're patient, I'm sure someone will come for you eventually," he sneered, then the two of them strode off to the other side of the Arid Oasis.

Barclay rested his head back against the ground and closed his eyes to block out the sky's brightness. His throat ached for water, and his thoughts seemed to blur around the edges. He didn't understand what had happened, how Shakulah wasn't really Shakulah.

For a while, no one spoke. It would've been a waste of energy. They would die of thirst or heatstroke before the sun rose the next morning.

Then Hasu appeared at Barclay's side, blood crusted against her cheek and ear. With a grunt, she slammed a rock down on one of his restraints, and the stone crumbled into gravel.

"How did you—"

"I woke up and pretended to still be unconscious. Very brave, I know." Then she reached into her pocket and pulled out a strange, prickly cactus bulb that bloomed with a white flower encased—impossibly—in ice. Bitti perched on one of the petals, cooling off. "But we need to hurry. I stole this from one of his jars while he was talking to Shazi and switched it with a regular cactus. We need to leave before they notice."

TWENTY

After Hasu freed the five other apprentices, they rested in the shade of the palm trees—but they knew they couldn't rest for long.

"I don't understand," Barclay rasped, his voice hoarse from lack of water. "If you were telling the truth and that isn't Shakulah, who is it?" The massive creature slumbering in the center of the Arid Oasis matched every painting and statue he'd seen of the Legendary Beast.

"It's an illusion, just like the entire oasis is an illusion," Shazi answered.

Tadg twiddled a blade of grass between his fingers. "What do you mean? It feels real to me."

"Remember when Yasha's fire Lore caught in the grass, then it vanished? That's when I realized it. What you're looking at and feeling isn't real. It's like a giant, very convincing mirage."

Barclay's eyes widened. "It's like what Dudnik said in class. The Arid Oasis is the only oasis in the world that doesn't have any water supply. Because it's fake." Maybe Dudnik's theories were cleverer than people gave her credit for.

"But what's making the illusion?" asked Hasu.

"Shakulah," Shazi said. "She's never actually lived in the Arid Oasis."

Viola gasped. "Then when Mom and the other Scholars said that Shakulah couldn't cause the Ever Storms because she's been asleep, and when Shakulah barely woke on Midwinter, it was all just . . . a lie." She cradled her head in her hands. Her forehead beaded with sweat. "It all makes sense now. This whole time, Shakulah has been trying to warn us that Keyes broke into the Library to discover how to bond with her. She *knew* what he was after. And no one realized it."

"Well, she could've been clearer, couldn't she?" Tadg grumbled.

"But if Shakulah isn't here, then where is she?" Barclay pressed.

"I don't know," Shazi said. "That's the one thing I can't figure out."

"But Keyes already *did* figure it out," Viola said urgently. "He's on his way to her right now. For real, this time."

"And what, we're supposed to stop him?" Cecily gestured around the oasis. She sounded more frightened than Barclay had ever heard her. "We tried that already! Barclay was nearly buried alive, and Hasu's brains almost got knocked out." Beside them, Hasu tenderly touched the cut on her temple where the stone had hit her. She winced.

"So you say we just do nothing?" Tadg demanded.

"Hasu already stole his rare flower thing. That counts for something."

"Sure, until he finds another!"

"We should go after Runa and Cyril," Viola said. "If we tell them—"

"But they're in the first Ever Storm," Barclay argued. "If we went in there, we'd never make it out!"

"Stop fighting, all of you!" Hasu shouted, and everyone turned to her in shock. Hasu never raised her voice. "We need to think. Dia told us that Legendary Beasts live in places full of Lore, places that act as the hearts of the Wilderlands. If that isn't the Arid Oasis, what is it?"

"The Ironwood Forest?" Barclay suggested weakly.

"Did *you* see a giant hyena prowling around on our field trip?" Tadg asked.

The group fell silent, everyone thinking hard.

Then Shazi's breath hitched. "The Library of Asfour."

Viola gaped. "You're saying that this whole time, Shakulah has been underneath the University?"

"But Keyes and Yasha were living down there for ages," Hasu said. "Wouldn't they have found her?"

"Not necessarily," answered Shazi. "The Library is a labyrinth, and it's full of old Lore that barely anyone understands. It all makes sense now, don't you see? The door that only appears to those who are worthy. The riddles and puzzles. The Library is *alive*, and it's because it's the true heart of the Wilderland."

"Perfect," Cecily said. "Then we tell someone. Your dad. Whatever Guardians are left in Menneset. Anyone. And they can—"

"But they won't be able to go inside," Viola reminded her. "The doors are locked to everyone except . . ." She swallowed. "Except us."

They looked between one another in horror. The edges of Shazi's tunic were singed from Yasha's fire Lore. Brownish-pink streaks dribbled down Hasu's jawline from blood-tinged sweat. Barclay was so covered in sand that he could feel it like crust in the corners of his eyes.

"Why us?" Shazi whispered, reminding Barclay of the similar question he'd asked Keyes earlier. Keyes's response still made him shudder. "The Library could've chosen anyone else."

Barclay staggered to his feet. "Because we *know* Keyes and Yasha, and unlike Runa and Cyril, we can work together."

"So it's up to us, then," Cecily said hoarsely. Hasu rested her hand on Cecily's shoulder, and gradually, Cecily stood up beside Barclay. The others did the same.

Viola clenched her fists. "Then let's go find our carrier dragon."

The return to Menneset was the most uncomfortable hour of Barclay's life. With the caravan destroyed, the apprentices could only tie themselves to Justine's humongous stomach like six human fanny packs. And though Justine felt better, the gurgles of her indigestion still rumbled at their backs.

The Ever Storm that engulfed the capital city loomed ahead.

"Brace yourselves," Viola told them, and Barclay squeezed his eyes shut as Justine soared straight into the writhing vortex. They lurched from the force of the winds, up and down and up again as Justine careened around buildings and aqueducts. Below them, the streets had never been so dead. They flew over an empty Menneset Market. Over entire neighborhoods where no lights shone in the windows. And when they touched down in the central campus of the University of Al Faradh, the campus looked like a wasteland of scattered leaves, papers, and shards of glass.

As much as they wanted to sprint directly for the Library, they had no choice but to steal into the cafeteria first. They rushed to glug down glass after glass of water, and they devoured whatever food they could find. Barclay was so starving that he didn't even realize the biscuits he'd gobbled up were for Beasts until Viola pointed out the paw print label on the container.

Reenergized, they dashed through the storming courtyards into the hall where they'd last seen the Library's door.

It waited for them, golden light seeping from its cracks.

The entrance to the Library of Asfour had always awed Barclay, and now he felt foolish for never realizing the truth of its power. Viola twisted the ruby knob, and as they entered, the sconces along the stairwell flared brighter. As though Shakulah recognized them.

"Remember," Viola whispered, "we can run into Keyes and Yasha again at any moment." Though she didn't go on, her unspoken warning hung in the air.

Keyes might've spared them in the Arid Oasis, but he wouldn't show them mercy again.

With his Mark throbbing in warning, Barclay retraced the familiar steps down the carpeted stairs. While the others gawked at the enormous statue of Faiza Asfour, Shazi and

Barclay made straight for the podium, where the same riddle awaited them as before—the riddle that granted entrance into the labyrinth.

I have spoken every story ever told,
From the ones of fable to the histories of old.
Though I may bleed or fade away, I can never die.
Look upon me as I ask of you—what am I?

"Do you remember the answer?" Shazi asked him.

"How could I forget?" he muttered, then he shakily picked up the quill, dipped it in the glass bottle, and wrote the gift that Keyes had given him.

Ink

At first, nothing happened, and Barclay worried that the answer was some trick after all. Then the magnificent double doors groaned as they spread open. Behind them awaited an impossibly long hallway, stretching for what looked like miles into the distance. Wooden doors lined it at either side. Each was intricately carved, none the same as the one beside it.

Dangling from a chain at eye level was a giant ring of keys.

"Whoa," Shazi breathed.

The six of them walked into the hallway, marveling at the length of it.

"That can't be real, right?" Hasu asked. "It looks like it goes on forever."

"After the Arid Oasis, I think we should assume that nothing is real just because it looks it," said Barclay.

With a *thud*, the golden entrance slammed shut behind them. They jumped.

Cecily twisted the handles of several of the wooden doors, but none budged. "Are we trapped in here?"

"Only until we find the exit." Shazi snatched the ring from the chain and sifted through the keys. There must've been hundreds of them, some brass, some silver, others iron . . . and one of them gold. She tried that one first on the door beside her, but it didn't fit. She moved on to the next key.

"You're going to try all of them?" Tadg asked. "That will take hours!"

"Do you have a better plan?" Shazi shot back.

"Well, no, but—"

"Then shut up. I'm trying to concentrate."

While Shazi tried key after key, the others jangled more of the knobs, hoping to find a single one unlocked. They were disappointed, and as minutes ticked past, they also grew bored. Cecily and Tadg gave up and plopped onto the floor.

"Are you really just going to sit there?" Viola demanded.

"What else are we supposed to do?" asked Cecily. "Hover over Shazi's shoulder and watch?"

"Yeah, that's pretty annoying, actually," Shazi muttered, and Viola—who'd been doing just that—sheepishly backed away. Then Shazi shouted, "I got it! I got it!"

With a click, she swung the door open, and the six of them huddled together to peek at what mystery awaited them on the other side.

It was a wall.

Slumped against it was a skeleton.

They screamed and lurched back. Tadg tripped and fell.

"Well, that's just awesome," he said sarcastically, standing up and brushing himself off.

Viola leaned over the skeleton and pressed her palm against the wall, then pushed at it with a howl of frustration. "That isn't *fair*. Shakulah can't possibly expect us to do the same thing for every door. At that rate, we'd be here forever."

"Yeah," Barclay said warily, "like that guy."

"Here, I'll take a turn," Hasu offered, and Shazi bitterly handed her the keys.

While Hasu tried the next door, Shazi paced back and forth. "I don't get it. Dad said the Library was full of puzzles, but this isn't something we can solve."

"Maybe it is," Viola said. "Maybe we're just not thinking about it right." Once again, she hovered over Hasu's shoulder, her focus fixed thoughtfully on the keys. Then she turned back to the double doors they'd entered from. Their gold lacquer gleamed almost as bright as sunlight.

She snatched the ring from Hasu's hands.

"Hey!" Hasu protested. "You'll lose my place if—"

"This key has to be special. It's the only one that's gold. Just like those doors."

"But that's the way we came," Barclay said.

"We can't assume anything is real just because it looks it, remember?" Then, biting her lip, she slid the gold key into the lock.

It clicked.

She huffed as she pushed on the heavy doors, and Barclay, Cecily, and Hasu scrambled to her side to help her open them.

Despite Viola's words, Barclay still expected to be greeted

once again by the entrance hall. But they'd uncovered a new place entirely.

"Now *this* is a Library," Cecily said.

It was the largest room Barclay had ever seen, and every inch of it was packed with bookshelves.

The apprentices gaped as they roamed the aisles. The tomes and scrolls around them looked so old that Barclay feared a single touch would make them crumple into dust. Word mites like he and Shazi had seen when they first explored the Library skittered on every surface. And instead of carpet, parchment lined the stone floor, crinkling as they walked.

Viola wondrously grazed her fingertips across the spines of books, then she yelped as one spun around and snapped at her, its deckled pages biting down like teeth.

"What is that?" she asked as the book now scooted deeper into its shelf. Inky black eyes glared at them from its cover.

Tadg leaned closer. "I think it's a Beast."

He slowly reached a hand toward it, and it growled, a sound like a rustle of paper.

"Come on," Cecily said, grabbing Tadg by the arm and steering him away. "We don't have time to sightsee. We need to find Shakulah before Keyes and Yasha do, remember?"

The group continued on until the aisles opened at the center of the room. Here the shelves were so short that they barely reached Barclay's knees, far smaller than the ones behind them, which spiraled up and up until they disappeared into the darkness of the gigantic ceiling.

In the room's center stood a desk, and on the desk rested a book.

Shazi's brow furrowed as she leaned over it. "Half the

words at the top have faded too much to read. Look." She stepped aside so the others could peer at it.

of the beginning,

o she fell

darkness lives.

The wilds

death's to claim,

So with

ummoned us by name.

Below the strange words was a jumble of Lore script.

S	G	N	H	O	U	L	D	Y	O	U	S
E	R	A	A	J	N	A	V	A	R	E	K
T	A	V	O	S	T	E	A	R	L	T	H
I	V	R	S	K	N	O	W	D	L	E	D
G	A	A	E	L	O	S	H	R	T	T	O
T	L	S	I	M	E	A	I	O	T	W	I
L	D	H	L	B	L	E	A	M	R	A	H
E	O	T	A	U	V	Y	W	H	E	I	G
H	R	Y	K	T	O	N	Y	C	O	U	R
S	H	A	O	U	L	D	E	O	R	S	W
H	H	E	N	Y	O	U	C	L	L	I	M
S	E	S	I	A	D	N	O	M	I	D	B

"It's a bunch of nonsense," Cecily said.

"No, it's not," Shazi breathed, then she pointed to the left corner of the jumble. "Look. This spells 'Gravaldor.'"

"And there's 'Lochmordra,'" Tadg said, tracing his finger up the right half. "We must have to find the names of each of the Legendary Beasts. Here."

He handed Shazi the quill beside the book, but before she could mark the words they'd found, Barclay seized her hand.

"You can't write in a *library book*," he said, aghast. "It's probably hundreds of years old!"

Shazi shrugged him off. "Then why would the Library give us a quill?" Before Barclay could further protest, she circled the names of the two Legendary Beasts. Then, per Viola, Hasu, and Barclay shouting out more answers, she traced around all six.

As she lifted her quill from the page, the apprentices held their breath.

"Shouldn't some bookcase move and a door appear or something?" asked Cecily.

"Great," Tadg said flatly. "So that was pointless."

"We should check the walls," suggested Viola. "Maybe we'll find a door unlocked or—"

"Wait! There's a message in between the words. Look." Barclay cleared his throat and read aloud, "'Should you seek to steal this knowledge lost to time, it will be—no, bear—a heavy weight on your shoulders when you climb.'"

All of them tilted their heads up toward the endless ceiling, where the bookshelves spiraled into blackness.

Barclay dragged his gaze down to the littlest shelf, the one he'd thought was so ridiculously small. "They're stairs."

Tadg paled. "I'm not going first."

"I will," Barclay offered, hoping his voice sounded braver

than he felt. With a gulp, he climbed atop the first shelf. The steps weren't very wide, and no railing would protect him if he lost his balance.

Slowly and carefully, the six of them ascended, following the direction of the spiral. Barclay's heart hammered; he hoped he wasn't leading them on a dangerous mistake. Behind him, Shazi whispered, "Don't look down. Don't look down." It only grew darker the higher they scaled, and Viola shone a light to guide their steps.

"I see it," Barclay said between huffs. "I see the door." The rectangular shape awaited them only two more turns around the room, which sounded far shorter a journey than it actually was. "We just need—"

"Ahhhh!"

Barclay whipped his head around in time to watch Viola's arms flail, then she teetered backward and disappeared with a scream.

"Viola!" he shouted.

Viola's shriek cut off abruptly, and petrified, Barclay leaned out to peek over the edge. Viola hung perpendicular to the steps, as though lying sideways in midair. The only part of her still touching the bookshelves was the tip of her left boot, caught by Cecily's shadow.

"Pull me up!" she wailed. "Pull me up!"

The shadow dragged her back to standing, and Tadg and Shazi seized her as she regained her footing. Barclay sighed with relief.

"Thanks," Viola choked at Cecily.

Cecily's shadow slinked back beneath her. "Don't mention it."

After that terrifying episode, Barclay was so anxious to

leave this chamber behind that his hands trembled when he finally grasped the doorknob.

He clambered into the messiest room he'd ever seen. There was no furniture, only books, trinkets, and other curios piled everywhere like a dragon's hoard. A layer of dust coated it all thicker than a blanket—thicker than *five* blankets.

"This looks like my grandparents' house," Cecily said.

Across the room, another door awaited them, this one with a shiny gold plaque—the only object within sight that gleamed. They had to scale over the mounds of items to reach it, sending towers of books timbering with a crash and several globes rolling across the ground.

Knowledge is needed to pass this door.
Should you not know the answer, find it on the floor.

What is the most poisonous substance in the world?

Tadg snorted. "Toadles, probably."

"It's gotta be some sort of snake, right?" Shazi asked.

"It could be a Visharrow spider," Hasu suggested. "Or a Nagira. Maybe a Pinasar. My brother swears he saw one on an expedition once."

"It might not be a Beast at all," Viola pointed out. "It only says—"

"I know what it is!" Cecily blurted. When the others looked at her dubiously, she added, "I swear Instructor Dia mentioned it once. I've been taking better notes since I failed the first test."

"What is it?" Shazi asked.

Cecily's face scrunched as she racked her brain. "I don't remember. It had to do with one of our field trips." She squatted and rifled through the books scattered around their feet. "Just look for books about the Desert. Or about rocks. I feel like it has to do with rocks."

"Well, I'm going to look for books about the Sea," Tadg said. "There's some murderous jellyfish Beast that Dad always wanted to bond with."

"And I'm going to research Nagiras," said Hasu.

"I'm being serious," Cecily told them. "I *know* I'm right about this."

Judging from the awkward looks on the others' faces, no one believed her.

"We're just splitting up to cover more ground," Viola offered pleasantly.

Cecily groaned and shuffled through the books. Barclay knelt beside her.

"I believe you, though I don't remember anything Dia said about poison," he told her. "I'll go look on the other side of the room. We can divide and conquer."

Finding a single book within the mess proved no easy task. There must've been thousands of books in the room: cookbooks and adventure books, biographies, journals of Lore Keepers past, field notes and fairy tales. Poetry about romance or legends or tragedies. Play scripts and comics. Memoirs and essays. Stories no longer than a few words on a scrap of paper. Stories so large, their books weighed more than cinder blocks.

Time passed. Ten minutes, thirty, a whole hour. Barclay

felt his focus waning, and the others looked as tired as he did. Tadg's head bobbed as he slumped against the wall, a scroll unfurled in his hands, and even Viola's gaze had drifted off into the distance.

Only Cecily continued to study with the same vigor. She crouched in the corner of the room, scouring one pile before leaping to the next.

"That's it," Shazi said, standing up. "New idea: we bust down that door."

"You really think Shakulah would let you do that?" Viola asked.

"If she wants us to help her, then yeah, maybe she would."

She trekked across the room, kicking aside books and items to clear a berth. Then, with a running start, she threw her shoulder against the door . . . and crumpled to the floor.

Tadg jolted awake at the *thud*, and Barclay couldn't help it—he snickered.

"What are you looking at?" Shazi groaned as Cecily stood over her.

"You're kind of in my way," Cecily said smugly.

"You found the answer? And you couldn't have told me *before* I nearly broke my arm?"

"Well, you seemed so sure."

Shazi muttered under her breath and rolled to the side, letting Cecily stand in front of the door.

"The fruit of an Ironwood tree," Cecily said proudly.

The door swung open.

"Pretty sure you earned a free pass on our Wilderlands exam," Barclay told her, and she beamed.

Together they strolled into the next room, which was

thankfully far cleaner than the one before it. In fact, it was empty. The lone door on the right-hand wall was built of thick stone, similar to the entrance of a vault. Etched on its surface was a strange scribble of lines. A staff leaned against it.

Cecily ran her hand over the pattern's grooves. "This is the ugliest symbol I've ever seen."

"I don't think it's a symbol," Barclay said. "But I have no idea what it is."

"This map must be over a thousand years old," Viola said behind them, and Barclay turned to see her studying the floor. He'd been so focused on the exit that his eyes had glided over the mosaic of square tiles, painted like a map of the Desert.

"It looks a lot like the map in Dad's book." Tadg pointed down at the golden star at his feet. "This must be Menneset. And over there—that's the Lightning Plateaus."

"So this is Dakmana," said Viola.

Hasu tapped her sandal against a white tile. "The Salt Plains."

Barclay scanned the farthest edges of the room, wondering if they might glimpse the areas of the Wilderland that still had yet to be discovered. But the mysterious map was even smaller than the one in *A Traveler's Log*.

"So what are we supposed to do?" he asked.

Tadg frowned as he puzzled over it. "I've never noticed it before—the landmarks are all arranged in a similar shape. Look. Shipwreck Coast and the Lightning Plateaus, they're two corners. And the Ironwood Forest and the Death Corridor, they're also across from each other."

"So it's what, a diamond?" asked Shazi.

"No, that leaves out the other three in the middle." Tadg walked a straight line from Dakmana to the Salt Plains to Menneset.

"A diamond split in half," Cecily suggested.

Tadg glanced between the tiles and the etchings on the door. "I think we're supposed to draw the shape. It'll probably be one symbol. Something you can draw in a continuous line."

From Menneset, he walked to the Ironwood Forest. Then he shook his head and moved to the Lightning Plateaus.

The others did the same, bumping into one another and tripping over each other's feet.

Finally, Tadg broke away from the group and grabbed the staff. He swung it around and poised its tip at the top of the squiggled knot. Then he traced out a symbol. Down to the left, down again to the middle. Up to the right, up to the middle. A diamond. Then he repeated the process a second time, drawing a smaller diamond set inside the first. Finally, he dragged the staff to the dead center of the door.

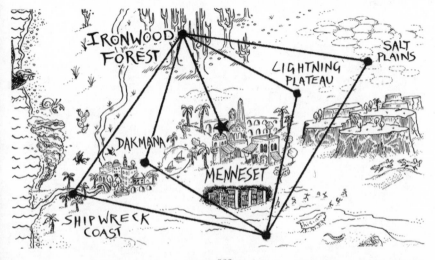

"What did you draw?" Hasu asked.

"An eye," Shazi said with realization, and she was right. Menneset was the pupil.

The floor rumbled as the stone door began to lower like a drawbridge, and Tadg let out a holler of victory.

But before the door finished opening, the torches along the walls snuffed out, throwing the room into blackness. The door fell—not with a gentle descent, but with a *slam*, making the apprentices cry out in alarm.

Ei-ah-ah-ah-ah-ah!

The cackling howl echoed off the walls. Barclay stumbled in terror, smacking into Hasu's back.

"I-is this supposed to happen?" she whispered, her voice hitching.

"I don't think so," he said darkly. "I think Keyes and Yasha got to Shakulah first."

TWENTY-ONE

Viola's light Lore glowed from her hands, illuminating surroundings that Barclay no longer recognized. The map on the floor had vanished. The staff Tadg had clutched, gone. And beyond the empty space where the door had fallen stretched a cavernous tunnel that had none of the Library's previous grandeur. The coarse walls resembled a cave, and trampled books and pages cluttered the damp floor.

Ahead, passages branched off in either direction.

A labyrinth.

Ei-ah-ah-ah-ah-ah!

Shakulah's howl thundered, shrill and piercing even through the earth.

"B-but I stole one of his ingredients," Hasu stammered. "Keyes couldn't have—is Shakulah . . . ?"

"We need to save her!" Shazi shouted, then she sprinted

down the hallway. The others followed as Shazi led them right, then left, then left again.

"How do you know where you're going?" Cecily asked.

"I don't—but the sound was that way."

"You could run ahead, Barclay," Tadg suggested. "You could see if—"

"And get separated from us?" Viola said. "No, we have to stick together."

But after countless turns and dead ends, their pace slowed to a walk. Twice Viola had to pause to catch her breath, while Hasu and Barclay stretched out their achy muscles. The day had left everyone sore and exhausted.

"We've already been down this direction," Barclay said, panting. "We're lost."

Which meant they had no way to get to Shakulah.

No way to get out of here.

Shazi groaned and slumped against the wall, rubbing her leg where her prosthetic joined her thigh. "I don't know how much longer I can walk."

"You can lean on us," Tadg said, offering his arm.

"Thanks, but it'll be faster this way." Shazi unsheathed her sword and pointed it toward the floor. The metal of the blade rippled, then lengthened into a cane.

"Will that be enough?" Barclay asked.

"Don't worry. I've got Saif to do the fighting for me."

At that, Saif appeared beside her. His pointy tail rested like a comforting hand on her shoulder.

Ei-ah-ah-ah-ah-ah!

Saif jolted, then, without warning, he abandoned his Keeper and scurried down the cavern.

"Saif!" Shazi called. "Where are you going?"

The Scormoddin disappeared around the next passage.

When Barclay and Root were in the Woods, Root had a connection to Gravaldor that Barclay didn't. Maybe the same was true for Saif and Shakulah.

"Saif is a Beast of the Desert," Barclay breathed. "He might be able to lead us to Shakulah."

Shazi's face brightened, and she trod forward, her cane clanking against the stone floor. "Come on. Let's follow him."

"Kulo, you too," Viola said, and her Skulkit appeared near the wall. Instantly, his large ears shot up, and he dashed ahead—in the same direction Saif had gone.

The six of them hurried to catch up to the Beasts, following the jingle of Kulo's earrings and the clatter of Saif's metal legs as he scuttled through the tunnels. After several minutes, the papers littering the floor began to rustle, and Barclay's hair blew into his face.

"Where is this wind coming from?" Hasu asked.

Then, as they sped around a corner, they saw it—a massive cavern, consumed in a powerful vortex. No papers covered the floor in this tunnel. Instead, veins of gold webbed through the stone, growing all the more numerous closer to the labyrinth's end. Succulents sprouted like fungi on the tunnel walls. Some of them glowed a soft, otherworldly green, lanterns lighting their path.

Ahead, Saif and Kulo vanished into the vortex.

"Kulo!" Viola called, running after him.

"Wait," Barclay said. "Keyes and Yasha could be . . ."

But Viola didn't listen. She disappeared into the gusts.

Shazi muttered something under her breath, then followed after her. Then she twisted her head around and called, "Well? Are you all coming or not?"

Hasu gulped but strode ahead next, Barclay and Tadg at her heels. The gusts were so fierce that he could feel them sucking them all forward, and Root's Mark throbbed so painfully that tears stung at Barclay's eyes. Then, once Shazi had disappeared into the cyclone, and Hasu and Tadg after her, Barclay looked back at Cecily. She hovered at a distance.

"Come on!" he called.

"I-I've never been in one of the Ever Storms," she yelled back.

"It'll be fine. Take my hand."

"But what if Keyes is in there? At the Oasis, I . . . I could've escaped from those shackles. But I was too scared, and now I—"

"It's all right," Barclay told her, though her words had surprised him. In the rush of it all, he hadn't realized Cecily could've freed herself by turning into shadow. "We're all scared. But if Keyes is in there, then we'll stop him. Together."

Cecily inched forward. Trembling, she grabbed his hand and interlaced her fingers with his. With a final, frantic inhale, they plunged into the tempest.

Blackness swallowed them. Barclay couldn't see Cecily, couldn't see anything. Sand and dust and tiny scraps of paper blasted through the air, a blizzard of filth. The wind blew them sideways, and Cecily's hand tore from his grasp as he fell to the ground.

"Cecily!" he shouted, but even he couldn't hear his voice over the roar of the gales. This was more powerful than any Ever Storm he'd explored. Only the first one could've compared with this. Even after he yanked up his shirt collar to cover his mouth and nose, he still choked on all the debris. Tears streamed from his eyes, and he had no choice but to shut them tight.

Panic clawed through him. Keyes and Yasha were in here. Shakulah was in here. Any of them could be standing beside him, and he'd have no idea.

He wondered if Shakulah ever ate her victims. Gravaldor did.

His arms shaking with effort, Barclay pushed himself to his knees. Then he raised his hands to either side.

Wind!

The vortex slowed, and a pressure heavier than any he'd ever felt before pressed against his chest. Like being buried alive—for real this time. He gasped as his Lore broke. The storm resumed as powerful as ever.

He considered summoning Root, as they were stronger together. But he doubted even the two of them combined could slow these winds. Which meant he was helpless. His friends were gone. The cavern's exit could've been anywhere, but he had no idea how he'd find it.

Then a murky figure appeared before him. It walked through the storm as though it were merely a light breeze, and Barclay braced himself for Keyes or Yasha. He was so tired, but he'd fight for as long as he had to.

Then the figure stepped into view, and Barclay realized with shock that it wasn't an enemy.

"Mom?" he croaked.

It couldn't be—Barclay barely remembered her face, only her long, dark hair and the way she used to braid it. Yet it *was* her, as though she'd been plucked straight out of his haziest memories, as though she was still alive beside him.

The ground rumbled, one beat after another. Footsteps, coming closer.

His mom disappeared, and Barclay tried to stand so he could race after her, but something heavy weighed him down. A fallen beam, he was certain, even though no such thing was really there. But his mind believed otherwise, as though reliving that terrible Midsummer's Day.

"Mom! I'm trapped!" he called out. "Mom! Can you hear me?"

She continued on, oblivious.

A roar sounded overhead. A crash. A scream.

Another figure appeared to his left. A man. He warily walked forward, an axe slung over his shoulder. Neither his clothes nor his light brown hair flapped in the wind.

"D-Dad," Barclay blubbered. "That won't stop Gravaldor. He's too powerful to . . ."

Then his father vanished as well, as though he'd never been there at all.

Barclay couldn't stop shaking. His memory of that day had long since gone foggy around its edges, yet now the events were starkly clear. The neighbor who'd carried him out of the rubble. The hours he'd spent looking for his family, only they never—

His family. The word jolted him back to his senses. His parents might've been gone, but he still had a family, and they needed him now.

A scream cried out from somewhere in the cavern.

"Dad! You can't do this! Lochmordra isn't—*Dad!*"

Next Barclay heard a sob.

"I can't move it. It hurts. . . . It hurts so bad. I'm going to die, aren't I? I don't want to die."

Someone else cried softly to themselves.

"I shouldn't have left. I can't do this. *Why* did I think I could do this?"

"Maybe you were wrong about me!" another person shouted angrily. "Maybe I won't ever be ready, no matter *how* special I am!"

A fifth, frazzled voice moaned, "No, I didn't steal these— I-I earned them. I'm not lying! I swear I'm not!"

They were his friends, Barclay realized. Each one of them was trapped in a different awful memory, with no way of finding one another.

He needed to stop the illusion, but he couldn't control these winds. The only person who could calm this storm was the one who'd created it.

Shakulah.

Barclay turned. Faintly, he could still feel the ground quake, still hear the booms of other houses crashing around his. Terror coursed through him, but he ignored it. He needed to walk toward whatever scared him. Toward Gravaldor. Toward the unknown.

Then a huge shadow loomed into view.

Shakulah looked the same as her mirage in the Arid Oasis, from her brown fur to her jagged black stripes and mane. Except she was no longer sleeping. She crouched, her mouth open in a moan. Her head whipped violently from side to side.

When Barclay took a cautious step closer, Shakulah stilled. Her eyelids peeled open, and Barclay realized that her right eye—her golden eye—was missing.

Shakulah hadn't caused all this destruction to hurt them. She'd done it because she was in pain.

Hasu's plan had paid off; Keyes hadn't been able to bond with her, not without the right ingredient to his snare. But Keyes and Yasha were already gone, and for reasons Barclay didn't understand, they'd taken Shakulah's golden eye with them. And though there was no chance of capturing them now, Barclay *could* fix the mess they'd left behind.

Shakulah still stared at him through one narrowed, suspicious eye. Then she bent low and opened her mouth in a vicious snarl. Her sharpest fangs were longer than Barclay stood tall.

He froze, his blood rushing in his ears. He was about to be eaten.

Several tense seconds passed. Barclay's knees trembled against the force of the winds. His clothes flapped. His sand-crusted hair scratched against his cheeks.

Finally seeing he meant no harm, Shakulah snapped her jaw closed. Barclay summoned Root, who stepped protectively in front of his Keeper.

"Go find Viola or Shazi. Better yet, find both of them."

But Root didn't move. He bared his own fangs at the Legendary Beast, who watched him warily in return.

"I'll be fine," Barclay promised. "Go."

Root huffed and sped off into the storm.

As time ticked past, Barclay realized how foolish it'd been to ever mistake the illusion in the Arid Oasis for Shakulah.

The power that radiated off her was even fiercer than the storm. It was heat like the burn of direct sunlight. Her surroundings danced in a blurry haze, as though the world was a mirage and she was the only thing that was real.

Shazi stumbled to Barclay's side first, guided with her fist clutched in Root's fur. She craned her neck up at Shakulah and gasped. The trails of old tears streaked down her face.

"Are you all right?" Barclay asked.

"It was like I was . . ." She shuddered, then seized Barclay's arm to keep from toppling over in the wind. "What's wrong with her?"

"Keyes stole her eye. Do you think you and Saif could calm her?"

"*Calm* her? She's a Legendary Beast! How are we supposed to—"

"Root calmed Gravaldor once, in the Woods."

Shazi swallowed. "All right. I returned him to his Mark once I came in here." Saif appeared, once again at Shazi's side.

Shakulah stared at the pair of them as they approached her. Twice, Shazi stumbled, and when her knee struck the ground, Barclay first thought she'd lost her balance. But then when Saif lowered himself as well, he realized she hadn't fallen—she was kneeling.

Saif's tail curled up until it pointed at Shakulah. Then it grew longer and longer, stretching high enough that they could almost touch.

Barclay froze, worried Shakulah would see it as an attack.

Instead, the Legendary Beast leaned forward. Saif's tail pressed against the center of her forehead.

Around them, the winds began to slow. They never stilled, but Barclay no longer had to fight to remain upright. It was working.

A moment later, Root and Viola reached his other side.

"She's . . ." Viola gaped. "Incredible." Then she noticed Shakulah's missing eye, and her face contorted in rage. "He *stole* it, didn't he? He left her like this."

"Can you calm her?" Barclay asked.

"Calm her? She's hurt. I don't know how to heal her." Then her breath hitched. "But maybe . . . I can try something else."

She knelt, sitting against her heels. Kulo materialized in front of her, and Mitzi poked her head over Viola's shoulder.

"What's happening?" Tadg asked. He clutched Hasu's hand, who held Cecily's with her other.

Viola hushed them. "I need to concentrate. Mitzi, light."

While Mitzi shone a beam from her mouth, Viola held her hands in front of her. A single bead of glass glimmered between her palms. It spun in the air, growing larger and larger with every rotation. Across from her, Kulo dropped his head low in concentration. They might've managed a few tricks together, but never had they attempted anything on this scale.

"What is it?" Hasu asked. "A sphere?"

Barclay didn't know either, until he gasped with realization. "It's an eye."

Viola's arms quivered from the effort, and Barclay held his breath, braced for a crack to spread across the glass.

When Viola rose to standing, the sphere only continued

to grow. A light shimmered inside it. Both of Viola's Lore had mixed together, creating an object so marvelous, it deserved a shelf in the Library. It belonged here.

Then she strode forward, and the sphere floated down, slowly coming to rest in her hands. She wobbled.

"Shazi," Viola said. "It's heavy. Can you help me?"

Shazi pushed herself up, and the two girls held the glowing eye between them. The light danced across their faces, illuminating the dirt and sand crusted in their eyebrows and the sweat dappled on their foreheads.

Together, they hoisted it up toward the Legendary Beast.

"Don't drop it," Hasu whispered nervously from where she and the others watched behind them.

At first, Barclay thought Shakulah didn't understand, but Shakulah lived in the largest library in the world, surrounded by knowledge. There was likely nothing that Shakulah didn't understand.

Then she lowered her head, and Viola and Shazi pressed the sphere against her empty socket.

"Gross," Cecily said wondrously.

Barclay agreed—though he was far less captivated by it. His stomach clenched as the flesh around Shakulah's socket gave way, and the eye slid into place.

At once, the winds died. The grit in the air fell, and torches ignited with flames, flooding the cavern in light.

Except the cavern was no longer a cavern at all. Bookshelves encircled the room, and grand pillars rose up to a ceiling that twinkled like the night sky. In fact, if not for the treacherous journey to reach here, Barclay might've forgotten they were underground at all. The temperature cooled.

Lemon and olive trees sprouted from the dirt floor. A pond glistened to their right.

An oasis, a true one.

Shakulah rose. Her right eye gleamed golden, and even if she couldn't see from it, and though it wasn't identical to the one Keyes had stolen, it seemed to please her.

Then her head drooped. She lowered herself to the ground. With a final, shining look at the six apprentices, she closed both her eyes and went to sleep.

"If this Ever Storm is gone, do you think that means they all are?" Tadg asked.

"I think so," Barclay answered.

"But Keyes and Yasha got away," said Cecily. "By tomorrow they could be halfway across the world."

That was true, but Barclay couldn't bring himself to worry about the fight tomorrow, not after all they'd survived today. They'd escaped an Ever Storm. They'd faced Keyes and Yasha in the Death Corridor and still left with their lives. And now they'd saved Shakulah and the entire Desert with her.

"Come on." Viola gestured to a passage between the bookcases that led to a stairwell. The steps climbed on and on, seemingly forever. "Let's go back to Menneset."

TWENTY-TWO

Today we have gathered together to celebrate the remarkable achievements of one hundred students," Chancellor Essam said from the amphitheater's stage. He wore his best, shiniest robes, with at least twenty tassels draped over his shoulders. "Another class has graduated from the Symposium."

The audience in the back of the theater—mostly parents, Lore Masters, and school faculty—applauded. The students at the front, however, cheered with hoots and hollers.

Rohan stood up on his bench and raised his fists into the air. "We did it! We did it!"

Everyone roared all the louder. Cecily jumped up and down. On Barclay's left, Viola threw her arms around him in a tight hug.

Essam cleared his throat. When the ruckus settled down, he continued, "Never before in my time as Chancellor have

I seen a Symposium so disrupted. Students having to miss class to fulfill duties to the Guild. The criminal actions of Audrian Keyes, who we've since learned was living beneath the very school. And, most dreadfully, the Ever Storm that forced us to evacuate and delayed this event for two weeks."

The attendees grew solemn, remembering the chaos that Menneset was still recovering from.

After Barclay and his friends had returned to the city, they'd gone straight to the Guild House. Asfour's team arrived only hours later, many of them wounded and shaken from their expedition into the first Ever Storm. According to Runa, over half of them had gotten lost and tricked by illusions of old memories. Until the Ever Storm settled, allowing them to reunite and escape.

The other Symposium students, meanwhile, had been a day into their flights when they received the message to turn back to Menneset. After spending the first week of Spring helping the University staff begin cleaning and repairing the school, they'd sat for their exams—and every one of them had passed.

"And so," Essam went on, "it is with great pride that I congratulate this year's class for finishing the Symposium. And now I welcome High Keeper Gamila Asfour, who will be awarding each student their diploma."

Essam returned to his seat beside the resident Lore Masters, and Asfour strode to the podium, her hands clasped behind her back. "It is my pleasure to present the graduates of this year's Symposium. When each individual is called, they will walk to the stage and receive their diploma from their resident Master. Will the Scholar apprentices please stand?"

While Asfour began reciting the names in alphabetical order, Tadg muttered to Barclay, "How much longer do you think this will take? I feel ridiculous." He scratched at the itchy fabric of his formal robes.

"At least yours fit," Barclay told him, yanking up the hem of his own gown, which trailed on the ground. "I can barely walk in mine."

Behind them, Rohan leaned forward and ruffled their hair. "It looks like this is going to be goodbye. The next time you see us, we'll be fully fledged Guardians."

"*If* we pass our licensing exam," Deirdre reminded him sternly.

"Cheerful as ever," Rohan grumbled.

"What are you going to do once you're Guardians?" Barclay asked.

"Well, Dumont has the whole Guild on watch, doesn't he? No one knows where Keyes will strike next." Rohan's face was unusually serious. "You don't always get to pick where you're assigned your first few years on rotation, but I'm going to request to go home. Some of the rarest, most important Beasts and plants are in the Jungle. I want to protect it."

"I'll probably request the Mountains," Deirdre said. "Keyes has already gone after Dimondaise once. Who's to say he won't try again?"

"That's . . . that's great," Barclay told them, forcing a smile.

After the Sea, Keyes had been branded a wanted criminal across all the Wilderlands. But the mood of the Lore Keeper world had still been hopeful. Just because he'd evaded capture once didn't mean he'd manage it again.

But he had, and he'd nearly destroyed a second Wilderland.

Things were changing—and not for the better. It scared Barclay.

The Guardian apprentices were called last, and Cyril rose from his seat to present each student with their diploma.

"Viola Dumont," Asfour said, and applause rang out across the amphitheater as all the Symposium students cheered for this year's Tourney victor. And they weren't the only ones. At the back of the audience, Runa and Viola's entire family were also in attendance. Leopold and Kadia clapped, both polite and dignified. Pemba sat atop Mory's shoulders, the two of them shrieking and waving wildly as Viola accepted her diploma.

"Shazi Essam."

Onstage, Shazi squeezed her father in a hug. Essam beamed with pride.

"Cecily Lloris."

Despite Cyril already assuring Cecily that she had indeed passed her final exams, Cecily sighed with relief as she walked down the aisle.

"Hasu Mayani."

As Hasu shook Cyril's hand, she grinned to one of the rows behind them, where two of her older siblings had come to support her.

"Tadg Murdock."

Viola's family cheered again as Tadg strode up to the stage. He earned an extra handshake from Instructor Dia, who sat with the other teachers in the front row.

"Barclay Thorne."

Barclay had to hitch up his robes as he walked. His stomach churned with a mixture of embarrassment and happiness as Viola's family once again clapped and hollered.

Cyril presented Barclay a scroll with an official Guild insignia branded on it in foiled gold. Then he awkwardly shook Barclay's left hand, as Cyril's right wrist hung in a sling, still healing from his mission.

"Well done," Cyril told him. He sounded like he meant it.

After all the diplomas had been awarded, the students squirmed restlessly in their seats, ready to celebrate with their friends and family. But Asfour had yet to leave the podium.

"Before we conclude today's ceremony, I'd like to say a few additional words," she announced. The whispers among the theater silenced. "First, though I don't have the authority to award medals of honor, as that privilege belongs to the Grand Keeper alone and historically does not apply to apprentices, I believe there are several students who deserve special recognition for their exceptional service to the Guild. It is thanks to them that Audrian Keyes's attempts to bond with Shakulah were thwarted and that the Ever Storms were put to an end. Would Viola Dumont, Shazi Essam, Hasu Mayani, Barclay Thorne, Cecily Lloris, and Tadg Murdock please stand?"

Barclay and his friends exchanged a shocked glance before they rose from their seats.

"Did you know she was going to do this?" Barclay whispered to Viola.

"I had no idea."

"What you did would've been a tremendous risk for

experienced Guardians, let alone apprentices of thirteen and fourteen," Asfour said. "As the High Keeper of the Desert, I would like to offer you my sincerest thanks."

The amphitheater applauded once more, and the six of them smiled shakily at one another, flustered.

After the clapping stopped and Barclay and his friends sat down, Asfour said, "Like the Sea, the Desert has had to endure a time of great peril as the result of Keyes. And I am proud that, despite being exhausted and undersupplied, we have emerged from this troubled period stronger than ever, thanks to the tireless efforts of the Lore Keepers of the Desert—as well as those who have come to our aid."

The applause reignited, but Asfour continued on.

"However, I am also frustrated. How much of this turmoil could've been avoided had the Desert's chapter of the Guild been provided the Guardians and Surveyors it needed? Even after the destruction faced at the Sea, the threat of Keyes has been consistently downplayed. Part of the reason is that for the past several hundred years, the Wilderlands have only known peace. But the blame also lies with the Guild."

Viola met Barclay's eyes warily. Around them, the happy atmosphere of the graduation had turned serious and bleak.

"As High Keeper, I've had to ask apprentices to devote time away from their studies to undertake dangerous missions. I've had to ask Guild members to work around the clock, beyond the point of exhaustion. I've had to ask a brave team of Guardians and Surveyors to venture with me into the first Ever Storm, a mission that could've easily claimed all our lives. These are requests that I should've never had to make. And yet I did, because while the Sea has had to rebuild and the Desert has faced annihilation, the Grand Keeper has wished to avoid drawing attention to the matter of Keyes due to his personal history as his Lore Master."

Viola stiffened, and she kept her gaze locked on Asfour even as many of the students turned to stare at her. Those who didn't gawk at Viola peered snoopily into the audience, where Leopold Dumont watched from the back.

In the corner of the amphitheater, Tristan Navarre scribbled eagerly into his notebook.

"It is my belief that Audrian Keyes must be treated as what he truly is—a villain whose actions threaten the very existence of the Wilderlands. It is also my belief that, with a united effort across the Guild, we can and *will* apprehend him," Asfour said firmly. "Which is why I am declaring my candidacy for the upcoming election of Grand Keeper. Thank you, and congratulations again to the students of the Symposium."

The applause was tremendous. Barclay froze, unsure whether or not to join it. He agreed with all of Asfour's words, yet he knew what this news would mean for Viola and her father.

With that, the ceremony officially ended, and Barclay, Viola, and Tadg had to squeeze up the stairs to reach Runa and Viola's family. It wasn't hard to find them. Because of his height, Leopold's furious crimson face stood half a foot above the crowd.

However, someone beat them there first.

"Runa? Runa, is that you?" a shrill voice called.

Looking as though she'd swallowed a Dungwasp, Runa

plastered on a smile and turned around as Instructor Dudnik clambered up the steps past Barclay and his friends. "Grusha, what a pleasant surprise."

"Thought you'd sneak away without a single hello for your only family? After ignoring all of my invitations to tea?" Dudnik inspected Runa with narrowed eyes. "Have you been eating? Sleeping? I've read the most frightening reports of a plague brewing in the Mountains—only infects you if you're left-handed. And I've been so worried that you—"

"There's no plague, Grusha, and I'm right-handed."

Barclay coughed to hide his snickering.

"Your poor mother wasn't! And with our luck, you never know when disaster could strike. Now when will you come visit me in Permafrosk? I have more than enough room for you and your students."

"Sometime, I'm sure. And look at that—they're here now. Well, unfortunately, we really ought to be going. . . ." Runa frantically motioned for her three apprentices, but it was Kadia who saved her, marching past Dudnik and throwing her arms around her daughter.

"I'm so proud of you," she told Viola. "But come on. Let's find a more private spot to talk, why don't we?"

With awkward goodbyes to Dudnik, their group slipped across campus to a shaded grove of palm trees.

"Special recognition from the High Keeper!" Mory said cheerfully. "That's quite an honor. Were the three of you surprised?"

"Not as surprised as hearing Asfour is running for *Grand Keeper*," Viola said tightly. She turned to her father. "What does this mean? The Dumonts have been the Grand Keepers for—"

"For three generations." Leopold pressed his hand to his mouth, breathing deeply. He seemed a hair's breadth from shouting. "But not forever. She has every right to run. She's qualified, respected, popular. . . ." Then, without warning, he snapped. "*I* am the one who appointed her as High Keeper. What would she have had me do? Send every last Guardian to Menneset? What of the floods in the Jungle? The rabid Eberocks outside Sycomore? I came here myself to face Keyes! What more could I have done?"

Kadia rested her hand on Leopold's shoulder. "This isn't the place."

"Nor was it hers! At my own daughter's graduation. She knew I'd be here. She *wanted* me to hear it."

"Some would consider that more honorable," Runa said stiffly. "Better to hear it first from her than to read it in the *Khronicle*."

Leopold loomed over Runa. "You knew about this, didn't you? You've been loyal to her from the start."

"Asfour has my respect, not my loyalty," Runa said coolly. "The only people who have my loyalty are those three." She nodded to Barclay, Tadg, and Viola. "Now if you'll excuse me, I'd like to talk to them—"

"Leopold," a voice said, and their group spun around. Cyril and his three apprentices joined them. "I'm sorry to interrupt. I realize this isn't the best time."

"No, no, I'm glad you're here, Cyril," Leopold said gruffly. "I'd like to issue a response as soon as possible, and—"

"With respect, sir, I didn't come here to speak to you. I came to speak to Runa."

Leopold blinked, looking boggled.

Runa crossed her arms. "This should be good."

Cyril opened his mouth, but before he could say anything, Leopold cut him off. "I'm going to find Essam and ask if he could lend me use of his office again." He wrapped his arms around Viola. "I'm sorry. I'm so, so proud of you, and I feel terrible leaving when—"

"I could come with you," Viola said. "I want to help."

"No, this is your day. You should celebrate. I'll swing by your mom's house this evening before I return to Halois."

Then, with a final, perplexed look at Cyril, Leopold strode away.

For several seconds, no one spoke. Kadia pursed her lips, and Viola fiddled with the few golden baubles she'd pinned to her graduation robes, trying to hide her disappointment. She wasn't doing a great job of it.

"Runa?" Cyril asked, breaking the silence. "Do you have a moment?"

"I suppose," she answered.

He glanced over his shoulder. "Um, in private?"

"Whatever you want to say, you can say it here."

Cyril's gaze roamed over the apprentices and Viola's family. He shifted from side to side, then finally he said, his voice strained, "I've come to apologize. For our duel, for the way I've treated you, for all of it."

Mory made a funny noise in the back of his throat. With a hand on either shoulder, he steered Pemba away. "Why don't you summon Bulu so he can play in that fountain over there?" As they walked, he jerked his head for the others to follow.

They did, but they did so slowly. Barclay and Viola locked eyes in astonishment. A few paces away, Cecily silently mouthed, "Whoa."

The apprentices and the Tolos retreated near a bubbling fountain. But while Pemba and her parents played with Bulu splashing in the water, the others strained to eavesdrop on their teachers.

"When we confronted Audrian in the Mountains, I thought he had only lost his way," Cyril said. His words sounded rehearsed, like he'd been thinking about them for a long time. "I thought he was still our friend, that we could change him and return to what it was like before. And when you killed him—almost killed him—I thought you'd betrayed him. I thought you were heartless. And—"

"Yeah, you don't need to remind me," Runa said flatly.

"Right, right. Well, I guess—I was wrong. I was naive, and I chose to believe the worst in you instead of the worst in him. If you hadn't done what you did that day, I'd probably be dead." When Runa didn't respond, Cyril stammered, "I—I know it took me a long time to realize my mistake. Too long. And I often wonder if Audrian ever would've managed to trick us at the Sea if the two of us had been friends again. Everything he's done in the past year and a half, I blame myself for. I'm the one who started this feud between the two of us, over something that didn't even happen the way I thought. And I want to be better. Not just to you, but because of the reasons I became a Guardian in the first place. And so I'm sorry. I know things might never be the same between us, but I'd like to try to go back to how we used to be, once you've forgiven me."

Barclay's chest swelled. Finally, the Horn of Dawn and the Fang of Dusk would no longer hate each other. Finally, Cyril had set things right.

"Took him long enough," Shazi muttered.

"I still think he's full of himself," Tadg said. "Though he *did* help me make my poison Lore a lot stronger."

"I'm so glad. I've always secretly liked Runa," said Hasu.

Amid all their happiness, it dawned on Barclay that Runa hadn't actually spoken.

"I don't forgive you," Runa told him.

"Wh-what?" Cyril stuttered. "But . . . Can I ask why?"

"No. I don't owe you an explanation. I don't owe you anything."

The six apprentices gasped and stared at one another with alarm.

"Ouch," Cecily said with a wince.

Barclay agreed with her. Cyril's apology had sounded like he meant it, but as much as Barclay wanted Runa and Cyril to get along again, he also understood why Runa had said no. Yasha had left his old friends in the Arid Oasis to die, and Barclay didn't think he'd ever forgive him. Some betrayals cut too deep.

Cyril shifted again, looking as though he wanted to add something. Then, seeming to think better of it, he strode toward the apprentices. His face was unreadable, and he met no one's eyes when he said, "Why don't you say your goodbyes? I'll be in the Chancellor's office with Leopold."

After he left, no one knew what to say. Then Barclay weakly managed, "Goodbyes? Are you leaving?"

"We're going to Valpur," Hasu said. "It's been ages since I've seen my whole family."

Barclay blinked in surprise. Valpur was the capital city of the Jungle, and he thought Cyril never left Leopold's side.

"Where will you be going, now that the Symposium is over?" Cecily asked morosely.

"We're staying here," answered Viola. "With my mom."

Shazi kicked a pebble on the ground. "You'll write to us, won't you?"

"Of course," Barclay said. "And we'll see each other again when . . ." Whenever and wherever Keyes next resurfaced, and Runa and Cyril were summoned to stop him.

The thought saddened Barclay. Shazi, Hasu, and Cecily were family to him, but they were only family of bitter circumstances.

"When we beat him," Tadg finished firmly.

The others nodded and echoed, "When we beat him."

That night, they gathered in the Tolo house for an after-dinner tea.

Leopold had already paid his visit and left, anxious to return to Halois. He planned to give a speech addressing Asfour's accusations on the steps of the Mountains' Guild House.

"It's very generous that you'd let us stay here," Runa told Kadia and Mory.

"Nonsense," Mory said, scratching the chin of one of the three Beasts snuggled atop his lap. "The more the merrier. As you can see, we already live in a menagerie."

"And I miss having my daughter home." Kadia squeezed Viola's hand fondly. "The three of you could probably help me with my work. I've never seen the University this excited. Shakulah! Living right underneath our offices! All my colleagues are racing to learn more about her illusion Lore and how she blends it with real phenomena in the Desert, like the Phantom Roar inside the Ever Storms—not to mention her famous laugh!"

"Now that you're staying here," Pemba told her sister excitedly, "I moved my bed so that you could share a room with me and Bulu. And I made up beds for Mitzi and Kulo, too."

Hearing their names, Mitzi and Kulo perked up from the room's corner, where they chased a glass marble that Kulo had made across the floor.

Viola grinned at her. "I think that sounds great. Did you make sure to hide all your shiny things?"

Pemba nodded vigorously. "I put them all under my bed."

Kadia's lips quirked into a smile. "Did you, now?"

"Speaking of bed," Mory said, shooting Pemba a pointed look. "It's two hours past your bedtime. Look, Bulu is already asleep."

On the couch in the next room, Bulu slumbered in a tight, glittery ball.

Pemba pouted. "But Viola is here!"

"And she'll be here in the morning," Kadia said, "and the next day, and the next day. Come on. If you want, you can pick out *two* books to read tonight."

Mory grinned. "Only if I get to do the voices."

Woefully, Pemba scooped Bulu from the couch and took her parents' hands. The three of them climbed up the stairs, leaving Barclay, Tadg, and Viola alone with Runa.

"I couldn't help but notice during the ceremony that you got a lot of applause, Viola." Runa smiled mischievously over her cup of tea. "I was wondering if that still means what it used to."

When Viola didn't respond right away, Barclay looked up from his packet of graduation documents and said brightly, "Viola won the Tourney."

Viola fiddled with her pins. "It was luck, really. I didn't even try before—"

"She rang the bell in the University tower," Tadg told Runa.

"Exactly," Viola said. "I mean, you did it first. It's what gave me the idea."

Runa looked surprisingly touched. "The secret stairs behind the bookcase?"

Viola nodded. "I noticed it when Dad came for Midwinter! I was looking through my magnifying glass, and I spotted a groove in the wall that didn't look right. I snuck up on the last day of class."

Tadg, who'd also been examining his folder, held up the second paper that'd come with his diploma. "What does this mean? 'All graduates of the Symposium are eligible to apply for their official Guild stamp at the Office of Records and Confidential Archives (ORCA).'"

"It means we have to design each of your special Guild seals," Runa said, "so you can qualify for higher-ranked assignments and send and receive letters through the Guild."

"Like . . . secret documents? Secret *missions*?" Tadg asked eagerly.

Runa snorted. "More like you have to start dealing with boring forms. Like all the documentation I get to fill out because the three of you and your friends broke University rules and went into the Library of Asfour. Next time you throw yourselves into danger to save the Wilderlands, you can do your own paperwork."

She laughed, but the mood in the room wasn't so light-hearted.

"What's going to happen now?" Viola asked. "We just wait to find out where Keyes and Yasha attack next?"

"I'm afraid so," Runa answered. "But we know more than we did before, thanks to you three. In fact, I have a theory now."

"What is it?" asked Barclay.

"You mentioned that they stole Shakulah's golden eye, just like they stole Lochmordra's trident at the Sea. I'm starting to think that they're after each of the golden possessions of the Legendary Beasts."

"Why?" Viola asked.

"I'm not sure. We don't know much about them, unfortunately. Some of them have significance, like the legend of Maedigan associated with Lochmordra's trident. Others, like Shakulah's eye, have no special story or powers. But I've shared my theory with Asfour, and now the best Scholars in the world, like your mom, are devoting themselves to finding the answer."

"Whatever it is," Barclay said darkly, "if Keyes wants it, it's probably not for anything good."

Runa looked between them seriously. "I can tell what the three of you are thinking, you know. You're thinking that things are going to change now."

The apprentices stared into their teacups.

"And you're right in a lot of ways. Stopping Keyes has become more important than ever. But I don't want that to get in the way of your lives or your apprenticeships."

"It already has," Tadg bit out. "We've faced him not once, but *twice*."

"And we want to help," Viola said. "We don't want to sit out the next time a Wilderland is in trouble."

"I know that," Runa told them. "Which is why I promise you that I won't keep you in the dark anymore. I never wanted any of you to get involved in my problems, but this problem is all of ours now, and I want us to be ready to face it. Together."

An hour later, when the rest of the house had gone to bed, Barclay and Root sat in their guest bedroom. Root gnawed on a bone. Barclay hunched over the desk, writing a new letter to Master Pilzmann.

At first, Barclay wasn't sure if he should tell him about the Library of Asfour, or their showdown with Keyes and Yasha in the Arid Oasis. He didn't want to scare Master Pilzmann into worrying that even more danger lurked beyond the edge of the Woods.

But danger was coming, whether Barclay admitted it or not. Adventure might be exciting and marvelous, but no adventure story would ring true without a bit of peril.

And so he scratched his quill against the parchment. He first wrote all the needful things: the date, the salutation, and the apologies for how much time had passed since his last letter. Then, scary or not, he told Master Pilzmann the truth:

I've been on an adventure.

AN EXCERPT FROM

A TRAVELER'S LOG OF

DANGEROUS BEASTS

VOL. 3

BY CONLEY MURDOCK

AGMOR

Wilderland: the Jungle
Class: Prime

These regal birds are best known for their colorful plumage, but admirers should be careful not to get too close, as their sharp feathers are highly toxic. One prick will turn you green with nausea to match!

ALCUNA

Wilderland: the Mountains, the Desert
Class: Prime

The wool of these llamalike Beasts will keep you warm even in the coldest temperatures. Now, those are some socks I'd love to receive as a birthday present.

ANTHORN

Wilderland: All
Class: Trite

Antlike Beasts with metallic bodies, whose exact color varies depending on which Wilderland they are from. Their burrows and hills often contain precious metals and minerals due to deposits found in their eggs.

ARACHADEE

Wilderland: All

Class: Familiar

These white, twelve-legged Beasts resemble spiders, and though most only measure a foot long, a queen Arachadee (Mythic class) can grow as large as a human man. Their webs make such a powerful adhesive that they often get stuck themselves.

ASPERHAYA

Wilderland: the Desert

Class: Mythic

These ferocious sand snakes swim underneath the Desert's dunes and can go a whole day without needing to surface for air.

BADACHIDIA

Wilderland: the Jungle

Class: Familiar

Because of the food fermenting their stomachs, one belch from these smelly hoatzinlike Beasts can knock out an entire expedition party. (This comes from firsthand experience.)

BILBOT

Wilderland: the Desert

Class: Familiar

These tiny marsupials have large ears and sound Lore that can detect predators from over ten miles away.

BOLIKONO

Wilderland: the Desert

Class: Familiar

These small birdlike Beasts might not be able to fly, but they can run faster than most humans on land. The fastest Bolikono on record once won a gold medal for completing a marathon in just under an hour.

CALAMEAR

Wilderland: the Sea

Class: Familiar

The bubble Lore of these octopus-like Beasts make them excellent bath companions.

CAPAMOO

Wilderland: the Desert

Class: Prime

These large flightless birds lay prized dark green eggs that look like giant avocados. Despite rumors of aggression and even war with Lore Keepers, Capamoos are not very clever and would make very poor military tacticians.

CHIMPACHIPA

Wilderland: the Jungle

Class: Prime

The debates wage on about whether these Beasts are more spider or more monkey. On one hand, they produce a web-like slime Lore from a single spinneret on their stomach, which resembles a belly button. On the other hand, they do appreciate a good banana.

DOLKARIS

Wilderland: the Tundra

Class: Mythic

Though their Elsewheres relative, the sabertooth tiger, has long gone extinct, Dolkarises remain a bloodcurdling monster of the Tundra. They can use their Lore to grow their icicle-like fangs over three feet long—large and sharp enough to pierce a man through.

DONKILISA

Wilderland: the Woods, the Mountains, the Desert

Class: Prime

These serpent Beasts have rattles on their tails that can lull prey asleep—and which are very useful to parents trying to soothe crying infants.

DRAGON

Wilderland: the Mountains

Class: varies

A collective term for Beasts of a mixture of reptilian and avian natures, who vary in size, power, and type of Lore.

EBEROCK

Wilderland: the Woods, the Mountains

Class: Prime

Look out! These powerful boarlike Beasts weigh as much as three tons and can cause earth tremors when running at full speed.

FWISHT

Wilderland: the Sea

Class: Familiar

Capable of carrying objects twice their size, these pelican-like Beasts make excellent postal birds. And their healing Lore might not work on humans, but it does just the trick for a Beast's minor scrapes or bruises.

GRAVALDOR

Wilderland: the Woods

Class: Legendary

Resembling a massive bear, the Legendary Beast of the Woods slumbers for most of the year, and some Keepers credit hearing a low rumbling in the forest that could be his snores. When awakened, he has been known to destroy entire towns, especially when feeling threatened.

HADABUMA

Wilderland: All
Class: Familiar

These tiny owl Beasts are famous for making a wide variety of noises, including squeaks, screeches, hoots, chirps, squawks, wails, and even giggles.

HADDISSS

Wilderland: the Desert, the Mountains, the Jungle
Class: Mythic

Being only skeleton, these serpentine Beasts have no brain, no stomach, and no insides at all. They don't seem to eat or age, and much about their lives remains a mystery. Though I'm positive I heard one burp once.

HOOKSHARK

Wilderland: the Sea
Class: Prime

The heads of these sharks resemble large hooks, which they use with their sand Lore to dig bottom-dwelling fish out from the seafloor. Beware—they are known to indulge in humans as well.

JACKAWA

Wilderland: the Jungle, the Desert

Class: Prime

These canine Beasts are highly territorial, and they mark their lands with frightening displays of bones and carcasses—and, often, with poop.

KABUSOON

Wilderland: All

Class: Mythic

These sometimes deadly Beasts make their homes in haunted places, such as abandoned houses or graveyards. If you ever notice the hairs on your arms prickle or goosebumps creep across your back, take heed. It could be a Kabusoon preparing to strike.

KARKADANN

Wilderland: the Desert, the Jungle

Class: Prime

A large, hairless horse with an ivory horn and the attitude of a wolverine. I desperately wished for one as a child only to later learn they are nothing like ponies.

LOCHMORDRA

Wilderland: the Sea

Class: Legendary

Lochmordra dwells in an unknown place deep within the

Sea, rising to terrorize sailors or devastate coastal villages. His mouth is so large, he can swallow ships whole.

LUFTHUND

Wilderland: the Woods
Class: Mythic
Tricky to find and trickier to tame, as they are fiercely independent. Resembling large black wolves, they can grow up to six feet long and four feet tall. They can turn entirely into wind, like a rush of smoke billowing past, and their Lore can conjure storms and wind gusts. Absolutely magnificent! Also highly dangerous.

MADHUCHABEE

Wilderland: the Jungle
Class: Mythic
Unlike the more common, Trite-class Stingurs, Madhuchabees are exceptionally hard to find, as they can portal long distances with their spatial Lore. I would personally be honored to be stung by one.

MISKREAT

Wilderland: the Woods
Class: Familiar
Pesky little pests! Living in colonies at the edge of the Woods, these wrinkly creatures steal into nearby towns and smash any fields of pumpkin, squash, and—occasionally—turnips.

MUDARAT

Wilderland: the Desert, the Mountains, the Woods
Class: Prime
These armadillo-like Beasts are armored by unbreakable diamond plates, making them beautiful to behold and extraordinarily hard to maim. They live in several Wilderlands, but they are hardest to find in the Mountains, as many are accidentally kidnapped by dragons to live in their gemstone hoards.

MURROW

Wilderland: All
Class: Trite
These field mice have spikes protruding from their backs that whistle loudly when the wind blows through them, warning away predators.

NAGIRA

Wilderland: the Jungle, the Desert, the Sea
Class: Prime
These venomous snakes are among the deadliest Beasts in the world. Not only can they inject poison into their bites, but they can spit it into your eyes, leading to blindness or, in exceptionally rare cases, superhuman vision.

NATHERMARA

Wilderland: the Sea
Class: Mythic

A giant lamprey, capable of both water and electric Lore, that can only be found in the Sea's darkest depths. One also happens to be my most cherished friend.

NITWITT

Wilderland: the Jungle
Class: Familiar
This bird, previously believed to be extinct, uses its stone Lore by eating rocks to help digest its food. As you can imagine, this makes it impossible for them to fly, and they are easy prey to water-dwelling Beasts since they easily sink.

PHOENIX

Wilderland: the Mountains, the Desert
Class: Mythic
This fiery Beast exhibits an unusual form of immortality: it bursts into flame at old age and is reborn as a chick. Wild phoenixes are nearly impossible to bond with, but Lore Keepers have gotten lucky should they happen upon a rare egg.

OSTRELLO

Wilderland: the Desert
Class: Prime
Ready, set, go! These birds are among the fastest runners in the world. I do *not* recommend startling one, as they will chase you for hours—even days—on end.

PINASAR

Wilderland: the Jungle

Class: Prime

These tiny scorpion Beasts are considered the most venomous creature in the world. A single prick from their tails can cause every muscle in your body to turn to stone.

RAPTURA

Wilderland: the Desert

Class: Mythic

These falconlike Beasts can turn their bodies into sand to avoid being struck or to fly into hard-to-reach places. Raptura eggs have never been discovered, and it's theorized that they are born in the rare circumstance when lightning strikes the Desert dunes.

RITHIS

Wilderland: All

Class: Familiar

Don't let their spooky nature fool you—these ghost Beasts are exceptionally friendly. Proper lures aren't even needed to summon them, as they (like me) are easily tempted by chocolate candy.

SALADON

Wilderland: the Desert
Class: Prime
These large lizardlike Beasts charge their light Lore by sleeping out in the sun. Once fully charged, their scales glow a brilliant orange.

SANAMHISAN

Wilderland: the Desert
Class: Prime
These camellike Beasts help transport millions of kritters worth of cargo across the Desert and even into the neighboring Elsewheres. Their labor is so vital to the Wilderland that several cities have a Sanamhisan Workers Union to make sure they receive plenty of rest, treats, and vacation days.

SCORMODDIN

Wilderland: the Desert
Class: Mythic
With over three hundred individual steel plates covering their bodies, these scorpion Beasts are almost impossible to wound. Their long sharp tails make excellent blades. One even won the gold medal in Menneset's swordsmen competition for six years in a row.

SERPENSALA

Wilderland: the Mountains, the Desert, the Woods, the Jungle

Class: Familiar

These small snakelike Beasts burrow into floorboards and walls to lay their eggs, leaving homeowners with a nasty surprise when they do their Spring cleaning.

SHAKULAH

Wilderland: the Desert

Class: Legendary

The hyena-like Legendary Beast of the Desert is most famous for her mythical laugh, as rumors claim that hearing it foretells death and destruction.

SLEÁBEAK

Wilderland: the Sea, the Tundra

Class: Prime

This seagull Beast skewers fish out of the water with its long, spearlike beak. But when it comes to vexing the Sea's beaches, it's unclear which is worse: its front end or its back end!

SMYNX

Wilderland: the Tundra

Class: Mythic

These lynxlike Beasts can survive in the coldest parts of the Tundra due to their powerful fire Lore. Wandering travelers have often mistaken them for demons, as they can turn their entire body into flame.

STONETOAD (ENTRY BY TADG MURDOCK)
WILDERLAND: THE SEA
CLASS: ???
AN UGLY, WARTY TOAD WITH A GEMSTONE IN ITS FOREHEAD. ~~PEES~~ SECRETES POISON. DOES NOT RESPECT AUTHORITY.

TARMACEDON
Wilderland: the Mountains, the Woods
Class: Mythic
These massive creatures can stand comfortably on either four legs or two, a talent which I believe evolved from their ability to slam their front legs on the ground and generate earthquakes. They hibernate in the Winters by turning their entire bodies to stone. Warning: do not approach while wearing the color red.

TASUMABASA
Wilderland: the Desert, the Mountains
Class: Mythic
In the week after these lizardlike Beasts shed their skin every year, they have no body at all and are instead made entirely of ash.

TENEPIE

Wilderland: the Mountains, the Desert
Class: Mythic

These cunning crowlike Beasts can control their bodies and shadows separately, though each always remains attached to the other. Their shadows are especially ticklish.

TRICKANIS

Wilderland: the Woods, the Desert, the Tundra
Class: Prime

These coyote-like Beasts make so many sounds that many Scholars believe they have their own language. Their most famous, the howl, is probably meant to help a lost Trickanis find its pack.

TURTLETOT

Wilderland: the Sea
Class: Familiar

These turtlelike Beasts have large shells made of coral, and because coral makes a delightful, colorful home for all sorts of tiny creatures, at their adult size, Turtletots become miniature Beast and animal hotels. Buggy guests beware, though—your room service just might eat you!

VISHARROW

Wilderland: the Jungle
Class: Mythic

Though only the females of this spiderlike species are venomous, few Lore Keepers dare to approach their infamous black-and-red webs.

VOXEN

Wilderland: All
Class: Familiar
These Beasts may be large, but the only danger they pose to humans is their mighty kick. Voxen are useful to farmers for helping till their fields and providing milk.

VULTAN

Wilderland: the Mountains, the Desert, the Woods, the Jungle, the Tundra
Class: Prime
Because their diets solely consist of dead and decaying animals (or people), Vultans have a grisly reptuation. But their healing Lore makes them handy staff members in Wilderland hospitals.

WARAMASA

Wilderland: the Desert, the Jungle
Class: Mythic
Often considered the king of feline Beasts, their roars are so fearsome that even Beasts bonded with Lore Keepers will stop their attacks at the sound of one and lower into a bow.

ACKNOWLEDGMENTS

It is truly a childhood dream fulfilled to write a magical boarding school, and I have many people to thank who helped me ace it.

First, my world-class editor, Kate Prosswimmer, who is the most incredible champion of this series. Thank you for always greeting my chaotic spreadsheets and lengthy emails with such patience and enthusiasm. Without you, I'm quite sure *The Ever Storms* would remain the broken, unfinished manuscript it was after the initial draft.

Next, my agent, Whitney Ross, whom I am constantly grateful to have as both an advocate and a friend. Thank you for being someone I can depend on through any storm. And thank you as well to my foreign agent, Heather Baror-Shapiro, who has guided Barclay's adventure to new lands far and wide.

Thank you to my A+ team at McElderry Books, whose

tremendous creativity, passion, and tireless effort never cease to astound me. That includes Nicole Fiorica, Samantha McVeigh, Justin Chanda, Karen Wojtyla, Bridget Madsen, Caitlin Sweeny, Nicole Russo, and Alissa Nigro.

Thank you to Christine Lynn Herman, Axie Oh, and Tara Sim, whose feedback I have come to rely on so dearly amidst this Wilderlore adventure. To my writing group: you are all a class act.

Thank you to Petur Antonsson and Karyn Lee, who have designed yet another breathtaking cover.

Thank you to the authenticity readers who've helped me shape the world of the Wilderlands. Thank you as well to Heba Elsherief, Aminata Siby, and Sonia Varandani, whose Arabic, Bambara, and Hindi language expertise, respectively, have truly helped the Beast names shine.

Thank you to my husband, who so patiently listens to me ramble about the future of Barclay's story; as well my brother Connor, whose spontaneous FaceTime chats I greatly enjoy. And of course, Jelly Bean, the most legendary of Legendary Beasts.

Last, thank you to my readers. My most cherished memories of this journey include the messages I've received from kids, parents, teachers, booksellers, and librarians. I'm so grateful you've joined me and Barclay on this adventure.